Ellie Holmes writes commer   ic
   mysteries. She takes her
                countryside and tne suolime Cornisn coast.
Ellie is a member of the Alliance of Independent Authors and the
              Romantic Novelists' Association.

To find out more please visit ellieholmesauthor.co.uk

Also by the same author

The Flower Seller

The Tregelian Hoard (Book 1 – Jonquil Jones Mystery Series)

ELLIE HOLMES

White Lies

ELLIE HOLMES

White Lies

Print and distribution by IngramSpark
ISBN: 978-0-9934463-4-4
EBOOK ISBN: 978-0-9934463-5-1

This book is dedicated to Simon
– You were my 'Connor' and I miss you

Chapter One

Sam Davenport thought she'd imagined it: the driving rain, her husband Neil's shout of surprise, the sickening crunch of metal on metal, the explosion of inflating airbags.

A bad dream. That was all it was. Why, even now, they were on their way back to Meadowview Cottage with its thatched roof dipping low over leaded-glass windows and a welcoming fire burning in the TV room to keep the children and their sitter cosy in their absence.

Yes, it was a bad dream. Soon, they would be home and Neil would take off his clothes in the bedroom while she took off her make-up in the ensuite and together they would dissect the party and their friends.

Except, they wouldn't. Because she hadn't imagined it. The Range Rover was skewed at a crazy angle across one of the main roads of the Essex market town of Abbeyleigh and picked out in its headlights was the shape of a motorbike and, a few metres on, the body of its rider.

'Shit! I didn't see him! Did you see him?' Neil's voice was high-pitched.

'No. I was looking for my mobile,' Sam replied, flustered. Letting her bag fall to the floor, she threw open the door.

'What are you doing?' Neil grabbed her arm. 'We have to go.'

'We can't go!' She watched him looking at the large, executive-style houses that surrounded them. At midnight, they were all in darkness. For now.

'We sure as hell can't stay. What if he's dead? It'll ruin me.'

'For God's sake, Neil! Is that all you can think of?' Wrenching her arm free, she got out of the car. 'There's more to life than your bloody reputation.' The freezing January rain fell in torrents, soaking her Stella McCartney dress. 'I'm going to see if he's all right.'

The motorbike lay on its side and in the arc of its headlight Sam could see the body of a man in black riding leathers. Her cerise-coloured party shoes slapped on the wet tarmac as she ran towards him.

'*All right?*' Neil chased after her. 'I hit him at forty miles an hour. Of course he's not all right. Jesus!'

The man was on his back, rain streaming over the visor of his crash helmet. Sam stared at his chest. Was it moving? In her mind, she heard again the screech of brakes, the sickening bang.

Kneeling beside him, she unzipped his jacket and pressed her fingertips to his neck the way she'd seen them do on the television. His skin felt cold and clammy. Sam bit back a cry of relief when, at last, she found his pulse.

'Call an ambulance.'

'Can we say you were driving?'

'What?'

'I'm probably over the limit.'

'Will you just ring for the ambulance?'

'Of course, if we'd stayed at the Northey Hotel like I wanted this would never have happened.'

'Neil!'

'So can I say you were driving?'

'Say what you bloody well like, just ring!'

'Hello? Ambulance, please.'

It was true. He had wanted to stay at the Northey.

'They've got a spare room. Our sitter will be okay. I'll pay her double.'

'I have to go home, Neil. The children aren't well.'

'They've got colds not scarlet bloody fever.'

'And they need their mum. You can stay if you want.'

'A great way to celebrate my fortieth, spending the night alone,' he'd grumbled. 'No, we'll both go home.'

Sleet began to mingle with the rain. Sam shivered. 'Give me your jacket.'

Neil did as she asked and Sam placed it over the stricken man, pulling the collar up under his chin and tucking it in round his shoulders.

Sitting back on her haunches, she watched as Neil began to pace, talking urgently into his phone, his left hand thrusting continuously through his hair. His white silk shirt was plastered to his body, stretches of pink skin showing through, revealing the hint of a spare tyre.

He turned to Sam. 'They'll be here soon,' he said, yanking at his tie. His gaze moved to the injured man. 'They want to know if he's conscious.'

Nervously, Sam lifted the man's visor. To her relief, his face looked normal, peaceful even.

'He's unconscious.'

As Neil relayed this information, Sam studied the man in front of her. He was white. Early thirties, Sam guessed. With brown eyebrows and a long, thin nose.

'On his back,' Neil said. 'His left leg doesn't look good. There's . . . it looks like blood. A lot of it. Shit! I think that might be a bone.'

Sam was amazed that she hadn't noticed the injury to the man's leg. Now, as she looked, she could see the blood pooling on the ground, mixing with the rain, washing away along the road. Suddenly the smell of it hit her and she felt nauseous.

'My God, Neil! What have you done?'

Neil gave her a horrified look before turning and throwing up in the gutter.

'I'm sorry,' Sam whispered. She stroked the motor-cyclist's cheek.

Her hand froze as she suddenly found herself staring into the man's dark eyes. Instinctively, she reached for his gloved hand and gave it a squeeze. To her joy, he returned the pressure.

'The ambulance will be here soon. You're going to be okay.' As she stroked his cheek once more, his eyes flickered and closed. Alarmed, Sam checked his pulse. It was thin and weak, worryingly so.

'Shouldn't we be doing something about his leg?' she asked as Neil returned wiping spittle from his chin onto the sleeve of his shirt.

'She said the ambulance will be here soon and not to move him. We'd only make matters worse.'

Worse? Could they be any worse? Another fifteen minutes and they would have been home. Safe, inside Meadowview Cottage. Sam pictured its squat wooden front door and, within, thick, beamed walls painted in a variety of pastel colours, the open fireplaces so lovingly restored downstairs, the pretty patchwork quilts upstairs. Her beautiful home. Yet she'd move out tomorrow if only this man, this stranger, would live. If only his blood would stop running along the road.

She closed her eyes, willing him better. In the distance, she could hear sirens wailing and, when she opened her eyes again, the area was bathed in flashing lights.

'Remember, you were driving because I'd been drinking. The rain was heavy. You didn't see him until it was too late. Okay? Sam! Okay?'

'Yes.'

They'd been in the foyer of the hotel. 'Give me the keys,' Sam had said.

'No. I'm fine.'

'But we agreed, I'd drive tonight.' She'd tried to take the keys from him.

Grinning, he'd put his hand to her cheek. 'I love you so much.'

And she had thought: *But do I still love you?*

His kiss had tasted of scotch.

'Give me the keys,' she'd said again.

'There's no need. I'm okay.' He'd wrapped his arm round her waist and leaned against her. 'You want to go home. I'm going to take you home and, once we're there, I'm going to show you how much I love you.'

Sam looked down at the man in front of her. *I should have tried harder to stop Neil driving.*

Hands gripped her shoulders.

'We'll take over now, love.' The voice was gentle. 'I'm Mark. This is Terry.'

Sam managed a thin smile at the paramedics. 'I'm Sam. This is my husband, Neil.'

'Do you know who this is?'

Sam shook her head.

Mark draped a blanket round her shoulders. 'Who was driving?'

Sam glanced at Neil. 'I was,' Sam said.

'Any injuries?'

'No. My husband and I are fine.'

Terry, the other paramedic, was kneeling beside the motorcyclist on the opposite side from Sam. 'Has he regained consciousness at all?'

'Briefly. He opened his eyes and I spoke to him and he squeezed my hand.'

'Which hand were you holding?'

'His right hand. Is he going to be okay?'

'Why don't you go and sit in the back of the ambulance? The police will be along shortly to take statements.'

Neil helped her to her feet.

'Left leg looks nasty.'

'Fractured femur, open by the look of it.'

'Yeah. He's lost a lot of blood. Better get on to Abbeyleigh General; warn them we're coming in.'

Sam heard the radio crackle as the paramedic made contact with the hospital. Neil was trying to pull her along but her feet seemed frozen to the ground. Out of the corner of her eye, she saw what looked like a gym bag. Walking over, she picked it up. Sure enough, it was a drawstring bag, with Reebok written on it. Sam peered inside. There was clothing and a pair of trainers. She walked back to the paramedics.

'I think this belongs to him. It was over there.' Sam pointed.

'Thanks.' Terry drew out the man's wallet. 'His name's David McAllister.'

Sam watched as they removed the crash helmet. The motorcyclist hadn't shaved that morning. To Sam, the sight of his stubble made him seem even more vulnerable. She studied his face. His lower lip, fuller than the top lip, protruded slightly as if he were pouting. *And you've every right to be*, Sam thought. *There you were minding your own business and we come barrelling into you.*

'David? Can you hear me, mate? David, my name's Terry and this is Mark. We're going to get you to the hospital as soon as we can.'

'Is he awake?' Sam asked eagerly.

'No, but it helps to talk to him. We're never sure how much people can hear in a situation like this. David, we're just checking for other injuries and then we'll be on our way. Okay, mate? Just hold on, David. We won't be long.'

More sirens screamed out of the darkness. Sam stepped back and bumped into Neil. 'Remember, I'd been drinking. You were driving,' he hissed. 'You didn't see him. The rain must have obscured your view.'

David McAllister. On his motorbike with his gym bag on his back. On his way home? To a wife or a girlfriend? Now, on his back, his blood (his life?) seeping away.

'His name's David.'

'I heard. Did *you* hear what *I* said?'

'Yes.'

A mass of policemen arrived, shouting and pointing. Sam strained to hear what Mark was saying above the din.

'Classic T-bone . . . Abbeyleigh General . . . they're expecting us.'

She watched with trepidation as three officers approached.

'Hello, I'm Sergeant Morris from the Traffic Investigation Unit. PC Trent and PC Wareham are going to take statements from you both. Has anything been moved?'

'Only the man's gym bag. I found it over there.' Sam pointed. 'Is it okay if I ring my daughter, Cassie?'

Sergeant Morris nodded.

Neil handed Sam his phone and she made the call, giving her daughter the briefest of details and telling her they would be home as soon as they could. 'My bag's in the car,' she said to no one in particular as she passed the phone back to Neil.

'Shall we get out of the rain?' PC Trent ushered Sam towards one of the police cars. She looked nervously over her shoulder as Neil was led in the opposite direction.

'Nothing to worry about Mrs . . .'

'Davenport. Sam Davenport.' They sat in the front of the police car.

'The paramedics tell me you're not injured. Might be in shock, though? How do you feel?'

'Numb.'

'Perfectly understandable. Stu,' PC Trent yelled out of the window. 'Go and scare up a cup of hot, sweet tea from the petrol station on the corner. Tea always helps,' he said, turning back to Sam.

'I don't take sugar.'

'Little bit of sugar will help settle you down. I'm going to take a few details from you now and then we'll let you get home. I'll carry out a formal interview with you tomorrow. Okay?'

Sam nodded, barely processing what the officer was saying. Surely, this was all happening to someone else. It couldn't possibly be her car over there, could it?

They'd moved David onto a stretcher, Sam noted. She watched the paramedics lift him from the ground.

'I understand you were driving. What happened?' PC Trent looked over his shoulder, following Sam's gaze. 'They're taking him to hospital.'

'Can I go with him?'

'No.'

Sam watched the ambulance pull away. Its flashing blue lights blurred as tears clouded her eyes.

'Good! Tea.' PC Trent took the cup from his colleague. 'Drink this, Mrs Davenport. You'll feel better.'

Sam took the cup. Shocked, she stared down at herself as tea slopped over the blanket and into her lap. 'I'm sorry,' she gasped, embarrassed.

'It's okay. Here.' PC Trent rescued the cup. 'I'll hold it. Take a sip.'

Sam drank. The tea was indeed very hot and very sweet. She grimaced but continued to drink. When she got halfway, PC Trent trusted her to hold the cup for herself. She laced her fingers round it, hugging it. He was right. The tea did make her feel better.

'Take your time. Tell me what happened.'

Sam struggled to focus. 'We threw a party at the Northey Hotel to celebrate my husband's fortieth. We were heading home and we came down Market Street. We . . . I was getting ready to turn onto the Stebbingsford Road. I thought it was clear. The next thing I knew, he was right on top of us. He just seemed to come out of nowhere.' Sam bit her lip.

'Were you having any mechanical difficulties prior to the accident?'

'No.' Just sniping at one another. Gearing up for another row. Sam hadn't been able to stop herself, pushing in the way a person might tease a mouth ulcer with their tongue, knowing it would hurt but doing it nevertheless.

'I saw the way she looked at you,' she'd said softly.

'For God's sake, Sam! Not this again!' Neil had taken his left hand off the wheel and thrust it through his hair. 'I thought we'd agreed: New year, new start. I'm sorry she was at the party but I'd invited everyone else from work; how would it have looked if I'd left her off the list? I did warn you.' He'd said it as if that made all the difference. 'And I didn't speak to her. Christ, I barely even looked at her. Can't you let it go? Please?' he'd pleaded before adding, 'Why don't you ring our sitter, tell her we're on our way?'

Sam had reached into her bag and then bam! Had she made him lose concentration? Had she caused the crash?

'Is it your car?'

'Yes.'

Two years old. An unusually extravagant present from Neil. Now the car she'd so proudly polished had a man's blood on it. They'd only used her car because Neil's BMW was off the road. Would the man have been less badly injured if they'd been in the BMW and not the Range Rover? Sam massaged her eyes.

'Do you keep the car well maintained and serviced?'

'Yes.'

'Did you come to a complete standstill at the junction?'

I hit him at forty miles an hour. 'I think so.'

'You're not sure?'

Sam hesitated. How much would they be able to tell from the skid marks? 'I can't remember,' she hedged.

'What speed were you doing at the time of impact?'

The word *impact* made her feel nauseous again. 'I don't know.'

'How fast would you say?'

'Five, possibly ten, miles an hour.' Was that an acceptable answer? She had no idea.

'Was it raining?'

'Pouring.'

'Do you normally wear glasses, Mrs Davenport?'

'No.'

'When did you last have a sight test?'

'November.'

'What is it you do?'

'I run an interior design company with my business partner, Connor. Meadowview Designs. And I'm on the fundraising committee for the Abbeyleigh Hospice.' *Why had she told him that? To prove she was a good person? Was she? David McAllister probably didn't think so.*

'And your husband?'

'He's a lawyer with Brookes Davenport, the solicitors on the High Street.'

'I'm going to have to ask you to take a breath test. Do you consent to taking the test?'

'Yes. I had a glass of champagne at the toast.'

PC Trent smiled kindly. 'If you'd just like to blow into the tube and keep blowing until I tell you to stop.'

Sam started to blow. *If I lose my licence, how am I going to work or run the children about?* She derailed her train of thought. *Good God, woman! There's a man on his way to hospital, his leg mangled and you're worried about the bloody inconvenience.*

'You can stop blowing now.' PC Trent fiddled with the apparatus. 'You're not over the limit.'

Sam struggled not to feel guilty as relief surged through her.

'Have you got your driving licence and insurance details with you?'

'No.'

'Don't worry. You can give them to me tomorrow.' PC Trent laid down his pen. 'How old is your daughter? Cassie, wasn't it?'

'She's fifteen, and I have a son, Josh, who's twelve. They've got bad colds. That's why they stayed home tonight. Neil wanted to book us a room at the Northey.' Sam pulled the blanket tighter round her shoulders. 'I didn't want to leave Cassie and Josh all night with the sitter, knowing they weren't well. I wouldn't have gone out at all but for the fact it was Neil's fortieth and we had the party arranged.'

PC Trent nodded sympathetically. 'I just need to take some personal details from you and then we're done.'

A few moments later, Sergeant Morris tapped on the window. Sam lowered it. 'Your bag, Mrs Davenport.'

He handed it to her.

'Thank you.'

'I found it in the well of the front passenger seat.'

Sam opened her mouth and then closed it again. 'I grabbed my bag from the back to find my phone, to ring for the ambulance.' She looked from PC Trent to Sergeant Morris. 'But I knew Neil had his phone on him so I must have thrown my bag back down again.'

Sergeant Morris nodded. One of the other officers was motioning for Morris and Trent to join him. Sam watched them leave and then leaned forward, her head in her hands. She was never going to keep this up. She was going to say something to incriminate herself or Neil. What had she just said? Something about Neil? What if Neil had said something different? Instinctively, Sam reached for the gold ring she wore on the little finger of her left hand and began to twist it furiously. She strained to hear what the officers were saying above the din of the rain hammering on the roof.

'Any witnesses?'

'Not so far.'

Witnesses? Sam's blood ran cold. What if someone had looked out of their window and seen her husband get out of the driver's side? *I've just lied to the police.* The enormity of what she had done began to sink in.

'The motorcyclist is a David McAllister. Couldn't find a note of next of kin but there was a business card. He's an estate agent with Lewis Shaw on the High Street.'

'Better contact Mr Shaw. If they operate, they'll need to speak to someone and get on to PC Stiles at the hospital, see if he's been able to get a statement.'

'Mrs Davenport was the driver.' They all looked in Sam's direction.

Sam rested her elbow on the door and rubbed her eyes, pretending not to listen.

'She reckons five to ten miles an hour. Breath test was okay.'

'I've just spoken to Stiles at the hospital,' PC Wareham said. 'He was able to speak to McAllister briefly. He'd been playing football at the leisure centre. He and a mate bought Chinese afterwards. They'd gone back to the mate's house to eat it. He was making his way home from there. He lives in one of the posh flats in the Old Mill development. He remembers travelling south on the Stebbingsford Road. Then nothing until he woke up in the ambulance. Poor sod'll be lucky to play football again with that leg.'

'What about Mr Davenport? Does he corroborate his wife's story?'

'Yes, Sarge. The husband's Neil Davenport of Brookes Davenport, the lawyers. He's kicking up a bit of a stink. Wants to take his wife home.'

'Did you stick to the story?'

Sam jumped as Neil came up beside the car door. 'Yes.'

'You okay?'

Sam looked up at her husband. His blue eyes were haunted and with his light-brown hair made two shades darker by the rain, his face looked deathly pale. 'Yes,' she replied. 'You?'

Neil nodded and, reaching into the car, took her hand in his, giving it a quick squeeze.

'How fast were you going?'

'I don't know.'

'You said "I hit him at forty miles an hour".'

Neil frowned. 'When did I say that?'

'When we got out. Were you going that fast?'

'Of course not.'

'Why say that, then?'

'Figure of speech.' He sighed. 'All I wanted was to have a good time tonight.'

Sam heard the regret in his voice. She knew how hard he'd been working, racking up the hours, hoping that when his uncle retired in the autumn he would be in pole position to take over as senior partner. Tonight should have been a desperately needed respite. Instead, it had turned into a nightmare.

Sam's heart jolted. Neil looked lost and frightened. Getting out of the car, she put her arms round him.

'They'll let us go home soon.'

'What if I've killed him, Sam?' His hands gripped her skin through the back of her dress so tightly she thought the delicate material might rip.

'He's not going to die,' Sam said with as much conviction as she could muster.

'God, I hope you're right. I didn't mean for this to happen. Any of it.'

Were they still talking about the accident, she wondered?

Chapter Two

PC Trent's interview on the Sunday afternoon followed the same lines as the one the night before. Occasionally, Sam felt Neil squeeze her hand and whenever she looked his way, Murray Black, Brookes Davenport's leading criminal lawyer, nodded and smiled encouragingly.

They were seated at the wooden table in the kitchen at Meadowview Cottage. Sam had obsessively cleaned the Shaker-style kitchen that morning. The units were pristine. The brass saucepans, hanging above their heads, gleamed. But, however hard she'd scrubbed and polished, Sam had been unable to rid herself of the sights, sounds and smells of the night before: the sickening bang, the motorcyclist's mangled leg, the gym bag flung forlornly aside, the pungent smell of his blood.

'Do you remember what was going on in the car prior to the accident? Were you distracted in any way?'

The pressure of Neil's hand was a little harder this time. Sam resisted the urge to look at him. 'No. Everything was fine. I think my husband had his head back, asleep.' They had gone over every detail in the conservatory that morning, fuelled by coffee and guilt, until, finally, she'd felt as though she had indeed been driving.

'Thank you, Mrs Davenport. You've been very helpful.'

Sam walked PC Trent to the door. 'How is he?'

'They operated on his leg last night. That's all I know.'

Sam nodded. 'Thank you.'

'We'll be in touch.'

Sam walked back into the kitchen.

'Bottom line. What are we looking at here?' Neil asked Murray.

'Clean driving licence, sober, momentary loss of concentration. My guess is careless driving. A fine. A few points on the licence.'

Neil pushed his hands through his hair, anchoring them behind his neck. 'And if he's badly injured or, God forbid, he dies?' His gaze was focused on the oak table.

Sam sank down beside her husband, holding her breath.

Murray gave them both a sympathetic smile. 'I'm sure the young man will be fine. There's nothing to suggest otherwise. He had a broken leg. However nasty, people don't tend to die of broken legs. We'll put in a guilty plea and you'll soon be able to put all this unpleasantness behind you.'

Sam gave him a wan smile. He meant well but how could Murray know what it had felt like to look into the biker's eyes and know they were responsible for what had happened to him?

Sam splashed water into the kettle as Neil showed his partner out. 'He's an estate agent, you know, the motorcyclist. If I'd known that at the time, I'd have told her to put her foot down.' The two men laughed.

Sam arched her eyebrows as Neil returned. 'Put my foot down?' she said icily.

He looked embarrassed.

'You didn't stop at the junction, did you?'

Neil sat at the table and rubbed his hands over his face. 'It was late. The roads were quiet. I might have been driving a little fast.' He met Sam's gaze. 'You were worried about Cassie and Josh, eager to get home.'

'So this is my fault?'

'No.'

'You were drunk,' Sam said accusingly. 'I tried to stop you driving.'

'Yeah well, if you felt that strongly, you should have tried harder. For both our sakes.' Neil scraped the chair over the flagstone floor and stood. 'Christ, I didn't do it on purpose. I didn't see him.' He slammed his way out of the kitchen.

Last night, he'd wanted to make love. Practically begged her. With images of the accident circling in her mind, Sam hadn't felt able to. Instead, he'd clung to her and, when she'd rolled onto her side, he had pressed in tightly against her, not in a sexual way, but in a seeking succour way.

Regret lapped around her. There would have been a time, not so long ago, when anger would not have been her default position where Neil was concerned, only love.

Crossing to the phone, Sam ran her finger down the list of emergency numbers and reached for the receiver.

'Abbeyleigh General.'

'Hello, I'd like . . .'

The kitchen door swung open. Sam put the phone down.

'And another thing,' Neil said. 'We should be supporting one another in a time of crisis not tearing each other apart.'

'I've just lied to the police for you. What do you call that, if not support?'

His tense expression softened. 'It took a lot of guts to stand up and take the blame for me. I'm just sorry I had to ask you to do it.' He sighed. 'You know how impossible it is at work at the moment. Edward is so worried about cries of nepotism; I have to work twice as hard as anyone else to prove myself. An incident like this would have ruined my chances.'

'I know.'

Pulling her into his arms, Neil bent his head to hers. 'I lost my concentration. It could have happened to anyone.' His fingers tightened over her shoulders. 'I need you to tell me you don't blame me.'

Edging back, Sam studied his face. At forty, Neil was five years older than her and, at that moment, he looked every one of those extra years and more besides.

She felt her heart contract. He might have been behind the wheel but she was as much to blame, for letting him be there in the first place and then distracting him. 'Like you said, it could have happened to anyone but please, promise me you'll never drink and drive again.'

'I promise.' He kissed her cheek. 'I love you, Sam. You do know that, don't you?' He hugged her tightly. Then, easing back, he cupped her face in his hands. 'I'll be with you every step of the way. You won't have to do this alone. You have my word.' Behind him, the kettle began to boil. 'Why don't you go and put your feet up in the conservatory?' he suggested. 'I'll bring you a cup of tea when it's brewed.'

Chapter Three

Sam looked out of the conservatory window; the garden lay dank and dripping in front of her. Cobwebs laced the nearby conifers, raindrops hanging across them like strings of pearls. Beyond, fingers of mist were pushing their way round the old apple tree, obscuring everything that lay beyond. It was mid-afternoon but Sam could already feel the darkness creeping in.

She lit the Tiffany lamp on the small wicker table. The conservatory was a large, octagonal shape. Sam had stuck to a limited palette of colours, cream for the floor and the blinds, luscious greens, in varying hues, for the plants set off by the odd splash of colour; a hibiscus in bloom in one corner, a striking cerise bougainvillea in another. A sumptuous pastel-green wicker suite, with cream cushions, nestled invitingly among the plants. Sam sat on the sofa, twisting her ring back and forth.

The accident complicated everything but the fundamental problem remained. Neil had cheated on her and she had tried to forgive him. Had tried to forget. Four months on and she was still trying. Still failing. How long did she give it before conceding defeat?

'Has the policeman left?'

Turning, she found Josh in the doorway. Sam patted the seat beside her. 'Yes, he's gone.' She felt her son's forehead and frowned. 'You're still very hot, darling. How do you feel?'

'I'm okay.' He nestled into her side.

Sam put her arm round him. Twelve going on eight. How quickly children lost the desire to appear grown up when they felt under the weather.

'Are you going to prison?' Josh's eyes were large with fear as he looked up at her.

'No, sweetheart.' She hugged him to her fiercely, pressing a kiss to the top of his head.

'Truly?'

'Truly.'

'I heard you and Dad arguing. Everything's going to be okay, isn't it, Mum?'

Sam sighed. That wonderful childhood world where just a few words from a trusted adult could soothe away all fears. But who would soothe away her fears?

'Mum?'

'Everything's going to be fine, darling.'

*

Neil Davenport massaged his temples before popping two painkillers into his mouth, desperate to quell the jackhammer in his head. What a mess! Of all the things to happen. Why them? Why now? He knew men who drank heavily every weekend, nothing ever happened to them, while he'd had a few glasses of scotch and his world had caved in.

All he'd wanted was to celebrate his birthday. One lousy night. Surely, he deserved it after all the hours he'd devoted to chasing this blasted promotion?

The pain behind Neil's eyes worsened as his thoughts turned to the motorcyclist. Broken legs could be nasty and he was so young. Sam's age, maybe younger. What if there were head injuries, too? How was he going to live with himself if he'd ruined another man's life?

He sat down heavily at the kitchen table, head bent. It was all his fault. He'd let Sam's outburst about Megan distract him and now a man lay injured. Would the fallout from his adultery never end?

He had already spent the last four months feeling like a shit for the illicit tumble with Megan, which, if he was honest, he'd been too drunk even to appreciate.

Looking back, he tried to figure out how he'd got himself into such a mess. He'd been working long hours and Megan had been there, his assistant fee earner, ordering takeaway food to share across his desk, sympathising about the stress of a big case, willing to stay late to discuss tactics.

He'd spent more time with her than with his own family. Yes, he'd thought about sex with her. Like most men did about most women. She was so different to Sam: with exotic almond eyes and a pillowy chest.

He'd wondered what it would be like and, like a besotted fool, when the opportunity to find out had presented itself, he'd taken it and her. But it hadn't been planned and it certainly hadn't been worth it. At home or at work. He ought to have 'idiot' tattooed across his forehead or somewhere more delicate.

He was lucky Megan hadn't turned the whole thing on its head and had him up on sexual harassment charges. She'd been great, however. Kept quiet. Even cried when he'd told her he was happy with Sam, not looking to have an affair.

He rubbed his neck. One selfish mistake and so many damaged lives.

He roused himself to pour Sam's tea and, with a sigh, carried the mug through to the conservatory. Thank goodness for Sam. Her willingness to take the blame for the accident would see them through this latest drama.

As for the harm wrought on their relationship, that would take a lot longer. The pain on Sam's face when she'd spotted Megan at the party had been a knife to his heart. He had been crazy to think they were on their way to putting his infidelity behind them. He wondered now whether they'd even begun.

*

Sam watched Neil put her tea on the table.

He perched on the edge of the sofa. 'Where are the kids?'

'Cassie has gone to Sophie's. Josh is on his computer.'

'Last night, did the paramedics say anything about other injuries?'

'I think it was just the man's leg but I'm not sure.'

Neil pinched the bridge of his nose.

'I was thinking of ringing the hospital,' Sam admitted.

'They won't tell you anything.' He met her gaze. 'I've tried.'

'Then maybe we should go in person. Apologise.'

'No! The one thing you must never do is accept responsibility for an accident. If we did that, we'd be in trouble with our insurance company.'

'Don't you think we're in enough trouble already? I hated lying for you.'

'I know. I'm sorry I had to ask you to do it. If things were different at work, I would have done the right thing.' He met her gaze. 'Come on, you know that.'

Sam nodded.

'I should have listened to you. I should have let you drive. If I'd done that . . .' His voice faltered. 'All I wanted was a night off from everything.'

The urge to take Neil in her arms and comfort him was strong but Sam resisted and moved instead to stand in front of the window. Drizzle misted the glass. She watched as it turned to heavy rain, battering the pots of winter pansies she'd planted.

'I keep hearing that bang in my head, like an explosion, when I hit him. I've been driving since I was seventeen. I've never had an accident. Not a single bloody one. Last night I could have killed us all.'

The rain was torrential now. Sam watched it bounce off the patio. Suddenly, Neil was behind her, his arms round her waist, his chin resting on her shoulder. Sam tensed.

'I'll find a way to make it up to you.'

Was he still talking about the accident? She didn't think so. A pretty young woman had thrown herself at him four months earlier and, in a moment of weakness, temptation and curiosity had got the better of him.

It had been a one-night stand that had exploded in the midst of their marriage like a hand grenade. She'd fought valiantly to bind the wounds it had inflicted on her but, despite her best efforts, they were as raw now as the day Neil had confessed.

'I had no choice but to invite Megan to the party. I hoped she'd have the good sense not to show up. I guess I was wrong.'

Just hearing him say Megan's name was enough to plunge the dagger into Sam's heart afresh. She moved out of his embrace. One day, she might have built up enough armour to deflect the blows but not yet.

'She's in love with you,' she said tonelessly.

'No.'

His reply had come too quickly.

'Megan had a crush and I was a fool for being flattered by it. It meant nothing.'

Sam crossed the room to shut the conservatory door. 'You think because you say it meant nothing I should forget about it but I can't. God knows I've tried, but I can't.'

Neil recoiled.

'Darling, it was a stupid mistake. You and Josh were spending the weekend at Comic Con in London, Cassie was staying at Sophie's. Megan and I were working late. She ordered a takeaway and before I knew it, we were back at her place drinking wine. I was a fool. The biggest fool going but it meant . . .'

He fell silent.

'Would you have told me?'

'What?'

'If she hadn't answered your mobile and if I hadn't confronted you when I got home, would you have told me?'

'Yes. What happened was no reflection on you, on us. I was caught up in the moment. Drunk. One minute we were chatting, the next we were kissing.'

'And fucking.'

'It wasn't planned.' He put his hand to her cheek but she pulled away. 'I want to mend what I've broken, Sam. I just don't know how.'

She shook her head, fighting back the tears.

'Now that Megan has moved departments, I go days, weeks even, without seeing her. That's the God's honest truth.'

Sam fought the urge to clamp her hands over her ears and shut out the white noise of hows and whys and sorrys. They didn't help her deal with the here and now. They didn't show her how to start over or to trust again and he wasn't making it easy for her. Just last week he'd been at the office until eight one night, seven the next. When at last she'd heard his key in the door she'd confronted him. 'I thought you were going to work from home more?'

'I do, whenever I can.' He'd spread his hands in supplication.

And Sam had thought: *Was she there to hold your hand tonight? Is your lack of appetite because you grabbed a sandwich like you said or did she order a takeaway like she did before? Did she rub your shoulders while you ate?*

'Short of leaving the firm, I don't know what more I can do and you know I can never do that.'

Turning away from him, Sam stared at the lashing rain. What more *could* he do? Yet, all that he had done was still not enough to fill the well of pain that had been sunk in her soul. She needed to put some distance between them. It was the only way.

She hooked her hair behind her ears. Her thinking hairstyle Neil called it. *Watch out!* he'd declare. *Sam's going all serious on us.*

It was now or never, Sam realised. She could either keep up the pretence that she was dealing with the anguish or she could stop lying to Neil and to herself.

'I can't go on like this, Neil. I'm sorry. I've tried but I'm tired of trying. I want a break.'

'Darling, I . . .'

'Dad's affairs ripped my family apart.'

'I know . . .'

'I can't be my mother, constantly forgiving, constantly waiting for the next bad thing to happen.'

'You don't have to be. I promise I . . .'

'Dad made promises. He broke every promise he ever made.'

'I'm not your father, Sam. The way he treated you and your mum was unforgiveable. He was a bastard. Don't put me in the same league as him, please. I know how badly I've hurt you. Just tell me what you need me to do to make things right and I'll do it.'

'I'd like you to leave.'

Such momentous words and yet, in the end, they'd been much easier to say than she could ever have imagined. Sam felt a weight lift. She watched Neil's look of confusion turn to horror.

'What? No! Is this because of the accident? I'll go to the police now. I'll hold my hands up.'

'This isn't about the accident.'

'I don't understand. I thought we'd agreed: New year, new start.'

'It was you saying those things, not me.'

'Let's talk about this again tomorrow. I'm sure you'll feel differently.'

'I won't.'

'What about the children?'

Cassie and Josh had been the reason she'd delayed this long but how long did you suppress personal need for the greater good? She'd given it four months. Would four years have been better?

She'd thought about it last night as she'd watched the slow journey of the moon across the sky. The children would probably have left home by then, for them it would have been better, but what about for her? Four years of pretending, of living a lie, would have left her an empty shell. She'd seen what that had done to her mother.

'We'll tell them the truth. That we're going through a bad patch and we need to take a break from one another. It's not as if they don't know something's wrong. They've heard the raised voices. They've felt the tension. We've been pretending everything is fine but we've been fooling no one, least of all them.'

'Why don't I just move into the spare room?'

'No.' She ignored the pleading look in his eyes. 'Don't fight me on this Neil, please! I need you to do this.'

'You're not saying you want a divorce?'

'I'm saying I want some time apart.'

'A separation?'

Sam nodded.

'Can I have a couple of days to find somewhere?'

'Of course.'

'How long do you want me to move out for?'

'I don't know.'

'A few days? A week? A month?' he pressed.

'I don't know,' she said again more sharply.

'Should I pack a bag or a suitcase?'

'A suitcase.' She watched his face fall in the gloom of the winter's afternoon.

The rain drummed on the conservatory roof, filling the silence.

Chapter Four

Sam opened the door of Meadowview Cottage as her business partner, Connor Barrett, pulled up in his Audi A3. Pavarotti blasted out of the music system as Sam manhandled two overstuffed carrier bags onto the back seat.

'Rocking the knackered look, Samson,' Connor said.

'I love you, too.'

Sam had done her best to contain the damage six sleepless nights had done to her face but her blue eyes, usually her best feature, were puffy in spite of the light covering of make-up, and her graduated blonde bob lacked the vitality it normally had. A bad hair day. There had been a lot of those.

She had thought asking Neil to leave would be the hard part but the period leading up to his departure had been worse. The 'You'll come and visit me won't you, kids?' speeches had been designed to ratchet up the pressure on her as much as to cement future arrangements with the children.

They'd had the desired effect. She was already getting it in the neck from Cassie in particular. 'Why are you making Dad leave?' 'Can't you just sort things out?' And the kicker: 'Don't you love him any more?'

Neil and the children had hoped she'd relent and Sam had come close. There had been a series of lows: enduring the sullen silence round the breakfast table or, worse, Neil's forced jocularity; opening the wardrobe and being confronted by a row of empty hangers.

It would have been easy to change her mind, but the easy options in life were rarely the best ones. She'd spent four months pretending the adultery hadn't happened because it was easier to lie to herself than face the consequences. She couldn't go on like that.

'So Neil's gone then.' It was a statement not a question.

Sam turned the music down. 'Yes. How did you . . .'

'He's renting a flat two doors away from mine.'

'Your idea?'

'He asked if I could help him find somewhere *short term.*'

Sam shot Connor a look.

'I cooked him Bolognese—'

'You *cooked*?'

Connor laughed. 'Okay reheated. Waitrose do remarkably good Bolognese. Neil and I shared a bottle of red.'

'Sounds cosy.'

'He spent the evening talking about you.'

At least she knew he hadn't been at Megan's.

'Josh asked me if it would be forever,' Sam said.

'What did you say?'

'I told him I didn't know. Neil wants to keep it quiet for the time being. Just us.'

Connor nodded. 'My lips are sealed, hon. So a lot's happened while you've been taking some time. Mrs Cassell has changed her mind. Again. She wants to go for the peacock blue. Terrible choice. I'm trying to talk her down. We had three new clients. All promising. Phil Blunkett wants us to kit out a show flat at his new development. Those fabric swatches have arrived at last and Rhys has asked me out to dinner. In Paris.'

'The designer Rhys?'

'The very same.'

'When?'

'When he gets back from Tokyo.'

'Congratulations.'

Connor grinned. 'That will be you soon, hooking up on Tinder. Have you downloaded the app yet?'

'Behave.'

'You should. Live a little before you let Neil come home.'

'Who said Neil was coming home?'

Connor smiled.

'What have you got there?' Connor asked indicating the bags in the back. 'Neil's clothes?'

'Donations for the charity auction. I'm going to drop them off after I've been to the hospital.'

'About that . . .'

'I need to know how he is. Without any news, I feel as though I'm drowning in a vacuum.'

'Can you drown in a vacuum?'

'I lay in bed last night thinking about him, imagining all sorts.'

'Oh hello.'

'I meant about his leg. It was an open fracture. That means his thigh bone came through his skin. Think about it, Connor.'

'I'd rather not and neither should you, hon. Does Neil know you're doing this?'

'No. When I suggested it, he told me to stay away. Said the insurance company wouldn't like it.'

'He's right.'

'I need to say sorry. Maybe then I can get the accident out of my head.'

Connor patted her knee. 'Want me to come in with you?'

Sam threw him a smile. 'Thanks, but no. This is something I need to do on my own.'

'How are you going to get in? Don't you have to be a relative or something?'

'It's a hospital, Connor, not a prison. Although I thought I'd say I was his sister just in case it's restricted visiting or something.'

Connor laughed. 'In for a penny, in for a pound I suppose. Do you know which ward he's on?'

'Stebbingsford. Second floor. I rang this morning.'

'Well, I hope you've got your sackcloth and ashes on under that coat. After all, if a job's worth doing . . .'

'Very funny.'

'It was an accident, Sam.' He turned the car into the hospital grounds. 'You have to stop beating yourself up.'

'I want the guy to know that I care.'

'Which is laudable. Just don't go expecting him to be very receptive. Don't imagine he's in the best frame of mind right now, and however well-intentioned your apology is, he may not want to hear it.'

Sam nodded. 'It's a risk I have to take.'

Connor pulled up in the drop off/pick up zone and leaned over to kiss Sam's cheek. 'Good luck, hon. When you're done, you'll find me at the office running our business.'

Sam laughed. 'What would I do without you?' she asked as she picked up the bags from the back seat.

'A question I often ask myself. Bring me a Frappuccino when you're done.'

Chapter Five

Sam rubbed alcohol gel into her hands at the entrance to the Stebbingsford Ward. Then, taking a deep breath, she approached the nurses' station.

'I was hoping to see David McAllister. I'm his sister,' she added.

The young nurse smiled at her. 'David's in the room on the right.'

It was that easy. Somehow, she had imagined it would be harder. Perhaps she'd just hoped it would be. Apologising was a noble thing to do. The problem was finding the nerve to do it. Her hands were suddenly clammy and as she walked down the corridor her heart felt fit to jump out of her chest. What if she wasn't as noble as she wanted to be?

The door of David's room was open. She caught her breath. His hair was brown, with a floppy fringe that fell across his forehead. Unshaven, his stubble reminded her of how he'd looked on the night of the accident except the man she'd last seen on his back, eyelids flickering as the rain fell on him, was now sitting up in bed, dressed in a white tee shirt. He looked so well; Sam offered up a prayer of gratitude.

Her nerve faltering, she toyed with the idea of leaving. He seemed fine. What good would an apology do anyway? She jumped as David spoke.

'Hello, have you come to prod and poke me about as well?' He had a strong Scottish lilt. Every letter of every word was clearly pronounced.

'No. I'm . . .'

'Typical. The prettiest woman I've seen all week. I was hoping for a bed bath at the very least.'

Sam grinned. 'Sorry, you're out of luck.' Stepping into the room, she realised David had another visitor. The man looked to be in his thirties, overweight with dark hair and glasses.

'Don't mind him,' the man said, jerking his thumb at David with a smile. 'He's high on medication.'

'Not high enough,' David countered.

The large man stood and offered Sam his hand. 'I'm Tony.'

Sam shook hands. 'Sam.'

Both men were staring at her, clearly waiting for her to speak. Sam hadn't envisaged an audience while she apologised. What if this friend, Tony, turned nasty? The last dregs of her courage drained away. The apology would have to wait until she could get David on his own.

'So, what can we do for you?' David asked genially.

'I . . .' Sam looked down at the booklet open on the table across the bed. There was a section about Hospital Radio and beneath it another on Hospital Visitors.

'Are you a hospital visitor?' Tony asked following her gaze.

Sam hesitated, then nodded. 'But you've already got a visitor, so I'll go,' she added hastily and took a step towards the door. The apology would keep for another day.

'You're welcome to stay. Beats looking at his ugly mug. Tony, get the lady a chair.'

'Really, there's no need. I wouldn't want to interrupt.'

Despite her protestations, Tony was already fetching a chair from the corridor and setting it down beside her.

'We were only talking about football, nothing heavy.' David smiled. 'Please, sit down.'

Not wishing to appear rude, Sam sat. 'Thank you.' The room was very hot. Sam unwound her scarf.

'I'm David McAllister.' David raised his hand in greeting.

'Sam.' She bit her lip. 'I've already said that, haven't I?'

'Aye, you have. So, what do you do when you're not being a hospital visitor?' David asked.

'I run an interior design company.' She left the scarf in a bundle on her lap and undid a couple of the buttons of her coat. Should hospitals be this hot? Surely it just allowed the bugs to breed?

'Samples for your customers?' David nodded towards the two bags Sam had stowed beside her chair.

'No. I'm on the board at the Abbeyleigh Hospice. We're holding a charity auction in March. These are donations.'

'We raised three thousand pounds with a sponsored swim for the hospice last year,' Tony said. 'Not me personally,' he added, laughing as he clutched his girth. 'My colleagues at the council.'

'You decided to sit that one out, didn't you?' David said.

Tony smiled and pushed his glasses up his nose. 'I have a slow metabolism. Mum and Dad are both the same, larger than life.'

'He'll be telling you next he's big boned. Christ, man, you just eat too much. Admit it.'

Sam was disappointed. Did David have to be quite so disparaging towards his friend? She realised that perhaps she'd been guilty of eulogising David McAllister. Young, energetic (evidence the gym bag), handsome, hardworking (she'd imagined). She'd put him on a pedestal. The poor, tragic man who had been minding his own business until her husband had crashed into him. It had never crossed Sam's mind that she might not like him when she met him.

Remembering the grapes she had brought with her, Sam plucked them from the top of one of the carrier bags. 'These are for you.'

'You'll go bankrupt buying grapes for every person you visit,' David said.

'You were a special case.' She offered the grapes round before leaving them on the bed.

'Head case more like,' Tony retorted.

'Special, how?' David asked.

Sam clenched her fists beneath her thighs, her nails biting into her palms. *Idiot! Think before you speak.* She forced a smile. 'You're the first person I've visited.'

'I wondered why you didn't have a little name tag thingy. Everyone else does. I hate hospitals,' he said vehemently. 'I don't think I'd voluntarily come to one. How often do you have to visit?'

'Um.' Sam looked from one to the other. 'I can pretty much do what I want at the moment,' she said vaguely.

David raised his eyebrows. 'That's nice. How come?'

'Early days.'

'Why did you pick me?'

'I . . .' Sam's mind froze.

'Sam? Why me?'

David's voice cut through her jumbled thoughts.

'I just picked a name.'

'Nothing to do with me being handsome and charming then?'

'I'm afraid not.' She smiled.

'Have we met?' David asked suddenly.

Sam's heart stuttered. 'No, I don't think so.' She let her fringe fall forward, eager to shield her eyes from David's suddenly keen gaze.

'You look familiar.'

Could he have a memory buried somewhere in his subconscious of those few brief seconds when he'd looked into her eyes and squeezed her hand? She felt the heat creep into her face.

'You haven't asked me what I'm doing here,' David said. 'Normally, it's the first thing people ask.'

Of course it is. Except, I already know. 'I didn't like to pry,' Sam said.

David let out a shout of laughter. 'Believe me, all trace of privacy disappeared the minute I came in here. I was riding my motorbike when a car, one of those big four by fours, collided with me. I'd been playing football at the leisure centre. Tony's our goalie. Not the best but what he lacks in ability he makes up for with enthusiasm, don't you, mate?' David grinned. 'Anyway, me and one of the other lads picked up Chinese after and took it back to his house. I was on my way home from there when it happened.'

Sam knotted her hands together. The diamonds of her engagement ring bit into her skin as her ring slipped round. The heartbreak diet, worked every time. 'Can you remember the accident?'

'No. Only what the police told me. Apparently, this woman said she didn't see me. Didn't look properly more like. It was at a junction. The police are investigating. They don't think the stupid bitch stopped. Can you believe it? Who wouldn't stop at a stop junction?' David glowered. 'And my bike's a write off.'

'She was probably talking on her mobile,' Tony said.

'Aye or doing her make-up.' David glanced at Sam. 'No offence.'

'None taken,' Sam said quietly. So, the police had worked it out. She'd feared they would.

'Are you okay?' David asked.

Realising the two men were looking at her, Sam struggled to recover her composure. 'The bike can be replaced,' she said tremulously. 'How are you?'

'Busted my leg. Fractured my femur. That's the thighbone to you and me. They had to stick a rod down it and screw it into place.'

'He'll set off the detectors at the airport now, for sure.'

'Aye. I hadn't thought of that.'

'Is your leg the only injury?' Sam asked.

'Isn't that enough for you?'

Sam caught the twinkle in David's eye, the smile tugging at his lips. At least his sense of humour was intact.

'Cuts and bruises mostly. My left knee took a hammering, my left elbow. Across my ribs. It could have been worse.'

Sam's eyes widened.

'She could have driven off and left me. At that time of night, in that weather, I could have bled to death before anyone found me.'

Sam heard Neil's voice in her head. Determined. Scared. *'We sure as hell can't stay.'* If Neil had had his way . . .

Sam shuddered. 'But you're going to be all right?'

'Aye. They've already had me up and out of bed on crutches. My physio's a sadist, mind.'

'The physiotherapy's important, though, mate,' Tony said gently.

'I know.'

'I'm sorry,' Sam said.

Both men looked at her in surprise. 'You've got nothing to be sorry for,' David said. 'It's the bitch who was driving who's at fault.'

'You don't want to let his little sob story get to you,' Tony added.

'He's right. You'll hear worse stories than mine in here. You need to toughen up, Samantha.'

'Yes.' *Except that bitch you're talking about is me.*

Inwardly, Sam cringed. This charade had gone on long enough. If only Tony would leave, she could confess and get it over with. While she tried to think of a way to get Tony out of the room, Sam searched for something to say. Something banal. The sort of thing a real hospital visitor would ask. 'How long have you been down south?'

'Fourteen years. I moved down a couple of years after my parents died. They were killed in a coach crash in Italy when I was sixteen. My family don't have a whole lot of luck with automobiles.' David smiled sadly. 'It was just me, no other family, so I thought I'd make a clean start with my girlfriend at the time. I'm an estate agent, by the way.'

Tony made the sign of the cross.

David laughed. 'Highly regarded, as you can see.'

Maybe I should ask Tony to get me a drink? Sam looked up as the nurse she'd seen at the desk stuck her head round the door.

'Help, Jane,' David said. 'They're ganging up on me in here.'

'You're saved. Visiting time's over,' she said with a smile before withdrawing.

'Will you come again?' David asked looking at Sam.

'Would you like me to?' Sam asked surprised.

'Aye.' He helped himself to a grape. 'Don't forget, I'm your special case. You have a duty now.'

Flummoxed, Sam said, 'I'll do my best.'

Chapter Six

David threw aside the Lee Child novel. It wasn't holding him like it had before the accident but he suspected nothing would. For the umpteenth time he checked his watch. Lauren had told him she would visit on Saturday morning. Now, there was only ten minutes of the morning left. He fiddled anxiously with the strap of his watch. If she didn't get there soon the ward would be closed for lunch.

'Hello, David.'

'Lauren! Where have you been? I thought you'd be here hours ago.'

'It's a long way to come.'

'Not that far.'

He watched her gaze take in his dressing gown at the end of the bed, his slippers on the floor, the crutches beside the armchair.

'Darling, I wish you'd come sooner.'

'The traffic was bad.'

He'd meant sooner as in earlier in the week but he let it go. She was here now.

'The nurse said they'll be serving lunch in a minute. They were just wheeling the trolleys in when I got here.' She wrinkled her nose. 'Rather you than me. It smelt awful.'

'Come and sit down.' He indicated the seat beside him.

'No, I'm okay.'

She was bundled up against the February cold in a military-style great coat, pink gloves and a voluminous woollen scarf. 'Aren't you even going to take off your coat?' he asked.

'There's no point. I'll have to go soon.'

He tried to hide his disappointment. Didn't she realise how he'd longed to see her these past few days? A couple of rushed phone calls and one-line emails had been the extent of his contact with her. Now, all he wanted to do was run his fingers through her blonde hair, kiss her heart-shaped mouth and celebrate the fact he was still alive. Despite the pain and the drugs, he felt his body stir as it always did when Lauren was near.

'I've missed you.'

She showed no intention of leaving the doorway, as if to do so might expose her to some killer hospital bug.

Did he really have to ask her to kiss him? He'd been in a life-threatening accident, for God's sake. The least he'd expected was a tear-filled reunion, Lauren throwing herself at him, distraught at how close she'd come to losing him. David nobly shrugging off the pain to comfort her. The images dissolved in his mind.

'Marcus drove me here.'

'Your boss?' He was instantly suspicious.

'I was going to tell you last week but . . .' She gestured to the bed.

David cringed at her look of distaste as her gaze settled once again on his crutches. 'Tell me what?' he demanded.

'Marcus and I are an item. It happened very suddenly.'

'When?'

'A few weeks ago.'

'Not that suddenly then.' He turned away, pain and anger vying for supremacy.

'I was going to tell you,' she said again.

'Well now you have so you can bugger off.'

'Charming! I didn't have to come at all, you know.'

'Do you expect me to be grateful?'

'I'm sorry.'

'So am I.' He met her gaze. 'Sorry I ever let myself get mixed up with you. I should have known you wouldn't stick around. You were with someone else when we first got together, weren't you? Thanks for finishing with me, Lauren. While I'm in hospital. A few weeks too late but never mind. I'm fine by the way, thanks for asking.'

She pursed her lips. 'I hope you get better soon.'

With that, she was gone. Just as Jane came in with a tray.

'Beef stew and jelly and custard. Is that right?'

He nodded. His appetite gone.

*

As Sam parked her rental car in the hospital car park, snatches of her conversation with David came back to her. She smiled as she heard his accent in her head. First had become furst. Girl had become gurl. Look had become loook. However, as she stared up at the hospital building, her smile faded and the knot tightened in her stomach.

Telling him she was a hospital visitor had seemed like a harmless white lie but it had meant David had placed a degree of trust in her as a result. When he found out she'd abused that trust he was going to be as angry as hell and that was before a word of her apology had even been uttered.

Sam wanted to bury her face in shame as she replayed his words. *'You've got nothing to be sorry for. It's the bitch who was driving who's at fault.'*

Why hadn't she had the guts to speak up then and get it over with? She had to tell David the truth and accept the consequences, however unpleasant, and she had to do it quickly before someone recognised her and did it for her. It was only a matter of time until the police or the insurance company gave him enough details for him to work it out. If the insurance hadn't been in Neil's name alone it would already have been too late. Better by far that he heard it from her first. Squaring her shoulders, Sam set off.

You mustn't falter this time, even if Tony is there. Say your piece. Apologise and leave. No sense dragging this out for you or for him.

Sam paused at the entrance to David's room, taking

a moment to ready herself. David was sitting in the armchair which had been turned to face the window. As she stood there she saw him wipe the back of his hand under his eyes. There was no mistaking the action. He was crying.

God, I shouldn't be seeing this. She started to back away.

'Lauren? Is that you?'

Realising he must have seen the movement of her shadow, Sam reluctantly returned to the doorway. 'No. It's me,' she said and raised her hand in greeting.

'Oh hello.'

He'd shaved that morning. It made him look younger, she thought. Younger and lost. 'Fancy some company?' she asked, keeping her tone deliberately light as she held up the new bag of grapes she'd purchased. Perhaps if she stuck to the role of hospital visitor for just a little longer she could cheer him up.

'Not really.'

Undeterred, she proffered the grapes anyway. 'Could be just the time you need it most,' she said, determined now not to take no for an answer. She sat on the edge of the bed. His lunch was untouched on a tray on the table, she noticed. She inched the grapes closer.

David helped himself, threw a grape in the air, caught it on the back of his hand, flicked it and caught it again in his palm.

'Neat trick.'

'It's amazing what you do to fill in the time.' Elbow leaning on the windowsill, he rested his head against his fist. 'God, I could do with a drink. Next time, smuggle in a couple of beers, will you?'

'Painkillers and booze?' Sam raised her eyebrows.

'Oblivion sounds quite appealing just now.' He took another grape.

'Has something happened?' she asked, half afraid of what his answer might be. Had there been some kind of set back with his recovery?

'My girlfriend, Lauren, just broke up with me.'

Sam knew that look and the emptiness that accompanied it. He hadn't seen the break up coming. Blindsided by it, he was still reeling. She knew that after the shock would come hours of soul searching. Endless questions with no satisfactory answers. Then, anger would descend, weaving its way into the fabric of his being like a tapeworm, stealing away his peace of mind, replacing it with self-doubt.

Sam had lived through every stage. David was just beginning the journey. Her heart went out to him.

He met her gaze. 'Bad day,' he admitted quietly.

Sam watched as the muscles in his cheek worked to clamp down on his emotions. He had every right to be bitter, to feel sorry for himself.

Before she had chance to think about what she was doing, she leaned across and pressed a kiss to his cheek.

Both equally surprised by her actions, they stared at one another. Slowly, Sam drew back, as if by doing so gradually, David might be able to overlook what had just happened.

Turning, she stared intently at the window, watching

a raindrop as it raced down the pane, then another and another. Anything to avoid having to look at David.

What the hell was she doing? There was a boundary. A line over which she was not supposed to cross and certainly not with David. Men like her father and Neil might be able to break the rules with impunity. It didn't mean she could.

'I'm sorry.'

'I've never had a woman apologise for kissing me before,' he said wryly.

Slowly she lifted her gaze to find him smiling at her. 'At least it made you smile.'

He laughed. 'You've a kind heart, Sam.'

Embarrassed, Sam began to disagree.

'Believe me, it's nice to know there are still women like you out there.' He unscrewed the lid of a bottle of mineral water and took a long drink.

Sam watched his Adam's apple rise and fall as he drank, tried to ignore the flutter of attraction in her chest. She twisted the gold ring on her little finger.

'That woman who hit me hasn't even had the courtesy to send a card. You'd think after all the damage she's done it would be the least she could do. Whereas someone like you, with your own business to run, goes to all the trouble of coming here to spend time with complete strangers. You're a class act, Sam.'

Sam hunched her shoulders as David raised the bottle of water to her in salute.

'I should go,' she said, standing.

'No.' His hand shot out, gripping hers. 'Stay. Please.'

His gaze was intense, his eyes boring into hers. 'I could really use a friend.' He gave her hand a squeeze before releasing it.

Sam subsided back onto the bed, her heart beating discordantly. It had been a long time since a man other than her husband had held her hand or looked at her the way David had just looked at her, but she was separated now. The old rules didn't apply. She could flirt if she wanted to. And she wanted to. The realisation left her feeling lightheaded.

'You're married.'

Her new-found sense of freedom crashed and burned. She'd yet to take off her wedding ring. 'Yes.'

'For how long?'

'Sixteen years.' And holding. Their anniversary holiday to Sardinia in August had already been booked. Was there a sadder prospect than her and the children going alone?

'You don't look old enough.'

'You're very kind.'

'Kids?'

'Two. My daughter Cassie is fifteen and I have a son Josh who's twelve.'

'Are they good kids?'

'The best.' She smiled. 'But I guess every parent says that.'

'Tell me about them.'

'Cassie wants to be a pop star or a dancer or an actress depending on what day of the week it is.' Sam rolled her eyes and David chuckled. 'Josh is obsessed with computers. His father and I expect the FBI to come battering down the door one day because Josh has hacked into somewhere he shouldn't.'

David grinned before taking another drink. 'And your business?'

'I started it ten years ago in the back bedroom. It was just a hobby really and then I did a college course.'

Sam could still recall Neil's look of surprise. 'They do courses in scattering cushions?'

'There's a bit more to it than that.'

'I should bloody hope so at that price.'

'Once I finished the course, I joined up with my best friend, Connor. He was working as a window dresser and together we launched Meadowview Designs. Now, we rent a small office in Abbeyleigh.'

'Sorry, David. Didn't realise you had a visitor.'

They turned as the nurse, Jane, entered.

She picked up the lunch tray and tutted. 'Not hungry?'

'Not today.'

'You need to eat. Got to keep your strength up. Do you want me to see if they've got anything else?'

'Maybe later.'

'I haven't seen you doing a circuit of the ward recently. Must do it, you know. Every hour. It helps ward off blood clots and it's good practice on the crutches.'

David grimaced. 'I know. I'll go in a minute.'

'If I'm in the way, I can leave,' Sam offered, as Jane departed.

'No, stay. It's good to talk to someone new. Bill from across the corridor likes to come in and tell me about his operations, which have been many and varied. I am more familiar with his intestinal problems than I ever hoped to be.'

Sam laughed.

'And you're far prettier.' His eyes crinkled at the edges as he smiled.

There it was again, that look, intense and intimate, as if the world outside the door no longer existed.

'David!' Jane's voice echoed down the corridor.

'Okay. Stop bugging me, woman! I'm going. Isn't there anyone on the ward who needs an enema or something?'

'Don't tempt me.'

David grinned. 'I'd better go for that walk. You're welcome to join me.' He manoeuvred himself upright.

Instinctively, Sam reached out to help.

'Leave me be,' he said firmly.

Chastened, Sam backed away, watching as David made his way awkwardly round the end of the bed.

He paused in the doorway. 'Are you coming?'

'Sure.' She hurried after him.

'Do you live in Abbeyleigh?' he asked.

'Old Stebbing. You?'

'I've a flat in the Old Mill and a holiday home, a cottage on the coast. Up past The Hallows.'

'I know the area.'

'I was thinking of renting it out as a holiday let. A romantic retreat, that sort of thing. It'll need a makeover though. Maybe I'll give you a call when I get out of this place. Mates' rates?' He arched an eyebrow.

She spun her ring.

'If you're busy, I'm sure I could find someone else.'

'No, I'd be happy to help.'

'Who gave you the ring?'

Sam raised her eyebrows.

'The one you twist when you're not sure what to say.'

Nonplussed, Sam let go of the ring. 'My dad.'

'Are you close?'

'He's dead now but no, we weren't close.'

'I'm sorry.'

They had reached the end of the corridor. David balanced himself in front of the vending machine and fished in his pocket for change before buying a bar of chocolate. 'You want anything?'

She shook her head. 'Not sure that's what the nurse had in mind.'

'To my knowledge Jane didn't get her heart kicked to the kerb today. In the absence of alcohol, a Snickers bar will have to do.'

He turned neatly and they headed back up the corridor, his crutches clicking on the floor.

'Were you at the property exhibition at the Town Hall before Christmas, by any chance?'

'No. Why?'

'I thought maybe that was where I knew you from. How about Lewis Shaw's Christmas party, did you come to that?'

Sam shook her head.

David looked perplexed. 'I'm sure we've met. You don't remember?'

'Sorry, no.'

'What does your husband do?'

'He's a lawyer.'

'Really? I'm going to need a lawyer, help me sort this mess out.'

'Best to wait until you're home, surely? You don't want the stress of dealing with lawyers while you're still in hospital. Do you know when you might be able to go home?'

'A good while yet.' He let out a heavy sigh.

'Hard work,' she asked sympathetically.

'Aye, it is. Tough on the shoulders.'

They'd reached the threshold of David's room. Sam stood back as he swung his way in and gingerly lowered himself into the armchair, his face ruddy. 'Mission accomplished, Jane,' he called, ripping open the chocolate bar.

'Gold star.'

He sank back into the chair with a grimace. 'I thought I was in pretty good shape till this happened. We all think we're invincible, don't we? But the human body is more vulnerable than you think.

'My sadistic physio is teaching me to go up and down stairs tomorrow so that'll open up a whole new world of pain. It'll be good to see something other than this ward, though. God, I cannae wait to get home.'

He tore off the top of the chocolate bar and offered it to Sam.

She took it with a smile. 'Thanks.'

'Can't say I'm looking forward to going back to work though. It's funny how quickly things change. A couple of weeks ago my goals were all about how many sales I could generate, how much commission I'd pull in.' A frown drew his brows together and he gestured to his leg. 'That all seems so unimportant now.'

'You feel as though someone has changed all the rules without telling you,' Sam said quietly.

David looked at her in surprise. 'Aye. That's exactly how I feel. How did you know?'

'When you've suffered an upset it's hard to find a fixed point of reference. Everything has changed in the blink of an eye and you're struggling to come to terms with it.'

'Will I?'

'Eventually.'

'Did you?'

Sam smiled. 'Some of us are still trying.'

She broke the connection of their gaze, worried she'd said too much, that he was going to ask her a question she wouldn't want to answer.

'Life can be a bitch sometimes,' he said.

'Can't it just?'

She was shocked by the feel of David's hand resting on hers, his thumb gently stroking her skin. When she looked up, the compassion in his eyes took her by surprise.

This was all wrong. He shouldn't be the one offering sympathy and she shouldn't be enjoying his touch as much as she was. He gave her a smile, his fingers lingering on hers before he finally took his hand away. Sam's heart raced. *What is happening here?*

'I'm glad I have you in my life, Sam the hospital visitor, even if only briefly. Someone who cares. It's a rare thing.'

'I'm so sorry for what happened to you,' Sam blurted out, emotions bubbling dangerously close to the surface. 'You didn't deserve this. I just wish I could turn the clock back.'

'You and me both. I keep thinking, if only I hadn't played football that night or stopped for that takeaway. If only the driver of the four by four had taken more care.' He shrugged. 'The damage is done,' he said with a sigh. 'But I can't stop going over it all. I keep getting these dreams. More like nightmares, really. It's dark and I know I'm in danger but I can't figure out where the danger is coming from and then it's too late and something, I never see what, hits me and I cannae get back up.'

'You're reliving the accident.'

'Aye.' He dropped his gaze, colouring. 'I seem to be monopolising your time. Is that all right? Don't you have other patients to visit?'

'Not at the moment.'

'How come?'

She floundered. 'This is just a trial, you're my only patient.'

'Really?' He grinned. 'That makes me a special case, indeed.'

Sam swallowed. How had she ever got herself into such a mess? It had been easy to pass off the lies she'd told as white ones but if you told enough of them did they stop being white and become darker? Had she passed that point already? *Tell him the truth. Do it now.*

'I've never told anyone about the dreams before,' David said quietly. 'I've been getting flashbacks too although I guess they're feelings more than actual flashbacks. I'm cold and so scared I can't move.' He fiddled with the wrapper of the chocolate bar. 'I cannae seem to get the accident out of my head, which is ironic seeing as I can't remember anything. I feel like I'm going mad.'

Taken off guard, Sam said, 'Perhaps you should talk to one of the doctors.'

'A shrink?'

'I'm no expert but it could be post-traumatic stress disorder. I've heard my husband talk about it. There's stuff the doctors can do to help.'

'Drugs?'

'Drugs maybe, therapy.'

'Isn't therapy just talking? Like you and I are? I'd much rather talk to you than some shrink in a white coat.'

'The difference is they know what to say to help you feel better. I don't,' Sam said.

David smiled. 'Don't sell yourself short, Samantha. I was feeling pretty low before you turned up.'

Chapter Seven

Lifting the elastic band from her diary, Sam checked the time of her appointment. Then, closing her diary, she sorted through the contents of her briefcase: the samples and swatches she took to all new clients, the promotional material from her favourite designers, the glossy photographs giving examples of her work. She felt the nerves flutter in her stomach as they always did before a first meeting. Could she match the home-owner's hopes and dreams with her vision and talent? Would she be good enough to deliver what they wanted on a realistic budget? Would they like her enough to trust her with their home?

The house was a Victorian villa on one of the smarter streets of Stebbingsford and Mrs Mitchell had sounded charming, if a little nervous herself.

Sam saw the curtain twitch at the window to her left as she walked up the tiled path. The front door opened before she reached the porch. She smiled brightly and held out her hand.

'Mrs Mitchell?'

The lady nodded. 'Call me Daphne. You must be Sam. Please, come in.'

Daphne Mitchell was in her late sixties or early seventies, Sam guessed. Her white hair was fashionably cut and she wore smart white trousers and a flowing blue shirt that brought out the colour of her eyes. She showed Sam through to the sitting room where tea and biscuits were already set up on the low table between two sofas.

'Milk and sugar?' Daphne asked.

'Just milk. Thank you.'

Sam cast her eyes around the room. She was gratified to see all the original features remained – from the wooden shuttering, to the cornicing to the elaborate plasterwork moulding around the light. To her left a welcoming fire burned. Sam admired the honey-suckle tiles that set the fireplace off. There was too much furniture for the size of the room and the plain magnolia walls were a little dull but it was a lovely light room even in the gloom of a winter's afternoon.

Sam took a sip of her tea. A proper cup and saucer. Not something you saw very often now. Sam resolved to hunt out Neil's mother's china from the back of the cupboard when she got home.

'I have to confess I'm a little nervous, my dear. I've never done anything like this before.'

Setting her cup back in its saucer, Sam said, 'You've no need to be nervous. Why don't you start by telling me what you would like my help with?'

'Very well. I moved here last year after my husband died . . .'

'I'm sorry.'

'It was very sudden; a heart attack. He'd been working on his precious machines. I found him dead in his study.'

'How awful for you.'

'It was. Two more months and we would have celebrated fifty years together.' Daphne's eyes filled with tears. 'Silly of me,' she said, drawing a handkerchief from the sleeve of her shirt. 'I promised myself I wouldn't do this.'

Putting her cup and saucer on the table, Sam moved to sit next to Daphne and put her arm around the older woman's shoulders. 'Nothing wrong with letting a few tears out. Does more harm to hold them in.'

Daphne nodded, blotting her eyes. 'I cook too much food.'

'I'm sorry?'

'When I cook, I still prepare enough for two. I can't seem to get the portion sizes right. Not that Ted ate that much. He never was a big eater. We always used to sit at the dining table to eat though. He insisted on it. Now he's gone it seems silly to set a place just for me so I eat in the kitchen.'

Not sure how to respond, Sam gave Daphne's shoulder a rub.

'I moved here to be closer to my friends. I don't drive, you see, and Ted and I never had any children. We always hoped it would happen one day but it never did. Ted's machines became his children. Whilst I . . .' Her gaze drifted to the fire. 'Do you have children?' she asked, turning back to Sam.

'Yes, two. A boy and a girl.'

'How lovely. You're very lucky.' Daphne squeezed Sam's hand. 'And very kind. But you didn't come here to listen to an old woman reminisce. You'd better drink your tea before it gets cold. We both should.'

Sam returned to the other sofa and picked up her cup and saucer as Daphne did the same.

'Place needs a makeover,' Daphne said between sips. 'Every room. All the walls are pale. There's no colour. I like colour. I could do it on my own, I suppose. Bit extravagant hiring a designer. Not sure what Ted would say. But I don't want to do it on my own and money's not a problem.'

Sam lifted out her notepad and began to make discreet notes. 'Have you any particular style or look in mind?'

'I want it to be welcoming, cosy but with an edge. I don't want anything too modern. It wouldn't suit the house or me and it has to be comfortable. At my age I don't want to live in a place that's more like a gallery than a home. Do you know what I mean?'

Sam smiled and nodded. 'I do.'

'I thought you could work on the two front rooms first.'

Sam looked at the TV in the corner of the room. 'Is this where you come to relax in the evenings?'

'Yes.'

'And the other room?' Sam looked up from her notepad. 'Daphne?'

'My reading chair is in there. I was hoping you could do something with it.'

'Reupholster it?' Sam suggested.

Daphne nodded. 'The only other things in the room are Ted's machines. I got the removal company to pack them up in boxes but . . . I don't like going in there. Could you take them away, please?'

Sam put down her pen. 'If you want me to but if they were Ted's wouldn't you rather keep them? I could incorporate them into my designs and . . .'

'I can't look at them. I don't even want to go into the room. I just want them to go to a good home, to someone who will appreciate them. Ted loved them so much, you see.' She stopped abruptly and drank her tea.

'Why don't I arrange for them to go into storage for a little while so you can make a final decision in a few months' time?'

'I don't want them,' Daphne said sharply. 'He was working on one of them the day he died. Just promise me you'll find them a good home, that's all I ask.'

Sam nodded. 'If you're sure that's what you want.'

'Will you be able to take them with you today?'

Sam saw the hope leap in Daphne's eyes.

'Why don't I take a look at them first, see if they'll fit in my car?'

'Yes, of course. I'll wait here.'

Crossing the hall, Sam opened the door. The room was a mirror image of the sitting room except this one had no furniture in it bar the chair and six boxes. Sam lifted the flaps of the nearest box. Inside was what looked like a metal monkey holding a candle. Sam picked the box up to test its weight. It was heavier than she'd imagined but not too heavy to carry to the car.

She opened the rest of the boxes. There were four more models: a boy, a girl, a jester and another monkey. In the last box Sam could see an old-fashioned till but it was incomplete with pieces scattered around.

Sam went back to Daphne. 'I can take them with me if you would like me to.'

'Yes, please, dear. You would be doing me a great favour. I just want them gone.'

Sam nodded. 'Why don't you take a look at the samples I've brought with me? You can let me know if anything catches your eye and while you're doing that I'll take some quick measurements.' She lifted her laser measuring device from her bag.

'And put the boxes in your car,' Daphne said pointedly.

'Would you like me to do that first?'

'Yes, please.'

Sam touched the woman's shoulder and nodded, putting her laser measurer down on the table.

She had just finished loading the last box into her car when her mobile vibrated in her pocket. Fishing it out, Sam answered.

'Hello?'

'Mrs Davenport?'

'Yes.'

'It's Susan, Neil's secretary.'

'Oh hello. Is everything okay?'

'Yes. Neil's meeting with a new client has overrun and he's asked me to pick the children up from school for him. I just wanted to check with you whether Josh has his maths club today or tomorrow. Neil couldn't remember.'

'It's tomorrow,' Sam said. 'Neil's asked you to pick them up?'

'Yes.'

Sam checked her watch and looked back at the house.

'He shouldn't have asked you to do that. I'll pick them up.'

'Are you sure? I don't mind.'

'No, it's fine. It's not your job.'

'Okay. Thanks. Bye.'

Sam headed back inside.

'Have you seen anything you like?'

'Lots.' Daphne smiled. 'I've separated them out.'

Daphne had picked several deep jewel colours, Sam noted.

'Boxes gone?' she asked lightly.

'The boxes have gone,' Sam confirmed.

Daphne reached across to squeeze her arm. 'Not part of the service, I know, but thank you, my dear.'

'It's no problem. What would you like to do with that room now?'

'I'd like to make it into a reading room with an area where I can do my crafts. I knit and sew.'

Sam smiled. 'It'll make a lovely reading and craft room, those big windows let in so much light. I'll just take those measurements I need and then I'll be on my way. I'll work up some sketches and a mood board for each room and then make an appointment to come back and see you.'

Daphne smiled. 'How exciting. I need something to look forward to. This is going to be just the ticket. Thank you, Sam.'

*

Sam pulled up outside the gates of Abbeyleigh High School. She was quick to spot Josh and flashed her lights.

'I thought Dad was picking us up?'

'So did I. Have you seen your sister?'

'No. What are all these boxes?'

'Things I'm looking after for a client. Just squeeze in as best you can. Do you need a hand?'

'No.'

'What happened to your trousers? They're covered in mud.'

'I fell over.'

'Did you hurt yourself?' Sam asked, concerned.

'No, I'm all right.'

'There's your sister.' Sam flashed her lights again.

'Where's Dad?'

'Busy. So you've got me.'

'There's nowhere to sit.'

Sam lifted the box off the front passenger seat. 'You can sit there but you'll have to hold this for me.' She passed the box back once Cassie was in the car.

'What is it?'

'An old-fashioned cash register, I think.'

'Is there any cash in it?'

Sam laughed. 'I doubt it.'

'Why can't you put all this stuff in the boot?' Cassie asked as she edged her rucksack between her legs.

'Boot's full of samples.'

Sam turned the car and headed for home.

'So, how often does Susan pick you up?'

'She's done it every night this week,' Josh said.

'Really?'

'Grass,' Cassie hissed.

In the rear-view mirror, Sam saw Josh pull a face at his sister. 'We go back to the office and do our homework in the conference room until Dad's ready to take us home.'

Not quite the quality time with the children I had in mind, Neil.

'Did you know there's a monkey holding a candle in this box?' Josh asked.

'Yes.'

'Cool. What are you going to do with him?'

'I have no idea.'

Chapter Eight

Sam set the table for breakfast. It was Saturday; Neil's day with the children. He'd arrived early, looking handsome in chinos and a Paul Smith shirt. Sam had caught the scent of his aftershave as he'd passed by and felt her heart contract.

'Am I allowed to sit down?'

'Of course you're allowed.'

'You're looking good.'

'You're looking tired.' She wondered how many hours he'd put in that week. Too many, probably. When he'd been at home, she had tried to put a brake on his obsession with work but now he had no one to stop him and it worried her. She squeezed his shoulder. 'Don't overdo it.'

He gave her an amused look. 'I think you lost the right to lecture me when you threw me out.'

'Neil . . .'

'Can I have a piece of toast?'

'You can have bacon and eggs if you want.'

'Toast will do. How come you've dug out Mum's china?' He nodded towards the cup and saucer on the worktop.

'I met with a new client last week. She had the most exquisite china. I decided we should use ours.'

Neil smiled. 'Is that why I can't get hold of you any more because you're busy with work?' he asked as he picked up the butter. 'The answer machine is always on here and your mobile's always off.'

The hospital had a policy. No mobiles. 'I must have forgotten to put it on.'

'Or you could be avoiding me.'

'Or I could be avoiding you,' she agreed, meeting his gaze. They smiled at one another.

Sam hugged her tea and watched her husband as he ate. Traces of the man he'd been remained. The brown hair was untouched by grey and his cheeks retained a boyish quality, a little on the podgy side, like puppy fat still waiting to fall off.

His eyes had aged though. The skin around them was lined and drawn and he needed glasses now for reading. Sam didn't mind them. They made him look distinguished.

The briefcase had done that when first they'd met at a café on the concourse of Liverpool Street Station. I'm being picked up by a man who works in the city, Sam had thought at the time and the idea had amused her because the people she worked with were so disparaging about the hordes of buttoned-up business people in their smart suits and shiny shoes, who swarmed, like ants, through the station every day.

Perhaps that was why she'd been so attracted to Neil or maybe it was because the handsome man with the gentle eyes had unexpectedly offered hot chocolate and sympathy just when she had needed it most.

'I'm Neil.'

'Sam.'

He had pushed the hot chocolate towards her. 'Drink this. You'll feel better.'

'How do you know?' Sam had challenged. 'You don't know what's wrong with me.'

He'd given her a kindly smile. 'I'm hoping that once you've drunk your chocolate, you'll tell me and I can help you sort it out.'

'I wish it were that simple.'

He'd waited patiently while she drank.

'Do you want to talk about it?' he had asked with impeccable timing as soon as she'd finished.

Sam had looked up into eyes that seemed genuinely interested. 'I've managed to lose a boyfriend and a job all in one day.' She'd quite enjoyed the look of surprise on his face.

'A boyfriend *and* a job? That's quite an achievement.'

'I never do anything by halves.'

'Why don't I buy you dinner and you can tell me all about it?'

Discovering they were both from Abbeyleigh, dinner had been at The Northey. Classic. Simple. No nouvelle cuisine at silly London prices. Just good food and a man with a nice smile to share it with.

He'd ordered the wine with authority. She was a champagne drinker normally. The people at the model agency where she worked never bothered with anything else but the silky smooth red was full of flavour and she didn't refuse when he topped up her glass. She felt comfortable. Not a position she'd expected to find herself in at the end of such a tumultuous day.

'Better?'

'Much.'

'You'll get another job,' he hesitated. 'And another boyfriend.'

'I daresay.'

'What happened?'

'I was a fool.'

'I find that hard to believe.'

She laughed. 'Don't. It's true. A star-struck fool. I was a booker at a modelling agency. SubZero.' She paused, half expecting him to say he'd heard of them. When he remained silent, she continued. 'I went there hoping to be taken on as a model but they said I didn't have what it takes.'

'I'd beg to differ,' he interjected.

Sam hadn't been fishing for a compliment and the sincerity of his smile took her by surprise. *Be careful, Samantha. Your heart is in pieces. Don't give it away again too soon.*

'They said I could have a job as a booker and I thought that was better than nothing. I got to work in the fashion industry, which is what I wanted.'

The chorus of 'tall but not tall enough', 'pretty in a wholesome way but not different enough' still rang in her ears. A booker, possibly, but never a looker. Backroom staff. Strictly admin only.

Sam ran her finger round the edge of her wine glass as she debated how much to tell him. 'I got a crush on one of the photographers the agency used. Pete. He was seeing one of our models but she finished with him. Then, he came on to me. Said I shouldn't be working behind a desk, that I should be in front of the camera.' She paused, blushing. 'I should have known better but I was flattered and stupid enough to believe him. Turns out he was just using me to make his former girlfriend jealous. It worked. They were reunited.' Sam took a swift drink of her wine. Neil didn't need to know how Pete had put her down in front of everyone or how all the models had laughed. Confession was good for the soul. Humiliation was best left out of the equation.

'What a git!'

Sam smiled. 'I didn't think you'd met.'

Neil mirrored her smile. Sitting back, he swirled the wine in his glass. 'I know his type. He was wrong for you.'

'Evidently.'

'You need a man you can rely on.'

'That'd be nice. Know any?'

Now, Sam tipped the remains of her tea away. After her father's actions, Pete's betrayal had left her devastated. She'd thought herself incapable of ever recovering, ever trusting again. But, of course, she had recovered. The passage of time had taken the sting out of the humiliation and an incident she had assumed would blight her life had barely encroached on her thoughts these past, happy years.

Looking back on it now, she could see it for what it was: an unpleasant experience that she had lived through and learned from. Was that how she'd feel about Neil's adultery in a few years' time? Would it all just fade into the fabric of her life? A dropped stitch and nothing more.

'Thanks for picking the kids up the other day.' Neil's voice broke into her thoughts.

'If you're struggling to do the school run, you should have told me. I only suggested it as a way for them to see you during the week. If you've got Susan doing it for you, it rather defeats the purpose.'

'Yeah, sorry.'

'Do you want me to go back to picking them up?'

'Could you? It does make things difficult at the office.'

'Okay.'

'I could do the morning run instead.'

'Sounds like a plan.' She smiled. 'I'll go and give the kids a shout.'

Before she had a chance, Josh came barrelling into the kitchen. He pulled the earphones from his ears. The tinny sound of drum and bass leaked out.

'Hi, Dad.'

'Hello, son.'

Sam walked into the hallway. 'Cassie! Your dad's here.'

Her daughter ran down the stairs, a whirlwind of limbs and long blonde hair. 'Hi, Dad. Do you mind if Sophie tags along today?'

'More the merrier. Josh, do you want to bring someone?'

'No, I'm cool.'

Cassie laughed. 'In your dreams, Joshua.'

Josh pulled a face.

'Where are you all off to?' Sam asked.

'Dad's taking us ice skating and then we're having lunch at that new Italian place in Stebbingsford.'

'I went there last week,' Neil said. 'Food was superb.'

He caught Sam's eye. It was clear he wanted her to ask him who he went with but she was too afraid to ask.

'I was hoping we could have a chat later,' she said. 'There are some things we need to discuss.'

'Impossible. Sorry. Once I drop the kids back here I'm needed at the office. The way things are going I won't be able to fit in a chat with you for at least a week. Maybe two.'

'I'll tell Park Place we won't be renewing our subscription to their health club and spa then, shall I?'

He crammed the last of the toast into his mouth. 'I barely have time to hit the running machine or go for a swim nowadays. I don't suppose I'll miss it. Come on, kids, fun and mayhem awaits.'

Sam watched from the kitchen window as they all piled into the BMW. Time was, she would have been going too. A chance to make memories. Now, she'd have to make do with the kids' status updates on their Facebook pages.

I'm needed at the office. Was that code for I'm back with her, she wondered?

Chapter Nine

Sam parked in front of Honeydews Auction House in Abbeyleigh. Gordon Honeydew raised his hand in greeting from the doorway.

'Nice to see you as always, Sam,' he said, kissing her cheek.

'And you, Gordon. Could you give me a hand to get these inside?'

'Yes, of course. Let's take them into my office.'

'Like I said on the phone, I'm looking after them for a client but I wanted to get a valuation done on them. Some of them look quite old. I thought they might be Victorian but you're the expert.'

Gordon smiled. 'Let me take a look.'

Sam looked out of Gordon's internal office window, watching the hustle and bustle on the floor of the auction house as they prepared for the next day's general sale.

'You're right. The monkey is a Victorian automaton, the other monkey too. The others are later, turn of the century, I would say, but still of value. Do any of them work?'

'I've no idea.' Sam turned back and watched as Gordon fiddled with the base of the monkey holding the candle.

'Ah, there it is.'

Suddenly the monkey's eyes rolled and the arm holding the candle began to lift. As it stopped the top of the candle began to glow. Then the light was extinguished and the arm lowered before beginning the movement again.

Sam laughed.

'These are really quite something,' Gordon said.

'My client's husband was an enthusiast.'

'Did he restore them?'

'He might have done. I'm not sure.'

'Can you leave them with me so I can do some research?'

'Yes.'

*

Sam was about to push open the door of David's room when she heard laughter coming from within and a woman's voice; light and teasing.

'I think you've made amazing progress,' the woman was saying.

Sam couldn't catch David's response.

'Behave yourself,' the woman retorted. Then, 'Sam's nice.'

Sam tensed.

'Aye, she's been terrific.'

'You and she are very different.'

'That's probably why we get on so well.'

'How is it that you're . . .'

'David!' Sam flung open the door. Jane was in the process of taking David's blood pressure.

'We were just talking about you,' David said with a smile.

'All good I hope,' Sam said lightly.

'I was just saying . . .'

'There's nothing wrong is there?' Sam cut her off, nodding towards the blood pressure monitor.

'No. Just routine.'

Sam painted a smile on her face. 'I think I heard one of the other nurses asking for you at the desk as I came by.'

Jane grimaced. 'No peace for the wicked.' She trundled the blood pressure machine out of the door. 'See you later.'

'Not if I see you first,' David joked.

Sam let out the breath she'd been holding.

David laughed. 'Don't look so put out, Sam. I know, as your special case, you want me all to yourself but you'll just have to learn to share.'

'I never was very good at that.'

'Come and sit down.' David patted the seat beside him. 'I have news. The consultant came by after you left yesterday. I can go home tomorrow.'

Sam didn't know whether to be happy or disappointed. For three weeks now she'd been visiting David in the hospital and somewhere along the way, the visits had become the highlight of her day. Now they were about to come to an end.

Realising that David was waiting for a response, Sam forced a smile. 'Home tomorrow? That is good news.'

Her attraction to him had taken her by surprise at first but after all the heartache of the previous months it had been a relief to have someone to laugh with again. Her heart might beat a little faster when he smiled at her but that just proved she still had a heart. What harm could it do?

Yes, she fancied him but she was hardly about to act on it. Sam the hospital visitor might be able to get away with it but Sam Davenport, the guilty party, certainly couldn't.

Every day, she had resolved to tell David the truth about the accident but each time they'd fallen so easily into conversation that it had seemed a shame to spoil things with an ugly confession and so it had gone on until now.

Sam was conscious of just how much she was going to miss him and felt the prick of irrational tears behind her eyes. *Maybe he never had to know?*

'I want you to come round for dinner once I'm settled.'

'What? No.'

'I want to say thank you for everything you've done.'

'I can't.'

'Why? Are there rules against that kind of thing?' He lowered his voice. 'Are hospital visitors banned from fraternising with patients outside the hospital grounds?'

'Something like that. You have no need to thank me.'

'Yes, I do. You've been like a guardian angel, helping me to get through this.'

'David . . .'

'So what do you say? Dinner at mine in a week's time? Come on, Angel. I won't take no for an answer. In my book rules are made to be broken.'

Chapter Ten

The bar at the Park Place Hotel and Spa was quiet for a Sunday afternoon.

'Are you sure you're okay with mineral water?'

Neil nodded. He'd promised Sam he would never drink and drive again. It was a promise he intended to keep, even if she wasn't around to see it.

Lewis Shaw shrugged. 'Cheap round for me, then.'

The ebullient estate agent returned a few minutes later with a double scotch.

'How's that man we had the accident with?' Neil asked, mustering as much nonchalance as he could while his insides churned.

'Home now but his leg's still a mess. Christ knows when I'll get him back. I hope your wife realises she's cost me my best man.'

'She was very upset.'

Lewis nodded. 'Accidents happen,' he said, adopting a less bullish tone.

Neil sipped his mineral water and watched the sunlight filter through the trees. Nasty breaks – and an open fracture of the femur was one of the nastiest – could lead to all sorts of additional problems. He'd been reading up on it. And motorcycle accidents were often the worst. Young men with ruined lives.

'Sure I can't tempt you?' Lewis asked, waggling his glass.

Neil hesitated. 'No,' he said with a sigh. 'I can't.'

'I haven't seen Samantha since your birthday party. We should have dinner sometime.'

'Sounds good. Perhaps once work calms down a bit.'

'I thought you had this promotion in the bag. You're the old man's nephew after all.'

'It doesn't work like that any more,' Neil said, tilting his glass and watching the sliver of lemon pitch back and forth. 'It's a democracy nowadays. Every partner has an equal say.'

'Surely your uncle can persuade them?'

'I'm not sure he wants to. He knows I hate his guts. The feeling's probably mutual.'

'How come?'

'My grandfather started the firm. When they were old enough, Edward and my father both went to work there. It was a family firm back then. My dad, being the eldest, was the rightful successor but my uncle had different ideas. He did all he could to cast my dad in a bad light. He'd palm off the less profitable cases to him and if they went out drinking, it would only ever be my dad who wound up coming into work late with a hangover. You get the picture.'

Lewis nodded. 'Standard business hardball.'

Neil pursed his lips. 'Maybe my dad was naïve,' he conceded. 'He certainly didn't see what was happening until it was too late. When my grandfather retired he handed the firm to Edward on a plate, saying he didn't think my dad was up to the job.'

'Ouch!'

'Yeah.'

'Did your father carry on working there?'

'Yes until he drank himself to death.' Neil grimaced. 'So you see, I want this promotion not just for myself but for my dad, too.'

'That's quite a weight to carry. Makes me glad I'm my own boss.'

Neil smiled. 'It must be nice to call the shots.'

'Here's to you setting your own agenda very soon.' Lewis lifted his glass.

Neil lifted his own in response.

'Who are you up against?'

'A guy called Tilden. The man's a machine. I don't know how he does it. I billed sixty hours last week.' Neil hunched over the table. 'But I don't know how I'm going to keep up that sort of pace.' Maybe it was a blessing in disguise that Sam wasn't around to nag him about his hours. She'd be appalled if she knew the truth.

'Can't you get something on him?'

Neil gave Lewis a hard stare.

'You want to play it straight,' Lewis said.

'Is there any other way?'

Lewis saluted him with his glass. 'I admire you.'

'Do you?'

'Yeah. There aren't many men who would choose to better themselves through hard work if there was an easier option. I admire your integrity. Bit lacking on that front myself.'

Neil smiled, feeling good about himself. Then he remembered the accident and his unwillingness to take the blame and the feeling evaporated.

'Bet you could do with a little pick me up, though?'

'Absolutely.' Neil nodded enthusiastically. 'Got one?'

'I might have. Ever considered taking the odd toot to see you through? Charlie's your man.' Lewis tapped his nose and gave an exaggerated sniff.

'Are you serious?'

'If you need to pull down sixty-hour weeks on a regular basis, trust me, that's the stuff to make it happen. Boundless energy. Confidence off the scale. It's the best stress buster I know,' Lewis said. 'And sex when you're high.' He rolled his eyes. 'There's nothing like it. Believe me, Sam won't know what hit her and neither will you.'

Neil mulled it over. The idea that a simple substance could make his life better than it was now was enticing. Lewis certainly didn't look like an addict, and if Lewis could handle it, surely he could? Then again, it was addictive not to mention illegal and Sam would kill him.

'Thanks but I'll pass,' Neil said.

Lewis shrugged. 'Suit yourself. The offer stands if you change your mind.'

*

It was one o'clock in the morning when Neil finally left the office. He'd gone there straight from Park Place pausing only to buy a bag of chips having eschewed the spa's healthier options.

Now, he opened the door of his rented flat and went through to the bedroom. His gaze settled on the empty bed. From the bedside cabinet he took out a pink silk scarf and, wrapping it around his hand, brought it up to his nose. Only a faint trace of Sam's perfume remained. He closed his eyes, breathing it in.

With a weary sigh, he returned to the living room and opened the first of a heap of files. It was too early to face a double bed alone.

Chapter Eleven

Sam stared out of her office window. The view consisted of a collection of uninspiring rooftops and a municipal car park.

'If you're seeking inspiration out there, we're in more trouble than I thought,' Connor said as he placed a mug of tea on her desk.

Sam smiled.

Standing beside her, Connor looked down at the mood board Sam had been working on.

'Looking good, Mrs D. You never know, you might be able to make a living at this.'

She stuck her tongue out at him.

'Seriously loving that lamp. You've got the brief nailed. Daphne Mitchell's going to love it. Which makes me wonder, if it's not Mrs Mitchell's mood board that's got you wistfully staring over rooftops what has? Spill!' He nudged the mood board out of the way as he sat on the edge of her desk.

'I was just taking a break. Boss's perks.'

'And daydreaming.'

'A little,' she conceded, sipping her tea.

'About anyone in particular? A certain someone whose name begins with N by any chance?'

'N?' Sam looked confused. 'Oh you mean Neil.'

'Of course I mean Neil. The love of your life, remember? How are things between you? And before you answer that question please remember I am a sucker for a happy ending.' He batted his eyelashes at her.

Sam stared at her tea. 'It's complicated.'

'You don't say?'

'It took Mum years to throw Dad out. When she finally did it, I remember begging her to make it up with him. Do you know what she said to me?'

Connor shook his head.

'She said she would always be waiting for him to cheat again. She said she would rather live in hope of good things happening than in fear of bad and for that reason she would never take him back. I don't want the cost of saving my marriage to be the loss of my peace of mind. Neil was full of promises but Dad made promises too and look what happened to those.'

'People don't come with lifetime guarantees, Sam. More's the pity.'

'I've never put a foot wrong in all the years I've been married. He took our vows and threw them aside like they meant nothing.'

'If you started over with somebody new, there'd be no guarantees with them either and try as I might I can't see you in a nunnery.' Connor squeezed her hand.

'For what it's worth, if I'd found a good, kind man like Neil, I'd put a ring on it.'

'Rhys still not phoned?'

Connor shook his head. 'There's playing hard to get and then there's Rhys. One weekend in Paris and two in London and then nothing.'

'Time to move on, perhaps?'

'Perhaps. But then I think about his cute arse in those tight jeans and all my good intentions go out the window.'

Sam laughed.

'Neil loves you, Sam. I know he had a funny way of showing it but you and the kids are all he cares about.'

'Us and work.'

'Once he gets this promotion things will settle down.'

Sam arched her eyebrows. 'If he wasn't so careful with money, I'd think Neil was paying you, Connor Barrett.'

Connor held up his hands. 'I am not on the payroll, I swear. I'm just a sucker for happy endings, like I said.' He sipped his tea. 'So if you weren't thinking about Neil what has got you staring pensively over rooftops? Is it the accident? Have you heard from the police yet?'

'No.'

'They're taking their time.'

'They can take as long as they like so far as I'm concerned.'

'It was a lapse of judgement. We all have them. Even you, Samson. The weather was awful that night.

Visibility must have been a nightmare. The magistrates will understand.'

'Let's hope you're right.'

'Is there something you're not telling me . . .'

'No.'

'Sam . . .'

'I'm fine,' she snapped.

'No, you're not. If you spin that ring any faster you'll get a blister. What is it? What's wrong?'

'I'm just tired of taking the blame with the kids for making Neil leave,' she admitted. 'And I'm tired of taking the blame for . . .' She bit her lip.

'For?'

Sam was shocked at how close to tears she was.

'Sam?'

Neil had drummed it into her. *No one must know.*

'Sam?'

'Neil was driving on the night of the accident.' She felt a tremendous weight lift from her shoulders as she spoke.

'*What?* Why did you tell everyone it was you?'

'Why do you think? If Neil had been breathalysed, he'd have been over the limit. He didn't want the scandal. It would have blown all chance of his promotion.'

'So he let you take the rap for him? Bloody hell, Sam!'

'What else could I do? He was yelling at me to say I was driving. All I wanted him to do was ring for an ambulance.'

'What a shit!'

'I was so scared of saying the wrong thing to the police.' Sam shuddered. 'The whole thing's been a nightmare. I don't think Neil stopped at the junction and I'm sure the police will figure that out from the skid marks. God knows what they'll do then.'

'Can't you come clean?'

'It's gone too far for that. Besides, Neil's promotion . . .'

'Bugger Neil's promotion.'

Sam met Connor's gaze. 'It would be a poor way to get back at him. I won't do it.'

'What does Neil say?'

'Stick to the story and carry on.'

'What a prince!'

'You wanted to put a ring on it a minute ago,' Sam reminded him.

'That was before I knew he was making you lie for him.'

'I could have said no.'

Connor put down his mug. 'Why didn't you?'

'Right before the crash we were arguing about Megan.'

'So this is your penance?'

'Something like that.'

'And Neil?'

Sam shrugged. 'Neil seemed to be able to put the accident behind him so quickly. He was back to his old work-obsessed self within a couple of days. He can't understand why I want to sell the Range Rover but how can I ever drive it again? I can barely look at it, let alone get behind the wheel. His view is: "I was the one driving; it's got nothing to do with you". But it has everything to do with me. David's blood was on the front of *my* car.'

'David? He was the guy on the bike, right?'

Sam nodded.

'You told me you saw him the day I dropped you at the hospital and that you apologised.'

Another white lie. Sam's gaze slid back to the chimney pots.

'Samantha . . .'

Knotting her fingers, Sam turned back to face him. Floodgates open, her words poured forth in an emotional torrent until she'd told Connor everything.

'And he still doesn't know who you are?'

'No.'

'Why haven't you told him?'

Reaching for her mug, Sam cradled it. 'On that first visit, I lost my nerve. I didn't want to do it with his friend there and after that we started talking, he'd say how much he looked forward to my visits and I figured it would be cruel to tell him then, better to wait until he was home. I should have done it on that first visit,' she conceded. 'The longer I've left it and the more I've got to know him, the harder it's become.'

Connor shook his head. 'I'm amazed he hasn't discovered the truth for himself. Surely, his insurance company have been in touch with him? They must have put your details in the letter.'

'The insurance is in Neil's name and while David knows I live in Old Stebbing, he doesn't know where exactly and I've been careful not to tell him Neil's name or our surname. I figured the less he knew about me, the less likely he was to stumble on to something that could give me away.'

'He's never asked?'

'I've become adept at fielding his questions and diverting the conversation on to safer topics.'

'Sounds exhausting.'

She nodded. 'I just didn't want to tell him until I was ready.'

'Will you ever be ready?' Connor asked sceptically. 'Do you want someone else to tell him? I'll do it.'

'No!'

'You can't carry on like this, Sam.'

'Once he knows the truth, I'll never see him again,' she said quietly. She lifted her gaze to meet Connor's.

'Hot, is he? When I suggested you live a little before letting Neil come home, I had in mind a little tit-for-tat revenge fuck, I certainly didn't mean you should do it with the guy you . . . Neil ran over. For goodness' sake, Sam, choose someone less complicated.'

'Even if I was going to do that, which I'm not, David would be the last person I'd choose. I like him too much to use him like that.'

Connor sighed. 'You can be an idiot sometimes, girl. You've fallen for him, haven't you? When I caught you daydreaming just now, it wasn't about Neil at all, it was about this David.

'You have to tell him the truth. Or at least your version of the truth, that you were driving that night. You can't be completely honest with him because if you are you don't know how he might react. He could go to the police. You and Neil could both wind up in jail.'

Sam blanched. Connor was right. 'Now he's home it's only a question of time until someone lets something slip, I realise that. He works for Lewis Shaw for God's sake and Lewis and Neil have been friends for years. I want to tell him but then I think about the way he'll look at me once he knows and I just can't bring myself to say the words.'

Connor reached for her hand. 'Face it, hon, he's going to be angry enough when he hears it from you. Imagine how angry he'll be if he hears it from someone else. When are you seeing him next?'

'Friday night. He's invited me to dinner. Neil's coming over to mind the kids.'

'I'm guessing he doesn't know who you are having dinner with?'

'I told him I was meeting you.'

Connor raised his eyebrows. 'Another white lie? This isn't who you are, Sam.'

'I know. I hate it and yet I keep on doing it. I thought I was too old to develop a crush on someone. I guess not.'

'Would you like your oldest friend to give you some sage advice?'

'Yes, please.'

'Meet him on Friday, tell him you were driving, then leave and never go back.'

She knew it was good advice but it was the last thing she wanted to hear.

'Where are we meant to be going for dinner, just in case Neil asks?'

'The new Italian place in Stebbingsford.'

Connor winked. 'I'll be sure to wear something nice.'

Chapter Twelve

'Thanks for popping in, Sam,' Gordon Honeydew ushered her into his office.

'Perfect timing, I'm due to see Mrs Mitchell this afternoon. She's the owner of the automatons.'

'Well you can tell Mrs Mitchell she has quite a collection here. Her husband clearly had a good eye. Even the later pieces are of remarkably good quality and two of them, the monkey automatons, are actually quite rare. I've prepared a written valuation for you.' He handed over a piece of paper. 'If Mrs Mitchell is keen to sell, we'd be happy to find them all new homes.'

'I wouldn't want to suggest a sale to her, Gordon. She's grieving for her husband. In a few months' time she may feel very differently about them and want them back.'

'Well, if she's more philanthropically minded, she might want to loan them out to the Abbeyleigh Museum. From my work with them, I can tell you their Victorian rooms could do with some brightening up. Would you like me to make some enquiries?'

Sam smiled. 'Yes, please. What about the box of broken bits?'

'The box of broken bits, as you put it, is very interesting. The cash register is an original. My guess is your client's husband was in the process of turning it into an automaton when he died.'

'You mean it wasn't one to begin with?'

'No. The others are all originals. That one's different. The broken bits aren't broken at all. They are the innards of the cash register. He was taking it apart in order to put it back together as an automaton. I haven't had the opportunity to examine it properly yet but I wonder how your client would feel if I took the project over and finished it off? No charge. I just love fiddling about with bits and pieces like this. What do you think?'

'I don't think she would mind.'

'Excellent. You speak to your client about what she would like to do with them long term and I will get to work on the cash register, see if I can figure out what her husband had in mind for it.'

'How much do I owe you for the valuation?' Sam asked.

'No charge.'

'Gordon . . .'

'You and Connor give us enough business, Sam. I'm happy to do you a favour now and then.'

'That's very good of you, thank you.'

*

The meeting with Daphne Mitchell had gone even better than Sam had hoped. Daphne had been delighted with the mood boards Sam had prepared and had embraced her ideas for the two rooms, even wanting to go a shade darker for the green paint in the reading end of the reading and craft room.

'I love the colours and this material just brings it all together perfectly.' Daphne stroked the red, green and mustard-yellow check fabric Sam planned to use to reupholster the wing-backed chair. 'How quickly can you begin work, my dear?'

'I should be able to start early next month.'

'That would be wonderful. Can you leave the mood boards with me?'

Sam nodded.

'I shall admire them during the day and occasionally stroke the fabulous fabrics you plan to use.' Daphne smiled. 'They're all so tactile. Just what I wanted.'

Sam gathered her things. Then, remembering the valuation, she paused. 'There is one more thing I need to speak to you about, Daphne. You remember the boxes you asked me to take away with me?' Sam saw the shadow pass over Daphne's sunny demeanour. 'It turns out your husband's machines are actually quite valuable and I . . .'

Daphne held up her hand. 'Please, Sam, find them good homes, that's all I ask. You can give the money to charity.'

Sam watched Daphne glance at her husband's picture on the mantelpiece.

'What was it like being married for fifty years?'

Daphne laughed. 'Wonderful, infuriating, astonishing. It doesn't feel like fifty years, of course. You think you'll remember all those days, weeks, months and years but you don't. Somehow they slip by and when they're gone you wonder how you let that happen, why you can't remember. It's hard to recognise happiness when you're living through it. Much easier to see it when you look back.' Daphne smiled. 'In our minds, we're forever thirty something, ready to take on the world. Then one day, you wake up old. And alone.'

'I'm sorry, I shouldn't have asked.'

Daphne touched her arm. 'It's okay. I'm glad you did. I loved Ted but it wasn't all wine and roses; there was many a time I could cheerfully have strangled him. But – what's that expression? We had each other's backs. And that was a nice feeling. I miss it. What I wouldn't give to hold Ted's hand again now just for a little while. We got very comfortable in our own little worlds, him with his machines and me with my crafts. Now I wish we'd spent more time together.' Daphne smiled. 'How long have you been married?'

'Sixteen years.'

'Is it a happy marriage?'

Sam stacked her paint cards and returned them to their holder. 'I thought it was. We're separated at the moment.'

'I'm sorry to hear that. Can I ask why?'

'He cheated on me with another woman.'

'And left you for her?' Daphne tutted.

Sam looked up. 'No, I asked him to leave. I needed space to come to terms with what he'd done.'

'Has he said he's sorry?'

'Yes.'

'But you don't believe him?'

'No, I do believe him.'

Daphne looked surprised. 'Then why haven't you asked him to come home?'

Sam bit her lip. 'I'm afraid he'll do it again.'

'So it's your fear that's holding you back not something your husband has or hasn't done.'

'I guess.' Sam put the paint cards into her bag along with the swatches of material they had been discussing.

'Has he done it before?'

'Not to my knowledge.'

'Then what's making you so afraid?'

Standing her bag on the floor, Sam told Daphne about her father. 'I can still hear the click of the garden gate the day he left for good.'

Daphne patted Sam's hand. 'What your father did was unforgiveable, my dear, but if you truly love your husband perhaps it's time for you to stop punishing him for another man's mistakes and ask him to come home. When I was young, I spent too much time worrying about things that never happened instead of just living. Don't be like me, Sam.'

Chapter Thirteen

Dressed in black jeans and a white shirt, Sam was applying blusher as Cassie bounced into the bedroom. The teenager threw herself down on her stomach on the bed, her head resting in her hands.

'You look nice.'

'Thanks.'

Sam watched Cassie trace her finger over the roses on the quilt. 'When you met Dad, how did you know he liked you?'

'He told me.'

'Straight out?'

'Yes. Why?'

'There's this boy. He's going to Sophie's party next weekend.'

Sam's gaze connected with her daughter's in the mirror.

'I think he likes me. I think he might ask me out. I'm fifteen now. You and Dad said I had to wait until I was fifteen. So if he asks me I can go, right?'

Her little girl. Too beautiful for words. Now, the object of attention from teenage boys; testosterone on legs.

Sam turned away from the mirror and stroked her daughter's cheek. 'Yes, for a date. Nothing more.'

Cassie laughed. 'If Dad had his way I'd have to keep my legs crossed until I was thirty.'

'At least.' Sam grinned. 'Don't let this boy or any boy for that matter pressure you into doing something you don't feel ready for. When the time is right, you'll know.'

'We had the birds and bees talk years ago, Mum.' Cassie rolled her eyes. 'Do you think I'm pretty?'

'Come here.' Sam patted the stool she was sitting on. As Cassie sat Sam moved to stand behind her. Lifting Cassie's long blonde hair away from her face, she clipped it up. Then, she traced her fingers over her daughter's brow and down her cheekbones. 'You see that bone structure?'

Cassie nodded.

'There are Hollywood actresses who have paid thousands of dollars for surgery to give them what you have naturally. You're not just pretty, Cassie. You're beautiful, which is why I don't want you to be in too much of a hurry, darling.' Sam rested her hands on Cassie's shoulders. 'Concentrate on your schoolwork and have fun with your hobbies and your friends. There's a whole world out there to explore. I don't want you to spend all your time fretting about whether some boy will call you or let you down.' Sam dropped a kiss to Cassie's head. 'Time enough for that.'

'Like Dad let you down? We know he's been up to something with someone from work,' Cassie continued. 'There was one time when Josh heard you shouting.'

They had thought they'd been so clever, keeping up a front, and all the time Cassie and Josh had known the truth about Megan. She felt the heat flame in her cheeks.

'I can understand why you're angry,' Cassie said. 'Milo's mum poured petrol over his dad's clothes and set them alight when he cheated on her.'

Sam raised her eyebrows.

'They're getting a divorce now. They both want Milo and his brother to live with them. Is that going to happen to us, because I just want things to be the way they were.'

Sam stroked her daughter's cheek. Cassie suddenly looked very young.

'Me, too,' Sam admitted.

'Can they be?'

The hope in Cassie's eyes was a dagger to Sam's heart. 'I don't know. I'm sorry, I know it's not what you wanted to hear,' she said quickly and she wrapped her arms around her daughter's shoulders, hugging her tightly. 'Your dad and I love you as much as ever. You'll still have us both, whatever happens.'

'It won't be the same,' Cassie said petulantly.

'Has your dad said anything to you?'

'Only that it's his fault and we're not to blame you.'

'Whatever decision we take about the future you have to trust us that it's the right one. Okay?'

She nodded.

Did Cassie believe her? Sam wondered. Was it possible to convince someone of something if you didn't entirely believe it yourself? For the first time in her life, Sam found it impossible to read the look in her daughter's eyes.

Chapter Fourteen

David leaned against the breakfast bar and watched Sam check the chicken roasting in the oven. He felt positively underdressed as he looked down at his tracksuit bottoms and Reebok tee shirt.

He'd never seen Sam look anything less than immaculate; eyes beautifully made up, lips pearly pink, great hair, loose and swingy, the sort of hair you wanted to touch, knowing it would be soft. He swallowed. She's married. *Very* married. Sixteen years and two kids married.

He turned away abruptly and, balancing himself, opened the wine.

'Not for me, remember, I'm driving.'

David nodded. Pulling the carton of orange juice from the fridge, he poured her a glass. He thought about pouring himself one but there was only so much orange juice a man could drink.

His gaze followed Sam as she put a cloth on the table.

'I'm supposed to be treating you to dinner, remember?'

'I'm happy to help.'

'Soon as I'm free of these blasted crutches we'll do this again except then I will do all the work and you can sit on the sofa and eat grapes and drink wine.'

She laughed but he could see a sadness in her eyes that pulled him up and made him wonder. *Are we on a clock?*

'Where does your husband think you are?'

'Having dinner with Connor.'

'He wouldn't have understood, about tonight?' David asked gently. He watched a frown settle on her face.

'I never got round to telling him about helping you. I think in the circumstances my having dinner with you might have come as a bit of a shock.'

Her husband didn't know? Why keep it from him? Unless . . . David's pulse quickened.

'Is he still working as hard?'

'Yes.'

'That must be tough.'

'It's only temporary.'

'Is that what he tells you?'

'Yes.'

'And you believe him?'

'I have to.'

'He shouldn't take you for granted.' It was on the tip of his tongue to add, *I wouldn't*. But he held back. 'Why have you done so much for me, Sam?' he asked. 'Don't think I'm not grateful,' he added quickly. 'But you only met me a few weeks ago and you've given up so much time for me. Why?'

'It's a terrible thing that happened to you and I wanted to help,' she said as she checked the chicken once more.

He'd given it a lot of thought since he'd been home. Why was a busy woman like Sam, with all her commitments, devoting so much time to him, a virtual stranger?

'Is that really all there is to it?'

He saw her hesitate, her frown deepening. *Say it, Sam. Say that you like me and you enjoy spending time with me.* His heart beat a little faster as he waited for her response.

She looked up, a smile on her face. 'I just wanted to help.'

She looked uncomfortable. Disappointed, David decided not to push her. He watched as she smoothed out a crease in the tablecloth. Mesmerised by the sight of her slender fingers moving across the crisp white surface he wondered what it would feel like to have those same fingers run through his hair.

Her husband wasn't giving her the attention she deserved. Maybe she was weighing up the pros and cons of having an affair. It was what Lauren had done, sought attention elsewhere. Maybe that had been his fault for putting work first, and if Sam chose to have an affair with him that would be her husband's fault.

As much as David tried to justify it to himself, he knew the situation was different. There were children involved and because of that, he shouldn't encourage her, however much he might want to. The question was, could he stop himself?

'David, there's something I need to say.'

He snapped his head up. Embarrassed that she'd found him watching her, he gave her a nervous grin. 'Sounds serious.' She was frowning again. His smile faded. 'What is it?'

'I . . .'

He laid his hand on her shoulder. The warmth of her skin burned his fingers.

'I'm so glad you're better now.' Her words came out in a rush followed by a quick, unconvincing smile.

'Thanks to you,' he said evenly. He didn't believe that was what she'd intended to say. There was something else.

Her smile was back. Dazzling. Vivacious. He longed to move his hand from her shoulder to her cheek. If he leaned in to kiss her, how would her luscious pink lips react? Would they yield to his, as eager for his touch as he was for hers or would they rebuke him with a sharp retort? Could one kiss, stolen in a fleeting moment, cause that much harm? It was only one kiss, after all. Perhaps he was right and she, too, harboured fantasies of the two of them becoming more than just friends.

He saw her smile waver, a question appear in her gorgeous blue eyes. *Just give me a sign, Sam. One sign.* She lowered her gaze, breaking the spell. The moment had gone but still he didn't want to be the one to turn away. His hand lay heavy on her shoulder now.

On impulse, he gave her shoulder a squeeze before releasing her.

She returned to the kitchen, all hustle and bustle, as if nothing had happened between them, as if he hadn't been about to kiss her and confess exactly how he felt about her; his guardian angel.

Perhaps she was ignorant of anything other than his friendship, until tonight he had been careful to hide his true feelings. Possibly, she had no idea, even now, and perhaps that was for the best. What good would it do to lay bare his soul? Married with children, an illicit affair would be the best he could hope for and instinctively he knew a little piece of her would never be enough for him. In a situation like that nobody ever won.

His stomach tightened first with disappointment and then with fear. What had she been about to tell him before she'd changed her mind? Had she been about to say she wouldn't be visiting again? He dreaded those words falling from her lips, knew it was only a matter of time until they did. Maybe he should take the lead; tell her that she didn't have to visit any more. Release them both from temptation.

He poured a glass of wine and took a sip. *Don't be such a selfish bastard. Tell her.*

'Sam.' She turned to him expectantly. The words stuck in his throat. He couldn't do it. He couldn't be without her. Not yet. 'Thanks. For everything.'

'You're welcome.'

She was another man's wife, not his to cherish, hold or love, and one day, probably very soon, she would

110

walk away. When that day came he had to be strong enough to let her go he realised. His punishment for meeting her too late.

*

Sam basted the chicken before perching on one of the kitchen stools. She took a sip of her orange juice. The Old Mill situated by the River Stebbing had been converted into flats the previous year. She and Connor had been invited by the developer, Phil Blunkett, to style the show flat and the penthouse so she knew enough about the development to know that David had bought one of the most expensive apartments.

The open-plan living area had wooden floors and large floor-to-ceiling windows with breathtaking views over the river and the fields beyond. The kitchen was stainless steel. To the left, patio doors led onto the balcony which ran the length of the flat.

At the other end of the living room was another door. Recalling the floor plans, Sam knew it led to a corridor, off which were two bedrooms and a bathroom. Another set of patio doors gave access to the balcony from the master bedroom.

The flat was the antithesis of Meadowview Cottage. No ornate fireplaces or pretty throws. Sam nevertheless liked its clean lines and minimalist, modern look. The living area was a mixture of coffees and creams, dominated by two squashy cream-leather sofas. A giant television hung on one wall and beneath it boxes of technology were piled on top of one another, many of which Sam couldn't readily identify. David was fiddling with one of them. Suddenly music filled the room. A piano concerto. He smiled at her.

'Dinner will be ready soon. Where do you keep the cutlery?'

'Drawer next to the sink.'

Sam opened the drawer. Something was catching at the back. She reached inside, her fingers closing round an envelope. She pulled it free. Inside the envelope she could see the embossed letterhead of a city law firm *Perkins Ronin* and beneath David's address the heading of the letter, visible above the fold, *'Re: Our Client – Lauren Brightwell'*.

Sam stowed the letter back in the drawer and took out the cutlery she needed. She had no wish to know what lay beneath the fold, it was David's private business. Most likely, Lauren was seeking the return of some of her belongings, their break-up had been rather abrupt as Sam recalled.

She took the cutlery over to the table. A bookcase stood nearby. Sam took the opportunity to scan the books and trophies. On top was a photograph of a football team. Muddy boys in blue-and-white hooped shirts, all grinning for the camera. It wasn't hard to spot David in the middle of the group with his foot on the ball. Sam's heart caved in at the sight of it. *He'll be lucky to play football again with that leg.*

'I was the top goal scorer that season,' David said, following her gaze. 'I got a ten-pound Woolworths voucher.'

They smiled at one another.

She wanted to ask if he would play again. Didn't dare. Beside the football photograph was a picture of a middle-aged couple. 'Your parents?'

He nodded.

'What were they like?'

'Incredibly loving. I didn't realise how much until I lost them. For years after they were gone it helped to imagine they were still at home. Dad making things in the garage, Mum cooking up a storm in the kitchen. It wasn't all plain sailing, mind. Dad liked a drink and Mum would give him hell about it.' David smiled. 'I miss them. Even now. They've been on my mind a lot since the accident.'

She watched his hands tense into fists, relax, then tense again. 'It must have been tough to lose them so young.'

'Aye. Sympathy bought me a couple of months with the landlord but it couldnae buy me forever. I had to watch them pack my parents' things in the repo van. Nothing I could do about it. A friend's sofa sufficed until the compensation payment from the accident came through. It was enough for me to start again.

He sat down at the table. 'Ever since, I've been in the business of making money. As much money as I could. Evenings. Weekends. When the other guys wanted to be with their families, I'd be doing the extra viewings. I was determined I'd never see my own stuff loaded into a repo van. Only my boss, Lewis Shaw, brings in more money than I do but that scramble to stay on top, it makes you do things that . . .' he paused.

Sam raised her eyebrows.

'Lewis sometimes gets me to undervalue properties for him. Usually probate sales. I value it. Lewis buys it. Then he sells it on a few months' later at the full price for a tasty profit and gives me a cut. Not exactly kosher. I've done well out of it, mind. My Audi TT, my Harley, a bunch of buy to lets and the holiday cottage but . . .'

'But?'

'When something like this happens it makes you think.' He patted his leg. 'The buy to lets are profitable but they're also a pain in the backside. I have to rent a lock-up for the car and the Harley and the insurances are eye-watering. When you step back you realise you're spending a fortune just to maintain the things you've bought. How crazy is that?' He gestured to the photograph of his parents. 'I can imagine my dad saying, "How much did you pay for that TV, lad?" They wouldn't understand my world. Truth is, I'm not sure I do any more.' He sipped his wine. 'I've decided to take some time. Offload the buy to lets. Do up the holiday cottage, maybe buy another, slow down some.'

'Hand in your notice?'

He nodded. 'I don't fancy being Lewis's patsy any longer and there's more to life than working twenty-four-seven.'

'I'll drink to that,' Sam said.

As they sat down to eat, David raised his wine glass.

'Thank you for everything you've done for me. You've been an angel. My angel.'

Sam tapped her glass against his, her gaze firmly fixed on the table. 'It was the least I could do.' She could feel the heat burning in her cheeks and prayed he would think it was just the residual heat from the kitchen that was making her glow.

'I heard from the police this morning. They've finished their investigation.'

She jerked her head up.

'The papers are with the CPS for consideration. They don't think the woman stopped at the junction. What sort of stupid bitch doesn't stop at a stop junction?' He shook his head in disgust. 'I hope they throw the book at her.'

Sam felt sick. 'Do you know when it might come to court?'

'No idea. The sooner the better as far as I'm concerned. I just want to put the whole sorry business behind me. Anyway, let's not dwell on the depressing stuff. When can you come out and take a look at the holiday cottage? Give me some tips for the makeover.'

What could she say? No would be the right answer. *No because I'm the stupid bitch who didn't stop at the stop junction* would be a better one.

'I've still got months of rehab ahead of me and I need something positive to focus on. I thought it might be fun, something you and I could work on together. What do you say?'

The music that had been playing in the background suddenly seemed a lot louder as the silence between them lengthened.

'Not quite the response I was looking for,' he said finally.

'I'm sorry, I . . .'

'You don't have to explain, Sam. You've given me so much of your time already. It was selfish of me to ask for any more.'

'It wasn't selfish,' she said quickly. She felt like an insect pinned under a microscope. She could feel his gaze beating down on her, knew if she looked up his brown eyes would be giving her that intense look of his. *Don't look up!*

'I could really do with an expert to help me get the look right.'

Against her better judgement, she met his gaze. It was twin beam, full on. Just as she knew it would be. Her heart heaved. The police knew they hadn't stopped. The papers had gone to the CPS. She was going to face prosecution. This charade was about to come to an end one way or another. It was time she stepped up and took responsibility for her actions. The words drummed in her brain.

'So what do you say; will you take a look? One visit. I'll take notes. That'll be it. I promise.'

Tell him no. Say you're too busy. Send Connor instead.

'I'd be happy to help.'

The strength of his smile was her reward. She'd think about the consequences tomorrow.

'Tell me about your dad. I'm guessing there's a story there.' He nodded towards her ring.

Self-conscious, Sam let go of it. 'When I was a little girl my dad was my hero. He left when I was eleven. The ring was my birthday present that year. I wore it on my middle finger back then. It was the last birthday present he gave me. He promised to keep in touch.' She shrugged. 'He promised a lot of things but then he married again, and had a new family. I'd just had Josh when he came back into my life. By then he was dying . . .'

'Were you reconciled before he died?'

She nodded. 'I visited him every day at the Abbeyleigh Hospice until he passed away. That's how I became involved with them.'

'Is your mum still alive?'

'Yes. She remarried. They retired to Spain ten years ago.' She smiled. 'I'd better see about dessert.'

She returned with two portions of cheesecake.

David topped up his wine. 'Not quite what I had in mind when I invited you to dinner. Again, I'm sorry you've ended up doing all the work.'

'I've only done a little.'

'It'll be easier when I can get shot of these damn crutches.' He pulled a face. 'The insurance company have been in touch. They've offered me money for the bike. I need to get it checked out, make sure I'm

117

not being ripped off and I need to see someone about making a claim.'

'You should have compensation,' Sam said firmly.

'The commission I earned on the sales I made before the accident is still coming through, so I'm okay just now but that money's going to run out soon. I'll be back to a basic salary then until I hand in my notice and then it'll just be the rental money. Not something I'd budgeted for. I used to let the money flow through my fingers like water. See it, want it, buy it. I guess I always thought it would be like that. I never imagined the tap being turned off.'

'I don't think anyone does,' Sam said.

'Things are going to be tight until I can offload the buy to lets. I've never had a compunction to save. I don't have a pension or shares. Just two massive credit card bills from mine and Lauren's trips to Ghana and Tahiti. She always did love an exotic holiday that one, not to mention her designer labels.

'Anyway. The past is the past. Bottom line, I could really use some sound advice. I thought maybe your husband could help. He's a lawyer, isn't he? Then I realised I don't know your surname. Daft, isn't it? I know so much about you and yet I don't think you've ever told me your surname. If you have, I've forgotten it.'

Sam put down her orange juice. David was looking at her expectantly. With a smile, Sam began to clear the table. 'My husband wouldn't be able to help.' She called over her shoulder. 'He's up to his eyes in work at the moment. Smith Mathers are very good though. I'll give you their number.'

When she returned to the table, David reached out, his hand on hers.

'You still haven't told me your surname,' he said, a smile on his lips.

His words crushed the thrill of his touch.

'It's Denney,' she said, choosing her maiden name. The white lies had just become a shade darker. She inched her fingers from under his. 'I need to spend a penny.'

Escaping to the bathroom, Sam leaned against the locked door. She had to call a halt to this. For goodness' sake, she'd almost kissed him earlier. This was not how the evening was supposed to go. She ran water into the basin and cooled the insides of her wrists under the tap. Not wanting to look at her reflection in the mirrored door of the vanity unit above the sink, Sam opened the door and reached for a towel from the rail to dry her hands.

Her gaze wandered over David's shaving foam, moisturiser and aftershave. There were two boxes of powerful painkillers next to them and a packet of anti-depressants. Her conscience tweaked.

What the hell was she doing here? She was thirty-five years old. Too old to be infatuated, too married to stay. Whatever problems she and Neil had, they were not going to be solved by her having dinner with another man.

She closed the vanity unit door and met her gaze in the mirror. David had his life to get on with and she had hers. It was time to stop playing games with another man's heart. She should go home and figure out if she still had a marriage worth saving.

*

It was late by the time Sam got home. She poured herself a glass of wine from the open bottle in the fridge. She'd had the perfect opportunity to come clean with David but the words had deserted her. Worse, she'd panicked when he'd asked about her surname and given him her maiden name.

She had been a friend when David had needed one most. She had done it to assuage her guilt for not staying at the Northey that night, for not taking the keys from Neil and, if she was brutally honest with herself, to get back at Neil over Megan.

Flirting with David had restored a little of her battered self-confidence, made her feel attractive again. But what had it done to the vulnerable young man she'd been flirting with? She had noticed him watching her that evening. The weight of his gaze had left her feeling flattered and flustered in equal measure.

She had enjoyed the flirting, the mutual attraction. She had wanted him to kiss her tonight. She took a sip of her wine. She was in far deeper than even she had appreciated. Her contact with David had to end. Connor was right. It was far too complicated.

She knew it would be a gamble to delay her confession much longer but maybe her assistance with the holiday cottage would be enough to take the edge off his anger.

Make it special. A fitting goodbye present. Then, tell him the truth and walk away. Your life will be a little darker without his smile but at least your conscience will be clear at last.

Chapter Fifteen

Neil heard the car sweep over the gravel, the hum of the electric garage door, the sound of the internal door opening and closing. Sam was home. He lifted his glasses to massage his eyes. It was twelve forty. Late for an evening with Connor. For just a moment he caught himself wondering if that's where she'd been.

Was it conceivable that Sam had decided to get her own back? An affair to even the score. Neil started to think about their friends, singling out any likely candidates. Surely, even if she'd decided to do such a thing, she'd be discreet enough not to choose someone from their immediate circle.

Her business brought her into contact with lots of people outside his sphere. Dismayed, he rammed the papers he'd been working on into their file and tossed it to the floor. It would serve him right if she had but the thought made him feel sick.

*

Sam stowed her empty wine glass on the drainer and went through to the TV room. Neil was sitting in his usual armchair, surrounded by files.

'Sorry,' she said. 'It's later than I intended.'

'Good time?'

'Yes.' She was unnerved by the question and her reaction to it. Feeling reckless, she was tempted to tell him where she'd been and with whom. Let him know that after sixteen years of marriage she had let herself look at another man and that she'd liked what she had seen. Part of her wanted to see the shock and hurt on Neil's face. She had drunk too much wine, too quickly, she realised.

'I see you decided to renew the subscription to Park Place. I had a letter.'

He nodded. 'Cassie likes to use the pool and once I've secured the promotion I want to start using the gym again.' He patted his spare tyre before taking off his glasses. 'I brought a stack of files to work on but Josh wanted to play the new Grand Prix game he'd bought. Even Cassie joined in. We had a good time. Josh won, naturally. I only started work an hour or so ago.' He stretched and yawned. 'If someone had told me I'd spend more quality time with my kids once I moved out, I wouldn't have believed them, but it's true.'

Sam remained silent.

'Just goes to show how things have been going wrong for some time,' he continued candidly. He laid his glasses on the side table. 'I've been thinking about going to the police, telling them the truth about the accident.'

'You can't go to the police now. I've lied, you've lied. It wouldn't just be a driving offence we'd have to worry about.'

'I don't care if it makes things right between us.' He stood and with a sigh pushed his hands through his hair. 'I shouldn't have asked you to cover for me. I wish I hadn't.'

'What's done is done.'

She could see again Neil, wide-eyed with panic. *'We sure as hell can't stay. What if he's dead? It'll ruin me.'*

Then, David in the hospital. *'That time of night, in that weather, I could have bled to death before anyone found me.'*

If Neil had had his way that might indeed have been the case. But it wasn't. Help had been called. They'd done the right thing. Moreover, Neil wasn't a bad man. In different circumstances, he would have been the first to stop and help, she reminded herself.

'I need to know why,' she said suddenly.

'Why what?'

'Why you needed her.'

She steeled herself for whatever he said next.

'This again? It's in the past. Leave it there,' he said wearily.

'I can't. I've tried but I can't.'

Neil shifted from one foot to the other. 'I was an idiot. It's all you need to know.'

'It's not enough.'

'I enjoyed her company. I can't talk to you about work because whenever I do you always say the same thing. "Don't work so hard. Spend more time at home".' He pulled a face.

'What's wrong with that?' Sam asked, stung. 'I worry about you.'

'It doesn't pay the bills, that's what's wrong with it. It doesn't buy membership to fancy spas. It doesn't get me my promotion.'

'That bloody promotion,' Sam muttered under her breath.

'When I talked to Megan about work she didn't criticise me or put me under more pressure. She tried to help.' He met her gaze. 'She didn't nag, Sam. She didn't rant at me whenever I got home too tired to string a sentence together. She didn't make me feel bad for missing the kids' parents' evenings. She didn't yell at me because I forgot to take the rubbish out, or mow the lawn or pick up the bloody dry cleaning. Sometimes I'd barely get in the front door and you'd be on at me. You wonder why I spent so much time at the office? Part of it was to put in the hours I needed to stand the vaguest hope of winning this sodding promotion but the other part of it, if I'm honest, was to get some peace and bloody quiet.'

Hands on hips, she stared at him. 'Do you think I wanted to be that person? I was just so damn tired all the time. I had a business to run, the kids and this place to look after. We were supposed to be a team and yet it all seemed to be falling on my shoulders and there wasn't enough of me to go around.'

'I wasn't pulling my weight here, I know that. You had every right to resent me for it but it would only have been for a short while.'

'Tell me about that night.'

He bent to gather his files. Then, hoisting them into his arms he made as if to walk by her. 'It isn't going to help.'

'It might. I want to know.'

'What do you want to know?'

'What was she wearing?'

Neil looked perplexed. 'A black suit, I think.'

'Skirt or trousers?'

'Skirt.'

'And a blouse?'

'Yes.'

'What colour?'

'Who gives a shit?'

'I do.'

His mouth was a thin line. 'It was purple, I think.'

'What was her house like?'

'It's a small new-build semi on the edge of town.'

'I don't mean its construction, you idiot. What was it like inside?'

'Neat. Tidy.'

'Had you been there before?'

'No.'

'So, you ate . . .'

'Yes, and then I helped her clear up.' Turning away, Neil began to pace the room. 'We were both in the kitchen and she touched my arm and we looked at one another and the next thing I knew we were kissing.'

'And in that moment you thought, *I'm going to risk my marriage and everything I've worked for just so I can fuck this woman.*'

'Not exactly.' He stopped and met her gaze. 'If I'd been thinking any of that do you think I would have stayed? I'd have run a fucking mile.'

'Did you take her blouse off or did she?'

Neil stared at the ceiling, shaking his head.

'Damn it, Neil!'

He levelled his gaze at her, the files held in front of him like a barrier. 'You really want to do this, Sam?'

She nodded.

'Fine. Have it your way,' he retorted angrily. 'I ripped it open.'

Sam's eyes widened.

'Were you still in the kitchen?'

'Yes.'

'Where did you take her? Across the table?'

'She doesn't have a table. The kitchen's too small.'

Sam felt a ridiculous surge of triumph. *You may have had sex with my husband, you slut, but at least my kitchen is big enough to have a table in it.* She turned away from him, closing her eyes. *Is this what I've been reduced to? Infantile point scoring to shore up my battered pride?*

'It was frantic, clumsy, drunken sex and it was over practically before it began.'

'And afterwards?' Sam asked quietly.

'I crashed out on her sofa with her on top of me. I only came to when my mobile started to ring and she answered it.'

'What were you thinking then?'

He broke eye contact and put the files on the floor. 'I was thinking, *Fucking hell! What have I done?*' he admitted ruefully.

Sam had a dozen different questions on the tip of her tongue about Megan – from her jewellery, to her perfume, to the way she made Neil feel – but would they help? Neil was already looking more uncomfortable than she had ever seen him look. Didn't that tell her everything she needed to know? And yet there was one more question she had to ask, one she couldn't let go.

'Was she better than me?'

'Sweetheart!' The word was a ragged sigh. 'She wasn't even close. For the first time in my married life I put myself in a position where I could be tempted and I was too weak to walk away . . .'

'Don't you think I've been tempted?' Sam asked, remembering David's hand on her shoulder, the look in his eyes when she'd thought he was going to kiss her and she'd thought about letting him.

'You . . .' Neil blustered.

'Don't look so surprised. Do you think it's only men who get to look and wonder?'

'But you didn't?'

She could see the horror in his eyes. So it was all right for him to have strayed but not for her to have done the same thing.

'Sam, have you?'

She lifted her chin. 'Not yet.'

His relief was palpable.

'I want us to have a future together, Sam. It's not too late. When you first found out, I'd listen to you sobbing your heart out, night after night. Knowing I had caused you such pain turned me inside out. All I can do is promise you I will never put myself in that position again and I do promise that. I do.'

'My father promised my mother a hundred times,' Sam replied stonily. 'Mum believed him and forgave him and he broke her heart again and again until finally she found the courage to throw him out.'

'Your father was a bastard. He went from one bed to another. I'm not him.'

She opened her mouth to speak before shutting it again. There would always be one more question, Sam realised, or worse the same question posed in a hundred different ways. If she kept picking the scab off this wound they would be having this conversation again in a month's time, a year, ten. It would never end until Neil tired of it, of her and gave up on them. A self-fulfilling prophecy. She spun her father's ring.

'If you truly love your husband perhaps it's time for you to stop punishing him for another man's mistakes.'

129

'I'm standing here, afraid to touch you in case you slap me or knock my hand away,' Neil admitted. 'But I don't want to be afraid to touch you, Sam, because I'm desperate to touch you, to kiss you, to love you.' His voice cracked with emotion as he leaned towards her. 'What do you need me to do to make things right between us?'

'If I knew, I'd tell you.' She balled her fists. 'I just get so scared.'

'I know, darling.' He bent his head to hers. 'And it's all my fault. I'm sorry.'

His lips brushed her neck. Then, his tongue began to tease her ear, just the way she liked. Sam shivered with sudden desire. They'd had sex infrequently since Megan. On each occasion, it had been awkward, often tearful.

With a jolt, Sam realised just how much she wanted to make love again. Her fantasies about David were just that, fantasies. Neil was the real world. Her world. One sign from her and they could start again. Part of her wanted him to rip her top off the way he'd done to Megan, jealous that he'd wanted to touch another woman so desperately, but was she ready? Neil was kissing her temple now. It would be so easy to let him carry on.

'I love you.' He edged his lips towards hers, captured them. His kiss was tender, questing. 'Always have, always will.'

Eager to take him in her arms, Sam's desire fought with her power of reason. After so many years, they would be incapable of sex without strings. As night followed day, sex with him would lead to a reconciliation and she hadn't yet made up her mind that was what she wanted. Gently, reluctantly, she pushed him away.

'It's too soon,' she said struggling to ignore the fire he'd started inside her.

He stroked her cheek. Then, with a sigh, he withdrew his hand. 'I'd better go,' he said and knelt to retrieve his files.

'Why don't you stay in the spare room tonight? It's the hospice auction tomorrow. You promised you'd help get things ready. It seems silly to travel to Abbeyleigh tonight just to come back in the morning.'

He nodded eagerly, his smile touching her heart. Was she mad? The children would doubtless jump to the wrong conclusion when they woke to find their father still in the house. Yet Sam couldn't banish the memory of Neil's kisses. Though tentative, they'd reminded her of what she had lost. It was too soon to pick up where they had left off, but maybe, just maybe, it was time to stop holding him at arm's length.

Chapter Sixteen

Sam opened her eyes, stretched and yawned. She'd overslept. The pretty, pastel-yellow walls of her bedroom, interspersed with ancient oak beams, greeted her bleary gaze. She rubbed her eyes. The voile canopy overhead went in and out of focus.

Pulling on her silk robe, she went downstairs. 'She Loves You' by The Beatles was blaring from the kitchen radio. Sam leaned, unnoticed, against the doorjamb. Neil was still dressed in his suit trousers and work shirt, with the sleeves rolled up. He was cooking bacon and singing along to the track whilst Cassie and Josh were buttering bread in time to the music, joining in on the chorus.

Tears clouded Sam's eyes and she retreated, unseen, to the hallway. What she'd witnessed was a family happy in each other's company. Did she have any right to let her fears stand in the way of such unity?

But I have to be sure. Neil's kisses had reminded her how good they had once been together and yet, confusingly, in her dreams, it had not been Neil kissing her neck. It had been David.

'What are you doing out here?' Neil asked, surprised.

'I was just . . .'

Neil grabbed her hand. 'Come on.' He pulled her in to the kitchen. 'I was just going to call you. Breakfast is ready.'

*

Park Place had donated their largest function room for the Abbeyleigh Hospice to hold its auction. David had managed to wrangle a ticket from his soon to be ex-employer, Lewis Shaw. Now, he bought himself a beer and cast his gaze round the packed room.

'David?' He turned to find Sam walking towards him. Was it his imagination or had her tone been a little sharp?

'Hello.'

'I didn't expect to see you here.'

He saw the worried look she threw over her shoulder.

'What do you think?' he asked, shamelessly fishing for a compliment. He'd made a bit of an effort. Baggy black suit, white shirt. The crutches spoilt the look but he couldn't manage without them yet.

'Very smart.'

Her smile was fleeting and stole all the joy her words should have given him.

'Can I get you a drink?'

'No, I'm fine. I should get back.'

'You look nice.' She was wearing a red woollen dress with a slashed neckline. 'You always do,' he added.

Her brows drew together in a frown.

'David . . .'

'You don't seem very pleased to see me,' he said, trying not to sound hurt.

Sam scowled. 'My husband and children are here.'

'You could introduce me.'

'That wouldn't be a good idea.'

Her tone was positively arctic now. He felt as though she'd slapped him. She had been so careful to keep him separate from the rest of her life, he realised, and here he was pushing at the boundaries, in the same room as her husband, her children, her friends. He was annoyed at the way she kept throwing worried glances over her shoulder.

She didn't want the two worlds to collide. But why? What was she afraid of? He'd only thought about kissing her. He hadn't actually done it. Friendship wasn't a crime. They'd done nothing wrong, so why did they have to hide?

'Are you ashamed to be seen with me?'

'What? No. Don't be ridiculous.'

'Then let me buy you a drink.'

'I have a drink waiting for me.'

He watched her hook her hair behind her ears. She looked edgy and uncomfortable. He hated to see her like that, to know he was responsible. And yet he couldn't stop himself from pressing.

'There's probably a lot of people here we both know. Lewis Shaw, for instance. He's just over there.' He gestured with his beer glass. 'Why don't you come over and say hello?'

'I'm not going to do that,' she said firmly.

'Sam.' He laid his hand on her arm.

She snatched her arm away. 'Don't touch me.'

'For God's sake, Sam. We're just two friends standing here chatting. What are you so afraid of? Come and say hello to Lewis.'

'No. Goodnight, David.'

'Sam.'

David turned to find a man in his late sixties walking towards them.

'Chris.'

David watched enviously as the man kissed Sam's cheeks. 'Fabulous turnout. I live in awe at how you and the committee pull this off year after year.'

The man turned to David and held out his hand. 'Sorry, Chris Hatton. I work at the hospice.'

'David McAllister.'

'This woman is a bloody marvel. Don't know what the hospice would do without her.'

David smiled.

'It's a team effort,' Sam said.

'How do you two know each other?' Hatton asked.

'We're friends.'

'David's a client.'

Hatton looked from one to the other. 'Well, the auction should be starting soon. I'd better take my seat. Don't be long, Sam.' He cast another glance at David before walking away.

'*Friends?*' she said.

'Aren't we?' he challenged.

'Are you deliberately trying to make me feel uncomfortable?'

'Of course not.'

'I need to get back.'

'Before you go, I was hoping we could pin down that date for you to come out and see the cottage at The Hallows.'

'Yes,' she said absently, edging away.

'When?'

'What?'

'When do you want to come out?'

'Soon.'

'Why are you so unhappy at me being here?'

'David . . .'

'Do you want me to leave, is that it?'

He saw the hope leap into her eyes. The sight of it crushed his heart.

'I think that would be a good idea.'

'If that's what you want.'

'Please.'

He gave a curt nod and watched her walk away. His was not the only pair of eyes on her, he noticed. Lewis Shaw, in particular, was watching her lasciviously as she passed by his table. Who could blame him? She looked gorgeous as she made her way across the room, swapping small talk as she went.

Eventually, she sat at one of the front tables. David craned his neck for a better look. There was a young boy, playing with his phone. Josh. A pretty girl, the image of Sam. Cassie. Plus a brown-haired man in a suit who, as David watched, reached across to Sam, took her hand in his and kissed the inside of her wrist. The husband.

David felt his heart tug at the sight of them together and turned away. He'd seen enough. He knew his place now. It was on the periphery of her life. He'd been a fool to hope for anything more. Perhaps one day he'd find someone whose hand he could hold like that. But it couldn't be Sam's. His guardian angel belonged to another man.

'David? Hi. It's Jane. From the hospital.' She laughed. 'You didn't recognise me without my uniform.'

'Sorry!' He kissed her cheek. 'It's good to see you.'

'And you. You're looking well. Here to support your sister?'

David looked puzzled. 'My sister?'

'Sam. She told me she was your sister. I have to admit I was rather curious, your accents being so different but I guessed you had separate upbringings. Anyway, lovely to see you. Have a good evening.'

'You, too.'

With a smile, Jane went back to her table, leaving David to stare, bewildered, in Sam's direction. *His sister?* Why would she say such a thing?

He'd thought her appearing at his bedside in hospital had been a happy coincidence. He'd been so thankful for her company, a friend when he'd needed one most. But if she hadn't picked his name from a list like she'd said, was it fate that had brought her into his life or had she deliberately sought him out? If so, why? What did she want from him?

His mind racing, he thought about confronting her, but as she briefly met his gaze, frowned and looked away, he knew there would be no point. How she was with him in a crowd was completely different to how she was with him when alone. If he wanted answers, they wouldn't be forthcoming tonight. He would have to wait until he could get her on her own. It seemed his guardian angel was a keeper of secrets and he intended to find out why.

Chapter Seventeen

Sam placed the breakfast cereals on the table and went back to the fridge for the milk and the juice, pausing only to stab the button down on the toaster.

Neil, tie hanging loose, grabbed the cornflakes. 'Thanks for letting me stay again last night.'

He'd taken the children to London for the weekend. Back late on the Sunday night, Sam had cooked them all a meal. It had seemed churlish to make Neil drive back to Abbeyleigh, especially as he would have to be back in a matter of hours to do the school run.

He'd stayed over a couple of times since the charity auction. Sam had given up trying to apply logic to their situation. She just followed her heart. If it felt right, she did it.

Making up a bed for him in the spare room felt right. Letting him kiss her did not and she had stopped him whenever he'd tried. He'd taken her rejections with good humour. It was obvious he considered the sleepovers a victory in themselves.

'Cassie. Josh. Breakfast.'

The children came shuffling in, gazes fixed on their phones.

'No electronic devices during meals. Come on, you know the rules.' She took Josh's phone and held her hand out to her daughter. 'Cassie.'

'I want you all to call me Cass from now on,' she said, handing over the phone.

'Why?' Sam asked as she stowed the phones beside the bread bin.

'It's cooler. Edgier. I like it.'

'Well, I don't,' Neil declared.

'Mum shortened her name.'

Neil looked at Sam for help.

Sam shrugged and smiled. 'She's got a point.'

'Nothing wrong with Cassandra,' Neil said. 'It was my grandmother's name.'

'Cass Davenport will look better on the magazines.'

'Which magazine?' Josh asked. 'The school one?' He sniggered. 'Pass me the butter, Cassandra.'

'Get it yourself,' she said, kicking her brother under the table.

'What are you having, Cass? Toast or cereal?' Sam asked.

'I'm not eating breakfast any more,' she announced.

'Of course you are. Most important meal of the day.' Neil pushed the cornflakes towards her as Sam put the toast on the table.

'You should eat something, darling,' Sam said.

'I need to watch my weight. As a singer . . .'

'I thought you were going to be a dancer, Cassandra,' Josh said, scooping his finger across the pat of butter and receiving a slap on the back of his hand from Neil.

'Use the knife.'

'I'm going to do both,' Cass said, shooting her brother a withering glance. 'And act.' She pushed the cornflakes away.

Neil opened his mouth to speak but Sam placed her hand on his shoulder. 'When I worked at the modelling agency, the models always ate breakfast. They needed the energy of eating little and often.'

Cass looked sceptical. 'They ate breakfast every day?'

'Yep.' Sam edged the cornflakes towards her.

'Little and often?' Cass repeated.

'It worked for them.'

With a shrug, Cass poured cornflakes into a bowl. Neil gave Sam a grateful smile.

'You just want to impress Tobyn,' Josh said. 'I saw the two of you outside the canteen last week.'

'Tobyn? What the hell kind of name is that?' Neil asked.

'It's cool,' Cass replied.

'And edgy, don't forget edgy,' Josh chipped in.

Cass threw a soggy cornflake at him.

'Cassie loves Tobyn. Cassie loves Tobyn,' Josh chanted.

'Shut up!'

'This Tobyn . . .' Neil began.

'He's really nice, Dad. He and his friend Tom are taking Sophie and me to the cinema on Friday.'

'What? Like on a date?' Neil cast Sam a horrified look.

'I'm fifteen, Dad.'

'Did you know about this?' Neil asked.

'Mum's agreed to give me and Sophie a lift into town.'

'Is that right?'

Sam nodded. 'Better we know where she is and who she's meeting, don't you think?'

'Cassie loves Tobyn. Cassie loves Tobyn,' Josh chanted again.

'Shut up, you horrible little boy! At least I have friends.'

'I want you home by eleven.'

'Dad!'

'Eleven. On the dot.'

'Can I have my pocket money early?' Josh asked through a mouthful of toast.

'Why?' Neil asked.

'I need something for the computer.'

'You always need something for the computer. Why can't it wait until the weekend?'

Sam poured herself a cup of tea and raised her eyebrows as Neil looked up.

'Okay.' He plucked a ten-pound note from his wallet. 'Of course, I didn't get any pocket money when I was your age. I had a paper round.'

Sam exchanged smiles with the children.

'If you two are finished, go and clean your teeth.' She smiled fondly as the children trailed out.

Dusting off his hands, Neil stood. 'Does that apply to me, too?' he asked with a smile.

'Absolutely. If you don't want to lose your teeth.'

'Our daughter is growing up too fast.'

'She can't stay seven forever.'

'More's the pity. Have you met this Tobyn?'

'Briefly. He seems nice.'

Neil grunted. 'They all seem nice until they get what they want.'

Ain't that the truth.

'Why is she worried about her weight all of a sudden?'

'Not sure. I'm going to pop up and see if I can get to the bottom of it.'

Sam found Cass plaiting her hair in the bedroom.

'Can I come in?'

'Sure.'

'What was all that about breakfast?'

'Nothing.'

'Didn't seem like nothing. You can tell me, Cass. I was fifteen once. Hard to imagine, I know.' Sam smiled. 'But I do remember what it was like.'

Cass met her gaze in the dressing table mirror. 'Tobyn's band need a new singer and its between me and another girl. You should see her, Mum. She's the sister of the lead guitarist. She's older than us and she's so cool and she's like a size zero. Next to her I look fat.'

'You're not fat,' Sam said firmly. 'You're beautiful. Don't skip meals, Cass. Things can get out of control so quickly if you start doing that. Half the models I worked with were bulimic or anorexic. They went through hell and they didn't look any better for it. They just looked ill. Remember that.'

Cass nodded.

'The band should pick the best singer and if they don't pick you, find another band or start your own.'

When Sam returned to the kitchen Neil was waiting for her with a bag in his hand. 'How'd the pep talk go?'

'Not sure. Did she eat when you took her skating the other day?'

'Big bowl of pasta.'

'Did she go to the loo afterwards?'

'You mean to . . .' He simulated sticking his fingers down his throat. 'No. How can she have body image issues, Sam? She's gorgeous.'

'Pressures of modern life. It's always been hard but with social media and airbrushed celebrities, it's even harder now.'

He shook his head.

'If we keep an eye on her we can hopefully nip it in the bud before it gets serious.'

'You don't really think she's throwing up in secret, do you?'

'No, but we have to be vigilant.'

'Just as well I got you this yesterday.'

Sam looked bemused as he drew out a mobile phone.

'I've already got a phone.'

'I know but just lately, it always seems to be engaged or switched to voicemail. I think it's important the family can always get hold of you. Keep it with you always. Please.'

Sam nodded. A stab of guilt striking her. She had kept the phone turned off for practical reasons when at the hospital. Since then, she'd got into the habit of switching the phone off whenever she was with David.

David. He'd left a message on her voicemail the day after the charity auction. His tone insistent *We need to talk.* She'd rung him back, making an excuse about how busy she was and that she'd call him when things calmed down. He'd implored her not to leave it too long.

She had been horrified to see him at the auction. Gripped by fear, she'd treated him shabbily. He'd made such an effort to look nice for her big night and she had repaid him by asking him to leave. Part of her was surprised he was talking to her at all after that. Make the most of it, she thought wryly, he won't be for much longer.

She looked up to find Neil watching her.

'Do you like it?'

Sam turned the phone over. 'It's great. Thanks.'

'Can I ask you something?'

Sam nodded.

'What's the going rate for getting someone to wash and iron my shirts?'

'I've no idea. Struggling to stay on top of the laundry?' she asked with a smile.

'I'm spending a fortune on new shirts – it's easier,' he admitted ruefully.

Sam laughed. 'For goodness' sake, what are you like? Just bring them home, and I'll do them for you.'

'Yeah? Thanks, Sam.' He rubbed his neck. 'That wasn't why I asked, you know.'

'I know.'

'Is there anything I can do to return the favour?'

'There is actually. I have a client who has asked me to find a home for her husband's automatons. The Abbeyleigh Museum are interested but I want my client to be able to ask for them back if she wishes. The museum has drawn up an agreement. Would you be able to check it over for me?'

'Sure, I can do that.'

'How's work?'

'Hectic.'

'I imagine the weekend away won't have helped.'

'My kids come first.'

Sam nodded. 'You'll make up the time though I'm guessing?'

'No choice.' He grimaced. 'It's going to be a long week,' he admitted.

'You can't keep working like this.'

'I have to keep working like this,' he said tetchily. 'It's the only way I can bill more than that bastard Tilden.'

Sam tried to quell the fear that rose within her. The last time he'd had a lot on, Megan had been there. She's not there now though, Sam reminded herself. Anyway, why should you care? But the truth was, she did. Little by little, Neil was inching his way back into her heart. Soon she would have to make a decision about whether or not he stayed there.

'Is it worth it, Neil?'

He looked at her in amazement. 'Let's not do this again, Sam. Of course it's worth it.'

'I worry about the toll it's taking on you. Right now, you're like a hamster on a wheel and I'm afraid that, when you get this promotion, it'll be more of the same. The only difference is you'll be a more important hamster on a bigger wheel.'

'What you have to remember is that the more important hamsters get to delegate to other less important hamsters.'

Sam nodded.

'Thanks, by the way.'

'For what?'

'Saying "when" not "if" about the promotion.'

'You work so hard. You deserve it.'

'Thank you. Come on, kids. Your father's taxi service is leaving shortly.'

Sam chuckled. In a flurry of kisses, shouted goodbyes and swinging bags, husband and children made their way out of the door. She gave them a wave. Just time for one more cuppa before she, too, had to leave.

Sam was halfway through when the post arrived and with it a summons to appear at Abbeyleigh Magistrates Court. Her heart dropped like a penny in a slot machine, bouncing against every rib on the way down to her stomach. She tipped the rest of her tea away and rang Neil on her new phone.

When she got to Neil's office he and Murray, the firm's leading criminal lawyer, were discussing the case. Murray stood to kiss Sam's cheek as she entered.

Fishing the summons out of her bag, Sam handed it to him. 'I won't go to prison, will I?'

'Now, Samantha.' He took her hands in his. 'No one is going to prison.'

'Are you sure?'

'Yes.'

His answer was so emphatic that Sam felt herself begin to relax.

He scanned the summons before tossing it down. 'In order to reduce the sentence, we need to convince the magistrates that you didn't intend to drive carelessly. The weather that night was atrocious – we can use that in your defence.'

'I don't need a defence. I'm guilty.'

'And he was probably going too fast,' Neil cut in.

'You don't know that,' Sam said sharply.

'Young guy on a Harley at that time of night? Call it an educated guess,' Neil said belligerently.

'It's not his fault.'

'If you're convicted, you're paving the way for a civil action,' Murray said.

'Good.'

'Sam!'

'I want to plead guilty and for it to be over,' she said.

'I'll send the summons back together with your driving licence. Then a hearing will take place in your absence and you'll be convicted of careless driving.

148

If the magistrates are minded to impose a ban they'll adjourn and a new date will be set for sentencing when you'll have to appear. If the magistrates aren't considering a ban, they'll sentence you on the day. My guess is the magistrates will impose a fine and put points on your licence.' Murray rubbed his chin. 'There might be some stuff in the Abbeyleigh Gazette.'

'What stuff?' Sam asked, alarmed.

'About you . . . the accident. They'll make a bit of a fuss because of Neil. I'm sorry.'

For a moment, Sam considered the viability of buying every issue of the Gazette the week of the prosecution, wondering how much it would cost. 'That'll be good for clients.'

'Yours or mine?' Neil asked mischievously.

'There'll be some interest for a week and then it'll die down,' Murray said soothingly.

'People will soon forget,' Neil said. 'Besides, you're offering to do up people's houses not drive their kids to school.'

'That's not funny, Neil. Will the victim be present?' Sam asked.

'If he wants to be, certainly he has the right to be.'

'Would . . .' Sam cleared her throat. 'Would the victim know about the hearing?' She tried to keep the alarm out of her voice.

'Yes, of course.'

'Now?' she whispered.

'I'm sorry?'

'Would he know now? At the same time as me?'

Murray looked taken aback at her tone. 'I don't know, Sam. He would have to be told but when would be up to the CPS.'

'Who cares what the victim knows or when he knows it? What difference does it make?' Neil asked.

'Are you worried about some kind of retaliation?' Murray asked, eyes narrowing. 'Because I have to say, it would be highly unlikely. I've certainly never come across it in relation to a motoring offence.'

'No, I just wanted to know, that's all,' she said, struggling to maintain her composure. Thank you, Murray,' Sam said.

He kissed her cheek once more. 'Trust me, my dear, you have nothing to worry about.'

Nothing to worry about? Sam spun the ring on her finger. If the CPS had already spoken to David, if he had worked out who she really was . . . It was too awful to contemplate.

*

The ensuite bathroom was Sam's sanctuary. Neil, when home, was banished to the family bathroom, down the hall. This was her retreat. The place where she came to light a multitude of candles and wallow in the bath while she read a book.

Now, Sam filled her wine glass for the third time and settled back in the deliciously scented, foamy water. Thank goodness for Molton Brown. Greedily, she sought the feeling of calm that usually descended upon her whenever she took up residence. Tonight, it stubbornly eluded her.

The four-piece suite was ostentatiously grand, the bath, in particular, revelling in its roll-topped, claw-footed glory. Her gaze took in the white wicker chair with its green-and-white, willow-patterned throw, the soft light from the group of church candles on the windowsill. All familiar. All good. She willed the sense of calm to come, for the knots in her back to untie. She felt the steam rise, opening her pores, but inside, her muscles were as tense as when she'd first entered the room.

There was no one to admit it to, but Sam was scared. What if the magistrates decided David's injuries were severe enough to give her a custodial sentence? The thought made her feel sick.

She drank deeply once more before checking her mobile. There was a missed call from David. With trepidation, she keyed in the answer phone. *You've got to stop avoiding me, Sam. We have to talk. I'm sending you the details of the holiday cottage. Meet me there tomorrow morning at ten. If you get there first the key is under the biggest of the three plant pots by the front door.* The message was blunt. The tone businesslike.

What would happen tomorrow? Sam pictured David's face, distorted with anger. '*You bitch! I'm going to walk with a limp for the rest of my life because of what happened that night.*'

Or, sobbing, would he grab her and say, '*How could you lie like that? I thought you fancied me. I thought we were going to have an affair.*'

Maybe he would just stare straight through her and yell at her to get out.

Sam reached for the bottle. Upending it, she eyed the trickle of wine with disappointment. *Should have opened two.*

Chapter Eighteen

David's cottage, Hallows End, stood in an elevated position. Sam knew from its location on the map that the coastal path was only ten minutes away and that the beaches along this stretch were small but quiet. Hallows End would make a great romantic retreat with the right fixtures and fittings.

She felt for the key under the largest plant pot and let herself in. It was only nine fifteen. She'd figured if she got there early enough she could sketch out a few quick ideas for the cottage and leave them with David as a parting gift even though there was a chance, when he found out who she was, that he'd simply rip them up.

She quickly scoped out the cottage. It had a small but functional kitchen and a large homely sitting room with an open fire. Upstairs there were two bedrooms and a bathroom. It wouldn't win awards for the most beautiful property in the world but it had potential.

She looked out over the back garden from the back bedroom window. It was large and mostly overgrown.

The part closest to the house had a ramshackle patio and there was a shed, which had seen better days, to the right-hand side.

The garden would definitely need a makeover too. If David was selling the dream of a romantic retreat, an overgrown wilderness in the garden would not fit the brief.

Returning to the sitting room, Sam set her pad and coloured pencils up on the table and began sketching out some room plans: lots of cosy throws, soft rugs and warm lighting for the sitting room, sumptuous bedding and a five-star-hotel-standard bathroom upstairs.

It was half an hour later when she heard a car approaching up the lane and went to the window. So, this was it. She went back to the table and tidied away her paraphernalia leaving just her sketches behind.

Working on the room plans had taken her mind off the summons. Now, the thought of it came back with a vengeance. What if David had known about the court summons before she had? What if he had figured out who she really was? Maybe she would not have the luxury of giving him the explanation she had been rehearsing, the apology that had been spooling through her mind all night. All of that could be taken away from her in the white heat of his rage if he already knew.

Apprehensive, she watched as David got out of his car. Dressed in jeans and a black tee shirt, he looked relaxed.

Sam clenched her fist and sagged against the wall. He didn't know. Not yet.

'Morning, Sam.'

'Hi.' He'd gelled his hair that morning. It was fashionably wayward and she loved every strand of it. His smile was warm and, as he looked at her, his brown eyes were soft with humour and gratitude. *Remember it all,* Sam commanded herself. *Especially the way he looks at you. He wanted to kiss you, maybe even make love to you. Remember that.*

'You found the key okay then?'

She nodded.

'What do you think?'

'It has potential.'

He chuckled and so did she.

'I don't mean in an estate agent doublespeak kind of way,' she said. 'I mean real potential.'

'It needs work though.'

She nodded. 'It's functional as it is but to make it what you want it to be it needs a top-to-tail makeover. A romantic retreat has to strike the right tone from the moment you drive up. The gardens have to look fantastic, the rooms need softening, the right lighting, the right furniture.'

'Just as well I know a first-rate designer.'

She watched him cross to the table.

'Who has already started work by the look of things.'

'They're just preliminary sketches, my initial thoughts . . .'

Who was she kidding? They would be her *only* thoughts.

'These are good,' he said, flicking through the sketches. 'You're right, it's all about the ambience. I also need to make a virtue of the dodgy Wi-Fi signal and the fact there are no shops or pubs within walking distance.'

'Market it as a place where couples come to get away from it all, to decompress from modern life.'

'Between us we should be able to pull it off, don't you think?'

She pretended to study the tiles on the Victorian fireplace.

'Sam?'

God, I'm going to miss you, she thought as she turned to look at him.

'I've so enjoyed the time we've spent together, Sam.' Steadying himself on his crutches he reached out to cup her cheek in his palm. 'It's meant a lot to me.'

'Me, too.'

'I'm excited at the prospect of doing this place up; you and I working together to make it happen. It's going to be fun, don't you think?' he grinned.

'Yes.'

She was about to lose that smile, she realised, and the man behind it. No more easy banter and gentle teasing. No more flirting with racing hearts and stolen glances.

David's smile faded. 'What's wrong?'

'Nothing. I'm fine.'

'I had lunch with Lewis yesterday.'

Sam's heart began to thump.

'He was talking about me having a desk job for a while.'

'It doesn't appeal?'

David snorted. 'The phoney grins. The dodgy deals.'

'When you put it like that.' Sam smiled.

'If you'd met me back then, you wouldn't have liked me very much. I was a prick. A rich prick but a prick nevertheless.'

Sam thought back to the initial disappointment she'd felt on meeting David, the offhand way he'd treated Tony. It seemed a long time ago.

'Do you still see Tony?'

'Aye. Lost touch with the others when I stopped playing football but Tony and I meet up for a drink now and then.'

She watched as David moved to sit on the sofa, taking her designs with him.

'These are very good,' he said, looking up at her with a smile.

'Thank you.'

'So, what's the matter?' he asked.

She caught her breath. 'I didn't say anything was.'

'You didn't have to.' He gestured to her hands.

Sam hadn't even been aware that she was fiddling with her father's ring. She let it go.

'It can't have been easy, finding the time to spend with me.'

'I wanted to do it.'

'Why, Sam?'

There was something in the way he spoke, the way he looked at her, as if he were trying to look beyond her eyes and into her soul.

Something was wrong. She hadn't noticed it before but it was obvious now, the tracing of fine lines around his eyes told her she was not alone in her sleepless nights. His hands, usually so relaxed, were tightly balled.

'You've been through so much. I wanted to balance things up a little by doing something nice for you.'

He took her words on board. 'It was nice. Thank you.'

'I was happy to do it.'

'*Was?*' David queried with a smile. 'Now I'm getting better, I can look after myself, is that it?' The smile became a grin.

'I didn't mean it like that.' Suddenly hot, Sam cast off her jacket. Beneath she wore jeans and a check shirt.

'We're friends, right?'

'Yes.' Unable to meet his eyes, she stared at the floor.

'So, if something was troubling you, you'd tell me.'

Feeling as though her chest was constricting, Sam began to pace the room. There could be no putting things off. The moment had finally come. But where to begin? How? *Don't be such a coward. Just tell him.*

'Something's wrong, I know it is.' David patted the sofa beside him. 'Sit down. Tell me what it is.'

With difficulty, Sam resisted. Better to keep a safe distance. Get it over with. She opened her mouth.

'I never had you down as a woman who kept secrets.'

'I don't, ordinarily.' Coming to a halt, she shot him an anxious glance.

'There's something you need to tell me, isn't there?'

Horrified, Sam froze. She tried to gauge his expression. He looked perplexed but not angry. Definitely not angry. 'How did you find out?'

'One of the nurses told me.'

'*What?*'

'Jane. She said you'd told her you were my sister.'

Stunned, Sam tucked her hair behind her ears, buying herself some time to think, her mind in a whirl.

'Why did you lie?'

'I needed to see you and I thought it would be easier if I told them I was your sister.'

'But you were a hospital visitor. Surely, you could have visited anyone you wanted?'

His face was so open, so without guile, it took her breath away. He clearly had no idea of the extent of her deception. Sam wanted the floor to open up and swallow her, for her never to have to confront the truth and witness the pain it would cause this man who had come to mean so much to her.

'I wasn't a hospital visitor,' she said tonelessly. She concentrated on the fireplace.

'But you said . . .'

'I know what I said.' Embarrassment made her tone sharp.

David frowned. 'I don't understand. Why did you say you were if you weren't?'

Sam rubbed her forehead. 'Because I had to see you.'

'You didn't pick my name from a list?'

'No.'

'You sought me out?'

'Yes.'

'Why?'

The silence lengthened. Sam was unable to drag her gaze from the floor. *Tell him. Just tell him and be done with it, with him.* Her tongue clove to the roof of her mouth.

'Did you know I was Scottish when you first told them you were my sister?'

She shook her head.

David snickered. 'I bet you had a shock then.'

'Yes.'

'And they didn't query it with you?'

Sam shrugged.

It was something she'd come to realise over the last few weeks; if you said something with enough conviction people believed you.

David chuckled. 'You certainly don't look like a Celt. A Viking, maybe. I bet there's been raping and pillaging in your bloodline.' His jovial look disappeared. 'What's going on, Sam?'

She felt the band around her chest tighten. *This is what it's like to drown. Not in water but in lies. This is my punishment for not telling him the truth sooner.*

'Things got out of hand.' She walked to the window and straightened the curtain. 'All I wanted to do was come to the hospital and apologise but Tony was there and I didn't want to do it in front of him and one thing led to another and you seemed to enjoy our chats and I did too and then . . .'

'Sam.'

David's voice cut through her jumbled words.

'Slow down. You're not making any sense.'

She turned round.

'Come over here.'

He looked so young, she thought. And scared. Against her better judgement, Sam joined him on the sofa.

Grabbing her shoulders, David turned her to face him.

'What are you talking about?'

His touch was a lifeline she didn't deserve, and unable to endure being that close to him, she tore herself free. She wasn't sure exactly when she'd fallen for him. Had it been in the hospital when she'd found him devastated and on the verge of tears after Lauren had left him or had it been on their very first meeting, when he'd been hurt and scared and she'd reassured him with a squeeze of her hand?

Now, she was frightened by the strength of her feelings for him. If he took her in his arms and kissed her, could she stop herself from responding? Shocked, she acknowledged just how much she longed for his touch. Closing her eyes, she imagined him slipping the buttons of her shirt undone, then losing patience and ripping her shirt open, as desperate for her as Neil had been for Megan.

Passion stirred within her and choking back a sob of frustration, she looked away across the room. She could never give in to her feelings because when he knew the truth about her, he would never love her back. To deceive him with words was bad enough but to deceive him with her body? She couldn't do that.

'Sam?'

She jumped as he touched her hand. Snatching it away, she made herself think of Neil. Her anger towards him was diluting a little more every day. His carefully judged attitude of regret and his obvious love for her were winning her over. She was married to Neil. Loved Neil. She felt her heart stutter. There was no room in her life for David. It had to end.

Steeling herself, she turned to face him. She was touched by the concern flooding from his eyes. Never, in all her years of marriage, had she felt this way about a man other than Neil. Nevertheless, she was desperate to let her fingers wander into David's hair, to watch the smile leap into those soulful brown eyes, to know the warmth of his mouth. It was as well she would never see him again.

'Tell me.' His voice was gentle, cajoling. He rubbed her shoulder.

It was an act of solidarity. Of friendship. However, his fingers burned through the thin cotton of her shirt. Could he feel the same electricity she could?

'I don't care that you lied. I'd just like to know why.' His eyes were full of questions.

'You have every right to be angry with me.'

'I'm not angry, Sam,' he said gently. 'Just confused.'

'I had to apologise.'

'For what?'

She wanted to take the fear from his eyes, to save him from the heartache of what he was about to hear. But there was no going back now.

'I want . . .' She stumbled over her words. 'I'm going to miss you.'

The tears she had hoped to keep at bay began to fall and, feeling wretched, she did nothing to stop them.

'Don't cry, Sam. I hate to see you so upset.' Reaching out to brush aside her tears, his fingers lingered on her cheek.

His hand was warm and so very gentle. Somehow, she had known it would be. *Kiss his palm and let yourself go. What harm can it do? Act on your feelings, let a breathless embrace be followed by a passionate kiss. You want to know what it feels like to have his hands on your body. Find out. Neil did. Why can't you?*

David's eyes were watchful. Sam could see the puzzlement in them but there was compassion there, too. Her words had left him bewildered but her tears had moved him. His fingers continued to stroke her cheek and automatically she turned towards his touch so that her cheek rested in the palm of his hand. Shutting her eyes, she gave herself up to the pleasure of his touch.

'Sam,' he said softly. There was a longing in his voice.

His lips brushed hers so gently she ached for more. She felt his fingers run through her hair, his body move closer, leaning into hers. Hot and strong.

He was going to kiss her again and she wanted him to. A parting gift to keep in her heart. A memory to cherish in the days, weeks and months that lay ahead without him. She leapt up, shaking.

'Sam?'

'I'm sorry, David.' She lifted her gaze to his and then quickly away. 'I've let things go too far.'

'I don't understand. I thought you wanted me to kiss you.'

'I did.' She took a deep breath and standing, swept up her jacket, holding it in front of her like a barrier. Meeting his gaze, she said, 'I came to the hospital to apologise to you for putting you there in the first place. I was the woman in the four by four. That bitch was me. My name isn't Samantha Denney, not any more. My name is Samantha Davenport and my husband is Neil Davenport.' Striding to the door, Sam cast it open. 'I'm so very sorry for everything I've done.'

'Sam, wait!'

She ran along the path. Behind her, she could hear David calling to her. Ignoring him, Sam wrenched open the door of the car and flung herself inside, fired the engine and drove.

She parked in a lay-by a couple of miles from the cottage, her tears coalescing. She would never see David again or, if she did chance upon him, he would have nothing but contempt for her. Sam crossed her arms over the steering wheel and wept at the thought.

Chapter Nineteen

The weather-beaten bricks of the terrace glowed in the early summer sun; pale golds and rusty reds set off by velvety moss. Ahead, the garden, full of mature trees and shrubs, hummed with the activity of birds and bugs. Sam made her way up the lawn, enjoying the feel of the grass under her bare feet.

'This is the height of decadence,' she declared as she placed a pitcher of martinis on the table.

'Long may it continue,' Connor replied, helping himself to a strawberry from the bowl at his elbow. 'I can't believe Neil's indoors watching football on a glorious day like this.'

'The cup final hasn't even begun yet. He and Cass are still watching the build-up.' Sam mulled over the strawberries before choosing one.

'Very cosy, you letting Neil watch the football here,' Connor commented.

'The telly in the flat isn't as big as ours.'

'Pubs have pretty big screens.' Connor nudged her foot with his own. 'Can't you just admit you like having him around, Samson?'

'I like having him around,' Sam parroted with a smile.

'Enough to have him back?'

'That's the million-dollar question.'

'Confronting him helped, though?' Connor asked.

'Yes. In fact, I wish I'd had the courage to do it sooner. I still have loads of questions about Megan. Sometimes I ask them and, although he hates it, he does his best to answer them. Other times, I realise I'm about to ask him the same question I've asked him a dozen times before, but in a slightly different way, and I bite my tongue. I'm beginning to think I'm more obsessed with her than he ever was.'

Connor laughed.

'It's knowing when to stop. Asking the questions was cathartic. To keep on asking them . . .' she let the sentence hang.

'Sounds like it's time to put it behind you, hon.'

She nodded.

'In the meantime, you let him sleep in the spare room and watch your TV.'

'It's his TV, too.'

Sam refilled their glasses.

'He's begun sending me letters.'

'Love letters?'

'Of a sort.'

'Sweet. You've got to admit the guy's a trier.'

166

'Yes, he can be very trying.'

Connor laughed. 'Where's Josh?'

'On his computer. Neil wanted him to watch the football but Josh isn't interested. He's working on a new computer game he's developing. Something to do with zombies.'

'You still worried about Cass?'

'A little. She lost out to that girl I told you about.'

'The lead guitarist's sister?'

Sam nodded.

'That was down to nepotism then – nothing to do with her voice or her weight.'

'Tobyn left the band in protest. They're starting their own now. That brings a new sort of pressure with it.'

'Well she polished off a hotdog and a doughnut when she was with me the other day and there were no mysterious trips to the loo afterwards. I think she's okay, Sam.'

'So do I. For now, but we need to keep an eye out.'

Connor nodded. 'Understood. Have you decided what to do with Daphne Mitchell's automatons yet?'

'Yes. The Abbeyleigh Museum have agreed to take them on loan. I've called them the Edward Mitchell Collection. Neil checked over the museum's agreement for me. It basically means that Mrs Mitchell can ask for the machines back at any time. All she has to do is give them two months' notice.'

'Does she know?'

Sam shook her head. 'Every time I bring the subject up she shuts me down. Her grief is still so raw. I'm hoping that as I continue to work with her and time passes she might become a little more receptive.

'I finished her sitting room yesterday and I've just got a few things to tidy up in her reading and craft room and then that's done as well.'

'What then?'

'I've already put mood boards together for her master bedroom and the guest bedroom at the front of the house and she's looking through samples for the second guest bedroom.'

'That's you sorted for a while then. I've given Rhys the old heave-ho.'

'Good. You deserve someone better.'

'I think I might have found him. His name's Warren. He's an insurance broker. Fabulous blue eyes.'

Sam smiled. 'I'm pleased for you.' She tilted her martini in salute. 'Murray's completed all the paperwork for court.'

'I hope Neil's being supportive.'

Sam nodded. 'He's told me not to fret about the court case. That it's his fault I'm in this mess and he's going to do everything he can to make it easier.'

'Except take the blame,' Connor said sourly. He gripped Sam's hand and gave it a squeeze. 'It'll be over soon.'

If only.

Her gaze tracked the progress of a bee along the nearby flower border. The pain of losing David had put a tear in Sam's heart; jagged and deep. A mocking reminder, the wound bore the memories of their time together, the sight and sound of him. With every day that passed, Sam hoped the constant beating of her heart and the relentless routine of her life would force the tear to heal. If anything, however, it was growing more painful, reinforced by the reality of life without him.

'I wish I could snap my fingers and go back to the end of last year, before the accident,' she said quietly.

'Have you heard from him?'

Sam stared at her fingernails. They were a mess. She needed to book a manicure.

'I only told him the truth last month after which I fled in tears,' Sam confessed. 'I haven't spoken to him since. Then, last night, out of the blue, he left a message on my mobile. It was after midnight. He sounded angry. I think he'd been drinking.'

'What did he say?'

'That I should have told him at the outset who I was and why I'd gone to see him.' Sam twisted a stalk off a strawberry and began picking off the leaves one by one. 'He says he needs to know what happened that night.' She let the leaves fall on the table.

'What will you do?'

'I don't know. I don't want a scene.'

Connor pulled a face. 'I don't think you can avoid a scene. The best you can hope for is to control where and when it takes place.'

'You think?'

'If you ignore him he'll track you down, possibly even come here. Do you want that?'

'Definitely not.'

'Then you need to go to him, hon. The court case has got him as stirred up as it has you. Go and see him. Get it over with.'

'Should I tell him what really happened?'

Connor lowered his sunglasses and met Sam's gaze. 'That rather depends on whether you think he can be trusted with that information. I wouldn't tell him if I were you. That said, I do think you have to see him even if it's just to repeat what you told the police. Look at it from his point of view. If it were you, you'd want as much information as possible. Achieving closure, that's what the Americans call it. Better to have ten minutes of unpleasantness than weeks of diving for cover every time the phone rings or the doorbell goes.'

She watched him take off his sunglasses and swing them in his hand.

'Why do you insist on wearing that ring?'

Sam glanced down. Her fingers were anchored around it. 'It's the only thing of Dad's I have left.'

'You say it like that's a bad thing.'

'Connor!'

'What? You only ever touch it when you're sad or anxious.'

'Do I? I suppose they're the feelings I associate with him.'

'All the more reason to take the bloody thing off then.' Connor topped up their drinks. 'When are you going to let Neil come home properly?'

'When I'm ready.'

'Are you secretly harbouring some fantasy that you and David might still get together, is that it?'

'No. I don't even know how that happened. I've never so much as looked twice at another man before this.'

'You were lonely. Vulnerable. Maybe David reminded you a little of Neil when he still had time for you. Did you and he ever . . .'

'No.'

'Maybe you should have.'

'Weren't you the one who told me he would be too complicated for a tit-for-tat revenge fuck?'

'Yes, but with hindsight, it might have been the ideal opportunity to get him out of your system and even the score with Neil, all in one go.'

'I'm not keeping score with Neil.'

'Yes you are.' Connor put his sunglasses back on and tilted his head back. 'Even if you don't realise it. Did David fall for you too?'

Sam closed her eyes remembering the feel of his lips on hers, the warmth of his body as he'd held her. 'I think so.'

'I'll come with you if you want me to, when you see him again.'

Sam gave Connor a grateful smile. 'Thanks, but this is my mess. I'm the only one who can sort it out.'

Chapter Twenty

Sam had decided not to tell David she was coming. Better to simply turn up, she'd reasoned. She could prepare and he wouldn't have time to rehearse his recriminations.

Fortune was smiling on her when she arrived at the Old Mill. One of the other residents, with whom she was on nodding terms, was just leaving and let her in.

Connor was right. She had to see David. To ignore him would be to risk him turning up on the doorstep of Meadowview Cottage. The children would ask questions. News of David's visit would get back to Neil. The web of lies would twist a little tighter. It was time to face up to her responsibilities, to be as truthful with David as it was possible to be. She owed him that.

Heart racing, Sam pressed the doorbell.

David answered quickly. However, his expression of pleasant curiosity soon disappeared behind a stony stare when he saw it was her.

'At least you had the decency to come.' His voice was strangely unemotional. 'But it isn't a good time just now.'

'This won't take long.'

He looked at her coldly, his eyes flattened by anger. Then, shrugging he turned away from her, leaving the door open.

Sam had steeled herself for this moment but his animosity was worse than she'd imagined. She wanted to say something about how wonderful it was to see him walking unaided but she didn't dare, afraid of what his reaction might be.

'I'm . . .'

'Don't tell me you're sorry.' He cut her off sharply. 'I don't want to hear it.'

Contrite, she held her hands in front of her. 'What do you want to hear?' she asked. He clearly wasn't going to make this easy for her. Why should he?

'The truth. Not your strong point, I know.' He sneered.

'David . . .' An icy stare cut her to the quick.

'Tell me what happened,' he demanded.

So, that's how you want to play it, is it? Impersonal. Cold. As though we never laughed together. As though we never kissed. She cleared her throat. The memory of his lips on hers was as real as if it had happened just a moment before. She tried to blot it out.

There could be no revealing the ultimate truth to him, she realised. It was a shame because she'd wanted to be completely honest, to achieve closure for herself as well as for him. However, one look at his surly face told her it was not to be. If he went to the police, she and Neil would be in even more trouble. She couldn't risk it before the prosecution took place. Possibly not even then.

'I was driving down Market Street,' she began.

'Where had you been?' He barked the question at her.

'What?'

'Where had you been?' he asked tersely. 'Where were you going? Who did you have with you?'

Flustered, Sam hooked her hair behind her ears. 'Neil and I had been at the Northey Hotel to celebrate his birthday. We left close to midnight. Josh and Cass had colds and I was eager to check on them.'

'How much had you had to drink?' His mouth was a mean line.

'One glass of champagne. For the toast. The police breathalysed me at the scene. It was negative.'

'Go on.'

'Neil was going to drive but he'd been drinking. I took the keys off him.'

'Thank God for that. You succeeded in shattering my leg on one glass of champagne. If your husband was drunk, he'd probably have killed me.'

'David, I . . .' She thought she saw him wince at the sound of his name and hesitated. 'I don't blame you for hating me.'

His hands tensed into fists. 'Good.'

She couldn't believe that one simple word could unleash such a tidal wave of emotion within her. She walked across to the patio doors and stared at the river.

'I just want to hear what happened,' he said. 'I'm not interested in excuses or apologies.'

'I drove along Market Street and . . .'

'It was raining.'

'Pouring,' she agreed.

'Stop leaving things out.'

'I'm not,' she said plaintively, turning to him. 'Not intentionally.'

His face betrayed cold fury, barely suppressed. 'Did you have the radio on? What was playing? Were you and your husband talking? What about? Were the windscreen wipers going double time?'

The questions were aimed at her one after the other. Rat-a-tat-tat. Like machine-gun fire. She fought the urge to dive for cover. She'd been naïve to think that by turning up unexpectedly she'd catch him unawares. He had clearly been rehearsing this conversation since the moment she had told him she was driving.

'The radio wasn't on,' she said edgily. 'The windscreen wipers were going double time, I think.'

'You think?' David's voice was incredulous. 'Don't you know?'

'No, I don't know,' Sam replied, upset. 'Not every detail of that night is imprinted on my brain.'

'Well it damn well should be,' he retaliated. 'Every detail of that night is imprinted on my leg.'

'I know and I'm sorry.' She walked towards him but he backed away abruptly.

'Damn it! I told you I didn't want to hear you say that.' He brushed by her and took a beer from the fridge.

'The windscreen wipers were going double time. I'm sure I would have put them on that fast with the rain as hard as it was.' In truth, she couldn't remember what the windscreen wipers had been doing but she thought it better to choose the path of least resistance.

Sam had never seen him looking so hostile. *Oh, David, what have we done to you?* Had this hatred always been there, she wondered, festering away as they'd talked in the hospital, merely awaiting a target? Would he have been this angry with a stranger or had she made everything ten times worse by her clumsy attempts to make amends?

'You didn't stop at the junction,' he said, sitting down.

'I might have been going a little fast,' she edged.

'You didn't fucking stop!' He thundered.

'I checked both ways. I thought it was clear. The next thing I knew you were right on top of us and I . . .'

'Did you swerve to avoid me? Did you brake?' Bang. Bang.

'Yes.'

'Which?'

'Both.' She hugged her arms round her, cold despite the sunlight pouring in. 'It all happened so fast. There was nothing I could do,' she said helplessly.

Contempt emanated from every pore of his body.

'When did you first see me?'

'When you were in front of me.'

'Not before?'

'No.'

'You tried to swerve?'

'Yes.' Her voice was becoming shrill. She made herself take a breath. 'I braked and I swerved but it was too late.'

'What happened then?'

'I got out to check on you. Neil phoned for an ambulance.'

'Where was I?'

'You were on your back.' Sam could feel again the cold rain soaking her skin, the terrified pounding of her heart. 'I knelt beside you and felt for a pulse. The rain was torrential. I put Neil's jacket over your chest. The operator wanted to know if you were conscious so I lifted your visor. Your eyes were shut. You looked peaceful. As though you were asleep. Then, suddenly, you opened your eyes and looked at me.'

'I looked at you?' David repeated sharply.

Sam nodded. 'I squeezed your hand and you squeezed mine back.'

'How long was I conscious for?'

'A few seconds.'

'I don't remember,' he said quietly, frowning. 'And yet, part of me must have remembered because that's where I knew you from, isn't it?'

Sam nodded. 'I think so.'

David's face hardened. 'You must have been laughing at me when I suggested places where we might have met.'

'I never laughed at you and I never set out to deceive you. It just happened that way and if I could do it again I'd do it differently.'

His frown deepened.

'Did I open my eyes again?'

'Not while I was with you.'

He nodded. Implacable, once more he said, 'What then?'

'We waited for the paramedics and the police. I tried to keep you as dry as possible.'

'My leg?'

'There was a lot of blood,' Sam said quietly.

David drank his beer. 'They're charging you with careless driving.' He pointed the beer bottle at her.

'Yes.'

'Will you plead guilty?'

'Yes, of course. I'm not trying to weasel out of anything. I've already pleaded guilty by post.'

'By post? So, you won't even be at court?'

She watched the white heat of fresh anger spurt from his eyes. 'I'll go and plead guilty in person if that's what you want,' she said quickly.

'I don't want anything from you,' he replied contemptuously.

'I know you're upset.'

'You don't know anything.'

Sam persevered. Somewhere behind this façade of indifference was the man she had known, fallen for. 'You have every right to be upset but it was an accident.' As she spoke, Sam was reminded of the desperate look in Neil's eyes as he'd tried to convince her that she should forgive him. Had she been this unmoved? 'It was an accident,' she repeated.

'You should have been more careful,' he said tersely.

Losing her patience, Sam said, 'Yes, I should but have you never lost concentration while you've been driving?'

'I've never had an accident.'

'That's not what I asked you,' she said pointedly. 'Every lapse of concentration you've ever had was a potential accident.'

'You can go now,' he said coldly.

Sam's eyes widened in disbelief. 'That's it? I'm dismissed. How can you be like this with me?'

'Och, it's easy.' Standing, he came close enough to her that she could smell the beer on his breath, see the misery in his eyes. 'I just remember how you sat beside my hospital bed and told me you were a hospital visitor or I think on how you exclaimed about the accident as if you were some innocent bystander and not the guilty party.

'I let you into my life when I was at my most vulnerable. I trusted you. Christ, when I managed to walk down the stairs for the first time, it was you I wanted to tell. How pathetic is that?' He strode past her and, snatching up the beer bottle, threw it into the bin with such force the glass shattered.

'It wasn't pathetic. We were friends.' She reached for his arm as he returned, felt the tight cord of his muscles.

'Well, you've got that right.' He jerked away from her. '*Were* friends.'

'David, please.' Tears flecked her cheeks. 'I can't stand this! I know you don't want to hear it but that's tough because I need to say it. I'm sorry, from the bottom of my heart. There isn't a day goes by that I don't think about what happened that night. If I could live that night again, I'd do everything differently. If I could swap places with you, I would.'

'I seriously doubt that.' He pressed out two pain-killers from the blister pack on the table catching her eye as he did so. 'Don't even think about lecturing me about painkillers and booze. I've been checking up on you, Samantha Davenport. Your husband's Neil Davenport. Works at Brookes Davenport in the High Street. He's the Head of their Personal Injury Department.' He threw the pills back. 'If it wasn't so sad it would be funny. I've been thinking about paying him a visit, telling him about us.'

'What? No!'

'You've been lying to him too, haven't you? I thought I could enlighten him.'

'Please don't do that.'

'They say confession is good for the soul but you wouldn't know too much about that, would you?'

'I wanted to tell you the truth so many times. I was too much of a coward to do it the first time with Tony there. The next time I visited you, I discovered Lauren had left you. It would have been heartless of me to tell you the truth that day and, whatever you think of me now, I'm not heartless. I'll admit part of me hoped I'd never have to tell you. You became my friend.' She saw him frown. 'I didn't want to lose you. Then I got the summons and I knew I had no choice.' Her eyes bored into his. 'While I may have deceived you about why I was visiting you, the things I shared with you, I shared as a friend. We became friends. Maybe more than friends. Deny it all you want now, but it's the truth.'

'But that's the worst of it, can't you see that?' he asked bitterly.

'Yes,' she said softly. Everything she had felt, he had felt too. That much was obvious. After all, it had been his lips that had brushed hers, not the other way round. 'It still tears me apart, what happened to you.'

He regarded her sullenly. 'What do you want me to say? That everything's okay and I forgive you? Because I can't. You see, everything's not okay and I don't forgive you.'

Fresh tears welled in Sam's eyes.

'I think you should go now.'

Slowly Sam walked to the door, praying with each step that he would call her back but no call came. She paused in the doorway. He'd sat on one of the sofas and flicked on the television. Nonchalant, or so it seemed, but the clenched fist that rested on his thigh, the knuckles showing white from across the room, betrayed how he was really feeling. Devastated, Sam realised there was nothing more she could say.

*

Lost in thought, Sam hadn't heard Daphne come into the room.

'I thought you could do with a break, my dear. I've brought you some orange juice. Freshly squeezed.'

Sam put down her paint brush. 'Thank you.'

Daphne stood looking at her old bookcase, her head tilted to one side.

'Have you changed your mind about the colour?' Sam asked.

'Not at all. I'm just wondering why it never occurred to me to paint it red in the first place.' Daphne looked at Sam and smiled.

Sam stood her glass of juice on the dustsheet. 'There's something you should know, Daphne. I was involved in a car accident in January. I was driving and I hit a motorcyclist.'

'How awful.'

Sam nodded. 'I broke his leg. I . . . I'm being taken to court later this week. There might be some stuff about it in the local press.'

'You poor thing. How's the motorcyclist?'

'Better now but he'll always walk with a limp. It was a horrible thing that happened.'

Daphne nodded. 'I had a feeling something wasn't right. You haven't seemed yourself for a while now. Is there anything I can do to help?'

'No. I just wanted you to be aware in case you saw anything.'

Daphne patted Sam's hand. 'Accidents happen. I burnt poor Ted's arm when he got too close while I was doing the ironing one time. I'm sure you didn't mean to do any harm.'

Sam shook her head.

'How are things at home now?'

'Fine.'

'Has Neil moved back in?'

'Not yet.'

Daphne gave her a searching look. 'Ted liked to go fishing. Used to spend hours on the riverbank in all weathers. Never spoke to a soul. Just sat there, staring at the water waiting to see if the fish would bite. Mad if you ask me but he enjoyed it. He said the secret was patience, letting out the line slowly then when the time was right reeling it in.'

Sam sipped her juice.

'Seems to me you're doing the same thing. Letting out the line, giving your husband a little bit of freedom, waiting to see if he'll stray again.'

Sam met Daphne's gaze.

'Perhaps it's time to reel him back in, dear, don't you think? Before he slips away for good.' She gave Sam a smile. 'Loving that red.'

Chapter Twenty-One

It should have been raining, Sam thought as she stared up at a cloudless blue sky on the day of the court case. *Raining as hard as the night of the accident.*

She turned at the thunder of footsteps down the stairs. Cass and Josh were wielding overstuffed sports bags. Sam knew her brain was addled today but surely neither of them had sport on Thursdays?

'Kids, go and wait in the car. I want to talk to your mother.'

'Good luck, Mum,' Josh said, giving her a fleeting smile before ducking out of the door.

'You'll be okay, Mum,' Cass said before disappearing.

'What's going on?'

'I thought it'd be a good idea for the children to stay with Connor this weekend. Don't look so worried, he's already agreed. It means I can take you away . . .'

'Away?' Sam was stunned.

Neil took her in his arms. 'Everything's planned. We're off to a little hotel in Dorset for a long weekend.'

Avoiding the implications of what that might mean, Sam said, 'I'm meeting clients this afternoon.'

'Connor's rearranged them. Please, Sam, let me do this for you. You've been miserable for weeks, sweetheart. You need a break. I've asked for a room with twin beds in case you're worried on that score.' He gave her shoulders a rub. 'I hope it'll give us the opportunity to talk without the court case hanging over us but, if you don't feel like talking, that's fine too. It's your weekend. We'll spend it any way you choose.'

Sam was conscious that Neil was waiting, eyes full of eager anticipation. 'Are you sure you can afford the time away?' she asked doubtfully.

'I've made time. I want you to go into Stebbingsford and indulge in a little retail therapy while we're waiting for the verdict.' He pulled out a wad of notes from his wallet. 'I'll meet you at the office at one. Murray should be back from court by then. He can update us and then we'll be on our way.' He kissed her cheek. 'A few more hours and this will all be over, darling.'

*

Sam thought about her husband's parting words as she drove into the car park at Brookes Davenport a few hours later. It was nice to think that she could put the accident and all that had flowed from it behind her but somehow she doubted it would be that easy.

The image of David's face, sallow and angry, was never far from her mind and the guilt would always be there. Hers by association, by default, but hers nonetheless. Nothing could make that right. No court case brought to a conclusion. No fine or ban.

With a heavy heart, she climbed the stairs to her husband's office.

'Any news?' she asked nervously.

'Not yet. Bought some nice stuff?'

Sam nodded. Her heart hadn't really been in it but she'd bought a few things.

She fumbled in her bag as her business phone began to ring.

'Hello? Mrs Booth? Thanks for calling me back. Yes, I've put together the swatches of material we talked about. I have a lovely set of pinks and lilacs to show you and I've managed to get hold of some samples from that designer I was telling you about. They're from his new range. Yes.' Sam took out her diary. 'Next Wednesday. Eleven o'clock. Great. I'll see you then. Bye.'

Neil gave her a smile as she snapped the elastic band back over her diary. 'Busy?' he commented.

Sam nodded. 'We're booking into September.'

Neil's smile faded. 'What about our trip to Sardinia in August?'

'What about it?'

'I thought, at the very least, you and the children would still go.'

'I'm not sure I can face it,' Sam admitted, walking to the window.

'But it's paid for. We won't get our money back.'

'I don't care. Maybe the children and I will go somewhere else instead.'

'That's madness,' Neil said.

'Is it?' She turned to face him. 'We booked the holiday in Sardinia to celebrate our wedding anniversary. It's the same hotel we stayed in on our honeymoon, for God's sake. How could I walk through the door when everything we dreamed of, everything we worked for, has fallen apart? You go with the children, if you can bear it. I can't!'

Neil moved to stand beside her but stopped short of touching her.

'Who's to say things won't get better, eh? We just need to put Megan and this bloody court case behind us. If we can do that, maybe we can all go to Sardinia.'

Sam edged away from him.

'If you want to,' he added.

In the leaden silence that followed Sam watched the pedestrians walking along the High Street. One, in particular, she recognised.

'Murray's on his way back,' she said.

A few moments later, Murray joined them.

Neil reached for Sam's hand and gripped it tightly. Grateful for the support she gripped his back.

'What did I tell you?' Murray exclaimed. 'Points and a fine. They didn't even contemplate a ban.' He kissed Sam's cheek.

'Really?' She hardly dared to let out the breath she'd been holding since Murray had walked in.

'I joke about many things, my dear, but not verdicts.'

Whooping with delight, Neil picked Sam up and swung her round before setting her down and planting a kiss on her forehead. 'Thank Christ for that. How much?' he asked, directing the question at Murray.

'Four points and an eight-hundred-pound fine. It could've been a lot worse.'

Neil grinned. 'You'd better take those clothes back.'

'Was the motorcyclist there?' Sam asked quietly.

'Yes.'

Sam pictured David's face, his eyes and mouth hardened by anger. Four points and eight hundred pounds for a shattered leg. It didn't seem very much. What had he made of the verdict? Sam wondered. Surely, he'd hate her even more now, if that were possible.

'Did he say anything to you?'

'Nothing of importance.'

'He said something, though?' she persisted.

'As I was leaving, he asked how I could defend the indefensible.'

Distraught, Sam turned to look out of the window.

'It's not the first time I've had that said to me. Don't suppose it'll be the last.'

Neil's hand was in the small of Sam's back. 'It's over now, sweetheart.' He bent his head to hers. Then, turning to Murray, he said, 'Great result, Murray. You've done a fantastic job.'

Recovering herself, Sam said, 'Yes, I'm sorry, Murray. Where are my manners?' She shook his hand. 'Thank you for everything.'

Chapter Twenty-Two

The country house hotel looked out over a dazzling blue sea that sparkled in the late afternoon sunshine. Their suite was luxurious. A small sitting room dominated by an opulent white sofa. A balcony with table and chairs to enjoy the view. A bathroom with gold fittings and thick cotton bathrobes and the bedroom with a king-sized, four-poster bed.

Sam surveyed the bed as Neil walked into the room.

'Oh no! They must have put us in the wrong suite. I definitely asked for twin beds.'

She watched him walk across the sitting room to the patio doors. Sliding them open, he stepped onto the balcony. 'I'll go down to reception and sort it out if you want me to. Although it'd be a shame to lose this view.'

Sam suppressed a smile. Neil would never make an actor. 'The room's fine.'

Neil grinned.

'You can sleep on the sofa.'

He beckoned for her to join him on the balcony. He'd been on his best behaviour on the journey, talking

189

about Meadowview Designs while the Lightning Seeds had played in the background. It was always the same with Neil; the Lightning Seeds in the summer, REM for the rest of the year. Sam would have preferred to listen to Radio Four but she had to admit the Lightning Seeds' swirling harmonies suited the weather.

Sam had noticed that Neil had turned off his mobile and stowed it in his pocket when he left the office. The message was clear: you're my priority. It had been a long time since she'd been that and she had appreciated the gesture.

Now, she joined him on the balcony, loving the warmth of the sun on her skin. Sam sighed. It was time to let the court case go and with it, David. Neil was right. It was over.

*

It was a balmy evening. The French doors of the dining room had been thrown open and tables placed on the patio. Sam and Neil sat in one secluded corner, the ivy-covered stone balustrade wrapping around them. The hotel, lit by spotlights, looked magnificent draped in a cloak of lilac wisteria. In the distance they could hear the gentle murmuring of the sea.

The food had been delicious and the conversation had stayed on safe topics: the children, the hotel, Meadowview Designs. Now, as the fairy lights twinkled into life around the balustrade, Neil stroked the stem of his wine glass, a contemplative look on his face.

'The letters I've sent you, I meant every word.'

The letters had touched Sam. It was so unlike Neil to put his innermost thoughts on paper. Sam had pictured him drafting and redrafting the letters, as he did with his legal documents, assiduously striving for perfection, seeking that magic formula of words that would quell her fears and unlock her heart.

How sad that the first love letters she'd received from her husband had been sent during their separation but then Neil had never been given to showy displays of affection. His was a deeper, more steadfast love. She looked up to find him watching her with sombre eyes.

'I know I broke something that was precious.'

He stopped abruptly and, as he looked away, Sam could see the sheen of tears in his eyes.

When he turned to face her once more, his expression was grave. 'I hurt the most important person in my life and I will never forgive myself for that but, if you can find it within your heart to give me another chance, I promise you I won't let you down again.' He reached for her hand across the table. 'I want you back.'

'I know.'

She could feel the electricity sparking between them like old times.

I want you back, too. The words were in her mind. A heartbeat away from her lips. She thought of the fantasies she'd harboured about David. As hard as she'd fallen for him, she had never removed Neil's wedding ring from her finger. Safe perhaps in the knowledge that she and David could never be because of their circumstances, she'd enjoyed their time together for what it was: a pseudo affair destined never to be consummated. Had that realisation subconsciously made it all right to fall in love with him? Had it been the release of emotion she'd needed to cope with Neil's betrayal?

Sam didn't know if she and Neil could overcome her fear of another betrayal but she realised she wanted to try. They had so much history together. It didn't feel right to throw it away without a second attempt.

Daphne's words came back to her. *'Time to reel him back in, dear, don't you think?'*

They climbed the stairs to their suite, hand in hand. Then, Neil led her into the bedroom.

Bringing her into his arms, he bent his head to hers with a sigh. 'I can't tell you how much I've missed holding you like this,' he whispered. 'All those nights alone.' He touched her lips with his own. Faintly. Tenderly. As if he were afraid she might pull away. 'I want to fix what I've broken.' He kissed her again more confidently this time.

Sam felt the fire in his kiss searing its way to her belly, igniting her own desire so that she was suddenly consumed by her need for him.

The strength of her feelings took her by surprise. As though a long journey had been dispensed with, she wanted to wrap him in her arms and remember what passion had been like before there was doubt and fear.

His lips were on her neck and she held him there, letting the scent of his aftershave fill her senses. They'd had sex since his one night stand with Megan, but it had been perfunctory. A bodily function to be endured.

Her heart had been a bystander but not this time. This time, she wanted him too.

She pushed his jacket off his shoulders, caught it as it slipped from his arms, tossing it on to the upholstered chair that stood by the window. Beneath, he wore a white short-sleeved linen shirt and beige chinos.

Sam pressed her hand against his chest, could feel his heart racing beneath her fingertips. Their gaze met and locked. He took her hand, drew it up to his mouth, held it tightly as he kissed the delicate skin on the inside of her wrist. Then, he moved her hand to his cheek, cradled it there as he turned his lips into her palm.

'I'm sorry for everything I put you through. I was a thoughtless, heartless bastard. I . . .'

'Kiss me,' she commanded.

'What?'

'I don't want you to talk. I want you to kiss me. We can talk later.'

She pulled him back into her arms, afraid that if he continued to apologise she would lose her desire for reunification. This new love of theirs was a vulnerable, fragile thing.

He obeyed and his kisses had an edge to them now that filled her with longing. They were the kisses of a younger Neil. A man seeking to impress and undress was how she had thought of him back then.

Some men never bothered to learn the art of kissing, seeing it merely as a step on the road to sex. Some men, however, knew the true value of kissing as an event in itself. Neil was one of those men. Over the years, however, even he had practised the art less often. Familiarity had stopped him trying. But not now. Now, he was putting his heart and soul into every kiss.

Sam surrendered herself to him, basking in the glory of his full attention. At that moment, she knew instinctively that if she chose to request something of him he would seek to make it happen. Whilst he was the one taking the lead, she was the one in control. She could ask anything of him, she realised. Like his resignation from Brookes Davenport for instance. Truly, they could then begin again.

He kissed the skin behind her ear and she sighed with pleasure. Could she ask him to abandon temptation and ambition at a stroke? Dare she? Was it fair? He was kissing his way down to the hollow of her throat now. Sam felt her knees grow weak.

He was holding her so carefully, like a delicate piece of his mum's china, his attitude reverential. Doubtless, he was afraid that she might turn away from him sobbing. She couldn't blame him. She'd done it half a dozen times before. She was determined, however, that it wouldn't happen tonight. Marriage 2.0. Sam's fingers tightened in Neil's hair.

There was a fresh vigour to his touch as his hands skimmed her shoulders and neck, seeking the zip that would release her from her new peony-patterned dress. Triumphantly he located the zip and lowered it before sweeping the dress from her shoulders and helping it to slide down her body.

Sam felt the fire in her belly leap anew as she watched his gaze move greedily over her skin.

'How can you be more beautiful than I remember?' His voice cracked.

Suddenly, his lips and hands were everywhere: seeking, touching, grasping, grabbing. Loving. She was no longer china to be held with care, she was a woman to be loved. *His* woman.

Swept up by the maelstrom of passion, Sam slipped the buttons of his shirt before pulling at the loop on the belt of his trousers. Her senses were heightened to such an extent that just the casual brush of his hand across her collarbone was enough to make her groan with pleasure.

They cast off the rest of their clothes and Neil crushed Sam to him, all reverence gone as he picked her up and threw her down on the bed, entering her almost immediately.

That sweet moment had become a thing of dread for Sam, so often accompanied by tears and tension since his confession, but not this time. Now, the joy of it was back in all its heart-stopping glory and she revelled in it, dragging her nails down Neil's back, urging him on.

As she came, the tears squeezed from her eyes. If she had climaxed at all post-Megan, they had been sorry excuses for the real thing; like the backbeat to a melody that never completely broke into song. She had feared that was the way it would always be, that somehow she had lost the ability to let herself go enough to know those heights again. That she was broken. How wrong she had been.

She was vaguely aware that he had come too but, like a selfish child, she was less concerned with his satisfaction. Her own fulfilment was all that mattered. There were so many cracks in her heart that his love needed to fill.

Afterwards, aglow, she lay in his arms staring at the peony-patterned dress on the floor. As she had put it on that evening, she had wondered whether it would be Neil's hand or her own on the zip that night. She was glad it had been Neil's. What they had shared had once been so beautiful. If they could just hold on to one another and the memories, then perhaps, there was a chance for it to be beautiful again.

They made love for a second time during the night. This union was altogether more tender as gently, slowly, they savoured one another.

When the morning light spread fingers of sunshine across the bed, Neil encircled Sam in his arms, one leg hooked possessively over hers as he kissed her temple.

Settled. Content. For the moment, at least, reassured, she lay with her head against Neil's chest and wondered about the feeling of lightness that was engulfing her. It had been so long, it took her a while to recognise it for what it was: happiness.

She was truly happy for the first time since Megan. Since David. Her heart swooped and she curled deeper into Neil's embrace.

They chose room service and ate breakfast on the balcony. Sam poured herself a cup of tea and weighed her words carefully. 'You should move back in.' She could see the muscles in Neil's cheek working as he clamped down on his emotions.

'If you want to wait . . .'

'I don't want to wait.'

He squeezed her hand and then looked quickly away.

He appeared to be studying a boat on the horizon but Sam could see that his brows were drawn together. She let him regain his composure before she said, 'Some things have to change.'

'What things?' he asked warily.

Now, it was Sam's turn to look out to sea. Last night, she could have asked anything of him and he would have agreed. Not so, this morning. His guard was up. She had let the opportunity slip. There would be no asking him to resign from Brookes Davenport now. The best she could hope for was to apply a brake to the insane hours he had been working.

'I know how much this promotion means to you, how much you want it, not just for yourself but for your dad. I know you feel your uncle stole the business from him and you want to right that wrong but . . .'

'I'm so close, Sam. Just a few months away.'

'Surely you can at least cut down on the number of hours at the office . . .' Sam saw him wince.

'Megan works in the probate department now. I rarely see her.'

'I'm not talking about Megan.'

'Tilden is breathing down my neck. He's billing so many hours. I don't know how he does it. If I'm going to compete . . .'

'Why do you have to?' Sam asked, exasperated.

'You know why. I watched my dad drink himself to death, hectored all the way there by my mother because of what happened. Can you imagine the ignominy of losing out to your younger brother in a town as small as Abbeyleigh? Everyone knew he'd been passed over, that he wasn't considered good enough.'

'I wish I could make you see that if you stepped off the treadmill it wouldn't necessarily mean the end of the world as you know it. It might mean a better world. I tried to make you see that last year, long before Megan. I don't care if you're the senior partner or a junior associate. What matters is us, having time for each other.'

'We will.'

'We didn't before.'

'I'll make the effort. I'll find the time.'

'That will just increase the pressure you're under. I don't want that.'

'I can't walk away, Sam. I'd do pretty much anything for you but please don't ask me to do that.'

She fell silent. As desperate as Neil was for their reconciliation there were still limits. In the dark enchantment of last night, there might have been a chance to turn him away from the promotion, but not now. Although she understood his reasons, she was still hurt.

'I'll try to work from home more,' he said and kissed her lips.

It was something.

'It will be different when I'm senior partner, I promise.'

She forced a smile, lost in the memory of the promises she'd listened to in the past.

'Dad promised everything would be okay after he left. Better, in fact. No more rows. Just good times. I believed him. He promised he'd come and see me every couple of weeks, take me out and he did, for a while. Then, two weeks became six and then twelve. Once he took me to the zoo. He bought me an ice cream, I dropped it, and he told me off. The visits stopped altogether after that. I thought there had to be a reason why he didn't want to see me any more, why he loved his new wife's children more than me. I thought it was because I'd dropped the ice cream.' She met Neil's gaze. 'He promised he'd always be there and he lied. Please don't do that to me.'

'I won't.'

'I'd rather you told me to my face that you were going than slip away from me inch by inch like he did. I couldn't bear it.'

'It won't happen.' Neil reached for her hand. 'You have my word.'

Time would tell. It wasn't that she didn't believe him. At that moment, she did. But if he'd cheated once, wasn't there a greater chance of it happening again? By taking him back, was she belittling what he had done?

Would he feel he could cheat again with impunity, that she'd always forgive him?

With a crushing disappointment, Sam realised the fear would always be there, suffocating her if she chose to let it. What had once been precious was damaged. It could never be as it had been before. Theirs was a new world now and she'd have to learn to live in it.

She moved to Neil's side of the table and encircled him in her arms, needing to smell his scent, feel the heat of his skin. If her senses were intoxicated by him, overloaded, surely there would be no air left for her fears to breathe?

She was gripped suddenly by an urgent need to be better than Megan: sexier, funnier, more beautiful. If she were everything that Neil desired, why would he ever need to look at another woman?

She kissed him ardently. It was easy to feel sexy when Neil's response was so instant. Sam's body reacted with the electricity of attraction. He pulled her robe apart, his mouth roaming over her breasts. She clasped him to her, her heart thumping so fiercely she was certain he must surely feel its echo beneath his lips.

'I have to be all that you want,' she said huskily.

'You are,' he gasped. 'God, you are!'

She rose then, majestic and padded back inside, letting the robe fall as soon as she was over the threshold. Neil was behind her in an instant, one arm curved around her breasts, the other fondling her bottom. She knew he'd take her there if she let him but she laughed, extricating herself, turning, grabbing his hand, leading him on.

He paused by the bed but she shook her head, guiding him instead to the bathroom and into the oversized shower cubicle. The jets of water fell like gentle rain, softly beguiling.

Finally, she let him take charge, gasping as he plunged her under the water, his tongue chasing the droplets down her neck and over her collarbone, to the peak of her nipples, then lower, across her stomach, between her legs and, exquisitely, down the inside of her thighs.

Leaning into him, Sam shut her eyes. Running her hands over his shoulders, she could feel the muscles moving beneath his skin; strong, resolute. The blood was thundering through her body now.

He fell away from her and she opened her eyes to find him on his knees before her, looking up at her with a sexy smile, his blue eyes vivid and engaging. Once, her whole world had been encapsulated in those eyes. She reached down to touch his face.

'With my body I thee worship,' Neil said with a grin as his fingers began to caress her thighs. Sam tilted her head back, covering his hands with her own, urging him on. She gave a yelp of desire as he kissed the curve of her belly before moving lower. Gasping, Sam felt her legs quiver as her body opened itself up for him.

His hands gripped her bottom, holding her close so that his tongue could work its magic. On and on he went, driving her to the brink, only to slow and settle her before starting again, harder and faster.

Desperately, she clutched him to her, almost senseless with longing, until she could stand it no longer. On the point of collapse, she begged him to bring her off and, with perfect timing, he was quick to oblige, sending her world spiralling gloriously out of control.

Drained, Sam slid to the floor of the shower, the last throes of her orgasm still rippling through her.

'You're the only woman I'll ever want.'

Spent, Sam was too exhausted to respond.

✻

On the Sunday morning, as they lay once more in bed, Sam thought again of that moment of climax, recognising it as her triumph over the months of heartache that had gone before. As a couple, they had been reborn.

'That man you were attracted to . . .' Neil began suddenly.

'What man?' Sam asked sharply, jolted from her reverie.

'You said, it's not only men who get to look and wonder.'

'Oh that.'

'There was a man, I take it. One man in particular? When we were separated?'

'Yes.'

'But nothing came of it?'

'No.'

'Do you still see him?'

'No.'

'Do I know him?'

'Not really.'

Neil sighed. 'I'm glad nothing happened between you.' His grip on her body tightened. 'I can't bear to think of another man touching you, holding you like this.'

And yet I will always think of you with her, if I let myself, Sam thought sadly. Was a man's ego so much more fragile than a woman's? His pride so all-consuming no breach of faith could ever be forgiven? Sam feared it was true.

Neil kissed her temple. 'We needed this.'

Sam turned in his arms. 'We did,' she agreed. She let her fingers wander over his chest as Neil's hand gently stroked her hip, his touch soft, mesmeric.

He'd come back to her emotionally and physically. Another couple of months and he would be hers mentally too. Promotion secured, they could move on. That better world he'd promised would, at last, be theirs.

'Why don't we extend our stay?' Sam suggested. She felt him tense beneath her.

'I'd like nothing better but . . .'

'You have to get back.' She cut him off, crashing back down to earth.

'I'm afraid so.'

Patience, Sam thought.

Chapter Twenty-Three

They were home by five o'clock. Josh was standing in the kitchen, eating a sandwich and dropping crumbs on the floor.

'Have we run out of plates?' Sam asked archly.

He smiled. 'You look like you've had a good time.'

She saw his gaze linger on their joined hands.

'We have,' Neil said jovially as he kissed Sam's cheek.

'When did Connor bring you back?' Sam asked.

'About an hour ago. Is this what it looks like?' Josh asked, looking from one to the other.

Sam nodded and saw the joy leap into her son's face.

'I'm going to be moving back in,' Neil announced, giving Josh a hug.

'That's great, Dad.'

Neil grinned. 'Where's Cass? I can't wait to tell her.'

'She's watching TV.'

Josh waited for Neil to leave before turning to Sam with nervous eyes. 'Is it great, Mum?'

'Yes.'

He gave her a hug. 'Congrats on the result at court. I knew you'd be okay.'

Sam kissed her son's cheek. 'Thanks.'

By God, we'd better do all we can to make this reconciliation work.

Sam had kept her business phone turned off for the duration of their stay in Dorset just as Neil had done with his. Now, while she waited for the kettle to boil she turned the phone on to check her messages.

The email from David leapt out at her.

She flexed her fingers to stop them from shaking before clicking on his name.

Hello, Sam. We need to talk. Ring or email me, please.

Above it was another email from him. She opened it. He'd obviously read her out of the office message.

Hello, Sam. We have to talk. When you get back, please get in touch.

Sam hit the reply button. *I don't think that would be a good idea.* She pressed send.

What was the point in opening herself up to all that pain again? What was he going to do? Tear into her about how light the sentence had been? His emails had sounded friendly enough but that was no guarantee. No, she was better off avoiding him.

She remembered with fondness the dizzy heights she and Neil had regained that weekend. There could be no place for David in her life now.

JUNE

Chapter Twenty-Four

Honeydews Auction House held a general sale twice a month. Sam and Connor tried to attend whenever possible, on the lookout for bargains or unusual items they could incorporate into their designs.

Sam fanned herself with her bidding card as she watched Connor examine a writing bureau. They already had a list of items they were interested in bidding on and Connor's smile told her they were about to add another.

'Perfect for Mrs Cooper, don't you think?'

Sam nodded. She raised her hand in greeting as Gordon Honeydew approached.

'Hello, Sam. Connor. I was hoping to see you, Sam. I've heard from the Abbeyleigh Museum. They are planning to revamp their Victorian rooms so they can incorporate the automatons. Provisional date for the grand opening is December. Any chance you can persuade your client to come along as the guest of honour? Maybe say a few words, cut the ribbon, that sort of thing?'

'I can try but I doubt it.'

'Do your best.'

'How are you getting on with the cashier's till?'

'It's a fiendish box of tricks.' Gordon sighed. 'I still haven't been able to open the cash drawer but I have figured out what Ted Mitchell was trying to do. I finally made sense of some of the notes and diagrams he left in the box. The plan was, I think, that a person would tap the keys of the cash register and instead of a price popping up in the window at the top, a message would pop up instead.'

'What was the message?'

'Happy anniversary. At least I think that was the plan.'

Sam brought her hand up to her mouth. 'He died just a couple of months before the couple celebrated their fiftieth.'

'Ted Mitchell was an old romantic then.'

'Will you be able to get it working?'

'I hope so. Be easier once I figure out what's stopping the cash drawer from opening. I'll keep you updated.' He kissed Sam's cheek.

Connor raised his eyebrows. 'You'll have to tell her.'

'I know. I just need to pick the right time.'

'Hello, Sam.'

Sam froze. *David.*

'Hello.'

He smiled and thrust out a hand to Connor. 'I'm David.'

'Connor.'

'Pleased to meet you, Connor. I've heard a lot about you.'

Feeling as though all the oxygen had been sucked out of the room, Sam made as if to move off. 'Nice to see you again, David.'

He caught hold of her arm. 'I'd like a word.'

The touch of his hand electrified her, a lightning bolt that carried with it precious memories. Her gaze fell to his hand. She looked up, silently pleading. He took his hand away abruptly.

His manner was not at all threatening and he even gave her a smile, an echo of the warm smiles she had once been so used to.

'Sam . . .' Connor stepped forward.

'It's fine, Connor. Could you give us a moment?'

Throwing a warning look at David, Connor nodded and moved over to study the paintings on the nearby wall, still close enough to keep an eye on her, Sam noted.

'I told you in my email . . .'

'That you didn't think it would be a good idea,' he repeated. 'I know. There's something I need to ask you.'

'I've told you everything I can remember,' she said. She leaned against the writing bureau for support.

'I'm sorry about the way I was with you.'

'I deserved it,' she said candidly.

'Five minutes of your time.'

Sam looked around. They were drawing furtive glances from the auction house staff. 'Okay, but not here.'

'How about Spike's on the High Street?'

'Too public.'

'My flat, then?'

Sam nodded. 'I'll come over once the auction has finished.'

'I'll be waiting.'

Two hours later, against her better judgement and that of Connor's, Sam stood in the middle of the flat that had once been so familiar to her, feeling, for all the world, like an intruder.

'I don't know what I'm doing here,' she admitted, unsure whether to sit down or remain standing.

'Can I get you a drink?'

'No, thanks.'

Unshaven and dressed in jeans and a tee shirt, David looked tired, Sam thought. She watched him lever off the top of a bottle of beer. Sam frowned.

'What were you looking for at the auction?' he asked.

'Some pieces for work.' She bit her lip. One of them had to tackle the elephant in the room. 'How's your leg?'

'Aches a bit.' He looked preoccupied.

'What were *you* looking for at the auction?' Sam asked.

'You.' He took a swig of his beer.

She had expected as much. She'd told him how often she attended. Sam looked at him now. Seated in one of the armchairs, he had downed half a bottle of beer already. Dutch courage. She would have to be the one to bring the court case up, she realised.

'I'm sorry about the points on my licence and the fine.' The verdict had been niggling away at her. Moreover, if he was going to end up shouting at her again, better he did it sooner rather than later. 'In no way, did the punishment fit the crime,' she added.

She watched the strain come back into David's face. He was still thinner than he should have been and very pale. He strode across to the patio door and, flicking the lock, slid it along. A cool breeze played with the hem of Sam's floral dress. He stood with his back to her.

'I thought you were bored with your husband. I thought you were guarded with me because you were making up your mind whether or not to have an affair. I was flattered and excited. When I found out you'd told the nurse that you were my sister, I realised what an idiot I'd been, that there had to be another reason why you were spending so much time with me.'

Sam's cheeks burned.

'The last thing I expected you to say was that you were driving that night. It was such a shock.' Retrieving the beer bottle from the table, he took another swig. 'I wanted to hate you,' he said evenly.

His words, though not unexpected, still had the power to shake her.

'Part of me needed to hate you.' Agitated, he pushed a hand through his hair. 'At my worst, I succeeded,' he admitted flatly. 'I wanted the woman who was driving that night to suffer.' His gaze met Sam's and his expression softened. 'I just wasn't prepared for that woman to be you.'

What could she say but sorry and she'd already said that so many times. She opened her mouth to speak but then closed it again as she saw him give a slight shake of his head.

'The fact remains that you were my friend.' He set the empty beer bottle down. 'I'm not sure I'd have made it through those early days without you.'

She watched him press out two painkillers and throw them back.

'I was good at putting on a front but a front was all it was. I was tortured by those nightmares and flashbacks, I told you about.' His gentle eyes took on a haunted look. 'And I doubted myself on every level because of what Lauren did. You made it easier to bear. I thought of you as my guardian angel. That's why, when you told me the truth, it was so hard to take.'

'I can imagine.' Sam's heart shrank with fresh shame.

'It took guts for you to come and see me. I threw that back in your face.' He spoke slowly as if weighing each word before releasing it. 'My GP confirmed your suspicion. He thinks I'm suffering from post-traumatic stress disorder. I'd just found out when you arrived that day. It doesn't excuse the way I spoke to you but the mood swings and the anger are all part of the PTSD. I just wanted you to understand.'

'You don't have to explain. I deserved . . .'

'My solicitor's arranging for me to have counselling,' he said, cutting her off. She watched his Adam's apple rise and fall as he swallowed. 'Never thought I'd need to see a shrink.'

He looked so upset it was all Sam could do not to take him in her arms. 'If it helps,' she offered weakly.

'Aye.'

Her palms were hot and itchy. She desperately wanted to escape onto the balcony, to go out into the cool air but to do that she'd have to pass David. Unsure of herself, she didn't dare.

'There's something I need to ask you and I need an honest answer. Even if you think it's not what I want to hear.'

Sam felt the flush in her cheeks deepen.

'Was it my fault? Was I to blame for what happened that night?'

Sam's heart contracted with pity.

'No!'

'If it wasn't my fault then why did it happen, Sam?' he asked plaintively. 'I've never seen anything in your character that's the least bit reckless. I know it was late and that it was raining. You said you didn't see me, that the first you knew, I was right on top of you. Be honest now, was I driving too fast? Is that why it happened? I have to know, did I bring this on myself? I keep reliving that night through my nightmares and the damn flashbacks I keep getting but I cannae remember. So, I need you to tell me, so I can stop questioning myself. Was it my fault?' His troubled eyes bored into hers.

A little voice inside Sam screamed at her to tell David the truth, to tell him that Neil had been driving that night. But if David had succeeded in hating her, what would he be like with Neil? What if he went to the police? Could she take the risk?

Celts were passionate people, ruled by their emotions. David could be volatile and unpredictable, she'd seen it herself, and the PTSD would only make that worse. Yet, to tell him the truth would finally release her from the cage of lies in which she'd been trapped. In a quandary, she stared at him.

'No, David. It wasn't your fault.'

'But . . .'

'You wanted my honesty.' Sam massaged her eyes. 'Believe me when I say none of this was your fault.' She took a step towards him and then another until she was within touching distance. 'There's something else you should know about that night but I need you to promise me you won't take it further.'

Slowly, he nodded. 'You have my word.'

Sam drew a ragged breath. 'I wasn't driving that night.'

'What?' David looked stunned.

'Neil was. That's why I can say, categorically, it wasn't your fault. He'd had too much to drink. He didn't stop at the junction. You didn't stand a chance, whatever speed you were doing. So, you must stop torturing yourself. This accident was no more your fault than it was mine and that's the truth.' Desperate now to escape his suffocating presence, Sam left him where he stood and went out onto the balcony, letting the cool breeze wash over her.

He knew the truth. It felt scary but good. David could take her admission and cause all sorts of trouble if he chose to do so but telling him had been the right thing to do. How could she have let him go on living tormented by the idea that the accident had in some way been his fault?

'He was drunk?' There was incomprehension in David's eyes as he joined her on the balcony.

'I tried to stop him.'

'And you lied for him?'

She nodded.

'Why?' There was an ache to the word, a longing to understand.

'Because he asked me to,' Sam said quietly.

'Simple as that?' David was incredulous, his expression hovering between anger and amazement.

'There was nothing simple about that night.'

'Why did you do it?' David demanded.

'Because all chance of his promotion would have been lost if he'd been prosecuted.' Her words died under the weight of David's sullen stare.

'Fuck his promotion! What about my justice?' David shouted, banging his fist down on the rail.

Sam clawed at his arm, spinning him round. 'It was a spur of the moment decision but, once I'd made it, there was no going back.' She let her hand drop. 'There's still no going back,' she added firmly, a touch defensively.

'You're still protecting him?'

'I have to.'

Sam could see the muscles working in David's cheek. 'Whose idea was it?'

'His.'

'You should have told me.'

'You were angry. I was afraid.'

'I felt betrayed.' He leaned over the railing, stared at the river below. 'It wasn't my fault?' he said softly.

'No.' She put her hand on his back.

He turned to look at her.

Sam watched the relief flood into his eyes followed by something else. Compassion.

'It wasn't your fault, either?'

'No.'

'You lied to protect him?'

Sam nodded, not trusting her voice.

'And the bastard let you?' His touch to her cheek was tender. 'He doesn't deserve you.'

Embarrassed, Sam lowered her gaze before gently removing his hand. *I can't do this*, she thought. *I have to leave now.* Yet, she remained rooted to the spot. His hand warm in hers.

He gave her fingers a squeeze. 'We were both victims of what happened that night.'

'Yes.' It was more a sob than a word.

'Sweet Sam. My angel. Have you any idea how much I wanted you not to be the driver? Anyone but you.' He crushed her against him.

Her fingers tightened over his shoulders. She was shocked by the force of the feelings building inside her. Propriety quickly reasserting itself, she pulled away.

'Why didn't you tell me the truth before?'

'Because I wasn't sure how you'd react. I was worried in case you went to the police. I wanted the prosecution out of the way.'

He nodded. 'It wasn't your fault,' he said again, with a smile.

Coming closer, his lips met hers. His touch was so soft that Sam wondered if she'd been kissed at all. Then, his mouth sought hers again, a little more boldly this time and there was no mistaking his intention.

Sam edged away. While she may have indulged in fantasies about David, fantasies were all they could ever be. She couldn't act on them. Dare not. Especially now she had been reconciled with Neil.

'Sam?'

She could see the question in his eyes. Sam swallowed. A playground dalliance was how she had come to think of their time together. Had anyone ever been so misguided? It had been so much more than that.

She had tried to justify her feelings and belittle them to protect herself but now there was nowhere left to hide. She loved him as much, if not more, than ever and the realisation floored her because she had come so close to believing the lies she had told herself and surely they were the most destructive lies of all.

'Sam?'

As he reached out, she backed away. A touch now would be her undoing. She had given her heart, once more, to Neil. She had made him a promise to try again. The children were overjoyed. She couldn't renege.

'You're incredibly special to me.'

'Special? You'll be telling me next you like me only as a friend.' There was an edge to his voice. A challenge.

'Because friendship is all we can share.'

'Who are you trying to convince, you or me?' David asked bluntly.

She met his gaze and quickly wished she hadn't. His eyes, full of longing, beseeched her.

'You know I've fallen in love with you, don't you?' he said.

'David . . .'

'I can make you happy, Sam.'

If I leave now, she told herself, *I never have to see him again.* Try as she might, she couldn't make her feet move.

'You don't have to pretend any more, sweetheart. I can see it in your eyes. You love me too, don't you? Say it, Sam! Tell me you love me.'

'David, please!'

He grabbed her shoulders. 'Damn it, Sam! Don't lie to me any more. Say it!'

'I love you,' she cried, tearing herself free. 'There! Are you satisfied? You've been on my mind every day. My heart thumps at the very thought of you. Is that what you want to hear? We can never have anything more than what we have now and even this is too much.' She pushed past him preparing to leave.

He caught her as she fumbled with the front door, dragging her back into his arms. His kiss tasted of beer, determination and longing. A dangerous combination and yet her desire for him flared.

She had played out this scene a dozen times in her head but nothing could compare to the feeling of his body hard against hers, the breathless excitement his arousal sparked in her. She was overwhelmed by her hunger for him. It was a need beyond reason and as his tongue searched her mouth for answers, she gave them to him in kind.

It would be so simple to take him in her arms and avenge Neil's affair. However, she knew instinctively one day of passion with David would not be enough. She would always want more and that could never be, because of Neil and the children.

Finally, reluctantly, she found the strength to break away. 'I can't.'

'After all that coward's put you through? I don't see a whole lot of honour in asking you to lie for him.'

Sam remained silent.

'There was a sadness in you. I sensed it at the hospital. I recognised it because I was feeling it too. He's hurt you.'

'I have to go.'

'I was right all along, wasn't I? I know now that you came to me because of the accident but you stayed because you liked me. I didn't get the signals wrong. All those times I wanted to kiss you, you wanted that, too. You were too bound up by loyalty to him to make the first move but you would have been happy to respond if only I'd dared.'

'No.'

'Well, I'm ready to dare.'

'David!'

'You asked me a moment ago if I was satisfied.' He gripped her left hand and held it up between them. 'How can I ever be satisfied while you still wear his wedding ring? Now that I know you want me too, that you always did? Be mine.'

'I can't.' Sam snatched her hand away. She had stepped back from the brink. Now, all she had to do was make herself walk away.

He barred her way. 'Take off his ring and be mine.'

'I can't do that.'

'Yes, you can,' he said calmly. 'You're imagining yourself doing it right now. You'll slip the ring from your finger and lay it on the table and I'll tilt your chin up and kiss you on the lips. Then, I'll stand behind you. Like this.' Sam sensed him moving to stand as close behind her as it was possible to be without actually touching her. The air between them was suddenly charged. 'I'll run my fingers through your hair and kiss your temple.'

His breath fell hot against her skin and, trembling with longing, it was as much as Sam could do not to lean back against him.

'I'll wrap my arms around you and I'll hold your breasts through your dress and we'll both imagine what it will feel like when there are no clothes between us.'

'Stop it, David!' She willed herself to move away from him but, spellbound, stayed where she was.

'You want me to touch you like that, don't you?'

The tension between them grew to breaking point.

'Yes,' she said weakly.

She cried out as he seized her.

'I'll hold you tight against me so you can feel how much I want you and then I'll take off your dress. I'll lower the zip very slowly and, as I do, I'll kiss your neck and . . .'

'Stop it!' At last she moved away, breaking the spell.

'Take off his ring.'

'I can't.'

'You want me.'

'I do.'

'Then . . .'

'I can't take off my ring.'

'Damn it! Why not? It's only loyalty that's binding you to him.'

'Not just loyalty. Love, too.'

'But you love me,' David said petulantly. 'You just said you did.'

'I love you both,' she replied.

'How can you still love him?' David asked, bewildered. 'He'll never change. Working all hours. Neglecting you.'

'Once he gets his promotion . . .'

'The same promotion that nearly cost me my life?'

'Things will be different.'

'Things will never be different. Men like Neil are driven. Once he gets the promotion, what then? If you think he'll be satisfied with that, you're a fool. He'll keep on striving because that's what men like Neil do. They're never satisfied.'

'You don't know him.'

'I was like him, Sam. I know how he thinks, how he feels.'

'You walked away.'

'It took the accident to make me see sense. It didn't do the same for him, did it?'

'Neil says when he gets the promotion . . .'

'That everything will change,' David jeered. 'And you believe him? He will always want more. He will never put you first. Even if you asked him to.'

Sam lowered her gaze.

'You have asked him to, haven't you?'

'I have to go.'

David caught her wrist. 'What did he tell you?'

'Let me go.'

His grip tightened. 'He told you to wait, didn't he? To be patient until he gets the promotion. What then, Sam? You think it'll be your turn? How can it be when the whole firm will be his responsibility? You'll spend your life living on promises that will never come true. Is that what you want?'

'Let go, you're hurting me.'

He released her hand and quickly cupped her cheek. 'You could have everything with me. You could tell me your heart's desire, Angel, and I would make it happen. Would he?'

'I have to give Neil the benefit of the doubt.'

'Why?' The sheen of angry tears were in David's eyes.

'Because that's what husbands and wives do. I can't let him down, I'm sorry. I have to be strong enough to walk away from temptation. Otherwise, what's the point in making a commitment? How can I expect other people to honour their promises to me if I can't honour my promises to them?'

'Then what are we going to do, Sam?'

She backed away from him. 'Say goodbye.'

'I can't do that. I've only just got you back. I can't lose you again.'

'There's no other way.'

'If you weren't with Neil?'

'If I were single? Things would be different, but I'm not single.'

'I need you in my life.'

'David . . .'

'I'll take anything you want to give me: a phone call, a lunch date. Something. Anything. Let me be your friend.'

'It wouldn't work . . .'

'It has to,' he declared. 'If friendship is all I can have, then friendship will have to be enough.'

'How can it be? We'll live in torment.'

'I'll keep my distance like I did before.'

'We can't take back the things we've said today.'

'I don't want to take them back.' He hooked her hair behind her ears and kissed her forehead before settling his hands on her shoulders. 'But if I can't have you as a lover, then I *must* have you as a friend because I cannae lose you altogether. Please, Angel. I need you.

You'll help make me whole again, I know you will. And I won't cross the line with you, I swear.' He bent his forehead to hers. 'Please, Sam.'

'Friendship? Nothing more,' she said sceptically.

He nodded. 'If it means I can see you, spend time with you, I'll be the best damn friend you've ever had. What do you say, Sam?'

Did she have the strength of character to enjoy David's company and yet hold him at bay? Could she succeed where Neil had failed?

'You'll help make me whole again.' She knew for David's sake, she had to try.

'Friends,' she replied.

Chapter Twenty-Five

With her arms full of curtains, Sam negotiated her way carefully up the narrow staircase of David's holiday cottage.

'David?'

'In here.'

Carrying the curtains into the master bedroom, Sam followed the sound of pop music into the bathroom. David was standing in the bath, tiling the wall.

'Looking good,' Sam said.

David gave her a tired smile. 'You don't look so bad yourself.'

Sam pulled a face. 'I was talking about the wall.'

David smirked. 'You've got the things for the bedrooms?'

'Yes. I've just brought the curtains up. The bedding's in the car.'

'Do you need a hand?'

'No, I can manage.'

As she worked to put the curtains up, Sam marvelled at how easy it had been to incorporate David into her life. Spending time with him lightened her heart and nobody had suffered as a result. If anything, it had had a positive effect. Her relationship with Neil was going from strength to strength as they navigated the choppy waters back to a new sort of normality. David was keeping his distance from her physically and Sam was working hard to ignore the occasional flashes of longing that gripped her in his presence.

It took her forty minutes to fix the curtains in both bedrooms, put the quilt covers on and generally dress the rooms.

'I've got to hand it to you, Sam,' David said from the doorway. 'You know how to make a room look good. One day, when you're a big interior design star, I'll be able to say I worked with her way back when.'

She smiled.

'Taught her everything she knows,' David added.

Sam punched his arm.

'Today Abbeyleigh and Hallows End, tomorrow . . .'

'Abbeyleigh again,' Sam replied with a chuckle.

'I was going to say London or Paris or wherever it is you interior designers hang out when you're not designing interiors.'

Sam grinned. 'You can stop flattering me now.'

'I'm just praising your work,' David said coyly. 'I haven't started flattering *you* yet.'

Sam flushed.

'Don't forget to let me have the bill,' David said.

'I'm not going to invoice you.'

'Why ever not?' David asked. 'I won't take advantage of our friendship, Sam.'

'But . . .'

'If it makes you feel better, I'll settle for a discount.'

Sam nodded.

'Come downstairs, will you? There's something I want to show you.'

Sam followed David down the stairs. He was limping slightly as he walked across the sitting room, she noticed.

'Look what I found in one of the kitchen drawers.'

They were the sketches she had made of the rooms and the gardens on her first visit to the cottage.

'You kept them?' she said, amazed.

'I was in such a state after you confessed that day, I stuffed them in the drawer and then completely forgot about them.'

Sam swallowed the lump that had risen in her throat. She had pictured him ripping the drawings to shreds after she'd left. She wouldn't have blamed him if he had.

'I thought you could concentrate on the sitting room while I gut the kitchen and then we can work on the garden together. What do you think? Lewis Shaw has just paid me the last of the bonuses that were due to me so I have a bit of spare cash.'

Sam nodded. 'I'd be happy to.'

Chapter Twenty-Six

When she got home, Sam walked into uproar.

'What am I going to do?' Cass wailed.

'Are you sure you left it on the dresser?' Neil asked, his arm round his daughter's shoulders.

'Yes, it's gone.'

'What's gone?' Sam asked.

'Fifty pounds,' Cass said.

'Where have you been?' Neil asked. 'The family phone was switched off,' he added accusingly.

Before Sam could answer, Cass said, 'I was saving it to help pay for a guitar.'

'You were saving it for *what*?' Neil asked, turning back to his daughter.

Cass gave him a sour look. 'Tobyn is teaching me to play.'

'Cass thinks our cleaner took the money,' Josh said from the doorway.

'She wouldn't,' Sam said firmly.

'That's what Dad and I said.'

Cass glared at her brother. 'We've never had money go missing before,' she said.

'You can't go accusing people without proof.'

'It must be her. We're not going to steal from each other, are we?'

'And you've searched your room?' Sam asked.

'Twice,' she replied sullenly. 'I've looked everywhere. The money's gone.'

'When you say you've looked everywhere is that proper looking or looking for things like your father does, without moving anything?'

Neil pulled a face.

'I did it properly,' Cass replied.

'Well, I'll go and do it again. Just in case.'

'I'll help.' Josh offered. 'I don't think our cleaner took the money. You just didn't look properly, like Mum said.'

Cass stuck her tongue out at him.

'A guitar?' Neil said to Sam as the children went racing ahead of them up the stairs.

'They've started a band.'

'Her and whatsit?'

'Tobyn. Yes.'

'What sort of band?'

'Not sure, but if she wants to give it a go it's important we let her.'

Neil looked unconvinced. 'Why couldn't she dream of being a vet?' he asked as they reached the door of the bedroom.

'And stick my hand up a cow's backside? Not bloody likely!'

'Language,' Sam and Neil reprimanded in unison.

'Mum! I've found it!' Josh was holding the money aloft triumphantly when Sam and Neil walked in.

'Where was it?'

'Down the back of the dresser.'

'Cass!' Neil said sternly. 'You told me you'd searched everywhere.'

'I did,' she said plaintively, snatching the money from her brother.

'At least it's been found, that's the main thing,' Sam said.

'So where were you?' Neil asked. 'I tried ringing.'

'I was working on that holiday home project I told you about up at The Hallows.'

'And the phone?'

'The signal out there is a nightmare so I switched it off.'

Which was true but she had also wanted to avoid the awkwardness of speaking to her husband while she was with David. A stab of guilt knifed through her. What if it had been a real emergency and he'd needed her?

Chapter Twenty-Seven

Sam stood back to admire the wooden floorboards she had spent the past two hours sanding. The muscles in her arms ached but the result was impressive and worth all the effort. She lifted off the mask she had worn to protect herself from the dust, settling it on top of her head.

David was assembling kitchen units. She could hear him singing along to a pop tune blasting out of the radio and smiled as he went hopelessly off key.

The holiday cottage was coming along nicely. It wouldn't be too much longer before they were finished with the inside and could move on to the garden. She felt a surge of regret at the thought. Once the job had been completed there would be no need to spend as much time with him.

Pushing the thought out of her mind, she went through to the kitchen. 'Music's a bit loud,' she shouted.

'What?' he asked.

'I said . . .' She reached for the volume control. 'Music's a bit loud.'

He laughed. 'I couldn't hear it over the sander. You all done in there?'

'Yes, come and see.'

'Wow!' David bent to inspect the floor. 'Good job.' He grinned. 'You are one talented angel. Not sure about your fashion sense though,' he said, standing.

Sam looked down at her paint-stained tee shirt and battered jeans. 'You'd hardly expect me to wear anything smart while I'm sanding floors.'

'I wasn't talking about your clothes. I was referring to what's on top of your head. Is that some kind of fashion statement?' He laughed. 'If it is, I can't see it catching on.' He lifted the mask off her head.

Sam grinned.

His kiss was so quick she barely had time to react. Lips to lips. He reached out and she stepped back abruptly. 'David . . .'

'You've dust on your face.' He stroked her cheek. 'There, that's better. I'll go and put the kettle on. Least I can do after all your hard work is treat you to a cuppa.'

Chapter Twenty-Eight

Neil checked the dates again. The happy hum of office life beyond his door receded until all he was aware of was the clattering of his own heart. There had to be some mistake. He checked again. It was there in black and white. Accusing him. No mistake.

What the hell am I going to do? Neil pushed his hands through his hair. He had to think carefully. There had to be a way to deal with this without bringing the whole world down on his head.

He reached for the telephone and called home.

The answer machine kicked in.

He speed dialled Sam's personal mobile. It went straight to voicemail. *Damn it, Sam! I told you to keep that phone on. I need you.*

'Call me as soon as you get this message. It's urgent,' he barked.

He speed dialled her business mobile. That, too, went to voicemail.

He thumped the phone down. *Why did nobody answer their bloody phones any more?*

He sat back in despair just as Megan walked by. Her name left his lips before he knew what he was going to say next. She gave him a shy smile. It was clear she didn't know how to behave around him. Who could blame her after the way he'd frozen her out?

'Megan, there's something I need to talk to you about. A problem on one of my files.'

'Okay.'

'Not here.'

'You could come to mine later.'

Relieved, Neil said, 'I'd appreciate it. Thanks.'

Though young, Megan was a brilliant strategist. She'd assisted him on some of his biggest cases before he'd had to get her transferred. He shut the offending file and stowed it in his briefcase. He wasn't going to let one stupid mistake ruin all his hard work. He couldn't. There had to be a solution. Megan would help him find it.

Chapter Twenty-Nine

'Can you pass me two more hinges from that box on the table?'

David held out his hand, enjoying the brief touch of Sam's fingers as she deposited the hinges into his palm. Her nails were unpainted but neatly shaped. Unable to resist he took her hand in his.

'I'll treat you to a manicure when we're done here.'

She smiled. 'There's no point in my line of work.' She gently extricated her hand from his.

'You paint them sometimes. I remember at the charity auction they were blood red. They looked fantastic.'

'You remember that?'

'Of course.' Standing, he hooked her hair behind her ear. 'I remember everything.' He winced as a jolt of pain went through his leg. He turned, eager to hide it from her, but he wasn't quick enough.

'It's late. We should call it a day.'

'No need. I've just got two more doors to fix.'

'And they'll still be there tomorrow.'

But you won't be, he thought. She'd already told him that she couldn't work this weekend. Family time she'd called it. He'd asked her if Neil would be there. Her silence had told him everything he needed to know. Her husband was still spending too many hours at the office. More fool him. Still, the more hours he put in the better, so far as David was concerned. *When Sam realises the man is more wedded to the office than he is to her, she'll be mine.*

'Tell you what, why don't you drive over to Little Hallows and pick us up some fish and chips while I fix the last two doors. Then we can have an alfresco supper in the garden to celebrate all our hard work today.'

Anything to make this day last a little longer.

Sam smiled. 'Okeydoke.'

Chapter Thirty

'I made us some dinner,' Megan said. 'Pasta.'

'You didn't need to do that,' Neil said, embarrassed.

'I wanted to. There's wine in the fridge. Do you want to do the honours?'

Neil nodded. He followed Megan into the kitchen. Memories of the last time they had been there together flooded back. He grabbed the bottle of wine and fled to the living room.

'Where does Sam think you are?'

'Seeing a client.'

He recalled their brief conversation earlier that evening.

'Finally got my message and decided to give me a call then,' he'd said sullenly.

'I've just turned my phone on. You know the signal is rubbish out here. What's wrong?'

He'd paused, debating whether or not to tell her about his stuff-up and decided against it. 'Nothing. I had a problem at the office but a friend has promised to give me a hand to help sort it out.'

He'd expected to get the third degree about whether

Megan was the friend but instead Sam had said, 'That's good. I'm going to be a bit late. It's been a long day and I'm starving so I've just driven over to Little Hallows to get some fish and chips.'

'How late? I need to go out tonight to see a client.'

'You can still go.'

He'd heard the undertone of irritation in her voice.

'I'm sure Connor will look after the kids until one of us gets home. He won't mind. He is their godfather after all.'

Now, Neil looked at Megan and shifted uncomfortably. 'I know I have a cheek being here but I'm in a fix and I need your help.'

'That's what friends are for. Why don't we eat?' Megan suggested. 'You can tell me all about it.'

Relaxing a little, Neil uncorked the wine.

'I have a client, Mr Stewart. He had an accident at work. His general damages are likely to be between seven and eleven thousand pounds. Special damages of ten grand. There's only one problem,' Neil paused, loath to admit he'd made a rudimentary mistake. 'The accident happened three years and five months ago.'

Megan swirled her wine, a look of rapt attention on her face. 'And?'

'I haven't issued proceedings. I recorded the wrong year for the accident so I recorded the wrong limitation date. I thought I had seven months left. Instead of which I'm screwed.'

'There has to be a way . . .'

'You know as well as I do, the limitation date is

written in stone. I've missed the deadline. It's such a basic bloody mistake.'

'It's no good beating yourself up,' Megan said firmly. 'What we have to do is figure out what you do now.'

'What I should do is take the file to my uncle, admit the mistake, invite Stewart to sue me for negligence and put the matter in the hands of our insurers.' Neil met Megan's gaze. 'But if I do that I can kiss goodbye to my promotion.'

'Everyone makes mistakes,' Megan said reasonably.

'You know as well as I do that my uncle is just looking for an excuse to recommend Tilden over me.'

'Could you bluff it? You've only just found the mistake. It's possible the other side will overlook it too. You may be able to settle the case without them realising.'

'It'd be a hell of a gamble.'

'You only have to hold them off until August. If the mistake comes to light after you're senior partner, it's a bit of a dent to your pride but it can't hurt you because the promotion will be in the bag.'

'Not the most auspicious of starts.'

'Granted.'

'I'm not sure my nerves could take it,' Neil admitted.

'What were you thinking of doing?'

'Paying him out.'

Megan's eyes widened. 'You'd have to use your own money. You couldn't use your drawings from the firm.'

'I know.'

'And it would have to be at the top end of what he might get.'

'It'd have to be twenty grand,' Neil said glumly.

'So you tell him the other side have made an offer.'

'Yes.'

'The cheque would have your name on it.'

'I could say they'd made the settlement cheque payable to me instead of the firm.'

'What about the other side?' Megan asked.

'I could fall on my sword. Admit the error, tell them they were off the hook and that it was in the hands of my insurers.'

Megan shook her head. 'Let their correspondence go unanswered for a while then tell them you're without instructions and are going to close your file, suggest they do the same.'

'If they discovered the mistake in the meantime . . .'

'It's a dormant file. They won't look. You need to get rid of your file, though.'

'I'll burn it.'

'Are there disbursements on the ledger?'

'A little over two thousand pounds.'

'Do you clear them or write them off?'

'It's too much to write off,' Neil said. 'I could pay them off with another cheque. Tell the cashiers the same thing I tell Stewart: the other side made the cheque payable to me by mistake.'

'That's fine but what about the costs?'

'Bloody hell! If I pay the disbursements and don't render a bill the auditors are going to be all over it like a rash and if I can't produce the file they're going to know something's wrong.'

'The only alternative is to make up a dummy bill, put it through accounts and then pay it off using your own money when you pay off the disbursements.'

'Christ almighty. This is getting expensive.' Neil pushed his plate away, his food barely touched. 'Bang go our savings.'

Megan looked sympathetic. 'What will Sam say?'

'Sam's the least of my worries right now.'

'You could hang on to your savings and come clean.'

'I'd be handing the firm to Tilden on a plate.'

'There aren't any others, are there?'

'God, I hope not. I can't afford any more!'

'You need to go through every file. Make sure. I'll help you. It's Saturday tomorrow; we could do it then. No one would know. We could get a takeaway in. It'd be like old times,' Megan said wistfully. Blushing, she fell silent.

'I don't know how to thank you. I needed to talk this through with someone who would understand. There's no one else at the firm I could have . . .'

'I'm glad I could help.'

'It's more than I deserved,' Neil admitted.

Megan reached across to squeeze his hand. 'It's what friends are for.'

'I'm grateful.' He returned the squeeze before withdrawing his hand. 'I have to go.'

Megan nodded. 'How about ten, tomorrow?'

'Sounds great.'

Megan beamed. 'I'll bring wine.'

Chapter Thirty-One

Sam watched the darkness begin to creep across the tangled garden and stifled a yawn.

'Tired?' David smiled.

Sam nodded.

'Don't blame you. Hell of a job you've done on that floor. Not to mention all the sanding down you did on the porch this morning.'

'Team effort. The kitchen looks pretty damn good.'

'Funny you should say that, about it being a team effort. I've been thinking.'

'Oh yes?'

'How would you like to go into business with me? Buying holiday lets, renovating them, running them.'

Sam smiled. 'I already have a business.'

'But this would be something we could do together. Just you and me.'

'It's a sweet idea but it wouldn't work, David. I already have a business I love, with Connor. I can't go into business with you, too. Life's complicated enough already.' She tilted her head back against the armchair. 'We should get this furniture back inside.'

David pulled a face. 'It's going to be fine tonight. It could stay out. It's not like I plan on keeping any of it.'

'Have it your way, boss. I need to go home.' Rousing herself she gathered up the remains of their fish and chip supper and threw it in the bin.

'On second thoughts, I suppose we ought to put it back.'

'I hope you're not going to be this indecisive when it comes to picking colours for the walls in the sitting room.'

He laughed. 'No, because I'm leaving that to you, Angel.'

She saw him wince as he hoisted up one end of the armchair.

'Perhaps we should leave it.'

'No, let's get it done.'

She could tell by the determined look on his face that there was no point arguing. She felt guilty now for haranguing him about putting the furniture back. She should have realised he'd had enough. She had noticed how his limp had got progressively worse as the day had gone on. She should have known better.

They worked quickly to put the suite back. When they were done, Sam flopped onto the sofa with a sigh, feeling the day in her own muscles.

'How about I make us a nice cup of tea as a nightcap?' David suggested.

Sam checked her watch. It was nearly ten thirty. She really should be getting back. She opened her mouth to argue but David was already heading for the kitchen.

'Sam?'

His fingers on her arm were warm.

Rubbing her eyes, she sat up. 'God, I must have nodded off!'

'Here's your tea.'

'Thanks.'

She watched as he lowered himself gingerly into one of the armchairs. Sam knew he would be in a lot of pain tomorrow.

'If you're that tired, maybe you should think about staying over. You can have the master. I'll sleep in the box room.'

She shook her head. 'I need to go home.' She sipped her tea then wrinkled her nose. 'Has the milk gone off?'

'It's long life milk, sorry. We've run out of fresh. How long do you think it'll be until we finish the inside?'

'A couple more weeks. I need to get this floor varnished and I can't wait to give that fireplace a clean. Those tiles are going to look amazing when I've finished with them.'

'I'm looking forward to conquering the garden. I wonder how many skips it will take to clear it?'

'Half a dozen at least.' She stifled another yawn as she finished her tea.

'Are you sure you're going to be okay to drive?' David gave her a worried look. 'I don't want you falling asleep at the wheel.'

She laughed. 'I'll be fine.' She carried her cup through to the kitchen and ran it under the cold tap. Returning to the sitting room she picked up her bag from the second stair and pulled the zipper along to get her keys. The pocket was empty.

'That's odd.'

'What?' David flicked off the light in the kitchen.

'I could have sworn I put my car keys in my bag this morning.'

'Not on the fireplace, are they?'

Sam scanned the fireplace. 'No.'

'Wait. I was upstairs when you got here this morning. Maybe you put them down somewhere up there when you came up to see me.'

Sam began to climb the stairs.

'I'll come up, give you a hand to find them.'

'Thanks. Damn!' Sam cursed as she stumbled on the stairs.

David reached out to steady her. 'Are you sure you're okay?'

'I'm just so tired. We've both overdone it today.'

'Sit on the bed. I'll find your keys.'

Feeling groggy, Sam allowed David to steer her into the bedroom.

'I can't believe how quickly this has come on.' Through half open eyes she watched David search the room.

'I'll check the bathroom. I was tiling when you got here. I bet they're in there.'

'Okay.' Sam couldn't resist the urge to lie down. She was startled when, a few moments later, David shook her awake.

'I've found them, Sam. They were on the windowsill but I've got to tell you, I'm not happy about letting you drive like this. You can hardly keep your eyes open. I'd run you home but I had a couple of beers this afternoon and another this evening. I don't want to risk being pulled over.'

Sam nodded. She wanted to sit up. To take charge but she couldn't seem to rouse herself. 'Taxi,' she said even as her eyes shut once more.

'Don't be silly. It would cost a fortune. Stay here. Come on, I'll turn the bed down so you can get in.'

'I have to go home. Neil . . .'

'I'll text Neil from your phone, tell him you decided to stay over at the job. He thinks you're here alone so he won't be suspicious. You can sometimes get a signal at the top of the lane. I'll walk up there and give it a try once you're settled.'

David was already pulling at the laces of her trainers and easing them off. Wanting to protest but feeling as though there were weights attached to her eyelids, Sam crawled gratefully into bed, resting her head against the snowy pillow with a sigh.

Chapter Thirty-Two

At the top of the lane, David drew out Sam's iPhone and fired off a text to Neil.

Decided to work late and stay over at the cottage. See you in the morning. Kiss the kids.

Taking the opportunity to thumb through her contacts, calendar and photos, David whistled to himself as he walked back down the lane.

The cottage was quiet when he got back. He took the stairs slowly, wincing as his leg almost let him down. He paused on the threshold of the master bedroom. He'd left the bedside lamp on. In its gentle glow he could see that Sam was asleep. She looked beautiful. Almost serene. Her hair had fallen across one cheek, obscuring his view.

He limped forward and gently reached out to tease her hair back out of the way. His fingers lingered on her cheek. He quickly drew out his phone and took a couple of shots to add to his collection.

He knew he was taking a chance but the sight of her here in his bed made it worth the risk. He eased off his trainers and settled down beside her.

It was midnight when he woke. It took him a moment to remember where he was and who he was with and then he felt guilty. He hadn't wanted the day to end and so he'd crushed up two of the powerful sleeping pills his GP had prescribed to help him cope with the nightmares and dissolved them in Sam's tea.

He pressed his face against her hair, breathing in the citrusy freshness of her shampoo. As he'd slept so his arm had curved around her body, hugging her to him through the quilt. Now, he let his fingers sweep along the curve of her hip and her waist. If only she was his. Not through pretence or subterfuge but properly his. Forever.

He had tried to keep within the boundaries she had set but it was impossible. His feelings for her were too strong. He could only hope that when the time came for him to confess, his guardian angel would feel the same.

Reality crashed through his thoughts. He remembered the text he had sent to the husband from Sam's phone. What if Neil decided to drive out to Hallows End? He could brazen it out but he might lose Sam because of it and he couldn't allow that to happen.

Reluctantly, he peeled himself away from her. Better to check if the husband had responded. He quietly slipped on his trainers and with a glance over his shoulder crept out.

The moon was bright, the lane clear enough to navigate. After ten minutes he had a signal. Sure enough there was a reply from Neil.

You work too hard! I know – pot and kettle ☺ See you tomorrow. Love you.

David scoffed as he read the text. *You love her? Really? If you loved her like I do you'd spend more time with her.*

He was about to turn the phone off when he noticed an email from Connor. Out of curiosity he opened it.

I was with Neil when he got your message. We were sharing a bottle of red and putting the world to rights. I'm not judging you. Not after what he did.

So Connor knew that Neil had made Sam lie about the accident.

Get him out of your system. Tit for tat for Megan and then come home. I'm here if you want to talk.

David marked the email as unread. *Get him out of your system?* So, Sam had told Connor how she really felt about him. Excited, David smiled into the darkness. He knew he shouldn't have drugged her to make her stay but what he'd done wasn't such a bad thing. Not really. She wanted to be with him as much as he did her. She just didn't have the guts to make the first move. Paralysed by loyalty to a man who wasn't worthy of it. *All I have to do is be bold enough for both of us. I can do that.*

He thought about the rest of the message. *Tit for tat for Megan. Who the hell is Megan? Had her stupid prick of a husband cheated on her?* David grinned as he let himself back into the cottage and ran up the stairs ignoring the pain in his leg. A quick glance at Sam told him that she hadn't moved.

She looked so peaceful. Desperate to capture the moment, he drew out his phone again. Nerves made his fingers clumsy, but he managed to take a few shots. Elated, he eased back the quilt this time and climbing inside, settled down beside her, letting her measured breathing soothe his thumping heart.

Neil Davenport is making this so easy for me. He couldn't resist letting his fingers rest against Sam's hip. *Soon we'll be doing this for real, Angel.*

Chapter Thirty-Three

Sam felt as though she'd been kicked in the head. It must have been quite a party. She hadn't felt this hung over since her days at the agency and yet she couldn't remember drinking anything stronger than tea. She willed her eyes open.

There was no voile canopy over her head. Stunned, she sat up and immediately fell back against the pillows. Her head felt heavy, still thick with sleep. She massaged her brow and gingerly opened her eyes once more. Where was she? She moved her gaze slowly round the room. Sunlight was streaming through the window. She narrowed her eyes against the glare.

Slowly she edged herself up on her elbows. Her heart leapt, cutting through the fog of her brain. The master bedroom at the holiday cottage? The pillows had been bunched into the middle of the bed. Had she been the only occupant?

As if suddenly aware of her body, Sam assessed her clothing. She was fully dressed. She padded into the ensuite bathroom and splashed cold water onto her face. It all came back to her then, sanding the floor in the sitting room downstairs, helping David fix the kitchen units, their fish and chip supper in the garden, moving the furniture back inside. She'd sat down on the sofa intending to stay for a moment and get her breath back before driving home but she'd fallen asleep. She remembered stumbling on the stairs and David telling her he was worried about her driving home.

God! Where did Neil think she was?

There was a knock at the bedroom door. 'Sam?'

'Yes.' She walked back into the bedroom.

David opened the door. 'Hi.' He gave her a shy smile. 'I heard you get up. I've brought you some tea.'

He was dressed in a baggy white tee shirt and Calvin Klein underpants.

'I can't believe I stayed over. What's Neil going to say?'

'I walked to the end of the lane and texted him from your phone. I'm sure he'll be fine. He wouldn't have wanted you to have an accident, after all.'

Was it her imagination or had there been a slight tone to David's voice?

'I need to go home.'

'Have some breakfast first. I've got some bacon on. Come downstairs when you're ready.'

Ignoring the tea, Sam put her trainers on before picking up her car keys from the dresser where David had put them the night before. At the bottom of the stairs she collected her bag.

'David, I'm going.'

'I've just made you a bacon sandwich.'

'I need to go home.'

'I'm sure Neil will be fine about last night.'

Sam glared at him. 'Haven't you got any trousers you can put on?'

She saw his face fall.

'The scars are ugly, aren't they? I'll put my jeans on.'

She reached for his arm. 'I didn't mean . . .'

'It's okay. You don't want to be reminded of the accident. I understand. If I were you, I wouldn't want to be reminded of it either.'

There it was again, that tone.

'David . . .'

'Your breakfast is on the table.'

With a sigh, Sam put her bag down by the door. If she was already in trouble with Neil a few more minutes wouldn't make any difference.

'Good?' David asked when he returned.

She wasn't sure if he was referring to the bacon sandwich or the fact he'd put his jeans on but she nodded.

'No brown sauce,' David said. 'Not quite as good without it.'

'I wouldn't say that.' Sam licked her fingers catching the dribbles of melted butter. She saw the look David gave her, the naked longing in his eyes. Standing, she quickly washed her hands in the sink. 'I need to go home and face the music. I really don't know what happened last night. I've never felt so tired.'

'It's the country air and the hard work. It's a lethal combination.'

She nodded and dried her hands on a tea towel. 'Still, we got a lot done which is just as well as I probably can't make it back until Thursday.'

'Sam . . .'

She turned to face him.

'Thanks for everything you've done. Everyone should have an angel like you. I'm glad you're mine.'

Chapter Thirty-Four

'There's a gaming exhibition in London in August. I really want to go. Dad is bound to be too busy but you'll come with me, won't you, Mum? Mum?'

'I should think so,' Sam said. She gave her son a smile. 'Not sure you can cram any more computer kit into your bedroom though.'

Josh grinned. 'I'll have to put in a planning application to convert the attic.'

Knowing Josh he was probably only half joking, Sam thought as she waited for the dental receptionist to finish dealing with another client.

'Mrs Davenport and Josh.' The receptionist gave them both a bright smile before consulting her computer screen. 'So Josh's check-up went well.'

Sam ruffled her son's hair. He promptly ducked to one side.

'We'll see Josh again in six months' time.'

The receptionist gave Sam the date and she tapped it into her phone.

'Thank you.'

On exiting the air-conditioned office, the summer heat hit them both like a wall.

'Sam? I thought that was you.'

Sam's heart heaved. David. With a fleeting smile, she pushed Josh ahead of her. 'Lovely to see you again, David. Must dash.'

She saw the flash of annoyance on David's face. It was a shoddy way to treat a friend but she'd become adept at keeping the two sides of her life apart and wanted to keep it that way. She gave him a pleading look.

'Och it's too hot to be rushing around, Sam.'

She watched as his gaze settled on Josh.

'This must be Josh. Hello, young man. I've heard a lot about you. How are you?'

'I'm fine.' Josh glanced up at Sam.

Caught, Sam knew she had no option but to offer up an introduction but before she could speak David got in first.

'I'm David. Your mum's helping me to do up my holiday cottage. She's a fine designer.'

'Yes, she is.'

'Well, like I said, we really must be going,' Sam said. Gripping Josh's shoulders she propelled him forwards.

'Can I ask you a quick question before you go?'

Reluctantly, Sam nodded.

'I need to get a website sorted for the cottage, something that showcases the property and can handle the bookings. I was looking at your website. I really like the design. It's got a great layout. Can you tell me which designer you used? I'd like to hire them to do mine.'

'I did Mum and Connor's website,' Josh said.

'Really? Any chance I could hire you, young man?'

'Josh only does it as a hobby,' Sam interjected.

'I could do you a simple site for a few hundred pounds. If you want something like Mum and Connor's it will be a bit more.'

Sam stared at Josh. 'I think this is something we need to talk about, darling.'

'I'd be happy to pay you the going rate, Josh. I really like your work.'

'Please, Mum.'

'The school holidays are just around the corner so it wouldn't interfere with Josh's schoolwork. What do you say, Sam?' David asked.

'Go on, Mum. I'll do a good job,' Josh urged.

Livid with David but feeling as though she had no choice, Sam nodded. 'Okay.'

'Does Mum already have your email address?'

'She does.'

'Cool. I'll email you my rates. If you let me have a more detailed brief about what you are after I can mock up a few sample pages for you to have a look at.'

'Great stuff. Thanks, Josh. Nice to see you again, Sam.'

'Go ahead to the car, Josh. I'll catch you up.' Sam watched Josh amble off. 'What the hell was that about?' she demanded when Josh was out of earshot.

'I need a website.'

'And you just have to have my son design it for you?'

'I didn't know Josh did yours. How could I? Anyway, he's said yes now. You can't disappoint him.'

He looked infuriatingly pleased with himself.

'How did you know we'd be here?'

'I didn't. I'm just out getting some shopping.' He raised the carrier bag in his hand and smiled. 'Honestly, Sam, you make it sound like I ambushed you.'

Because that's exactly what it felt like, she thought as she walked away.

*

Two days later Josh Davenport was standing on the threshold of David's flat hugging a box file. 'Mr McAllister.'

'Call me David. Thanks for coming over. I thought it would be easier to chat about the website face-to-face.'

Josh nodded.

'Can I get you a drink?'

'I'll have a Coke if you've got one.'

'Sure. I'll join you.'

Josh looked ill at ease stood in the middle of the open-plan living room, and David guessed he found it easier dealing with people via a keyboard rather than face-to-face. Tall and skinny, Josh had his father's hair but Sam's stunning blue eyes. David watched as the boy threw back his fringe with a nervous flick of his head.

It had been a bit underhand of him to use Josh to inveigle his way further into Sam's life but it had been an opportunity to good to pass up he'd thought. Besides, if he and Sam were going to be together he needed to get to know her children, make friends with them.

As soon as he'd spotted Josh's dentist's appointment in Sam's phone the idea had begun to form in his mind. Having already studied Sam's website, he'd guessed JD Designs was Josh, particularly as he'd been unable to find any trace of the company elsewhere on the internet. The fact that Josh was a great designer was an added bonus.

David handed Josh his Coke. 'The computer's through here,' he said. 'Like I said in my email I need a site that looks fresh and is easy to use. I've got some fantastic photos of the interiors of the cottage, all your mum's hard work.'

Josh smiled.

'I want to show them off and I want a booking form that's nice and simple.' David opened the door of the spare bedroom which doubled as his office. 'Take a seat.'

Josh opened up the box folder and drew out a sheaf of papers and a portable hard drive. 'Give me a few minutes to load up the samples and then we can go through them. You can tell me what you like and what you don't like.'

'Righto. Give me a shout when you're ready.'

'Cool computer,' Josh called over his shoulder.

David smiled. 'Thanks.'

It took them forty minutes to work through the samples and pin down a look that David was happy with.

'I should be able to build the site for you before we go to Sardinia.'

'When is that? Sam did tell me but I've forgotten.'

'Third week of August.'

'Are you looking forward to it?'

Josh shrugged. 'Depends what the Wi-Fi's like.'

'Still it'll be nice to spend some time with your dad won't it?' David fished. 'Sam has told me how hard he works.' He saw the frown on Josh's face.

'Not sure if Dad will be coming yet.'

'Because of work?'

Josh nodded.

'That's too bad. You wouldn't get me passing up a holiday in Sardinia.'

Josh smiled. 'You've got a lot of computer games.' He motioned to the shelves above the desk.

'Bit of a games freak,' David admitted. 'Helps me relax. You?'

Josh swung back and forth on the chair, the Coke cradled in his lap. 'I design games,' he said nonchalantly. 'There's a company in London that like my stuff. When I leave school, I'm going there for a try-out. Are you going to the exhibition in London next month?'

'As a matter of fact, I am.'

'Cool. Mum and I are going. We might see you there.'

'Perhaps we could all go together?'

Josh continued to swing the chair back and forth. 'You and Mum have been emailing one another.'

'Aye. We've been working together on my cottage.'

Nothing in the emails suggested anything more than a professional relationship. Sam had been very careful about that despite his best intentions to subtly lead her astray.

'You've got photos of her on your computer. Lots of them.'

Damn! He should have moved those onto a flash drive.

'We're friends.'

Josh tapped his fingers against the desk. 'Like Dad was friends with that woman in the office? We're not supposed to know about her but we do.'

David hesitated. 'No, not like that. Just friends.'

Although, if I had my way, we would be more than that and what would that do to you? David mused with a sudden pang of guilt. It was one thing to dream about taking things further with Sam, quite another to hurt her children in the process. Could he live with himself if that happened?

Josh flicked his fringe back. 'Are you friends with my dad?'

'No, I don't know your dad.'

'He's going to be the senior partner in his firm.'

'That's nice.'

'Cass thinks they might split up again.'

Again?

'Has Mum said anything to you?'

'No.' David couldn't help himself. 'Why does Cass think that?'

'Back when things were bad last year we'd go and sit at the top of the stairs and listen to them shouting. They were shouting again the other night. Mum doesn't like how many hours Dad's spending at the office. Cass thinks they'll get divorced. She says they only got back

260

together because of us and we're not enough to keep them together.'

'When did they split up?'

'Beginning of the year.'

David was stunned. Sam had been separated when she'd come to see him?

'And when did they get back together?'

'May.'

If the marriage was in trouble, he stood a very real chance of making something happen. Realising the boy was watching him, David tried to kill his growing sense of excitement.

'It's difficult when your parents row, isn't it?'

Josh nodded.

'Mine used to, sometimes.'

'Do they still?'

'No, they died in a coach crash. Do you want to see a picture of them?'

Josh nodded. He followed David into the living room and from the bookcase David took down the picture of his parents.

'What did they row about?' Josh asked.

'My dad liked a drink. My mum hated it when he'd come home drunk.'

'Did you win all these trophies?' Josh's eyes widened.

'Aye.' David swapped the picture of his parents for the boys' football team. 'That's me, in the middle at the front, with my foot on the ball. I was a striker.'

'You must have been good to win all those trophies,' Josh said in awe.

'Not bad. Do you play?'

Josh shook his head. 'I'm hopeless. Everyone laughs at me.'

'I'm sure that's not true.'

Josh thrust the photograph back into David's hands. 'What do you know?'

The boy's vehemence took David by surprise. 'You cannae be good at everything,' David said quickly. 'I bet the kids in your class aren't as good with computers.'

'I wish I could leave school now.' Josh traced his finger along the books. 'I hate school.'

'They give you a hard time?'

Josh shrugged.

'Anyone in particular?' David asked, his eyes narrowing.

Another shrug.

'Do you still play football?' Josh asked.

'No.'

'Why not?'

'I had an accident.'

'What happened?'

'I was riding my motorbike and I got knocked off it.'

'My mum had an accident in January. She hit a man on a bike.' Josh paused, meeting his gaze. 'Was that you?'

David thought about lying but guessed the boy would be astute enough to see through it. 'Yes.'

'She didn't mean to do it.'

'I know.'

'She cried for days after it happened. Mum and Dad rowed then as well.'

'Sometimes it's hard for grownups to get along.'

Josh flicked his fringe. 'Is that why Mum doesn't want Dad to know I'm working on your website?'

'I guess so.'

Josh nodded. 'I need someone to help me try out the prototypes of my games. I usually get Cass to do it but she's in a band with her boyfriend now so she never has time. Would you like to do it instead?'

David smiled. 'I'd be honoured.'

Josh looked around the room as if seeing it for the first time. 'Nice place.'

'Thanks.'

'Is that the latest iPhone?'

'Aye.'

'Can I see?'

'Be my guest.' David watched the boy seize the iPhone with glee.

'I only ever get Mum and Dad's cast offs.'

'Would you like it?'

'Are you serious?'

'Sure.' David hoped it would go some way to assuaging his guilt.

'Instead of payment?' Josh asked hesitantly.

David smiled. 'As well as. Think of it as a bonus.'

'Cool,' Josh said with such enthusiasm that David smiled.

Chapter Thirty-Five

The Queen's Head pub lay between Stebbingsford and Abbeyleigh. It had seemed to Sam the perfect venue for lunch with David. The fact that it kept them away from prying eyes was an added bonus. She'd texted David the day before to suggest it.

R U free for lunch tomorrow? Queen's Head at one?
Great idea. Can't wait.

Now, as Sam parked she took a moment to check her appearance in the vanity mirror. Tired of the shorts and tee shirts which had become her uniform as she had worked on Daphne Mitchell's bedrooms these past few weeks, she'd changed into a floaty summer dress.

Despite her anger at David over using Josh for his website, Sam had barely been able to get him out of her mind lately. Neil was pushing himself harder than ever at work, a final effort for the promotion that was to be announced in August. It was a vicious circle. The less she saw of Neil, the more she thought about David.

And the firm's summer barbecue the previous weekend had hardly helped the situation. Megan had been there in a low cut dress that had left little to the imagination. And she and her impressive cleavage had followed Neil around wherever he went.

'What was I supposed to do?' Neil had asked angrily when they'd got home. 'She's a young girl with a crush. She's not a threat to you.'

'Do you ever think about what you did with her?'

'No.'

'Do you compare us. Me and her?'

'Sam. Stop it!'

He'd taken her in his arms then and tried to kiss her but she'd turned away, pictures of him and Megan circling in her mind. She hated the woman she was when she felt like this, the woman his infidelity had made her: frightened and shrill and unforgiving.

It was all because of the shirts. His bloody shirts. Without them she would never have known. But she did know, however hard she tried to make herself forget.

It had started up again last month. She wasn't sure exactly when but as she'd pulled his shirt from the laundry basket she had smelt the unmistakable smell of Megan's perfume. It was a scent she would never forget: roses and jasmine. She had smelt it several times since then. And each time the little girl inside the woman, the one who had cried at the sound of her father shutting the garden gate, had cried again.

Unable to bear the alternative, she had decided to follow Daphne Mitchell's fishing analogy and feed out the line, giving Neil his freedom, hoping he would come back to her.

Sam looked at her reflection in the car's vanity mirror. They said it happened to all women eventually. She'd turned into her mother. She snapped the vanity mirror back into place.

As she entered the pub garden, David rose, pushing his sunglasses into his hair as she approached. The sight of him, lean and handsome, smiling affectionately, warmed her aching heart.

'Hi.'

'Hello. Happy birthday.'

He looked surprised. 'You remembered.'

'Of course.'

A young girl came to take their order.

It was a beautiful day with the heat shimmering across the open fields that surrounded the pub. Apart from a man in a suit, his head buried in a newspaper, they were alone.

Sam took a card and a package from her bag. 'These are for you.'

David looked embarrassed. 'You shouldn't have.'

'Open them.' She encouraged.

She'd chosen the card carefully. It depicted a scene of the Highlands of Scotland.

'Great card.' He grinned.

Sam smiled. The girl returned with their order. David waited until she'd gone before he opened his present.

'I don't know what to say.'

'Say you like it.'

'Like it? I love it.'

'I know you were missing riding your bike. I thought this might help.'

'It's brilliant.'

'Apparently, they take you round the track in various souped-up cars and then there's a chance for you to go round on your own. Be careful though, please. I don't want any accidents,' she begged.

'Thanks, Sam.' He got up and kissed her cheek.

'I'm glad you like it.'

Her heart fluttered as he settled beside her on the bench rather than returning to the opposite side of the table. She watched him pull his plate of chips towards him and add salt and ketchup.

'Do you know when you'll be able to ride your bike again?' She saw him frown. 'I'm sorry, have I said something wrong?'

'The truth is, I could ride it now if I wanted. I just don't have the nerve. The counsellor said I have to be patient with myself.'

'It's good advice.'

David smiled. 'Aye and it's easier to give advice than it is to take it.'

Sam nodded sympathetically. 'Do you still get the nightmares?'

'Yes. The doc gave me some sleeping pills. They help . . . a bit.'

'How's the counselling going?'

'Waste of time.'

'David . . .'

'They can't fix me. No one can. Except maybe you.'
He took her hand and, turning it over, stroked her palm
with his thumb. 'It's a great present.'

Sam tried to ignore the feel of his thigh pressed
against hers and the yearning to kiss him that had
suddenly seized her. She pulled her hand away.

'How's Josh?'

'Fine. He loves that iPhone but you should never
have given it to him without asking me first. Once the
website is finished, I don't want you to see him again.'

'He's perfectly safe with me.'

'I know that but there are boundaries, David. My
children can't be around you.' Sam sipped her drink.
She had been thinking about what had happened, her
mind spinning theories, anything so she didn't have to
think about Neil and how he'd got the smell of roses
and jasmine on his shirt.

She decided to test one of her theories out. To see just
how far David had gone. 'That day you were outside
the dentist's, it was no coincidence, was it? You weren't
shopping like you said you were. You knew we'd be
there.' She levelled her gaze at him.

'How could I . . .'

'You saw it in my phone, didn't you? When you
texted Neil, the night I stayed at the cottage, you
looked through my calendar, didn't you?' At least he
had the decency to look embarrassed.

'I shouldn't have looked . . .'

'No, you shouldn't.'

He grabbed her hand. 'He has so much of you and I have so little. I just wanted to look into your world, to imagine the bits I never get to see. I meant no harm.'

She shot him an angry look and pulled her hand away. 'Our life together is this. This is all I can give you.'

'I got carried away. I won't do it again. Please, Sam, don't be angry with me.' He nudged her shoulder with his. 'Come on, it's too nice a day to be angry. And it's my birthday,' he wheedled.

'What else did you look at?'

'Your calendar. A couple of photos. That's it.'

'I don't like it, David. It makes me feel uncomfortable.'

'I can see that. I'm sorry.' He stroked her leg.

She slapped him away.

David sipped his beer. 'Josh is one talented kid. You should be very proud.'

'I am.'

'Does he get on okay at school?'

'Yes. Straight-A student.'

'I meant with the other kids.'

Sam pulled a face. 'Josh doesn't mix. Never has. I'm surprised you two got on as well as you did. He normally takes ages to be comfortable with people. You must have the knack.'

'Bribery helped.'

'No, he really liked you. You should be honoured.'

David looked pleased. 'I am. He's a great kid.'

Anger thawing, Sam smiled. 'He loved your flat. It made quite an impression. He wants the same TV, the same music system, the same everything.'

'The boy clearly has taste.' David grinned. 'My flat is the pinnacle of style. I'm sure you, as an expert, would agree.'

'It's a bit boys and their toys for me,' Sam admitted. 'In my professional opinion, it's crying out for a woman's touch.'

'Aren't we all.' David responded.

Sam rolled her eyes.

'So, what would you change? About the flat?' he added. 'Because obviously I'm perfect the way I am.'

'Of course you are,' Sam replied. 'I'd make it cosier.'

'Cosier?' David pulled a face. 'I imagine that involves flowers and things that are pink,' he teased.

'Not necessarily.'

'I like my flat the way it is. That's not to say I'm against a woman's touch, mind. Far from it.' He chuckled. 'Of course, my definition may be different to yours.'

'I'm talking about lamps and cushions,' Sam said.

'Aye, what I'm talking about could involve lamps and cushions.'

'Rugs and fires,' she said, mirroring his smile.

'Oh yes! Rugs and fires are very important. Maybe we're talking about the same thing after all.'

'Atmosphere.'

'Atmosphere is crucial,' David agreed.

'And colour schemes.'

David pretended to look disappointed. 'Colour schemes don't really do it for me. Can we go back to the rugs and the fire?'

Enjoying the exchange, Sam groaned as her mobile trilled. Taking it out, she checked the screen. It was Neil. She turned the phone to silent and thrust it back into her bag. 'I'll let the voicemail pick it up,' she said.

'When's your birthday?' David asked.

'Fifteenth of June.'

'I've missed it!'

'It doesn't matter.'

'Yeah, it does. I'd have bought you a present. Maybe I still will.' He smiled.

'Best not,' Sam said and sipped her drink.

'How was the barbecue at your husband's firm?'

'Okay.'

He raised his eyebrows.

'There's a girl there with a crush on Neil. She kept following him round. Neil didn't do anything to put her off.'

'Are you sure he noticed? Men can be a bit dense when it comes to these things.'

'He noticed. You couldn't miss her in that dress.'

'You don't think there's anything going on between them, do you?'

Sam ran her finger around the edge of her wineglass. 'Yes. No. Maybe.'

'Have you asked him?'

She shook her head. She'd said too much, certainly more than she'd intended. 'Too much wine on an empty stomach,' she said. 'Ignore me.' She began to eat her lunch.

'Impossible,' David said softly. His hand strayed to her thigh.

His fingers felt hot through the cotton of her dress as he squeezed her leg and then gently began to stroke it.

'David . . .'

'No one can see.'

'Please, don't!'

Stubbornly, he continued to touch her thigh. 'What are you afraid of?' he asked.

She turned to look at him, their faces just inches apart. 'That I'll throw caution to the wind and kiss you in front of other people,' she said bluntly.

'Would that really be so bad? You could kiss my cheek. Friends do.'

'Don't tease me.'

Sam let out a cry as David's hand slid to her inner thigh. Snatching his hand, she thrust it away and moved to sit opposite him.

'You promised me,' she hissed.

'Tell me you didn't like it,' he challenged, his face hardening.

His words hung on the summer breeze.

'Do you have to go back to work this afternoon?' he asked. 'It's a lovely day. We could take a walk along the riverbank.'

Sam knew the sensible thing would be to say no. But if she were sensible she wouldn't be here in the first place. Her gaze followed his fingers as they stroked his beer glass. She looked up to find him watching her. Feeling suddenly reckless, she nodded.

They set off along the riverbank, meandering slowly to take in the view. When David reached for her hand, Sam didn't resist. It seemed perfectly natural. Fingers entwined, they walked on, his hand warm in hers.

They hardly spoke, merely pausing occasionally to look at one another and smile. Anyone seeing them would have thought . . . Sam swallowed. Anyone seeing them would have thought they were lovers.

The willow trees formed a canopy over their heads, providing a welcome respite from the heat, as the trees dipped their branches into the dark-green water of the river. It was another world. Their world.

'Look there,' David exclaimed. He pointed with their joined hands. 'Do you see the dragonflies?'

Sam watched the colourful insects bob and weave above the water. Cerulean blue and blood red. She wasn't surprised to feel David's free hand stroke her hair a moment later, she'd half expected it. He lifted her hair away from her face and kissed her cheek. Then, hooking his finger under her chin, he turned her to face him.

'My beautiful angel.'

'Stop it,' she said bashfully.

'You're an angel to me.' He nudged her lips with his own.

'David. We mustn't.'

'Why not?' he asked bluntly. 'He did, didn't he? With that woman in the office? There's no point denying it, Sam. It's written all over your face. How could he hurt you like that?' He held his hand to her cheek.

Roses and jasmine. Four shirts and counting.

Taking David's head in her hands, she pulled his mouth down onto hers. To hell with the consequences. She wanted this man. Why did she have to keep denying it?

The kiss was everything she had known it would be. Conscious that she was standing on the edge of a precipice, she ran her fingers through his hair. As he pressed himself against her she could feel his attraction for her.

'Is this really happening, Sam, because I cannae believe it. It feels like a dream.'

She smiled. 'I cannae believe it either,' she said, copying his accent.

David laughed. 'Was that supposed to be a Scottish accent?'

'It was a perfect Scottish accent,' she said, mock-aggrieved.

'Perfect? Aye if you're talking to someone who's never been to Scotland. Thank God you didn't pretend to be Scottish when you came to the hospital. They'd never have let you in. They'd have called security.'

Sam laughed. 'My accent wasn't that bad.'

'Trust me. It was. Say it again.'

'No.' Giggling, Sam ran along the towpath.

'Och, come on! It's the funniest thing I've heard in ages. Say it again,' he commanded as he chased after her. Catching her, he swept her into his arms. 'Repeat after me, my Scottish accent is rubbish.'

274

'My Scottish accent is rubbish,' she said, laughing as she did so.

'But I know a man who can teach me to do better,' David said.

Grinning, Sam repeated his words.

'You have to work on the pronunciation of your vowels,' he said, setting her down. 'It's all to do with your lips.' He kissed her lightly. 'And your tongue. The tongue is very important.' The second kiss was deeper. He bent his head to hers. 'I can't be your friend, Sam. I've tried but I cannae do it. I'm too much in love with you.'

She knew there was a line. She knew also that she was about to cross it. She had fallen for a man who wasn't her husband. Did that make her a bad person? A weak one? The damage had been done long ago, she realised. There had been an inevitability about it, possibly even from the moment he had first squeezed her hand as he'd lain bleeding on the road.

He kissed her bare shoulder, his fingers playing with the strap of her dress. Drawing out his phone he took a photo of her, then another and another.

'What are you doing?'

'I want something to remind me of today.' He pulled her into his arms, kissed her, the phone aloft beside them.

'Stop it!'

'I just want a little piece of you to hold on to when you go back to him.'

She reached for the phone. 'Delete them.'

'What?'

'I said delete them.'

'Sam.'

'Give me the phone.'

'No!'

'Delete them, David.'

'Okay, calm down.' He fiddled with his phone. 'There. Deleted.'

'All of them?'

'Aye.' He thrust the phone away. 'We shouldn't have to hide, Angel.'

'I'm married.'

'To a man who doesn't appreciate you. To a man who asked you to lie for him, not caring what the consequences would be.' David took her face in his hands, forcing her to look at him. 'I'd never do that. I'd never cheat on you, either. I love you. If I gave you my promise to be faithful, it would be a promise I'd keep. Men like him don't change, Sam. He cheated once. He'll do it again. Maybe he never stopped.'

Roses and jasmine.

David's fingers were gentle against her collar bone. 'Why wait for him to hurt you again? Why not leave? I know how it feels to be betrayed. You had every right to believe your husband would keep his vows. You had no warning the first time. You have now. Act on it! Leave him.'

Sam twisted away. 'You're asking me to split up my family.'

'I'll take care of you and the children. I need you, Sam. Much more than he does. I've never felt like this about anyone before. The accident was fate bringing us together. Can't you see that? This was meant to be.'

She made herself concentrate on the dusty towpath. Anything to buy herself time. Time to make a decision that could change all their lives forever. The silence lengthened. She took a step forward, nudging his shoulder as she passed. He reached for her hand but Sam linked her hands in front of her. 'Someone might see.'

He arched his eyebrows. 'The dragonflies?' he mused but he didn't press her, content to walk along beside her.

They arrived at Lower Leigh, the air taut between them. Although she was anxious at what would happen next, Sam didn't want the afternoon to end. The towpath in the dappled sunlight had been a magical place. A place for lovers. The word burned in Sam's brain. She wanted to be David's lover.

She sneaked a look at him. He seemed content but as he walked she saw him wince. His limp was more pronounced now. It had been a long walk. How could she have been so thoughtless? 'I'll ring for a cab to take us back.'

'That'd be good.'

Her mobile informed her, accusingly, that she had four missed calls. All of them from Neil. Sam rang for the taxi and then put the phone away. She didn't want to think about Neil right now.

Soon they were back at The Queen's Head. The late afternoon sunshine was gentle now, throwing lengthening shadows across the car park.

They lingered between their cars. 'I don't want to say goodbye,' David admitted.

'Me neither,' Sam said.

David's hand was hot on her arm. 'Come back to mine.'

Torn, she closed her eyes.

'Are you really going to let him keep making a fool out of you? You're worth so much more than that, Sam.'

Weak at David's touch, Sam could think of nothing else other than to pull him into her arms.

They drove as if possessed back to the Old Mill, he leading the way in his car, she following on behind. When they parked, he held out his hand to her and Sam gripped it tightly. In the lift, they seized one another, the months of denial heightening their passion.

Once at the flat, Sam laughed as David fumbled his key to the floor. Then, finally, they were inside.

'You were telling me I needed a woman's touch in here.'

'Yes.'

'You were right. I do.'

Sam felt the breath slam out of her body as he grabbed her to him. Tongues entwined, Sam struggled with the buttons of his shirt. Halfway down, she abandoned the task, ripping the material. The buttons bounced off the wooden floor.

Roses and jasmine. Four shirts and counting.

'Sam.'

Her name was a cry of longing and as he kissed her lips his hands were on her back, seeking her zip. Impatient to have him touch her, she wanted to knock his hands away and unzip herself but when she tried to move she found she was locked tight in his embrace.

At last, he found the zip. Standing back, he pushed the delicate material off her shoulders and smiled at her as it fell in a swirling, colourful cascade to her feet. Taking her hands in his, he helped her to step out of it and then bent his head to kiss her neck, her throat, the rise of her breasts still encased in white lace and she held him there, her fingers tightening in his hair, the way he'd held her on the riverbank, gasping with longing as his hot lips journeyed over her skin.

Holding fast to her hand, David led her towards the bedroom.

They both jumped as the buzzer sounded.

'They'll go away,' David said, his mouth on hers once more.

The buzzer went again, longer, more insistent.

He continued to kiss her. Sam wrapped her arms round his neck.

At last, the buzzer stopped and Sam realised she had been holding herself tense while the intrusion lasted. Relaxing now, she stroked David's cheek.

'See,' David grinned. 'I told you they'd go away.' He was just reaching for her bra strap when the telephone began to ring. 'Bloody hell! Ignore it. The answer machine will pick it up.'

As he spoke so, too, did the machine: 'Hello, I'm either out or screening my calls. Either way, you'll have to leave a message. Here comes the tone.'

Sam chuckled into his shoulder.

'Sam.' It was Connor. 'I know you're in there because I'm standing beside your car. Sam, pick up. Please. Josh has been mugged. He's at the hospital.'

Chapter Thirty-Six

Sam and Connor drove to the hospital in Sam's car with Connor at the wheel. They journeyed in a silence that hung heavy between them, Sam's face burning with shame.

'What's going on with you, Sam?' Connor asked at last.

'I wish I knew.' She stared out of the window. 'When I'm with him, I seem to lose all my bearings.'

'I thought you and Neil were happy now. That you were putting everything behind you.'

'So did I until I smelt her perfume on his shirts. He's practically living at the office, doing crazy hours. She's not even in his department any more so it's not like they have a reason to be together unless . . .'

'Have you asked him?'

She shook her head. 'I didn't want to. The kids were so happy when he came home and so was I. I figured if I tried to ignore it, he'd get over her but it's so hard to do that. I don't know how my mother managed it all those years.'

'And David?'

'I wanted to break a few rules of my own, to know what it was like to do more than look and wonder. Now I do.'

Pulling into the car park, Connor turned to her. 'I'll say you were with a client.'

'Thank you.'

To her horror, Sam found that Josh had been admitted four hours earlier, while she had been enjoying lunch with David.

Pale, with a bandage round his head and another round his right hand, a swollen lower lip and a cut to his right cheek, Josh was sitting up in bed when Sam got there. Neil was beside him in a chair.

'Mum!'

'Darling!' Overcome, Sam stroked Josh's hair whilst gripping his good hand. When her tears subsided, she searched in her bag for a tissue. With a sigh, Neil shook out a handkerchief and passed it to her. It could have been a tender moment, an echo of how they'd first met but, when she looked into Neil's eyes, Sam found they were ice cold.

'Where were you?' he spat.

'With a client.'

'Why didn't you answer any of the phones? Your mobiles, *both* of them? God knows, I've been calling them all.'

'I'm sorry.'

'You're *sorry*?'

'Can we do this later? I want to know what happened.'

'Some boys jumped me,' Josh said quietly. 'They took my iPhone, Mum.' Josh's face crumpled.

'You should never have bought the damn thing for him,' Neil said accusingly, staring at Sam.

Sam and Josh exchanged guilty looks.

'I won't be able to go to the gaming exhibition now, will I?'

'I'll take you to the next one,' Neil said tightly. 'Would you like another drink?' he asked, his tone softening.

Josh nodded.

Sam watched Neil take a plastic cup, fill it with orange juice and pop in a straw. Then, he held the cup, one hand to the back of Josh's head, supporting him tenderly while he drank. Sam's lip quivered at the sight of them.

There was blood on the front of Neil's shirt and on his sleeves, Sam noticed. Josh's blood. No doubt from where Neil had cradled their son's head against his chest. Thank God he had been there to hold him like that. Sam felt a rush of love for her husband.

'Had enough?' Neil asked gently.

Josh nodded.

Neil put the cup on the cabinet. 'Why don't you let me tell your mum what happened, okay?'

Taking Sam firmly by the elbow, Neil guided her into the corridor, his fingers biting into her skin.

'You're hurting me,' Sam gasped as he swept her along.

'Good!'

'Neil, please!'

When they reached the corridor, he let her go with as much force as he'd used to propel her along. Sam ricocheted off the windowsill, drawing stares from a passing orderly.

'Where the hell were you?' Neil demanded, his face darkening with anger.

'With a client, I told you.'

'And you just decided not to answer when I rang?'

'My bag must have been in the other room and I . . .'

'Don't give me that!' Neil raged, slamming his hand against the wall beside her head. Sam cried out. 'Every time I rang I had to go outside because I couldn't get a signal. Every time I was away from Josh for at least ten minutes. When my son needed me most,' Neil thundered. 'He was crying for you and what could I tell him? Mum's on her way.'

Distraught, Sam began to cry. 'Please, Neil, just tell me how he is.'

Neil leaned against the windowsill. 'A group of boys knocked him down and kicked him while he was on the ground.'

Sam gasped, gripping her stomach, feeling sick. She sank onto the windowsill beside Neil.

'He wouldn't let go of that bloody iPhone so they stamped on his fingers.'

'Dear God,' Sam whimpered.

'I wish you'd never bought the fucking thing for him.'

Sam had explained it away as an impulse buy. Now she wished she'd never let Josh accept it from David.

'We're not sure how, but he took a blow to the head. He had some blurred vision when he first got here but that seems to have settled now. Poor lad has mild concussion. They could have split his skull.'

'Don't!'

'His fingers are badly swollen. The doctors want to keep him in to check on the head injury.'

'I want to see the doctor,' Sam said.

'Why? I've just told you everything,' Neil said.

'I want to hear it from him.'

'It's a bit late to start playing the concerned parent now, isn't it?' Neil stood, arms folded as he looked down at her disdainfully.

'That's not fair,' Sam said.

'Watching my son sob his heart out for his mother wasn't fair.'

'I'm sorry.' Sam went to lay her hand on Neil's shoulder but he flinched under her touch and moved away. 'The boys who did this, did anyone see them?'

'They came at Josh from behind. A woman walking with her kids in the park saw it. The boys ran off when she got close. The police have taken a statement. Josh has had some trouble with a group at school. They've been bullying him. Taking cash from him. It's possibly the same group who attacked him but if no one can make a positive ID, it'll be hard to prove.'

'Bullied?'

'Since February,' Neil said coolly.

'And we didn't see it? How could we not see it?'

Neil leaned over her, his hands either side of her. Sam could smell the sweat on him, could see the dark pools under his arms, could imagine the fear and the panic and the anger that had put them there. 'Josh has always been a mummy's boy. If anyone was going to spot what was going on, it should have been you.'

'You bastard.'

He raised his eyebrows. 'I was here within ten minutes of the call. Where were you?' he demanded, sullenly.

Sam pushed by him. 'I'm going to see my son.'

Chapter Thirty-Seven

That night, Sam lay staring up at the voile canopy above her bed. The room was bright with moonlight. It was two o'clock and she was alone with her guilt as a cavalcade of images processed through her mind.

She had replayed the scene in the pub garden so many times she knew it by heart but always she hoped the ending would be different. Her mobile ringing, seeing Neil's name on the display, deciding to ignore it. Why had she done that?

It had been his first call. The crucial call to tell her about Josh. If she had taken that call she could have been at the hospital within twenty minutes instead of which it had been hours later. There had been other unknown numbers lined up accusingly next to Neil's battery of missed calls which she now knew were the hospital and the police also trying to reach her.

The tears fell horizontally across her cheekbones as she tortured herself with the timeline. They would still have been at the pub when Neil must have arrived, scared and alone, at the hospital. By the time Josh was rushed into X-ray, she and David would have been walking, hand in hand, along the riverbank. As the consultant had been talking in grave tones to Neil about the possibility of concussion, she and David would have been kissing and by the time Josh was transferred to a ward, she would have been in David's flat, undressing for him.

Her tears became sobs. Animal sounds rising out of her from some deep, primeval place. She held Josh's pyjama top up to her face until her volcanic misery subsided.

Then, throwing back the quilt, she stood, pausing to stare at her reflection in the dressing table mirror. Her nightshirt, one of Neil's old shirts, was familiar. The face above it was not. She was a stranger to herself, this woman who had put her desire for another man ahead of her own family.

She'd lost her mind. It was the only explanation. She had become so besotted with David that all reason had left her. She padded downstairs, intending to get a glass of water and found Neil, hunched over the kitchen table, a mug of tea untouched in front of him.

'Sweetheart?' she said hesitantly, unsure of his mood.

They'd barely exchanged a word all evening, he still seething with anger at her. When she'd gone to bed, she'd left him in the study surrounded by files.

'Have you slept at all?' she asked gently.

'I crashed out on the sofa for a bit.'

Was he so angry he couldn't even bring himself to lie down beside her?

'Couldn't sleep, though. Every time I closed my eyes all I could see was Josh and how he was when I first got to the hospital. You have no idea,' he said, his voice bitter and strained as he looked at her. 'They had him all cleaned up by the time you got there but when I saw him there was blood everywhere. It was all over his face, it was in his hair, it was even in his ears.' Neil rubbed his eyes with the palms of his hands.

'Oh God! Neil.' Sam brought Josh's crumpled pyjama top up to her mouth.

'I just stood there, in Casualty, shaking, and do you know what was going through my head? That stupid bloody nursery rhyme. Humpty Dumpty. Josh was such a mess, you see. I couldn't understand how anyone could ever put him back together again. I thought our beautiful boy was gone for good.'

Sobbing, Sam wrapped her arms round Neil's shoulders and laid her head against his. 'I'm so sorry,' Sam said, stroking his face. 'I'd give anything to go back, to change what happened, for you not to have been at the hospital alone.' They stared into one another's tear-filled eyes. 'Will you ever forgive me?'

Turning, he drew her down and on to his lap. 'How could I not?' he asked softly. 'You and the children are the most important people in the world to me,' he said as he clung to her.

And you to me, Sam thought, wondering how she could ever have forgotten that, even for a moment.

Chapter Thirty-Eight

David tapped the steering wheel in time to the track on the radio, his gaze fixed on the entrance to Abbeyleigh General. He should have been at home catching up on paperwork or at the cottage clearing the garden. But the paperwork was still untouched on his desk and the garden could wait for another day. There was nowhere else he could be right now other than at the hospital. The one place in the world he'd thought he would never want to see again.

Try as he might, he couldn't get Sam's face out of his head. As Connor's voice had risen, spectre-like, from the answer machine, Sam had looked as though someone had poured ice down her spine.

She'd left him in a matter of minutes, grabbing clothes and fighting her way back into them, all fingers and thumbs from the shock. He'd tried to help by zipping her up but she'd knocked his hand away with so much force his skin had stung from the blow.

As he'd watched her hunt for her shoes, discarded on their passionate journey through the living room, he'd wondered if he would ever hold her like that again. Already, it was a distant memory and the signs weren't good. He thought of their rushed call that morning.

'It's the first chance I've had to ring.'

'Sam? I've been so worried. How is he?'

'They knocked him over. They kicked my baby while he was on the ground.'

'Bastards! How badly is he hurt?'

'Concussion. He wouldn't let go of that iPhone you gave him so they stamped on his hand. He's been bullied for months, David and I didn't know.'

'This isn't your fault.'

She'd made a sound like a sob.

'Have they kept him in?'

'For observation because of the head injury. Although we're hoping we can bring him home tomorrow.'

'How was Neil when you got there?'

'How do you think?' Sam's tone had hit him like a blow to the stomach. 'I'd been ignoring his calls all afternoon. I don't think he'll ever forgive me. I'm not sure I'll forgive myself.'

'Sam . . .'

'Don't say anything, David. There's nothing you *can* say. I've got to go, Neil's coming.'

'Sam, wait! Can I visit Josh this morning?'

'No, we're going.'

'After, then. Sam, please.'

'No.'

So, here he was, ignoring Sam's wishes, willing to take any opportunity to sneak a few minutes with her boy because Sam wasn't the only one feeling guilty. It was bad enough he'd urged Sam to leave Neil, even though that would cause Josh pain, but he'd suspected Josh was having trouble at school. Why hadn't he pushed the point with Sam? Too busy trying to figure out how to kiss her, he thought, ashamed of himself.

It was twenty minutes later when he saw Sam and Neil leave the hospital. They exchanged a few words before Neil set off on foot and Sam got into her car.

As he watched her drive out of the car park, David picked up the package from the passenger seat of his car and headed towards the foyer.

Taking a leaf from Sam's book, he went up to the reception desk. 'Hello. Can you tell me where I can find Josh Davenport? I'm his brother,' he said, adopting an English accent.

A few minutes later, David was standing in front of Josh's bed. The boy was dozing. His face was a mess, his head and right hand heavily bandaged. No wonder Sam was in such a state. Anger took hold as David thought about the boys who had done this. Anger at them and at himself. *I should have made him tell me what was going on. Maybe then I could have . . .*

'David!'

The obvious delight on Josh's face at the sight of him brought a lump to David's throat. He drew up a chair. 'Hello, Josh.'

'They took the iPhone, I'm sorry.' Tears swamped Josh's eyes and it was as much as David could do not to join him.

'You've got nothing to be sorry for,' he said. 'You just have to concentrate on getting well, young man.' He took Josh's good hand in his. 'Listen, mate, your mum doesn't know I'm here. Can we keep it that way?'

Josh nodded.

'You should have told me about the bullying,' David said quietly.

Josh's gaze dropped. 'I wanted to. I didn't know how.'

David's grip on Josh's hand tightened.

'Mum and Dad are angry.'

'Not with you.'

'But I caused it.'

'You didn't,' David said firmly. 'None of this is your fault.' Remembering the package, David retrieved it. 'I bought you a present.' He watched the joy flood into Josh's face as he drew out the new iPhone. 'I picked it up for you this morning.' David tapped Josh's thigh through the bedclothes. 'You've got to promise me if anyone gives you any trouble from now on you'll tell someone. Me, your mum. Someone.'

'I will. I promise. Thank you. It's brilliant.'

Beaming, David ruffled Josh's hair. 'You're welcome, Josh—'

'Who the hell are you?'

David turned to find Neil standing at the end of the bed. Realising he still had his hand resting on Josh's thigh David slowly withdrew it. Neil's stony gaze followed.

'Dad! What are you doing back so soon?'

'I left my phone on the cabinet.' Neil looked from David to Josh and raised his eyebrows.

'This is David.'

'What have you got there?'

'A new iPhone.'

'I should be going,' David said. 'Remember what I said, Josh, concentrate on getting better. That's all that matters.'

'Wait a minute. Who are you? How do you know my son?'

David's brain scrambled as he searched for a suitable response.

'David's my friend.'

Both men looked at Josh.

'Your *friend*? How did you meet?'

Josh glanced at David. 'I offered to make a website for his business,' Josh said proudly. 'I met with him, just like you meet with your clients, and took all the details. David was really pleased with it, weren't you?'

'Very pleased.'

'Where did this meeting take place?'

David shut his eyes, knowing what was coming next.

'At David's flat in the Old Mill. He's got ever such a cool flat.'

'I bet,' Neil said sarcastically.

'I really should be going. Take care, Josh.'

David was halfway along the corridor when a hand on his shoulder spun him round. The punch connected with his chin and sent him sprawling before he had a chance to react. Neil stood over him, glowering. In his hand was the iPhone David had just given Josh. He let it fall onto David's chest.

'What the . . .' David began, his hand to his chin.

'My son doesn't want your present.'

'It was to make up for the one he lost.' David scrambled to his feet.

'Yeah? If my son wants another gadget, I'll buy it for him. I've heard about your sort.'

'My sort?'

'Don't think I buy that bullshit about the website. I saw the shifty look that passed between you. You met over the Internet, didn't you? One of those disgusting chat rooms. You've been grooming my son, haven't you?'

'Don't be ridiculous.'

'You had your filthy hands all over him, you bastard.' Neil ran David back against the wall. 'I saw you, don't deny it, touching him up through the bedclothes.'

'I . . .'

Neil stabbed his finger into David's chest. 'Paedophiles, like you, should be castrated and then hung. I'm going to report this to the police but if I find you sniffing around my son again, it won't be the police you'll have to worry about. Do I make myself clear?'

'Crystal.'

Chapter Thirty-Nine

Sam opened her diary and scribbled a few quick entries, the telephone cradled against her ear. 'That's great, Daphne. Thank you for being so understanding. I really do appreciate it. Bye.'

She looked up to find Neil leaning against the kitchen doorjamb.

'What are you up to?' he asked.

'I've been making some calls. I've managed to clear my diary through to our holiday in Sardinia so that I can stay home and look after Josh.'

'You'll be able to stay with him the whole time?' Neil queried.

'Yes.'

Neil pinched the bridge of his nose. 'You don't know how glad I am to hear you say that. I was going to speak to you about cobbling together some kind of rota, you, me and Cass.'

'No need.'

Neil squeezed her shoulder. 'Thanks, Sam. It's such a relief to know you'll be with him.'

'I can't wait to bring him home.'

'Me neither,' Neil agreed.

'I've been thinking, Neil. I don't want him to go back to that school in September. Can't we send him to St Luke's instead.'

Neil looked alarmed. 'A private school? How much will that cost?'

'Does it matter?'

'It's not something we've budgeted for, Sam.'

'We can start budgeting for it and in the meantime we can pay the first term's fees out of our savings. The money's there for an emergency. What's this if not an emergency?'

Neil pushed his hands through his hair. 'I'd rather not touch the savings. You can't get an account on those sort of terms any more. If we make a big withdrawal they'll downgrade us. Why don't I take out a short-term loan instead to tide us over?'

'If you want. We're agreed then, he can go to St Luke's in September?'

Neil nodded. 'What about Cass?'

'Cass loves it at Abbeyleigh High. All her friends are there and she'll be taking her exams next year. I don't think there's any need to move Cass.'

'Okay.'

Sam watched Neil glance over his shoulder before shutting the door.

'There's something I need to talk to you about.' He pushed her papers back across the kitchen table and leaned against it. 'I had to go back to the hospital this morning after we visited Josh because I'd left my phone behind. When I got there, there was a man with Josh. As I walked down the ward, I saw him . . .' Neil grimaced.

'What?'

'Touch Josh up.'

'*What?*'

'Would you keep your voice down. I don't want Cass to hear.'

'Who was he?' Sam asked, struggling to moderate her tone.

'Josh said he was a friend. I think he was a paedophile.'

Sam's eyes widened in horror. 'Dear God! You're not serious?'

'Face it, Sam. Neither of us knows what Josh gets up to in that bedroom. The Internet is awash with chat rooms full of dirty old men pretending to be kids. He's so naïve. This guy probably pretended to be the same age as Josh and then lured him into a meeting. Grooming, that's what they call it. Our son was being groomed, I'm sure of it.' Neil pushed his hands through his hair. 'It scared me. I don't mind admitting it. What would have happened if I hadn't turned up? Do these people have no shame?'

'We've got to get him out of the hospital.' Sam stood.

Neil pressed her back down. 'It's okay. I've made it plain that no one is to visit Josh unless you or I are there and I've given a statement to the police.'

Sam's mind raced. Was it more than just bullying she'd been blind to?

'Poor kid's been through so much. I just want to keep him safe until we go to Sardinia and then, when we're back, look after him until he can start at his new school in September.'

'How do we keep him safe from someone like that?'

'By not leaving him on his own for a while, by talking to him about the dangers. I think I scared the man off but we can't take any chances.'

'What did you say to him?'

'I punched him in the mouth,' Neil said, a trace of pride in his voice. 'And I told him I knew what he was and what he was trying to do and that I'd report him to the police. He ran off when I said that. They're checking the CCTV at the hospital, said they'd be in touch.'

Sam watched Neil take down the photograph of him and Josh playing chess in the garden. 'Do you think Josh is gay?' he asked quietly as he cradled the photograph.

'No.'

'Would we know?'

'I'd know,' Sam said firmly.

'Like you knew about the bullying?' Neil asked archly.

Sam snatched the photograph from her husband's hands and hung it back on the wall. 'I'd know,' she said again. She bit her lip. 'You don't think this man's actually . . .' She couldn't bring herself to finish the sentence.

'When I went back and questioned Josh he stuck to the line that the man was a friend.'

'My poor baby.'

'To be honest, I think he was more upset that I took away the iPhone.'

'What iPhone?'

'The man tried to give Josh an iPhone. It's a classic sign, buying the boy's affection.' Neil shuddered. 'Josh openly admitted he'd visited the man at his flat.'

'He's been to his *flat*? What did this man look like?'

'Tall, brown hair, Scots accent.'

It was as much as Sam could do not to laugh with relief. It had to be David. Even though she had told him not to visit Josh, he'd gone ahead and done it anyway. But touching him up? That couldn't be right. Neil must have been mistaken.

'When you say, touching him up, what do you mean, exactly?'

'Isn't it bad enough I have to carry the picture in my mind, you want me to describe it to you?' Neil asked, shocked.

'Yes.'

'He had his hand on Josh's leg and was rubbing it through the bedclothes and then, as I approached, he reached out and ruffled Josh's hair.'

'That could have been innocent.'

'Not from where I was standing. It makes me sick just to think of it. He left pretty sharpish after I arrived.

I followed him and told him where he could stick his filthy present and that he should stay away from our son, but people like that, they're persistent. If they think they've got their hooks into someone vulnerable, they don't let go easily and Josh thinks this man is a friend. We must somehow convince him of the danger without scaring him. We have to protect him. We will, won't we?' There was a catch in Neil's voice.

Sam crossed the kitchen and put her arms round her husband. 'Josh'll be fine. I guarantee it.'

Chapter Forty

The following week, Neil was at his desk when Brookes Davenport's receptionist rang through. 'Patrick Sheldon is here.'

'Thanks.'

Neil went to greet him. 'Patrick. Thanks for coming.'

'No problem.' Sheldon laid aside the magazine he'd been looking at and shook Neil's hand. The private investigator was a grizzled man in his fifties with salt and pepper hair and tired eyes.

Neil ushered him into his office. 'I want you to find out about a Scottish guy called David. He lives in one of the flats in the Old Mill.'

Chapter Forty-One

David chewed the end of his pen as he studied the Excel spreadsheet. Four bookings for the autumn already. Things were going better than even he could have hoped. At the sound of the buzzer he strolled across to the intercom, distracted.

'Hello?'

'David? It's Josh. Can I come up?'

'Of course.'

Opening the door, David waited for the lift.

'Josh, what a surprise! How are you?'

'Better. Sore.'

The boy gave him a shy smile. His cuts and bruises looked less raw but he moved with obvious pain. David hovered on the threshold. The allegations that Neil Davenport had made, although clearly ridiculous, were serious and although the police had seemed prepared to believe him when he'd told them it was a misunderstanding, he didn't particularly want to test that idea.

'Is this a bad time?' Josh asked.

'I was doing some paperwork.' David watched Josh's shoulders slump. *You're really too busy to let him in, and letting him in could get you into a whole heap of trouble.* Even as these thoughts were crossing David's mind, he heard himself say, 'Nothing that can't wait. What can I do for you?' The boy's grateful smile banished the last of David's qualms as he held open the door.

'I thought we could give one of my games a try-out. If it's not a bad time.'

'No. Coke?'

'Please. You'll have to give me a head start, though. I can only use my left hand.'

'I'll use my left hand, too. It'll even things up.' David collected the drinks from the fridge. 'Where does your mum think you are?'

'At the library. She said I could have an hour in town while she had a meeting with Connor.'

The knife twisted in David's heart. He'd tried countless times to get hold of Sam on her mobile but she hadn't returned any of his calls. 'How is your mum?'

'Okay.' Josh took a long drink. 'I'm sorry Dad wouldn't let me keep your present.'

'That's okay. I'm sorry you were put in a position where you had to lie to him.'

'I don't think Dad would like it if he found out Mum's been working with you. They rowed a lot after the accident. That might start up again if he knew and there's already an atmosphere because Mum didn't

304

come to the hospital right away. Dad's banned me from seeing you.'

'If being here is going to get you into trouble . . .'

'Do you want me to go?'

'No but . . .'

'We're friends, aren't we?'

'Yes, Josh. We are.'

'We're going to Sardinia next week.'

'That's nice.'

'Then, I'll be starting at my new school.' Josh looked at the floor. 'They're sending me to St Luke's.'

'Just because you had trouble at one school doesn't mean you're going to have trouble at the next.'

'I know.'

'If you do though, you must tell someone. Don't try to handle it on your own this time. Okay?'

Josh nodded solemnly. 'That's part of the reason I'm here. I want you to teach me how to be cool, how to fit in.'

David spluttered over his Coke.

'Is the idea that crazy?' Josh coloured.

'No, I'm just flattered that you think *I'm* cool.'

Josh's eyes were so eager that David was in two minds what to say next. Sam had told him Josh had no interest in anything other than computers and frankly it showed.

'Why don't you go shopping for some new clothes. Take Cass along,' David suggested.

'Cass?'

'She's cool, right?'

He shrugged. 'I guess. What else?'

'Maybe a more modern haircut? Get Cass to take you to the barbers.'

'Can't you do it?' Josh asked plaintively.

'If your dad were to see us together . . .'

Josh nodded.

'The clothes and the hair will only take you so far though. Being cool is about a state of mind as much as anything else. You need to be friendly and confident in equal measure.'

'I have a problem with confidence. I haven't got any.'

'Then you need to do what the rest of us do, Josh. Pretend.'

Josh looked at him in astonishment. 'Pretend?'

'Aye. If you do it enough it'll eventually come naturally. Now, how about that game?'

Chapter Forty-Two

Neil Davenport stared unseeingly at the computer screen, replaying his uncle's words.

'I'm sorry, lad. The partners feel you're still too young. Tilden is more experienced. The firm needs that.'

Too young? Bastard! He'd given it his all. He'd risked his marriage and his sanity. And for what? Nothing!

What would Sam say? he wondered. She'd probably be relieved. She had never shared his ambition. It would still be hard to tell her, though. *I'm not as good as I thought I was. I'm a failure, like my dad.* The words circled viciously in his mind.

Was it possible to carry on working at Brookes Davenport? Everyone would know he'd been passed over. He wasn't sure he could bear the comparison: like father, like son.

'I just heard,' Megan said from the doorway. 'I can't believe it! I'm sorry.'

So, it had started already. Bad news, like good gossip, travelled fast. 'I was better,' Neil said petulantly. 'It should have been me.'

'Did he say why?'

'Too young, apparently.'

'Is that it?'

'That's what he said.'

'Could he have found out about that personal injury cock up?'

'No. I've dealt with that.' Neil pushed his glasses on top of his head and rubbed his eyes. 'The only thing I haven't done is told Sam about the thirty-five-thousand-pound hole in our savings.'

Megan winced. 'You haven't told her?'

He shook his head. 'I should have done it straight away,' Neil conceded. 'The longer I left it, the harder it got.'

'And there's no way your uncle could have found out?'

'No. Not unless . . .'

'I haven't told a soul.' She placed her hand on her heart. 'It's so wrong, Neil! You're his nephew. Tilden shouldn't have the firm. He has no claim to it.' She sat on the edge of his desk. 'What will you do?'

'I don't know.'

'But you'll stay?'

'I don't think I can.'

Her hand on his was warm, tender. 'Do you want to come back to mine?'

He pulled himself together and gently extricating his hand from hers said, 'Thanks, but no. I need to tell Sam what's happened. It's just as well we're going on holiday tomorrow. I'm sick of this bloody place.' He kicked out at the wastepaper basket and sent it skittering across the floor.

'If you need to talk, I'll always listen.'

'I know. Thank you.'

*

As it turned out, Megan was the first in a stream of colleagues to visit his office; most came to commiserate, a few to pretend to commiserate in order to gloat. Neil was magnanimous with them all. If any of them were there hoping for a juicy quote, they left disappointed.

By the time he got home the effort of hiding his true feelings had taken its toll. Consumed by anger and bitter at what he saw as the injustice of it all, he was itching to take out his frustration on someone.

Sam was cooking dinner.

'I didn't get it,' he said, slinging his briefcase down on the table before going through to the TV room. He grabbed the bottle of scotch and a glass from the drinks cabinet.

'Didn't get what?' Sam asked when he returned to the kitchen.

Neil threw himself into a chair. 'I didn't get the promotion.' He poured himself a double. 'Here's to Tilden. I hope he and my firm will be very happy together.' Downing the drink, he grimaced. 'Bastard!'

'What happened?' Sam asked, drying her hands on a tea towel.

'According to my uncle, I'm too young, too inexperienced.' He poured another drink, threw it back.

'Neil!' she reprimanded. 'Is that helping?'

'Yes.' Defiantly, he splashed more scotch into his glass. 'It should have been mine, Sam. I worked so bloody hard.'

'I know.'

He found her look of pity hard to bear.

'You could try again.'

Neil laughed sourly. 'You don't get it, do you? I've been humiliated, Sam. Edward did it on purpose. Carrying on the tradition of shafting my side of the family.' He banged his fist down on the table making the glass jump. 'It's all I've ever wanted.'

'I know,' she said again. 'I'm sorry.'

'Are you?' At least Megan had had the decency to look upset on his behalf. Although Sam obviously felt sorry for him, he could sense she was finding it hard to disguise her relief.

'Of course I am. It meant so much to you . . .'

'But?' he challenged.

'I didn't like what it was doing to you. To us.'

He lifted his glass and saluted her with it.

'Don't you think you've had enough?'

'Oh yeah!' he said sarcastically. 'I've had enough.' He downed the drink then, out of frustration, dashed the glass to the flagstone floor.

'For Christ's sake, Neil! Feel better?' Sam demanded.

'Much. Be honest, Sam. You never wanted me to get this.'

'That's not true. I just didn't like the hours you were working.'

'Maybe I didn't work enough hours, have you thought about that? Maybe if you had supported me more.' It was all that business with the accident and then the separation, especially the separation. He'd taken his eye off the ball. He'd been so busy trying to win Sam back he'd let the hours slide.

'Don't take this out on me. It's not my fault.'

'Maybe if you hadn't made me leave home and spend weeks in a shithole rented flat where I couldn't concentrate . . .'

Sam flung the tea towel down. 'You only have yourself to blame for that.'

He nodded grimly. 'Yeah, I forgot. It's all my fault.' He got up unsteadily. 'It always is.'

'Where are you going?'

'Out.'

'You can't drive!'

'Don't worry, if I hit someone, it'll be my fault this time.'

Neil drove fifty yards down the lane before slamming on the brakes. He had promised his father that he would win back the company. He'd failed. Why couldn't Sam have taken a little bit of the blame? Why did it have to be his fault entirely? *I am good enough, damn it!* Events had conspired against him, that was all. He needed Sam to know that. To know that he was good enough, not a loser like his father. Why couldn't she have reassured him?

He massaged his eyes. Megan would tell him what he needed to hear. She wouldn't be pissy with him. He gunned the engine and then, just as fast, he killed it again.

Sam was still in the kitchen, clearing up the broken glass, when he walked in. Why was it that loved ones, who so often saw the best of someone had to deal with the worst too, he wondered.

'I shouldn't have taken my anger out on you. I'm sorry.'

Running to him, Sam took him in her arms.

Humbled by her reaction, Neil hugged her.

That was the beauty of home, he realised. It was the place where you could be yourself. Good and bad and where, if you were lucky, there were people there who would love you either way.

Chapter Forty-Three

A week later, Neil sat on the balcony of their Sardinian hotel, a beer in his hand as he watched the sun bounce off the cobalt water in front of him. The distance, in miles and time, had helped him put his disappointment over the lost promotion into perspective. He'd even come to the conclusion that his uncle might have been right; perhaps he would have been out of his depth.

He took a swig of his beer. He had pursued the dream of senior partner because of his father. He had always told himself it was what he wanted too but was it? Would anybody choose that kind of relentless pressure? It was rewarding financially, of course, but so was robbing banks.

He'd been blinkered, he realised. Always striving. Risking everything. Would he have had sex with Megan if he hadn't been half crazed over work? Would he have endangered his practising certificate by paying out that personal injury file instead of admitting his mistake and letting the insurers handle it? Would he have missed the warning signs about Josh?

All his working life he'd been eager to make partner, then equity partner, then head of department. All with one aim in mind: senior partner. For what? More money? Prestige? To avenge the memory of a man long since dead? What did any of that truly matter when compared to Sam and the children? He already had the true prize; he'd just been too blind to see it.

He heard the door open. A moment later, Sam joined him, dazzling in white linen trousers and a matching top. She flopped into the lounger next to him.

'Good shopping trip?'

'Yes. You okay?'

'Yeah, I've just been sitting here thinking about work.'

'Neil!'

'I'm going to hand in my notice when we get back.'

Sam took off her sunglasses. 'I think that's a good idea,' she said cautiously.

'With my CV, I'll be able to get into one of the firms in Stebbingsford.'

He toyed with the idea of telling Sam about their missing savings but if he were to leave Brookes Davenport, they would have to pay him out. The money would more than plug the hole. Sam would never need to know. Every cloud had a silver lining.

She ran her hand lightly over his arm. 'And Megan?'

Neil looked at her in surprise. 'What about Megan?'

'Are you still together?'

'No.'

He saw Sam twist her father's ring. 'I've smelt her perfume on your shirts for the last couple of months. Roses and jasmine.'

He shifted uncomfortably. 'She helped me with a problem on one of my files. We spent some time together as a result but it was purely professional. I swear. I might not be worthy of the promotion but I'm not a total bloody idiot.' He thought about the night in the car, how close he'd come to driving to Megan's. Shamefacedly, he stared out to sea.

He'd been working like a demon. It would be a relief to scale back and have time for normal things again. He looked across at Sam. She was watching him guardedly.

'I got so caught up in the day to day; I stopped seeing the bigger picture.'

'We're all guilty of that sometimes.'

'A fresh start will do us good,' he said. 'It's time for work to take a back seat and for us to concentrate on us instead.' Taking her hand in his, he laced his fingers through hers. 'I love you.'

'I love you, too.'

He leaned over and kissed her.

'Where are the children?' he asked, drawing back.

'Kids' Club doesn't finish for another hour. Josh is taking part in a chess tournament. Cass is having a tennis lesson.'

Neil grinned and kissed her again. 'In that case how do you fancy joining me in the bedroom to practise a little ball control of our own?'

Chapter Forty-Four

Sam sat in the garden of The Queen's Head, a vodka and orange untouched in front of her. She'd emailed David, asking him to meet her. Now, as she waited for him to arrive, she rehearsed the speech she planned to deliver. She was only halfway through when he appeared, clutching a beer.

'Sorry I'm late.'

As he sat down next to her it was all Sam could do not to move along the picnic bench, so desperate was she to escape the ambit of his charm. She had done so well in the last couple of weeks to convince herself that he was actually quite ugly and that the attraction had been some sort of abomination.

Now, here he was, clean shaven in ripped jeans and a tee shirt that showed off his lean figure, spiky gelled hair and fashionable sunglasses and there was her heart. That poor pathetic thing that was melting now like an ice cream in the sun.

Sam gulped her drink. The nail polish she'd applied for her holiday looked as good as the day she had left the nail bar. Neil said the red nails were sexy. Sam knew they wouldn't survive when she went back to work but for now she was sexy Sam with the sassy red nails. The woman Neil had delighted in. The woman who had frolicked, laughed, and danced in the moonlight with a man who'd escaped the drudgery of the office and was desperate to turn his back on the rockiest rocky patch their marriage had ever known.

Devastated by the lost promotion, Neil needed her and, in these last few difficult weeks, she'd come to realise just how much she needed him, too. There was no room for anyone else.

Especially not David. He'd cast a spell over her. It was the only explanation she could come up with for the rash way in which she had been behaving.

She had missed the signs that Josh was being bullied in large part because of her growing infatuation with the man sitting next to her. If there had been no David, she was sure she would have realised what was happening to Josh and been able to put a stop to it.

David's hand was on her thigh. His self-assuredness annoyed her.

'Why don't we go down to the riverbank?' Sam suggested. The garden was busy and she knew there was a table, tucked away round the corner that would give them more privacy.

'Sure. Good holiday?'

'Yes.'

They settled at their new table, Sam taking the seat opposite him. She watched him push his sunglasses into his hair, his face serious. 'How's Josh?'

How was Josh? *Probably emotionally scarred for the rest of his life* – that was the thought that Sam tortured herself with on the bad days, and there were a lot of those.

'On the mend. Children have a remarkable capacity for recovery.' It was her stock response. From the surprise in David's eyes, it was clear he'd expected something more. 'I expressly told you not to go to the hospital and you ignored me.' Anger was good. It stopped her feeling anything else.

'I needed to see him. I felt guilty, too.'

'Good! You should. Another bloody phone? What were you thinking? Were you even thinking? It was a stupid thing to do. You know Neil thinks you're a paedophile?'

'Yes, I am aware of that. I've had the police round.'

Sam had hated not being able to alleviate Neil's fears but how could she without telling him about her visits to David? One revelation would have led to the next and the next. Neil would have been like a dog with a bone, worrying the truth out of her until eventually she would have said too much. Silence, she had decided, was the lesser of two evils, though both options had given her sleepless nights.

'Were you aware that Josh was being bullied?' she asked.

'No,' he said sullenly.

318

'No idea. At all?'

David rubbed his chin and looked away across the river. 'He said some things when he first came round to mine.'

'What things?'

'Stuff about not getting on with the other kids.'

'And you never thought to mention this to me?' she asked, horrified.

'I did,' he said, stung. 'The next time I saw you. Remember?'

He was right. He had. Tired of being judged, Sam lashed out anyway. 'So, it's my fault I didn't know he was being bullied?' she cried.

'I didn't say that.'

'You meant it though,' she said crossly but the fight was already seeping out of her, guilt dragging her back down. 'You're right. You shouldn't have needed to draw me a bloody diagram. You met my son for one afternoon and you knew.' Sam shook her head. 'What sort of mother does that make me?'

'A wonderful mother. No one could love those children more.'

'Blind love. Looking back, it's so obvious. He was always pressing Neil for his pocket money early and there was all that fuss over Cass's money when it went missing that time. I was so busy checking up on Cass and spending time with you, I missed it.'

'Did Cass know? Did Connor?'

Sam shook her head. 'He didn't tell any of us. Cass knew he didn't have many friends. She just thought he

319

was a loner. We all did. They've been bullying him since February, David.' She paused. 'The month I met you.'

She watched him run his fingers up and down his beer glass, his gaze fixed on it.

'You blame me,' he said flatly.

'I blame both of us.' Sam stared at her fingernails. 'I can't do this any more. See you. Be around you.'

'Sam . . .' He went to take her hands.

Sam withdrew them, swiftly anchoring them in her lap. 'You've brought such joy into my life,' she admitted with a sigh. 'And I will always be grateful for that, but I don't want the pain and the guilt that comes with it. We have to stay away from one another. Josh . . .'

'Didn't get beaten up because we spent the afternoon together.'

'But he did cry for his mother and she wasn't there because she was with you. I will never forgive myself for that. If I hadn't been infatuated with you, I would have seen the signs and Josh wouldn't have got hurt.'

'You don't know that.' An angry silence descended on them.

She watched his hands clench into fists, flex and flatten on the table.

'Infatuated with me?' he said at last. His tone cold. 'It was more than that.'

'No.'

'Don't kid yourself, Sam. It was more than that and you bloody know it. You're going to stay with him out of loyalty aren't you?' David said angrily.

'I love him.'

'You love me.'

'I don't love you,' she said defiantly.

'Your feelings haven't changed,' he replied boldly.

'Yes, they have. We can never be.'

'We already are.'

'You flatter yourself.'

'It's a failing of mine.'

'I've noticed.'

Unnerved by his steady gaze, Sam looked away. Just a few short weeks ago, they had stood together a little further along the riverbank, kissing one another. In that sun-dappled, enchanted world anything had seemed possible but not any more. She reminded herself that while she had been in his arms, Josh had been in the hospital.

'I've been counting the days until your holiday was over.' He moved to sit beside her, his legs straddling the seat so he could face her, his knee touching her thigh. 'I've missed you,' he said, reaching for her hands.

She tried to pull her hands away but he wouldn't let go.

'Did you miss me?'

'No.'

'You answered too quickly. The thought of not seeing each other is tearing you apart as much as it is me. At least I have the guts to admit it. I'd do anything for Josh not to have been mugged, but I don't see why it has to affect us.'

'And that's why I have to put a stop to this.' Standing, she tore her hands free and, taking up her bag, began to walk away.

'Sam!' He grabbed her arm. 'Don't do this.'

She could see the fear in his eyes.

'I have no choice.'

'There's always a choice.'

'We were holding hands and kissing while my son was crying for me. Later, if Connor hadn't found me, we would have made love and I would have broken my vows. All the while, my husband was trying to comfort our son because I wasn't there. Because I was with you.' Hot shame brought tears to Sam's eyes. 'When something is threatening to destroy everything you care about you have to remove yourself from it. Completely. How can I ever hope to make things right with my family, repair the damage I've done, if my head is full of you?' she asked. 'We were a mistake. Don't you understand? A terrible mistake.'

'Does it feel like a mistake when I hold you?' he asked, pulling her roughly into his arms. 'When I kiss you?' He ground his mouth down onto hers.

'Don't.' She twisted away from him. 'You have to let me go.'

'Leave him.'

Sam looked into his dark eyes. Pools of love willing her to dive in and admit that nothing had changed, that she could still be his. 'It's a physical thing. If we don't see each other, it'll go away.'

'You don't kiss a man the way you kissed me without feeling more than lust,' he said.

'You want me to tell you it's more than just a physical attraction?' she asked, backing away from him. 'Sorry, David. You obviously give me more credit than I'm due. I'll admit I thought about going to bed with you. Tit for tat to get my own back on Neil but that was all it was. I don't love you. I've never loved you.'

'If you're going to lie, Sam, you need to be much more convincing about it. Like you were the first time.'

She flashed him an angry look. 'I don't love you. I've never loved you.'

David regarded her stoically. 'Saying it louder doesn't make it any more true.'

'I don't love . . .' Sam's face crumpled. David gathered her swiftly into his arms. 'I don't love you,' she whispered against his chest. 'I've never loved you.'

'And I want you to never love me forever,' he said gruffly.

'You can't talk me round. Don't try,' she said tearfully, edging away.

'Why must I be the one to give you up? Can't we find a way? There must be a way.'

She watched hope flood into his eyes. Steeling herself, she shook her head. 'We tried that already. It didn't end well.'

Threading her fingers into his hair, she kissed him deeply, putting everything into the kiss she knew she could never put into words without breaking down. How she would always cherish the memory of their time together. How she would never forget him. How a part of her heart would always be his. Then, with a sigh, she forced herself to step back.

'We can't be together,' she said.

There was a long silence as he stood in front of her, head bent, before finally he said, 'I know.'

'You're a good-looking guy, you'll find someone else.'

He kicked out at a clump of grass. 'Spare me the speeches.'

'David . . .'

'Just go, Sam.'

Head bowed, she walked away. Every step was agony but she forced herself to keep going. She could feel his stare, heavy on her shoulders. Almost buckled under the weight of it as she imagined the look of hope that would leap into his eyes should she pause and turn around, how eager his arms would be to accept her.

She balled her fists, the sassy red nails biting into her palms. Don't look back, she told herself. Whatever you do, don't look back.

SEPTEMBER

Chapter Forty-Five

Neil looked at the bouquet of extravagant white peonies. Sam's favourites. His pen was poised over the florist's card as his secretary, Susan, entered. 'Patrick Sheldon is here.'

'Thanks.'

Neil went through to reception.

'Good holiday?' Patrick asked.

'Fantastic.' Neil showed Patrick into his office and shut the door.

'Your key.'

'Thanks. The police have been in touch. They told me there was nothing to worry about. That Josh's story about the website checks out. It would appear I have a budding Steve Jobs on my hands.' Neil saw the older man frown and his smile faded. 'Were they wrong? Did you find something?'

'Nothing on Josh's computer. To be sure, I checked your wife's computer in case Josh had used it to cover his tracks.'

'And?'

'He hadn't.'

Neil let out a sigh of relief. 'That's good. The police were right then.' He caught Patrick's eye and his apprehension returned. 'It is good, isn't it?'

Patrick rubbed his jaw. 'Sam's been swapping emails and texts with him.'

'Are you sure?'

'The last one suggested lunch at The Queen's Head.'

'Lunch?' Neil repeated, bewildered. 'I don't understand. Why would she be meeting this guy for lunch? Who is he?'

'The one thing I can say with absolute certainty is that I don't think your man is a paedophile.' Patrick placed his report on the table. 'His name's David McAllister.'

'McAllister?' Neil repeated sharply.

'You know the name?'

'Of course. He's the guy suing me over the accident.'

'You didn't recognise him at the hospital when he was with Josh? After all, you were with Sam on the night of the accident, weren't you?'

'I was so out of it,' Neil confessed sheepishly. 'I don't remember much.'

Images of that night spooled through his mind: Sam kneeling on the wet tarmac, holding the motorcyclist's hand. He remembered her lifting the man's visor but he couldn't recall his face. He'd been too preoccupied with the horrific injury to the man's leg, sick to his stomach by the amount of blood on the road.

'I've printed off the messages. Luckily all of Sam's texts are backed up and sent to her computer so you've got copies of those too.'

Gathering himself, Neil studied them.

Hello, Sam. We need to talk. Ring or email me, please.

Hello, Sam. We have to talk. When you get back, please get in touch.

And Sam's reply. *I don't think that would be a good idea.*

'Those emails were sent in May,' Patrick said.

'That's when she went to court.'

Neil returned his attention to the messages and the one Sam had sent the previous week.

Meet me at The Queen's Head at one. We have to talk.

And McAllister's reply. *Can't wait to see you again.*

Neil looked at the date and time of Sam's message. Shortly afterwards she'd joined him in the garden. They'd lazed on sun loungers, enjoying the balmy evening and reminiscing about their holiday. Later, they'd made love and all the time she'd arranged to meet this man the next day.

The message was informal but there was something about the way it was phrased. As if they often met at The Queen's Head. Neil felt his heart compress as though someone had grabbed it and was squeezing the life from it.

'Did she meet him?' he asked quietly.

Patrick nodded. 'She was already at a table in the garden when McAllister arrived. Then, they moved to a table out of sight from the others, on the riverbank. I could see the path beyond so I know they were there but I couldn't get close enough to see or hear them.'

'When you could see them . . .' Neil found it difficult to go on. What if Patrick told him something he didn't want to hear, something he would never be able to forget? He cleared his throat. 'How were they with one another?'

'They seemed friendly. Sam looked a little tense, I thought. McAllister appeared relaxed.'

'Friendly?' Neil seized on the word.

'There was no physical contact between them, not that I could see.'

'You mean they didn't kiss each other?' Neil said bluntly.

'Not while I could see them, no.'

The words were cold comfort. Is that what Patrick thought they were dealing with here; a lovers' tryst? Had he hurt Sam so much that she'd resorted to taking a lover of her own? And *him* of all people. Stunned, Neil stared unseeingly at the report.

'What happened then?'

'They were out of sight for ten minutes or so. Then, Sam left. She had her head down, her sunglasses on. She looked upset. I let a few minutes pass. McAllister hadn't appeared so I decided to take a look. He was throwing stones into the river. He was so lost in thought

I don't think he even realised I was there. Then, he set off along the towpath towards Lower Leigh.'

'What the hell's going on, Patrick?' Neil's stomach clenched with fear. *Can it be true? Is Sam having an affair?* His beautiful wife in the arms of another man? He felt sick at the thought.

'The messages are bland. The ones where he's urging her to get in contact with him could be the desire to make up after a tiff.'

Neil flinched. *'It's not only men who get to look and wonder.'*

'They could be wholly innocent. They could relate to the accident. There are accounts in her Excel program on the computer. Monies charged to DM Properties, that's the company McAllister runs. I've printed those out too. It could be that she was simply doing work through Meadowview Designs for McAllister's company and the messages related in some way to that. Although . . .'

'Although?' Neil demanded sharply.

'She charged DM a lot less than her other clients. Maybe it was a way to assuage her guilt.'

Neil mulled this over. 'Sam was very upset by the accident. Perhaps she sought him out.' It would explain why she'd had so much contact with him. There could be an innocent explanation after all. He felt ashamed for jumping to conclusions, judging her by his own poor standards.

'So far as Josh is concerned, I think he was telling the truth. He did the guy's website and that was that.

I've written down the email addresses and passwords Josh and Sam use to access their emails. I can show you how to check their messages from here and then mark them as unread so they'll never know you looked at them first. If this is something you want to pursue, I can keep digging.'

Neil nodded. 'Do you think she's having an affair?'

He could hardly bring himself to say the words. He remembered their holiday. The walks they'd taken hand in hand. The passionate nights when they'd tumbled back and forth. Everything had been fresh and exciting. She hadn't suggested anything new but there was stuff they hadn't done for a while. It was easy to fall into a routine. Great sex but comfortable. On holiday, there had been more time to relax, to rediscover one another but had there been more to it? Had she been making up as much as she'd been making out?

'For what it's worth, I'm not convinced she's having an affair.' Patrick's voice cut through Neil's misery.

He seized the words. 'What makes you say that?'

'She has no reason to think anyone is going to check her messages. She'd feel no need to be guarded in what she said in them and yet there's nothing incriminating there. In my experience, people get carried away. They put all sorts in texts and emails, thinking they'll only ever be read by the intended recipient and later it comes back to haunt them. That isn't the case here.'

Neil rubbed his chin. 'See what else you can find.'

'You could just ask her.'

Neil shook his head. He couldn't go off the deep end at her and then find it was all a misunderstanding. Not after Megan. 'I need evidence.'

After Patrick had gone, Neil took Sam's photo down from the bookshelf. He wanted to believe his wife had worked with McAllister for altruistic reasons but a little voice in his head told him there had to be more to it than that.

With a jolt, he remembered their conversation in the kitchen when he'd told Sam about the man at the hospital.

'Josh'll be fine. I guarantee it.'

She must have realised it was McAllister from the description he had given her and that Josh was in no danger and yet she had chosen to reassure him in the blandest sense rather than telling him straight out that she knew the man and he wasn't a paedophile.

How could you do that? What were you hiding that was so precious you couldn't put my mind at rest? You know how many nights I lay awake worrying about Josh. With just a few words you could have taken my pain away. But you didn't.

He searched through the messages looking for the date of Josh's accident. There was no contact on the day itself but there was an exchange from the day before.

R U free for lunch tomorrow? Queen's Head at one?
Great idea. Can't wait.

Neil closed his eyes. An image of his son's bruised and bloodied face hovered in his mind's eye. She'd met

McAllister at one. At one fifteen he'd had a call from the police. At one twenty he had tried to ring Sam and she hadn't picked up. *You let it go to voicemail because you were with him!*

That afternoon had been one of the longest, most miserable afternoons of his life. He couldn't now recall exactly when Sam had finally shown up but it had been a few hours after his first call. *Were you still with him when Connor found you?*

Neil looked down at the florist's card. The peonies mocked him from the edge of the desk. Grabbing his pen, he wrote: 'Dear Susan, Thanks for all your hard work while I was away.'

Chapter Forty-Six

As a show of solidarity, Sam and Neil decided they would take Josh to St Luke's together on his first morning.

'If we could just get him interested in rugby or football,' Neil mused as he tugged on his seatbelt.

'I was reading in the school's booklet that they're proud of their swimming team. All new pupils have a try-out for the squad. Josh has always been a strong swimmer, so perhaps . . .'

'That'd be good,' Neil agreed.

They were both nervous, Sam realised. As nervous maybe as the first time Josh had gone to school. It was going to be a long day for all of them.

She shot Neil a sideways glance. Since their holiday, he'd been increasingly tetchy with the children and quiet with her. Occasionally, she had caught him looking at her, deep in thought. She'd asked him what was wrong but he would only shrug and say it was post-holiday blues.

Sam thought there was more to it than that. It couldn't be easy for him, working out his notice, trying to be professional, when the whole office knew he'd been passed over for the top job. However, his unhappiness seemed more personal than that. Perhaps his anger at her over Josh had not fully dissipated.

'At least I know Josh is not in danger from that man,' he said suddenly, a look of distaste on his face. 'I've been making enquiries. Seems he's got a reputation but it's for women not little boys.'

Sam's mind raced. *Enquiries about David?* 'What sort of enquiries?' she asked lightly.

'I got Sheldon on the job. Good man. Very *thorough.*'

Sam caught her breath. 'What did he say?'

'Said the guy has a thing for blondes. Usually has three of them on the go at any one time.'

Sensing Neil was watching her, Sam stared intently at her phone, pretending to flick through her schedule.

'I've got a busy day,' she said airily. 'You?'

'Always. Lots to sort out before I leave.'

Sam felt his gaze boring into her. Sheldon had definitely found something. What she didn't know but enough to put a doubt in Neil's mind. The irony wasn't lost on her. He had found something to incriminate her when she hadn't actually done anything wrong and had already walked away.

The tear in her heart that Sam had experienced after her first separation from David had now returned, just as jagged, just as deep. There wasn't a morning she didn't wake and wonder how he was and what he was doing. Walking away from him had been the hardest thing she had ever done but it had been the right thing. She was certain of that. On impulse, she reached for Neil's hand and squeezed it.

She turned as Josh ambled towards the car, his school tie loosened, his top button undone. He seemed older since the attack and, although it surprised Sam, more at ease with himself.

'We were just talking about the swimming team, Josh,' Neil said, pulling his hand from Sam's. 'They make a big thing of it at this school. It'd be a good way to make friends, and don't forget to make enquiries about the chess team, too.'

Josh grunted, head down as he studied a brightly coloured map of the school.

All too soon, Neil drove through the wrought-iron gates that bore the school's crest, the one mirrored on Josh's jacket which, because of the heat, was hooked over his arm.

'Remember I'm proud of you and I love you,' Neil said, his voice a little off key.

'We both do,' Sam said. The tension headache that had been gnawing at her temple all morning, now pounded with increased severity.

She could hardly bear to let Josh out of the car and into the harsh world of teenagers where bullies waited seeking out the quiet ones. Rubbing her forehead, she fought the urge to ask Josh to ring her every hour. They would get through this day and somehow she would stay sane.

'Have a good day, Josh.'

'See you later.'

He sounded casual but Sam could see the muscles were tight in his jaw. The blazer that had been folded neatly over his arm a moment before was now casually slung over his shoulder and his rucksack was hooked loosely over the other as he walked away.

Sam's heart followed him, as she knew it would for the rest of the day.

*

Neil offered his cheek rather than his mouth as Sam leaned across to kiss him goodbye.

'Have a good day.'

'You, too,' he replied. He pulled into the traffic without waiting for her to reach the door of her office or turn and wave as he usually did whenever he dropped her off.

Since Patrick's revelations, it had been difficult to keep up a pretence that everything was okay. Making love with the same carefree abandon they'd enjoyed on holiday had become impossible. Every time he entered her, he wondered how he measured up and the pressure was almost too much to bear so that he'd been given to feigning excuses.

He found himself watching her in unguarded moments, his mind spiralling through the things he'd found out. Like the fact David McAllister's home and mobile numbers were in the office mobile's contacts. He had thrown the phone down in disgust but had nevertheless tried to console himself with the fact that the mobile was Sam's main point of contact with her clients. His peace of mind had been short lived, however, when he'd crosschecked her personal phone, the one he had given her for family use only. At the sight of David's name beneath Cass's and ahead of Josh's he had felt his world grow colder.

Parking the car, he swept into his office and turned on his computer.

He looked up as Megan stuck her head round the door. 'What?'

'Edward wants to talk to you about how the handover process is going to work.'

'He can wait.' *Damned if I am going to dance to his tune now!*

Megan ducked out again.

Neil's focus returned to Sam. Was she using McAllister for a tit-for-tat fling, to even the score because of his dalliance with Megan? Though the idea hurt like hell, he could hardly blame her. If that was all it was, could they get through it? He hated the thought of another man touching her. But did he hate it enough to end their marriage? She had dealt with her feelings about Megan; she had tried to rise above them. Could he, if the tables were turned?

And what if it went deeper than a fling? He found it hard to imagine that Sam could dabble in a meaningless affair. The coldness that such an act would require simply wasn't in her nature. What if she had fallen for this man?

'Josh'll be fine. I guarantee it.'

He'd thought she was being strong because she knew how scared he was when, actually, she had known no danger existed. Why hadn't she said that the man was a friend in order to put his mind at ease? *Because then you would have asked about him. A good-looking, younger man as a friend? You wouldn't have let that pass. You'd have wanted details.*

She could have told you he was a business associate, as it was obvious you hadn't recognised him from the night of the accident, but she hadn't done that either. What had she been afraid of? The truth, perhaps?

He looked up as Megan came back in, carrying a mug of coffee which she put down in front of him.

'You looked like you could use this. I've told Edward you'll be free after eleven.'

'Thanks. Sorry I snapped at you.'

'Bad day?'

'Josh's first day at his new school.' *And I think my wife is having an affair.*

'We could do lunch later if you want to talk?'

It would be so easy to say yes. Lunch might lead to dinner and then a nightcap back at hers. They could make love on the sofa or maybe even make it to the bed this time.

And how exactly is that going to help your train wreck of a marriage?

'Thanks. Another time, perhaps.'

Chapter Forty-Seven

'Worried about Josh?' Daphne asked as she poured a cup of tea for them both.

Sam gave her a strained smile and nodded.

'Would you like some pills for your headache?'

'I took couple earlier, but thanks.'

'You don't have to stay, if you'd rather not,' Daphne said.

'I'd prefer to be busy. If I was at home the day would seem even longer.'

Daphne sipped her tea. 'So, the guest bedrooms are almost finished.'

Sam nodded.

'Just the kitchen diner to go then.'

Sam looked around her. 'Far be it from me to talk myself out of work, Daphne, but I think this room looks pretty good already.'

'No.' The older woman was adamant. 'It needs a lot of work in here.'

Sam frowned. 'Why don't we take a little break once the bedrooms are finished? I can come back again next year if you still want to do something in here.'

Daphne settled her cup in its saucer. 'I told you I wanted to have the whole house done and once the kitchen diner is finished, I was thinking of maybe changing things around a little in the sitting room.'

'Aren't you happy with it?'

'Yes, of course.'

'But you want to change it?'

Daphne looked down at the table. 'I shall miss you, Sam. I look forward to our little tea breaks.'

'Oh, Daphne.' Sam reached out to clasp the older woman's hand. 'I'll still pop round for tea and cake each week and have a natter, if you'd like me to. You don't have to keep finding me work. You haven't been doing that, have you?'

Daphne patted Sam's hand and smiled. 'No, I really did want all of the rooms done.'

'I will change the sitting room if you're not happy with it. No charge.'

Daphne shook her head. 'I love it. I was just being silly, my dear. I didn't want to say goodbye.'

'Well, now you know you don't have to. There is something I need to talk to you about though. I managed to find a good home for your husband's automatons . . .'

'Thank you, Sam. I knew you wouldn't let me down.'

'I've arranged, on your behalf, for them to be loaned to the Abbeyleigh Museum. They're reorganising their

340

Victorian rooms and the automatons are going to have pride of place when it reopens in December.'

Daphne smiled. 'Ted would have liked that.'

'As I say, they're on loan. You would need to give the museum two months' notice but then you could have them back.'

'I told you, my dear, I don't want them.'

'They're very valuable, Daphne. I know you didn't want to talk about it earlier this year but you need to be aware.' Sam drew the valuation from her bag together with the loan agreement. 'You need to sign both copies of the loan agreement. I'll give one back to the museum. You should keep your copy and the valuation somewhere safe.'

Daphne nodded, casting the papers aside without looking at them.

'The museum would like you to be their guest of honour at the reopening. They want you to cut the ribbon and perhaps give a little speech about Ted.'

'Goodness me, no! I couldn't do that.'

'Well it's a long way off yet. Promise me you'll think about it.'

*

To celebrate Josh's first day Sam cooked a roast, making sure Josh got the crispiest of the roast potatoes and an extra helping of sage-and-onion stuffing. After dinner, Neil and the children went into the TV room to play on the Xbox, leaving Sam in the kitchen stacking the plates in the dishwasher.

Now, she jumped as Neil came back into the kitchen. 'Kids want to know where dessert is.' He picked up the bottle of chardonnay from the table and topped up his glass before waving the bottle at her. She nodded and he refilled hers too.

'I was just about to dish up,' Sam said. She took the peach trifle, Josh's favourite, out of the fridge. 'Do you think he enjoyed today as much as he said he did?'

Neil caught her eye as he took four bowls down from the cupboard and put them on the worktop. 'I think so but I've asked Cass to have a quiet word with him later.'

Sam nodded. 'Good idea.'

'Time was when Josh and I played chess, I'd let him win. Now, I'm struggling to beat him.'

'I thought you were all playing on the Xbox?'

'The kids wanted to wait for you.'

Walking over to him, Sam put her arms round his neck. She felt him tense. 'I love you,' she said and risked a quick kiss to his mouth. She pulled back almost instantly fearing rejection, wanting to retreat first to maintain her dignity, just in case.

*

The family tournament on the Xbox had been won by Sam and Josh who had high-fived each other in victory and celebrated with mugs of hot chocolate topped with whipped cream before everyone had got ready for bed.

Now, Neil tapped softly on Cass's door.

'Come in.'

The room was a mass of fairy lights. Cass was sitting on her bed, her face illuminated from the reflected light of her phone. Her new guitar stood against the wall.

'I was just wondering if you'd had a chance to talk to Josh, sweetheart?'

'Yeah I did the whole big sis thing.' She smiled. 'He's fine, Dad. You can stop worrying.'

'Once you're a parent, that's impossible, Cassie.'

'Cass.' She corrected him.

He sat on the bed. 'And how are you?'

'I'm fine.' She put the phone down. 'You okay?'

He nodded and hooked his arm around his daughter's shoulders. 'You'd tell me if anything was wrong, wouldn't you?'

'Course.'

He kissed her temple and hugged her tightly.

'I'm fine, Dad. Don't worry. And I'll keep an eye on Josh, I promise.'

'You're a good girl. So when am I going to be allowed to meet Tobyn?'

She shrugged.

'He's not putting you under any sort of pressure is he? Pressure to do things you might not be ready to do.'

Cass coloured. 'No, Dad. Can we not do this?'

Neil bit his lip. 'How's the band?'

'Great.'

'Got a name?'

'Global Warning.'

'That's good.' He grinned and so did Cass. 'What sort of songs do you play?'

'Rock mostly. We're writing our own material. It's important to be authentic.'

Neil smiled and nodded. 'Played any gigs?'

'Not yet. Spike's do an open mic night. We're thinking of making our debut there.'

'Would it be okay if your dad came along? Met the boyfriend, heard you sing.'

'Maybe. Would you give us a hand with our gear?'

'If that's what it takes to get a ticket.'

She nodded.

'Any chance you could do an REM song for me?'

'Don't push it.'

Laughing, he dropped a kiss to the top of Cass's head. 'Thanks for checking on your brother, tonight. Sleep well.'

'You, too, Dad.'

He shut the door gently. He had two brilliant kids but did he still have a wife?

OCTOBER

Chapter Forty-Eight

Neil kicked the door of his office shut, eager to take the call from Patrick Sheldon.

'I've got some good news. McAllister has been seeing a blonde for the past three weeks.'

Neil's heart lifted. 'Has he seen Sam at all?'

'No. If there was anything going on between them, I'd say it's over now.'

After the call, Neil pulled out Sheldon's original report and read through it again. When he'd finished he shoved it aside in frustration. The answers he sought weren't there. There was only one way he was going to get those and that was by asking her. But did he really want to open that box?

*

'Is it just us tonight?' Neil asked as he sat down to dinner in the kitchen.

'Yes. Cass has gone to Tobyn's. They're writing songs together.'

'Is that a euphemism I'm not familiar with?'

Sam smiled.

'She told me they're going to play at one of the open mic nights at Spike's, said I could go if I helped shift their gear. She said it was a rock band. This Tobyn got long hair?'

'Longish.'

'Our daughter is turning into Stevie Nicks.'

'I don't think our daughter would know who that is.'

Neil grimaced. 'And Josh?'

'He's at Tom Martin's.'

'The other new boy on the swimming team?'

Sam nodded. 'He's a lovely lad and keen on computers. He and Josh are like peas in a pod.'

'It's good to know he's making friends.'

Neil poured them both a glass of wine. He nudged his food around his plate.

'Not hungry?'

'No, sorry.' He pushed his plate away.

After dinner, Sam settled herself in the TV room while Neil went to the study. He opened three different files before he abandoned the task, his head too full of Sam and McAllister to concentrate.

He went to join Sam. She was watching one of her favourite shows. Neil sat on the sofa beside her. Curling up, Sam rested her head on his lap. Automatically his right hand dropped to stroke her shoulder, while he ran the fingers of his left hand through her hair. She was here and she was his. Wasn't that enough for him? His desire for confrontation waxed and waned with each beat of his heart. You should never ask a question if you can't cope with the answer, he told himself. *But what if you can't cope with the not knowing either?*

*

Sam woke and stretched. She had been so comfortable she had fallen asleep. She turned her head to smile up at Neil. He returned her smile but it never quite reached his eyes.

'What's wrong, sweetheart?'

She saw him hesitate. Her sudden sense of fear was out of proportion to the situation and yet where once her worries had been mostly mundane, the same vague worries as everyone else, now they had a focus. *Megan.* Would her sense of contentment always be so fragile?

'Neil?' She sat up.

He pushed his hands through his hair and sighed. 'Are we okay, Sam?'

She frowned. 'Of course we're okay. She was aware of his eyes boring into hers, searching her face. Seeking what? He'd been giving her the same intense looks since their holiday. Her heart began to thump uncomfortably in her chest.

'I want you to tell me about David McAllister.'

The shock of hearing David's name fall from Neil's lips almost winded her. 'David McAllister?' she repeated, buying herself time to think.

Standing, Neil began to pace, his gaze fixed to the floor. 'You've been seeing him, meeting him. I want to know why.'

Sam knotted her fingers together, the diamonds of her engagement ring biting into her skin. 'David McAllister was the motorcyclist hurt in our accident. I was so worried about what we'd done to him that I went to the hospital to see him. I wanted to help.'

'And how did you do that?'

His tone was withering, his all too brief look at her as cold as ice. Sam dropped her head. 'He wanted to renovate his holiday home so he could let it out. I did some work for him.'

'And you didn't tell me about it because?'

She looked up. 'You told me not to see him. I thought you'd be angry.'

'Damn right.'

'We worked together on the property and then the arrangement came to an end.'

'Just like that?'

'Yes. Debt repaid,' she said brightly.

'Really? Why do you look so bloody guilty then?'

Sam unclenched her fingers.

'What's he like?'

'How do you mean?'

'I mean, what's he like?' Neil snarled. 'Smart? Funny? Obnoxious?'

'He's pleasant.'

'Pleasant?' Neil's lip curled.

'Yes.'

'Did you fuck him?'

'Like you fucked Megan?'

He laughed. 'I wondered how long it would take you to throw that in my face.' Striding across to the sash window, he thumped his hand against the frame. 'So, did you? Tit for tat? Revenge for Megan?'

'No.'

He turned to face her. 'I don't believe you. I think you saw an opportunity to get your own back and you took it.'

'And maybe I would have been entitled,' Sam said, standing. 'But I didn't.'

'How often did you meet him at The Queen's Head?'

'What?'

'I know you met him there. Do they have rooms?'

'Have you been following me?'

'So is that where it happened? Is that where you let him have you? Please tell me you were drunk, Sam, like I was with Megan, that things got out of hand and one thing led to another.'

'It wasn't like that.'

'So you made a conscious decision to cheat on me when you were stone cold sober? Thanks.'

'I haven't cheated on you.'

'You want to tell your face that.'

'Neil . . .' She went to reach for him but he pushed her hand away.

'I asked Patrick Sheldon to investigate the man I caught touching Josh in the hospital. I did that because I wanted to protect our son from a man I thought was a monster. Turns out my son was safe, my marriage maybe less so.' He kicked out at the basket of logs beside the fireplace. 'Tit for tat? Is that it? Were you sleeping with him because of what I did with Megan? I need to know.'

'No.'

He pointed his finger at her, his hand shaking. 'From the moment I told you about the man at the hospital, you must have known it was McAllister and that Josh was in no danger. You could so easily have put my mind at rest. Why didn't you?'

Sam felt her heart shrink with shame. She had tossed and turned night after night agonising over what to do while Neil had lain awake beside her worrying about their son. She had been desperate to quell his fears but she had been too scared to do so in case he guessed how far things had gone between her and David, just how close she had come to taking a lover to bed.

Her fear of losing him had won out and silence had been the price she had paid. It had been a heavy price, and she had been the only one to blame, because the tangle of white lies that had held her so tightly bound had all been of her own making.

'I thought you'd be angry at my making contact with him and keeping it from you.' It sounded weak even to her.

Neil regarded her coldly. 'You let me worry myself sick over Josh when, but for the fact you'd have been caught out in a lie, you could have stopped it?' He grabbed her wrist. 'I don't believe you. What else were you covering up? If you don't tell me I'm going to think it anyway, so what have you got to lose?'

You, maybe. Tears flecked Sam's cheeks. This was the day she'd been dreading. The day when the lies caught her out. Individually, they had seemed so harmless, yet with an unstoppable momentum they had built up, trapping her in a prison of her own making.

She missed David, his absence was an ache in her heart, but she loved Neil. He was her life. Her future. Once, she had wanted to avenge Megan and hurt him like this but not any more. Now, she just wanted to take him in her arms and hold him.

'I'm sorry,' she whispered.

It was time for the lies to stop, she realised. If it cleared the air then, maybe, moving forward, the marriage would stand or fall because of what they did next not because of something either of them had done in the past.

'I need to know,' he said quietly.

Sam bent her head. She couldn't talk of her feelings for David and face Neil. She spun her father's ring. 'I should have told you I'd gone to see him but you were living in the flat and it was easier not to. I did genuinely want to help him. The attraction came later. Then, I admit, I thought about making things even between us.'

'By sleeping with him?'

'Yes. I wanted to blot out the hurt of what you did with Megan.' She glanced up. Neil was staring at her stony faced. 'But I didn't do it, Neil. I could have done but I didn't.'

He looked shell-shocked, Sam thought. He had been pushing for an admission and yet it was clear he'd hoped one would never come. She couldn't blame him. She had been devastated to discover the truth about Megan. Her worst fears realised but that wasn't the case here. She hadn't taken that final, fateful step. She looked at Neil's face, clouded with anger and hurt and wondered whether it would make any difference.

'How far did things go?'

'We kissed.'

'When?'

'In the summertime.' She watched him take this on board, fresh hurt pinching his face.

'After we'd been reconciled?' His voice was sharp.

Her gaze fell to the carpet. 'Yes.'

'Let me get this straight. You started visiting this guy after the accident?'

Sam nodded.

'And you carried on seeing him until the summer?'

'Yes.'

'And you were lying to me all that time?' His voice cracked.

Sam thought about trying to justify her actions. One look at Neil's face told her there was no point. 'Yes,' she said in a small voice.

'What did you find so attractive about him?'

'Neil . . .'

'Perfectly reasonable question, Sam,' he barked.

'He was easy to talk to.'

Neil laughed. 'So you did a lot of talking, did you, before you stuck your tongues down each other's throats?'

'He was there. You weren't.'

'I'm asking you to explain why you cheated on me and that's the best you can do? Have another dig at me because I was always at work? You're unbelievable, Sam! Why not just tell me the truth. I know you're a little out of practice on that score . . .'

'For God's sake, Neil!'

'Just admit it, what I did with Megan gave you a peg to hang your conscience on while your knickers came off.'

'I told you I never slept with him.'

'I always knew I'd married above myself, feared the day you might wake up and wonder what the hell you were doing with me. Is that what happened? You woke up and thought *I can do better*.'

'No!'

'I know I've put on a few pounds and I need glasses now to read. But I don't need my glasses to see what's staring me right in the face. You wanted a younger man, didn't you? A designer boyfriend to go with your designer interiors. You . . .'

'You've got this all wrong. I love you.'

'You've got a funny way of showing it.'

She clawed at his arm. 'All that matters is that I could have taken things further with him but I didn't. It was my choice and I chose to walk away.'

The silence between them lengthened.

'If I hadn't slept with Megan . . .'

Sam seized the olive branch. 'I would never have put myself in a position to be tempted. I was hurting Neil, smarting with anger. I thought if I broke a few rules of my own what you'd done would hurt a little less.'

'Did it?'

'No.' She threaded her arms round his waist, pressed her head to his chest, held him tightly. 'It made me realise what was important. You and the children. What we have.' She could feel the tension in his back. 'I'm sorry.' The word caught like a sob in her throat as she realised he wasn't going to put his arms round her in return.

'When did you finish with him?'

Sam forced herself to step away, the pain of being so close and yet not being held by him, unbearable. 'I ended it when we came back from holiday.'

'Only then?'

'What happened with Josh and our time away made me realise there is only one man I wanted to be with and that man is you.' She met his gaze. Held it. She reached out to stroke his face but he jerked away.

'I'm going to need time,' he said gruffly.

She knew that feeling.

He stalked to the door then turned around. 'I know you met him for lunch the day Josh was hurt. But later, were you with a client like you and Connor said or were you still with him? I need to know.'

Time stood still. It was the question she had dreaded the most. The one she had hoped he would never ask and yet in her heart she had always known that if he ever found out about David, he undoubtedly would.

'I met him for lunch that day.'

'That's why you let my calls go to voicemail?'

'Yes.'

'And after?'

Another lie now could shatter any chance they had of a meaningful reconciliation but the truth could just as easily tear them apart because it was a truth she hardly wanted to admit to herself, let alone to him. She was trapped inside a Gordian knot of her own duplicity.

There was only one answer that could buy her the second chance she craved.

'I was meeting with a new client. That's where Connor found me.'

*

It was late by the time Neil was ready to turn in. He edged open the door of Josh's room. His son was asleep, the quilt pulled up to his chin. Neil remembered the sight of him bloodied at the hospital and offered up a silent prayer of thanks. Quietly, he closed the door. Then he went to Cass's room. She, too, was sleeping peacefully. His beautiful, feisty daughter, so like her mother, it made his heart ache. Neil crept out.

He opened the door to his own room. Sam was curled into a foetal position. There was a handkerchief grasped in her hand as if she had cried herself to sleep. The sight of it moved him. She did care for him and for their marriage. She had chosen him over McAllister. Moreover, they had two beautiful children who still needed both their parents.

Quietly, so as not to wake her, Neil got into bed. He crooked his arm under his head as he lay watching her. He'd believed her when she'd said she hadn't slept with McAllister. He was ashamed that it made such a difference, but it did. They could get through this if they both wanted to.

He thought about the afternoon Josh had been attacked.

'I was meeting with a new client. That's where Connor found me.'

Had she told him what she thought he wanted to hear? He wondered how he would feel should he ever discover that she had in fact been with McAllister. Kissing, flirting, laughing and joking while his son had bled and he had wept.

Tentatively, Neil hooked his arm over Sam's waist and settled himself beside her, letting his nostrils fill with the citrusy scent of her shampoo. A moment later, he felt her hand curl into his, tugging his arm tighter around her.

It was better by far to give her the benefit of the doubt, he decided, because he wasn't at all sure he could live with the alternative.

Chapter Forty-Nine

'And he asked you flat out if you'd slept with him?'

Connor was sitting on the edge of Sam's desk.

Sam nodded. 'Please, Connor, if he asks you again where you found me the afternoon Josh was hurt . . .'

'I'll tell him you were with a new client.'

'Thank you.'

'Whether he believes me or not is another matter,' Connor added, raising his eyebrows.

'He has to. If he ever finds out the truth of what happened that afternoon I don't think he'll ever forgive me.'

She picked up her phone as it rang. Neil. Checking up on her. She couldn't blame him. She had done the same on learning about Megan. She had to be patient with him – as patient as he had been with her.

After the call, Sam flexed her hands in front of her, watching the spotlights glint on the diamonds in her engagement ring. All the hurt and fear she had gone through, he was now going through but she took heart from the way he had put his arm round her the previous night. The gesture had been encouraging and although she had longed for something more, it was a start.

*

Gordon Honeydew beckoned Sam into his office. 'Thanks for coming over. I wanted you to see this. I've finally got it working. Well, sort of.'

On a side table was Daphne Mitchell's cash register.

'Press a few of the numbers. Doesn't matter which ones.'

Sam did as she was told. As she pressed the keys, letters sprang up within the Perspex cover at the top of the cash register. The keys spelt out 'Happy Anniversary'.

'Isn't that wonderful?' Sam said. 'I have to show this to Daphne.'

'Wait. There's more.'

'Press another button.'

Sam pressed a button and the letters disappeared.

'Now press a few more.'

As Sam pressed more buttons a new message was spelt out. 'I love you'.

Sam felt tears spring to her eyes.

'I've had a devil of a job getting it to work. Had to take the back right off. Finally got it working in the right sequence last night. It's quite something, isn't it?'

Sam nodded. 'Can I take it to show, Daphne?'

'Of course. It's hers after all but is there any chance you could leave it with me for just a little longer. I still can't get the cash drawer open and I think I know why. Ted Mitchell's diagrams lead me to believe that the cash register is supposed to open when "Happy Anniversary" is spelt out and then when the cash drawer is closed "I love you" should come up. I couldn't get it to work like that because the cash drawer is jammed so I improvised but I can't help thinking Ted might have put something in the cash drawer for his wife. Why else would he set it to open automatically when "Happy Anniversary" came up.'

'You think he put a gift in there for her?'

Gordon nodded. 'Whatever it is, I reckon it's got caught up, which is why it won't open. I'm reluctant to force it in case I break whatever is inside but I have an idea. You know I said I'd had the back off it when I was sorting out the keys?'

Sam nodded.

'The cash drawer is a sealed unit but I could cut through the top and lift a piece out to see what's going on underneath, free the mechanism and then fix the piece back in place. It will be on the inside so no one will be able to see the repair. What do you think?'

'I think you should do it. If Ted Mitchell left his wife a gift or a message she deserves to have it.'

'My thoughts exactly. I'll get to work on it tonight.'

*

Connor was waiting for her when she got back to the office.

'There's someone here to see you although I'm not sure you'll want to see him.' He moved to one side.

David was pacing in her office.

'Need me to get rid?'

Sam shook her head.

'Need me to come with you?'

'No. I'll be fine. Thank you.'

Sam shut the door of her office and leaned against it.

'You can't be here. You need to go,' she said firmly.

'How's Josh? Is he getting on okay at his new school?'

'Josh is doing very well. David, please! You have to go.'

She watched him sit uninvited in one of the chairs facing her desk, wincing as he did so.

'I've been desperate to know how Josh has been getting on. He's a good kid.'

'Yes, he is. He loves his new school. He's made friends. He's happy.'

'And Cass? How's Cass? She still seeing that boy, Tobyn?'

'Yes.'

'And you? How are you?'

'I'm okay. What are you doing here, David?'

'I just needed to see you. You were a huge part of my life, Sam. When you walked away, I couldn't just turn my feelings off like a tap.'

'I realise that.'

He leapt up and started to look at the drawings on her desk. 'What are you working on?'

'Phil Blunkett's new development.' She edged the drawings away from him.

'I've started seeing Lauren again.'

'The woman who left you while you were in the hospital?' Sam was shocked.

He nodded. 'I bumped into her at a party. She'd split up with the guy she'd left me for. She wanted to try again, make up for what happened.' David met her gaze. 'I thought she could help. I thought being with her would get you out of my head.' He moved towards her.

Sam fled to the other side of the desk. 'You need to go, David.'

'You don't know what it's been like for me, Angel. When you walked away, you took the best part of me with you. You were all I wanted, all I could think of, all I had.' He leaned across the desk.

'It had to end. You know that.'

'Lauren could see I was hurting. She wanted to know why. I told her about you. About us. She made me promise I was over you and I promised because I wanted it to be true but . . .'

'David . . .' Sam said, a warning note in her voice.

'Is he good to you, Sam, or has he hurt you again?'

'Neil's a good man and we're in a good place.' She watched the pain crack and break in David's eyes. 'Why are you here, David?'

He sat down once more, throwing his bad leg out in front of him.

'Lauren's always been the jealous type. After I told her about you, she became obsessed, pestering me with questions. Tell me how Sam does her hair? What perfume does she wear? Do you think of her when you

361

kiss me? Every day, there are a hundred questions. She cannae seem to let it go.'

Sam remembered how she'd obsessed about Megan after Neil's confession. 'Keep reassuring her. Eventually, she'll come to terms with the feelings you had for me and then the two of you will be able to move beyond them and be happy.'

'I think she might try to speak to you about us, that's why I'm here.'

Sam looked at him, alarmed. 'Speak to me? You mean come to my home?'

He shrugged. 'Maybe. I don't know. I'm sorry to bring this trouble to your door but I thought you ought to know.'

Sam's mind raced. 'You've told her we're over?'

'Aye, but I'm not sure she believes it.'

'Make her believe it.'

'I'm trying. It's not that easy.'

Sam rubbed her forehead. 'Okay. Well, if she turns up, I'll handle it. She can't do any harm.'

'What about Neil?'

'He already knows about us. I told him.'

David raised his eyebrows. 'How did he take it?'

'How do you think? He was hurt. Angry. He has every right to be.'

'We didn't do anything wrong.'

Sam laughed. 'We both know that isn't true.'

'Are you still together?'

Sam nodded. 'It'll take more than an illicit affair on his part and an infatuation on mine to tear us apart.'

'An infatuation?' David looked stung. 'We were more than that. Come on, Angel.' He stood.

'Whatever, it's over now.'

'It doesn't have to be . . .'

Sam looked at him in astonishment. 'Is it any wonder you can't convince Lauren we're over when you come out with crap like that. Jesus, David.'

'It's not crap.'

Sam slammed her hands down on the desk. 'Get it into your head, we're finished. Go and be with Lauren, go and be with anyone. But you can't be with me and you can't come here again. If Neil sees you . . .'

'So things are bad between you then?'

'Well they're hardly going to be peachy, are they? He had a private investigator tailing you because he thought you were a bloody paedophile. He followed you to The Queen's Head in August. He saw us together.'

'He confronted you?'

'Yes.'

'Did you tell *him* it was an infatuation?'

'It doesn't matter what I told him. We're over. That's all that matters.'

'Lauren . . .'

'If Lauren wants to talk to me, she can talk to me. There's nothing she can do or say that can hurt Neil and me.'

David blew out a long breath. 'You deserve to be happy, Sam.'

'So do you, but I'm not sure Lauren is the one to make it happen. Not after what she did to you.'

'I needed someone and I couldn't have you.'

'So you chose Lauren? She broke your heart. You were in pieces in the hospital after she dumped you.'

'And I had a guardian angel to put me back together again.'

'David . . .'

'It's okay, Sam. I get the message. We're through and my happiness is not your responsibility. I guess it never was. I just wanted to warn you about Lauren.'

*

After David had gone, Connor came in.

'Want to talk about it?' he asked.

'No, thanks.'

There was nothing to say. Her heart had pulled at the sight of David but she had made her choice and it was the right one. David would find someone else in time. Not Lauren. She was a port in a storm, nothing more. No, he would find a sweet, kind girl to settle down with. It could just never be her.

'I'm going to start on the mood boards for Phil Blunkett,' Sam said, hoping it would take her mind off things.

An hour later, Sam cast a critical eye over the boards. There was enough for Phil Blunkett to get excited about. It was a start but she knew she could do better. Perhaps tomorrow with fresh eyes she would see what was currently lacking.

'I'm going to go and pick the kids up, Connor. I'll see you tomorrow.'

'Goodnight, hon.'

Sam's heels clicked on the worn concrete of the car park as she hurried towards her car. Thumbing the alarm, she quickly climbed inside. She just had time to swing by the supermarket and grab something nice for supper before she had to pick up the children.

She drummed her fingers on the steering wheel in frustration as she waited for a gap in the traffic. It was only as a friendly driver flashed his headlights to let her out and she began to move forward that she noticed the blonde-haired woman standing on the pavement opposite staring up intently at her office window.

Lauren? It was hard to imagine anyone else being so interested in her office. Sam's heart sunk. Whilst she had made light of the situation to David, the thought of a confrontation with Lauren filled her heart with dread.

Her relationship with Neil was fragile. His smiles were slow, his kisses fleeting. When they had tried to make love the other night he had lost his erection inside her. Ignoring her soothing words and attempts to revive him, he had withdrawn and rolled away from her, his shoulders a hunched testament to his misery.

The last thing they needed was Lauren turning up on the doorstep bringing the past with her.

Chapter Fifty

'I think they were even better than last year and that's saying something,' Connor declared as he followed Sam, Neil and the children through the front door of Meadowview Cottage. 'Even Cass enjoyed it, didn't you, sweetheart?'

Cass smiled. 'As firework displays go it was all right.'

'Mm, I was thinking more of the boy with the cute eyes who kept looking at you and smiling.'

'His name's Tobyn.' Neil said. 'They're in a band together.'

'Has he got the Neil Davenport seal of approval?'

'We haven't been formally introduced yet,' Neil replied.

Connor draped his arm round Neil's shoulders. 'Will any boy get your seal of approval?'

'Doubt it,' Neil growled.

Connor laughed. 'It's the nunnery for you then, my girl!'

'Does everyone want tomato soup and hotdogs?' Sam asked.

A chorus of approval met her suggestion. She had expected nothing less. It was a family tradition after the Abbeyleigh Fireworks Display to come home and indulge in warming comfort food.

'I'll give you a hand,' Connor said.

'You can't, Connor,' Josh proclaimed. 'It's you and me against Dad and Cass on the Xbox.'

Connor ruffled Josh's hair. 'You could beat those two singlehanded, mate.'

'Oi!' Cass thumped his shoulder. 'You're my godfather too, remember?'

'And I take my duties very seriously,' Connor responded. 'And whenever you need spiritual or moral guidance, my love, I will be there for you but when it comes to Josh versus anyone on the Xbox, I will always back the boy genius.'

'We are so going to kill you two,' Cass responded.

Sam squeezed Connor's shoulder. 'Go and join in the fun.'

'You sure?'

'Positive.'

Humming to herself, Sam set about cooking the sausages and warming the soup. She could hear raucous laughter coming from the TV room and felt the tension in her shoulders begin to relax.

All evening she had held herself ready in case Lauren should appear and accost her in front of her family. Constantly on the alert, she had scanned the crowds in the park, scrutinising every blonde-haired woman, dreading a tap on her shoulder, or worse, on Neil's.

Having confided in Connor the day after David's visit to their office, Connor had been quick to pick up on her discomfort.

'If the psycho bitch tries anything tonight, I'll get rid of her for you,' he'd whispered as Neil and the children had gone on ahead. 'I'll tell them she's an ex-girlfriend.'

Sam had laughed. 'That will make for an interesting conversation.'

'At least it made you smile.' He'd linked his arm through hers.

'I wish you didn't have to fly to New York tomorrow.'

'If you're really worried about Lauren, I'll cancel.'

She'd touched his face. 'You've been looking forward to going away with Warren ever since he suggested it. Ignore me. I'll be fine. I'm sure most of it is my over-active imagination running wild,' Sam had said, a little embarrassed. 'She was definitely outside the office two nights this week and I'm pretty sure she followed me to the auction house. But then I also thought I saw her outside a client's house, again on Abbeyleigh High Street, outside Josh's school and in the supermarket. She couldn't have been in all of those places! It's just not logical. It's my mind playing tricks on me. I need to get a grip.'

'Preferably round her throat,' Connor had quipped.

Sam had smiled. 'If I could just talk to her, I might be able to convince her that there's nothing between David and me now. But the last thing I want to do is have that conversation in front of Neil.'

'Are things no better between you?'

Sam had waggled her hand.

Now, as she buttered the rolls for the hotdogs, the outside light switched on, flooding the front garden and drive in light. Dropping the knife, Sam went to the window and peered out.

Common sense told her it was probably a neighbourhood cat or maybe a fox, but such was the jagged state of her nerves she wouldn't let herself be convinced without checking. What if the doorbell went and Neil answered?

And then she saw her. A silhouette standing in the shadows by Neil's car. Sam bit back a cry and throwing open the side door, she ran outside. By the time she got there the front garden was empty. She scanned the lane left and right. Nothing.

Had it come to this? Was she seeing things now? Tears of anger and frustration built up behind Sam's eyes but at the same time a frisson of fear spread across her shoulder blades.

'Please, leave me alone,' she called into the darkness unsure whether she was appealing to a real person or just a phantom in her mind.

Chapter Fifty-One

The next day Sam woke with a fragile head from too much wine. She had over indulged in an effort to wipe from her mind the vision of the figure she had spotted – or thought she had spotted – beside Neil's car.

Now, as she mixed two aspirin she heard the kitchen door open and turned to find Neil rubbing his forehead and yawning and her heart swelled with love.

'Have you got time for bacon and eggs?' she asked, swallowing the aspirin.

'Bacon and eggs on a weekday?'

'The kids have both got lifts today. I fancy a change and it's supposed to be good for a hangover, isn't it?'

He chuckled. 'You did seem to rather enjoy yourself with the Pinot Grigio last night. Well I'm certainly not going to eat toast if you're tucking into bacon. Why not? I'll give you a hand. I think I saw some mushrooms in the fridge. Might as well do things properly.'

She ran her hand across his shoulders.

'Take the day off, Neil.'

'What?'

'Let's spend the day together.'

'Doing what?'

'Anything. Nothing. Who cares. Let's just spend it together.'

Laughing, Neil opened the fridge and stared inside. 'Nice thought, but you know I've got a ton of stuff to finish at the office before I leave at Christmas.'

Sam's head throbbed with renewed intensity. 'Why do you give a damn about that bloody place after what Edward did to you?' she asked crossly.

'Because when I leave I want the satisfaction of knowing that all of my files are up to date.' He picked up the bag of mushrooms and a couple of tomatoes. 'I'll take you to lunch if you like although I'm not sure we'll have much appetite after this.'

*

When Sam reached her office, she phoned David.

'Sam? Is everything okay?'

'No! Everything is not okay. Lauren is practically stalking me, David. You've got to get her to stop this. It's driving me nuts.'

She heard him sigh.

'I was hoping that had all blown over.'

'Well it hasn't. If anything it's getting worse. I can't go on like this. She's making me a nervous bloody wreck.'

'Oh, Angel! I'm sorry.'

'Tell her I'll meet her. If I talk to her perhaps I can convince her there is nothing going on between us.'

'I cannae tell her that. She'll know we've been speaking to each other. That will only make her worse.'

'Is she dangerous? Are Neil and the children safe? Am I?'

'What? Of course you're safe. She wouldn't do anything. She's emotional, highly strung. Not psychotic.'

'I think I should go to the police.'

'No!'

'She was outside my house last night. At least, I think she was. It's got to stop, David.'

'Don't go to the police, Angel, please. There's no need for that. We're thinking of moving away, buying a place near the holiday cottage. I'm sure once we're out of the area, she'll stop obsessing about you.'

'When are you leaving?'

'As soon as the settlement money from my claim comes through. Your husband's insurance company are digging their heels in. Get Neil to push the settlement through and we'll be gone. You'll never have to see either one of us again, I promise.'

'I'll speak to Neil, see what I can do.'

Sam put the phone down. Neil was likely to be bullish about the settlement. It was in his nature not to back down, especially where David was concerned. If only there was another way she could reach out to Lauren. *If I could just speak to her woman to woman.*

Then it came to her. The lawyers' letter that she had seen in David's cutlery drawer. Lauren had instructed London lawyers after her break up with David, probably squabbling over assets. Sam hadn't read the letter but she had read the banner across the top of it that had included the lawyers' name. *Perkins Ronin.*

She did a Google search and quickly noted down their number before ringing it.

'Hello. My name is Sam Davenport and I need to get a message to one of your clients. Her name is Lauren Brightwell. I'm not sure which lawyer was dealing with her matter but could you ask them to pass my name and number on to Miss Brightwell and get her to call me. It really is very urgent.'

Perhaps if Lauren stopped skulking about in the shadows and met her for a coffee she could end this.

As her phone rang she answered it quickly even though logic told her there was no way it could be Lauren calling her already.

'Sam? It's Gordon Honeydew. Any chance you can come over? I have something rather fabulous to show you.'

'You've managed to open the cash drawer?'

'Yes.'

'And there's something inside?'

'Come and see.'

Sam was at the auction house within ten minutes, breathless but excited.

'I haven't had time to rewire it yet so you must imagine you have just seen "Happy Anniversary" pop up and then voila.' He pressed a button and the cash drawer flew open.

Nestled inside one of the compartments was an eternity ring. Sam picked it up to admire it. 'It's beautiful.'

'Top-quality stones.'

Sam put it back in the tray. Beside it was a piece of folded paper. It had a tear in one corner.

'It was the letter that got caught in the mechanism. It tore a little when I freed it but only in the corner. It hasn't damaged any of the script.'

'Have you read it?'

'No. I imagine Ted intended it for his wife's eyes alone.'

Sam nodded. 'Quite right.'

'I just need to rewire it so that it works as Ted intended and then you can take it to show Daphne. Would you be able to come back in the morning?'

'You bet. This is going to mean so much to her, Gordon. Thank you.'

*

Neil had booked them a table at Spike's. He stood as Sam approached through the packed lunchtime crowd and kissed her cheek.

'Good morning?' she asked.

'Yes. You?'

She nodded. 'Don't know that I've got much appetite. You?'

He shook his head. 'I did warn you. Shall we share a sandwich?'

'Yes, let's do that.'

'Last of the big spenders, us,' he said with a smile. 'How does smoked salmon and cream cheese grab you?'

'Sounds good.' She shed her scarf and coat as she sat. 'Talking of big spenders,' she said after Neil had placed their order. 'Where do things stand with David's personal injury claim?'

'Why?' Neil asked sharply.

'Because the sooner we are able to draw a line under the whole thing, the better I'll feel.' It wasn't a lie. It just wasn't the complete truth.

'Soon.'

'Soon as in the next few days?'

'Soon as in before Christmas, I hope.'

Sam sat back stunned. 'Can't you push it through. I don't want it hanging over us any longer.'

'It's not up to me. It's up to the insurers.'

'But you could push them to settle, couldn't you? Use your influence.'

'My influence?' Neil chuckled. 'Glad you think I've got some. Truth is, I don't blame them for holding out. McAllister's got unrealistic expectations of what he might achieve.'

'How far apart are you?'

'Fifty grand. My guess is he'll settle for another twenty-five on top of what we've offered. We just need to wear him down. These things are a war of attrition. You know that. It's a question of who will crack first.'

'And how long will that take?'

'A week, a month. Who knows? Frankly, who cares?'

I do.

*

Sam rang David's number on the way back to her office.

'They won't settle at the figure you want. They

375

reckon you'll walk away if they up their offer by another twenty-five.'

'Bastards. I deserve every penny of that fucking money. I shouldn't have to settle for less.'

'No, you shouldn't.' There was going to be no quick fix, Sam realised. She was going to have to live with the spectre of Lauren looming over her for a few more weeks if not months. Her heart sank at the prospect.

'My lawyer has already warned me that your husband's lot probably won't give in. This could drag on to the middle of next year if I let it.'

Sam tried to swallow her cry of frustration. 'Can't you talk to Lauren, convince her that there's nothing between us now?'

'Don't you think I've tried, Angel? Lauren's always been insecure. Reassuring her with words is like trying to fill a hole in the sand with sea water. The only way to truly convince her that you and I are over is if we move away. Fuck it! I'll tell my lawyer that I'll take the smaller sum and have done with it.'

'I can't ask you to do that!'

'You didn't.'

'But . . .'

'This has to end and I'm the only one who can end it. I don't want your last memories of me to be tainted by Lauren's actions. What we had was beautiful. That's what I want you to remember.'

'It was beautiful and I do remember,' Sam said softly.

'Then that's all that matters. The rest is just money, after all.'

Chapter Fifty-Two

Sam was at Honeydews Auction House before they opened.

Gordon greeted her with a smile. 'I've got it all working just as Ted Mitchell wanted. Press any key and "Happy Anniversary" will pop up letter by letter. When the last letter pops up the cash drawer automatically opens. As the cash drawer is pushed shut, "I love you" springs up.' He gently placed the cash register into a box. 'I shall miss the old thing. It's been a conundrum but an enjoyable one.' He patted the cash register fondly. 'Try to persuade Daphne Mitchell to come to the unveiling of the automatons next month.'

'I'll do my best.'

'If she doesn't come the museum have asked me to give a speech about the automatons and Ted's work on them. I feel as if I know him after all these months spent studying his notes and diagrams.'

'Great as your speech will doubtless be, Gordon, I hope it doesn't come to that.'

'Me neither, Sam. Let me carry that to the car for you.'

*

Sam had kept her word to Daphne Mitchell and each week she had found time in her diary to share a pot of tea with her and enjoy a slice of cake. Over the course of the year they had become firm friends.

Now as Sam waited for Daphne to open the door, she wondered how she would react to the sight of one of her husband's automatons back in the house.

'Sam? What a lovely surprise! I thought you were coming round on Thursday.'

'I was but I didn't think this could wait.'

'What on earth have you got there?'

'Let me set it up on the table in the reading room and then I'll tell you all about it.'

'I'll put the kettle on,' Daphne said.

Sam lifted the cash register out of the box and set it down on the desk Daphne used when working on her craft projects. She rehearsed the instructions Gordon had given her.

'Oh my!'

She turned to find Daphne in the doorway, a look of dismay on her face.

'Please don't be upset with me, Daphne. Come and sit down.'

'That's the automaton Ted was working on when he died, Sam,' Daphne said, backing away. 'I don't want it in the house.'

'He was working on it for you.'

'I don't understand.'

'It was going to be your anniversary present.'

Daphne raised her eyebrows. 'I don't think so, Sam. I never liked his machines. Truth be told, I resented the time and love he lavished on them all.'

'I think you'll like this one when you see what it does.' She held out her hand. 'Please, Daphne.'

'Very well.' Daphne took her hand. 'I'll humour you, Sam, but then I want it out of the house. Do you understand?'

Sam nodded. 'I took the automaton to a friend of mine, Gordon Honeydew of Honeydews Auction House in Abbeyleigh. He valued the other machines and spoke to the Abbeyleigh Museum on my behalf. This one, as you know, wasn't finished. Gordon told me this one wasn't an original. Your husband had taken an old cash register and was turning it into an automaton from scratch.'

As she spoke Sam watched Daphne stroke her fingers over the keys of the cash register.

'I worked in a shop when Ted and I first met. I used a cash register just like this one.'

Sam smiled. 'Your husband left several diagrams and notes which were in the box. Gordon asked if he could work on it, try to figure out what your husband was trying to do with it.'

'And did he?'

'It's taken him a long while but, yes, he finally figured it out and got it all working.'

Daphne took a deep breath. 'I suppose I had better give it a go then. What do I have to do?'

'Press the keys and it will spell out a message in the display. When you get to the end of the message the cash drawer will open. When you shut the drawer, another message will pop up. I'll be in the kitchen.' Sam touched Daphne's shoulder. 'Take as long as you need.'

Sam made the tea while she was waiting and poured herself a cup. It was twenty minutes later before Daphne emerged, red-eyed, wearing the ring and holding the letter.

'Did you read it?'

'No. Neither Gordon nor I felt it was right to do so.'

Daphne smiled. 'Thank you. We existed so much in our own little worlds, Ted and I. He'd spend hours fussing over his machines. Sometimes I thought he loved them more than me. I so wanted a message from him. Something to hold on to. He was a man of so few words and now I have this.' Daphne clutched the letter to her heart. 'I can't begin to tell you how precious this is for me. I resented the machines so bitterly for taking him from me and now I feel as though the machines have given him back to me. Thank you for caring so much, Sam, for making this happen.' Daphne threw her arms round Sam's neck.

'It was my pleasure.'

'Will you thank Gordon Honeydew as well?'

'You could thank him yourself. He's going to be at the unveiling of the other automatons at the museum next month. Do say you'll come.'

Daphne drew back. 'Ted would want me to, I suppose, but I can't give a speech.'

'Everyone will just be happy that you're there.'

'Perhaps we could go shopping together. You can help me find something to wear.'

'I'd be delighted to.' Sam smiled. 'I take it the cash register is staying?'

Daphne smiled. 'I never want to be parted from it again.'

*

As Sam drove back to the office her thoughts turned once more to Lauren. As much as she wanted her out of her life for good, it didn't sit right with Sam that David should settle for twenty-five thousand pounds less than he was entitled to just to bring his claim to an end so they could move away.

Why should he take the hit for her? It wasn't fair. Not after everything he had gone through. After a wrecked night, Sam had decided she would pay the balance to him herself from her and Neil's savings. It was the right thing to do.

Now, after parking her car at the office Sam made her way to the East Anglian Building Society.

'You have ten pounds in your account, Mrs Davenport.'

Taken aback, Sam said, 'There must be some mistake.'

Manicured nails clattered on the keys. 'There's no mistake, I'm sorry. Ten pounds. Exactly. There was a withdrawal of five thousand pounds in August.'

Sam felt light headed. Five thousand pounds taken from their account? 'We must have been the victims of a fraud.'

The woman frowned. 'It was Neil Davenport who authorised the withdrawal.'

Neil? What could he possibly have wanted with five thousand pounds? Sam realised the woman was staring at her. Colouring rapidly, she thanked her for her help and left. In a daze, she walked along the High Street to the Essex Building Society. They had two accounts there. A platinum deposit account with over thirty thousand and the new account they had set up for Josh's school fees.

She asked for the balance of the platinum deposit account. 'That account was downgraded in August following the withdrawal that was made.'

Sam almost swooned. 'Withdrawal?'

'Neil Davenport made a withdrawal of thirty thousand pounds.'

Sam swallowed. That made thirty-five thousand pounds in total.

'There's three hundred pounds left in the account.'

'What about our other account?'

'That has a balance of two thousand.'

So, Neil hadn't touched the school account and neither, she realised, could she. Her plan had been to take money from both the general deposit accounts so it wouldn't look quite so obvious. Then replace it with a loan from her business account once she had had a chance to talk to Connor. She had planned to explain the withdrawals on the statements as a banking error if Neil ever queried it. It seemed, however, that Neil had got there first.

'Three hundred pounds,' Sam repeated.

It was a drop in the ocean.

'Yes.'

'Thank you.'

Sam burned with anger. What the hell had Neil done with their savings?

Chapter Fifty-Three

Sam fished her phone from her bag. David's home number. She wondered for a moment if it might be Lauren responding to the message she'd left with the lawyers.

'Hello?'

'Where are you, Sam?'

'I'm on my way to see Neil. Why, what's wrong?' she asked, picking up on David's panicked tone.

'I'm sorry, Sam.'

'What's happened?'

'Lauren caught me looking at a picture of you I had on my phone. We got into a fight. She grabbed my phone and stormed out saying that Neil deserves to know the truth about us. I'm sorry. I know it's going to cause you all kinds of trouble. If I could stop her, I would but I don't even know where she is right now.'

Flustered, Sam said, 'It doesn't matter. I told you, Neil already knows what happened between us.'

'She took my phone, Sam.'

'Yes, I know. You said.'

'It had my pictures on it. The ones I took of you and I that afternoon on the towpath. What if she shows them to Neil? Do you think he's going to understand then?'

Sam came to an abrupt halt, the noise of the High Street fading away. 'You told me you deleted them.'

'I lied. I couldn't do it. I wanted them.'

'Does Lauren know what happened that afternoon, with Josh, I mean?'

'No. To her they'll just be pictures of us fooling around and kissing. I'd be surprised if she was vindictive enough to show them to Neil but then I didn't think she'd keep bothering you the way she has. All I know for certain is that she's pissed at me and she's pissed at you and if she wants to get back at us both for loving one another, she's found a pretty good way of doing it even if she doesn't realise it. The photos are time and date stamped, Sam. If Lauren shows them to Neil he'll know you were with me for the whole afternoon.'

Chapter Fifty-Four

Sam ran the rest of the way to her husband's firm. She had just walked through the front door when a text arrived from David's mobile.

Bitch! He told me you were over but you've been ringing one another for weeks! I hate people like you, people who destroy other people's lives. You think you can have everything, don't you, including David? A perfect life. It won't be so perfect when your husband sees these . . .

The first of four images pinged onto her phone showing her and David on that magical, fateful, awful afternoon. Sam stared at them. Their affection for one another shone out of each photograph. Her eyes were soft with love. His face so tender in response. Their hands touching, holding. At one point, his hand had strayed to stroke her hair. She couldn't remember that but it must have happened. It was there in front of her. Together with the kiss.

The date and time screamed out in condemnation of her.

She took the stairs to Neil's office two at a time. If she could just get to Neil first before he saw the images. If she could find some way to soften the blow they might just find a way out of this mess.

Unannounced, she flung open his office door. Megan was sitting on the edge of Neil's desk, practically in his lap. She was wearing a pin-striped mini skirt, exposing gym-honed legs, and her hand was on Neil's shoulder as they laughed together. Two half-filled champagne flutes stood on the desk alongside the bottle.

Roses and jasmine.

Sam froze in the doorway, all forward momentum lost by the sight of them together. She felt almost winded. Her gaze settled on Megan's hand. She watched as the young woman slowly removed it from Neil's shoulder. Noticed, in that instant, how close her husband's hand was to Megan's leg.

Had she been blind this whole time? Was her husband's lack of desire for her due to his anger at her over her dalliance with David or had it been caused by guilt over his own actions?

Striding forward, Sam snatched up the champagne flutes and threw the contents first at Neil and then at Megan.

Ignoring Megan's screams and Neil's astonished protestations, Sam said, 'You'll be seeing some photos I never wanted you to see.' She threw a withering glance at them both. 'Now, I wonder why I cared. I'll be at home.'

Chapter Fifty-Five

She had Neil's suitcase on the bed and was piling his clothes inside when she heard his car skid to a halt on the drive. Anger spiking, she pulled open another drawer and, with fresh impetus, threw the clothes in the general direction of the case, her vision blurred by tears.

Had they ever stopped seeing one another? she wondered. Had his declarations of guilt about what he'd done and his love for Sam been calculated to win her back only to restore the status quo?

She recalled their conversation about Megan whilst on holiday in Sardinia.

'She helped me with a problem on one of my files. We spent some time together as a result but it was purely professional.'

There had been a look of horror on his face when she'd mentioned Megan's name and then something else. Shame. Why had he looked ashamed? It had nagged at her at the time but she'd put it down to shame over his initial betrayal and forced it from her mind, but what if it was shame at a more recent betrayal?

David had warned her. *'He cheated once. He'll do it again.'*

She looked up as Neil flung open the bedroom door. He glared at the contents of the suitcase. 'You've got a bloody nerve!' he declared. 'Even though you're the one in the wrong, I'm the one who has to leave?'

'Can you blame me when I find you and her drinking champagne and touching one another, not caring who might see you.'

'I wasn't touching her.'

'Your fingers were an inch from her thigh.'

'I rest my case,' he said petulantly.

Sam's indignation flared. 'Don't get smart with me.' She let the next armful of clothes fall into the suitcase with a flourish. 'She had her hands all over you.'

'She was congratulating me.'

'Is that what you call it? Like she congratulated you in her kitchen that time?'

Neil shouldered her aside and began to repack the suitcase himself. 'Actually, you've done me a favour, making a start,' he said, indicating the case. 'I'd have been going anyway after what I've just seen.'

'To her?'

'Who knows? Maybe.'

'Was it ever over between you?' Sam asked quietly, the squall of her anger calming for a moment.

Neil looked at her. 'Is there any point in answering that question? You'll think what you want anyway,' he said tersely.

'You've been carrying on with her the whole time, haven't you?'

'Gives you a get-out-of-jail-free card, doesn't it? I can't believe you have the nerve to try and cling to the moral high ground right now. Not that I have to explain myself to you any more but for what it's worth, the champagne is an office tradition when we have a big win, and we had at least five colleagues with us just moments before you arrived. But thank you for humiliating me in front of everyone. I really appreciate it.'

The wet stain from the champagne was apparent down the front of his shirt, speckling his tie. 'I'm not sorry I did it,' Sam said defiantly, raising her chin.

'The champagne or the affair?' he quizzed.

'There wasn't . . .' Her voice trailed off as he raised a cynical eyebrow. She couldn't deny an affair, she realised because although she and David had never consummated their relationship, it had been whole in every other respect.

'This was hand-delivered to the office shortly after you left with a note telling me to look at the photos that were sent to you this morning.' He threw David's phone down on the bed between them. 'I've seen them, Sam. I know you were with him when I was at the hospital with Josh.' Neil's tone was bitter as he continued to neatly fold and stack his clothes. Only the quickness with which he snatched the hangers from the wardrobe betrayed his fury.

'I didn't think you'd ever be able to forgive me if you knew the truth,' Sam admitted.

Neil's shoulder crunched into hers as he passed by.

'While you were fooling around, Josh was sobbing for you. I kept telling him, "Mum'll be here soon, Mum's on her way".' Angry tears gathered in Neil's eyes. 'I'll never forget that day. I felt so bloody useless. There was nothing I could do because the only person he wanted was you.'

The thought of Josh hurt and calling for her was too much to bear. Sam began to cry.

'While you were kissing McAllister, Josh was being so brave. He was in pain but he was trying not to show how scared he was. It broke my heart.'

'Don't, Neil, please!'

'What's the matter?' he snarled. 'Is the truth too painful for you? I hope it is. You deserve for it to hurt like hell. You were his mother and you let him down. You let us all down.'

'Don't you think I know that?'

Neil's face was savage as he brought it close to hers. 'Where did Connor find you? Were you in a room at The Queen's Head? Back at his flat? In his bed?' Neil thumped his hand against the dresser. 'Is that where you were? Is that where Connor found you?' He grabbed the phone and threw it against the wall.

'Please, Neil! Don't!' She watched as Neil's fury subsided, contempt replacing it.

'I believed you when you said you hadn't slept with him but those photos . . . You've got your hands all over one another. Do you honestly expect me to believe you went back to his flat for a cup of tea after that?'

'I fought against it with all my might but I fell in love,' Sam said quietly. 'I didn't sleep with him but I

won't lie to you. I wanted to and maybe that's as bad.
I did go back to his flat that day and, yes, we would
have gone to bed together if Connor hadn't found us. I
thought you were with Megan again. The smell of her
perfume was on your shirts and I thought—'

'Here's my chance. He's given me the perfect excuse.'

'I walked away after those pictures were taken. I
told him I didn't want to see him any more. I wanted to
make it work with you, but what do you care anyway
if you've been sleeping with her the whole time?' Sam
asked, exasperated.

'I didn't say I was,' Neil responded coolly.

Could it be that she'd made a mistake? Had her
paranoia got the better of her? Sam was struck by how
vulnerable Neil looked at that moment as he methodi-
cally packed his suitcase. She reached for his arm.

'Don't touch me.'

Sam snatched her hand back.

'I always thought I could trust you,' he muttered.
'After what you saw your mum go through, I didn't
think you would ever do something like this.'

'Trust? You don't know the meaning of the word,' Sam
retaliated, stung, remembering her trip to the building
societies that morning. 'What have you done with our
money? Was it a deposit on a place for you and her?'

'Our money?' he asked, puzzled.

'Yes, our money,' she shouted. 'What the hell have
you done with our savings? There's over thirty grand
missing. Where is it?'

'Ah, that.'

'You took it in August. Why?'

'I had some trouble at work.'

'What trouble?'

'I made a mistake on a file. I didn't want it to come to light because it would have blown my chances of promotion so I covered it up by paying the client off myself.'

'Dear God, Neil! And you didn't tell me? Leaving aside the fact you could have been struck off, that was as much my money as yours. How dare you! How did you expect to get away with it? Surely you knew I'd find out eventually?'

'I was going to tell you but then when I handed in my notice I knew the firm would have to pay me out. I planned to use the money to plug the hole in our savings and hope you wouldn't notice in the meantime.'

'So I would never have known,' Sam said. She sat down at the dressing table, stunned.

'That was the idea,' Neil admitted. 'How did you find out?'

The irony of the situation hit Sam so hard she almost laughed. She had discovered his dishonesty whilst trying to perpetrate her own deceit. That was how far they had sunk.

'I wanted to make up David's settlement to the full amount. I didn't see why he had to settle for less, not after what we did to him.'

Neil's face hardened.

'I was going to replace it with a loan from the business account once Connor was home. How did we get like this, Neil?' she asked sadly. 'When did we stop believing in each other? When did we stop confiding?'

'I wanted to tell you about the problem at work when it happened back in the summertime but I couldn't get hold of you. You were at that client's house at The Hallows when it all blew up. You spent the night there.' He paused, his eyes narrowing. 'Wait a minute! Was that *McAllister's* property?'

Sam stared at the floor.

'And you wonder why I turned to Megan?'

Cut to the quick, Sam looked away. 'I would have helped you.'

'When you'd finished fucking him? It was too late by then.'

Sam sank onto the opposite corner of the bed. She watched Neil zip up the case. 'You used to be the first person I'd turn to, and vice versa,' Sam said sadly. 'What happened to us, Neil?'

'You mean besides Megan and David?'

Sam spun the ring on her little finger. 'I'm not proud of my actions but when it came to a choice between you and him, I chose you,' she said. 'I wanted to save our marriage.'

Neil regarded her coldly. 'Well I'm struggling to be in the same room as you right now so I'd say our marriage is already dead.' He hauled the suitcase off the bed. 'I'll be back later to speak to the children. If they want me in the meantime, I'll be at Megan's.'

DECEMBER

Chapter Fifty-Six

Sam gave Connor a hug. 'I am so glad you're back.'

He grinned. 'I come bearing gifts but you can't open them until Christmas.'

Sam watched him stack parcels wrapped in Christmas paper on the kitchen table as she poured two mugs of tea.

'Shall I leave Neil's here or . . .'

'You can leave it here. Cass is seeing him later,' Sam said, joining him at the kitchen table.

'Is he still at Megan's?'

'As far as I know. He won't talk to me. Every time I ring, he asks if the children are okay and when I say they are, he hangs up. I'm not going to get anywhere with him until he cools down.'

'It's been three weeks.'

Sam shrugged.

'And all the time he's sharing her bed.'

'I don't know that.'

'You suspect.'

She nodded. 'Even if I was wrong about them before, I've practically pushed him into her arms now.'

'And let him stay there,' Connor said reproachfully. 'Why have you done that? Do you feel you have to pay some kind of penance because of what happened to Josh that afternoon?'

Sam stared at him. 'What would you have me do? Go round there and cause a scene.'

'Yes, if you want him back.'

'He won't even speak to me on the telephone! How is that going to help? I know Neil. He'll calm down. Christmas is coming; he'll want to be with the children. If I push him, I'll only make matters worse.' She squeezed his arm. 'It's good to have you home.'

'Good to be home.'

'Are you doing anything tomorrow night?'

'Don't think so.'

'Global Warning are making their debut at Spike's.'

'Really? Wouldn't miss that for the world. Are they any good?'

'Rehearsals are a closely guarded secret which only take place in Tobyn's parents' garage, so I wouldn't know.'

'How about the psycho bitch? Heard any more from her?'

'No. After Neil left I rang David to let him know I had his phone albeit with a cracked screen. He'd tracked Lauren down to her sister's. He's only just got back.'

She replayed the call in her mind.

'Hi, Sam. I've had it out with Lauren. She won't be bothering you again.'

'Are you sure?'

'Positive. Are you free tomorrow?'

'Why?'

'I'm thinking of buying a property here in Abbeyleigh to do up and sell on and I was wondering if you'd meet me there to take a look. Plus I'd quite like my phone back.'

'I thought you were moving away.'

'Lauren always wanted that more than me. Let me give you the address.'

'And?' Connor asked, bringing her back to the present.

'And he's thinking of buying a property in Abbeyleigh. He wants me to take a look.' She shrugged. 'It'll give me the chance to give him his phone back.'

'Is that the only reason you're meeting him?'

'Yes.'

'Don't do anything hasty. I know you're angry with Neil . . .'

'This has nothing to do with Neil.'

Connor sighed. 'Lie to me if you must, hon. But please don't lie to yourself.'

Chapter Fifty-Seven

The Abbeyleigh Museum had done a fantastic job displaying the automatons. They had pride of place in the centre of the exhibition space with a sign behind them that said *The Edward Mitchell Automaton Collection*. Each machine had its own stand with an information card about the history of the machine and its maker. Between the stands was a card giving the history of automatons in general, and to the side was a little biography of Ted Mitchell and a photo that Daphne had let Sam have.

'Think she's going to be pleased?'

Sam turned to find Gordon beside her.

'I hope so. She told me the cash register had given her back a part of Ted she thought she had lost forever.'

Gordon smiled.

'These obviously aren't as personal but are special nonetheless.' Sam checked her watch. 'I'd better go and pick her up. Would you keep an eye on Cass and Josh for me?'

'Yes, of course.'

When Sam arrived at Daphne's, the older woman met her at the door.

'I can't come, Sam. I thought I could but I can't.'

Leaving the door ajar, Daphne fled into the sitting room. Sam followed her.

'I'm sorry you had a wasted trip.'

'Your dress looks nice.'

Daphne looked down at herself.

'Gordon is going to give the speech. All you have to do is cut the ribbon. You don't even need to do that if you'd really rather not.'

'I'm not a centre of attention type of person, Sam. Fancy dos and speeches and ribbons. It's not me. It wasn't Ted.'

'It's just the museum's way of thanking you. They are so happy with the new exhibits and they are going to give such joy to the local community. The museum's curator was telling me that Abbeyleigh Infants' School has already booked a visit for next week.'

Daphne smiled. 'Ted would be pleased.'

'I'd really like you to see the display and how much care everyone has taken of Ted's machines.'

Daphne took a deep breath. 'Okay, Sam, but I want to stand at the back. No fuss. No ribbons and definitely no speeches.'

Sam would never forget the look of astonishment and delight on Daphne's face when she saw the exhibits half an hour later. She reached for the older woman's hand and gave it a squeeze.

'Happy?'

Daphne nodded.

Sam continued to hold on to her hand as Gordon delivered his speech.

'And so I feel I have got to know this remarkable man a little over these last few months. His diligence, hard work and attention to detail are bar none and without his efforts these wonderful machines would have been lost to us. It is therefore with the greatest pleasure that I give you the Ted Mitchell Automaton Collection.' Gordon cut the ribbon and then picked up his champagne glass. 'To Ted Mitchell, ladies and gentlemen.'

'Ted Mitchell.'

Daphne turned to Sam. 'He would have been so proud to see all of this.'

Sam could see the tears glittering in Daphne's eyes, could feel them gathering in her own.

'Thank you for making this happen and for making me come.'

Sam gave her a hug. 'You're very welcome.'

Chapter Fifty-Eight

The next day as Sam crossed the main road opposite Spike's, she noticed the sold sign above the door. Spike's had been in Abbeyleigh for as long as Sam could remember. She hoped the new owner wasn't going to come in and rip the heart out of the place.

Glancing through the window Sam could see that Spike's was as busy as ever. Her heart leapt as she recognised the man sitting near the window, his shirt sleeves rolled up, his tie loosened, a pint of lager suspended halfway to his lips as he laughed at something someone was saying. Neil. He looked . . . Sam couldn't avoid the word. Happy. A knife twisted in her heart. She wanted him to be downbeat, she realised, as miserable as she was.

With fear, she let her gaze move on to his companion. The person making him laugh. Sure enough, it was Megan. Who else had she expected?

Wounded, Sam turned away, doubling her pace but with every step she saw again the way Neil had laughed and the way Megan had smiled adoringly at him.

Connor was right. She was punishing herself by giving Neil the chance to be with Megan. Her just desserts for not answering Neil's calls that afternoon, for not being there when Josh needed her. It felt right that she should endure pain as her husband and her son had done.

There was more to it than punishment, however. As much as Sam was punishing herself, she was testing Neil. Feeding out the line so that, should the day come when they were reconciled, Sam could believe Neil had chosen her unequivocally over Megan, as surely as she had once chosen him over David. It was the only way.

Her thoughts had delivered her to The Rectory. David had told her it was a detached four-bedroomed house. However, the scant description had not done the house justice. A five-minute walk from the High Street, yet peacefully situated in a cul-de-sac beside the church; its location was superb. Sam's spirits lifted. She could see beyond the ragged wisteria, the rotting window frames and the flaking plaster to what it could be. An absolute gem. David had chosen well.

Her mind teemed with ideas. She recognised it for what it was; a self-preservation technique. Concentrating on the familiar stopped her having to think of other, more difficult, things.

After she had parked the car she had taken out David's phone and studied the photos of the two of them together, knowing it would be the last time she would look at them, testing herself to see how much it would hurt. It had hurt. More than she had anticipated.

To get the images out of her mind she had scrolled through the other photos on his phone. She had spotted the holiday cottage at The Hallows, enjoyed once more the transformation of the property from dowdy and functional to beautiful and romantic. But as she had continued to flick through the photos alarm bells had started to ring. She had found photos of herself that she couldn't remember David taking. In one she had been painting the wall of the second bedroom. In another she had been ladling out soup from a saucepan on the stove. In a third she had been buttering bread. The shots were mundane, boring even. Why had he bothered taking them? *Because he loved you, stupid!*

There were so many photos from those long summer days they had spent working together at the property that she was taken aback. She had had no idea he had been snapping away. Every time she had thought he was checking his email or social media, he had actually been photographing her. No wonder Lauren had lost it big time when she'd looked at the phone.

Did Neil have photos of Megan on his phone?

As she had continued to scroll through David's photos, a feeling of unease had developed. There were so many photos. From every conceivable angle. Flattering and unflattering. He'd fallen for her hard, that much was plain to see, but what she was looking at now went beyond attraction or infatuation. This was obsession. There was no other word for it.

She had caught her breath as she had come to a series of photographs taken while she had been asleep in bed at the cottage, that night exhaustion had got the better of her. Her hair had fanned out across the pillow, one hand visible in the shape of a fist beneath her chin. Then, later, she was on her back, the covers a little lower, one arm flung over her head.

Now, as she waited on the doorstep of The Rectory, a shiver went down her spine as she thought of the photos again. It was one thing to take pictures of her when she was unaware but awake. Quite another to do so when she was asleep. It was almost . . . creepy.

She balled her fists, determined to confront David about them as soon as he answered the door. As he pulled open the door a moment later, she pushed past him into the hall. Sam stared at the floor. Parquet tiles. Original.

'Your phone.' She held it out to him. The tiles would look lovely once they were polished up.

'Thanks. Did you . . .'

'Yes.' She looked up.

He nodded, looking contrite. 'All of them?'

'Yes.'

'You were all I could think of. I just wanted something . . . a little piece of you to hold on to when you went back to him.'

'It isn't nice to take photos of someone when they have no idea they're being photographed.'

He hung his head. 'No, it's not. I'm sorry.'

'Especially when they're asleep. What were you even doing in the room? You told me you would be sleeping in the box room. Did you?' she asked sharply.

'Yes, of course. Nothing happened, Angel. I swear.'

'Then what were you doing there?' Sam persisted. The photos snapped in an unguarded moment had made her realise the depth of David's feelings for her but the night-time photos had made her feel dirty, as though what she and David had shared had somehow sullied her.

'Unlike you, I couldn't sleep. I'd overdone things and my leg was aching and cramping. I got up a couple of times to get some painkillers. When I passed by your door I couldn't resist looking in. I just wanted to check on you, Sam. I swear that's all I was doing.'

'And you just happened to have your phone with you?'

'I needed the photos because I didn't have you.'

'I've deleted them.' She saw the flash of pain cross his face.

'All of them?'

'Yes.'

Stoical, he nodded. 'How's Josh?'

'Changing schools was the best thing we ever did. He's in the swimming team. They just won a cup at a County gala.'

'That's wonderful. And Cass?'

'She's singing in a rock band. They're making their debut at Spike's tonight.'

She followed David through to the kitchen. It was easy talking about the children. She was on solid ground.

'How are things between you and Neil?' *So much for solid ground.*

'He moved out in November. He went to Megan's.' David didn't look surprised. For a moment she wondered if he already knew.

'Because of the photographs?'

She nodded.

'I'm sorry.'

'Are you?'

He smiled. 'No.'

'And you?' Sam ran her hand over the pitted surface of the wooden table that stood in the centre of the kitchen.

'Lauren and I are finished, for good this time. I'm so sorry for the things she did. If I had known she would be like that with you I would never have let her back into my life.'

'Why did you, after what she'd done to you?'

He shrugged. 'I needed someone. Anyone. But I should never have got back with her. We were always going to fall apart it was just a question of when.'

'Because she's so high maintenance?'

'Because she wasn't you.'

'David . . .'

She spoke his name as a warning but he took no heed. Moving to stand in front of her, he gripped her hands. Sam tried to resist even though her heart soared at his touch.

Nevertheless, she kept her gaze fixed on the chequerboard tiles of the kitchen floor because she feared that to stare into his eyes again might be the undoing of her. It would be so easy then to lift her hand into his hair, to bring his mouth down to hers and experience the thrill of his kiss once more.

And why shouldn't I? Roses and jasmine.

Sam let her gaze move from the tiles to the old dresser, which stood against the wall. One of the doors was missing. She could see a bowed shelf inside.

'Sam?'

Up above, where rows of china should have been displayed, a handful of plates remained. She could do a lot with that dresser, strip it back, paint it up.

'Sam!'

The pressure on her hands was a little stronger.

At last, she tore her gaze from the dresser and plucked up the courage to look at him. His eyes were all that she remembered; soulful and beguiling. Could this ever work? If she and Neil divorced, could she and David turn the dream into a reality?

This dashing Celt. He gives his heart so freely but am I worthy of it? I still have a husband. I may despair of Neil, be angry with him but I still love him. The revelation shook Sam to her core. Just as David brought her into his arms, held her fast against him. Those strong, loving arms, holding her close, squeezing her tight. It was heaven to have him hold her like that. To feel his heart beating for her. But . . .

David kissed her temple. Then, running his fingers through her hair, he lifted her hair away and kissed her neck. 'I never thought I'd get the chance to hold you like this again, Angel.'

When his mouth met hers a moment later, she was transported back to that magical summer's afternoon by the river, could feel again the heat of the sun, his loving hands on her bare skin as he'd held her close.

Then, she remembered. Saw again Neil's blood-stained shirt and Josh's bandages.

She broke away, stepped back.

'Sam?'

'David. I . . .'

'You're free now. Neil's with Megan.'

It was true and yet . . .

'It's my fault,' he said suddenly. 'I told myself I wouldn't rush you. I'm sorry but I couldn't help myself. Don't you see, this is our chance,' he said, reaching for her hand.

Sam allowed herself to be brought back into his arms.

'We could be together,' he said. 'You and me.'

'And the children?' she asked, momentarily buying into the fantasy.

'All of us,' he confirmed.

'Where would we live?'

'Why, here, of course. It's perfect.'

'Here?'

'It's a beautiful house. A grand house. You could make it glorious.' He touched her cheek and smiled.

Sam thought about the house and how appealing the façade would look freshly painted, with new windows and the wisteria in full bloom. She had passed through a generous entrance hall, glanced briefly at the sitting room before arriving here, in the kitchen. The rooms were all large. She could do a lot with a house like this.

'It could be our next project. We could work on it together,' he said enthusiastically. 'Just like we did the holiday cottage.'

Sam's spirits soared.

'Let me show you the rest.'

They went from room to room. All bore the hallmarks of neglect but the fireplaces were intact, the cornicing undamaged. David was right; it was a grand house and together they could make it beautiful.

They walked up the stairs. Sam's enthusiasm ignited by David's own. They could live in this house. Husband and wife. It needn't be a dream.

As they reached the landing, David put his arm round her shoulders, before pressing a kiss to her temple.

'This could be Cass's room,' David threw open the door.

'You've obviously given this some thought,' Sam said, amused.

'I hoped,' David admitted bashfully.

Sam stepped inside. It was a large room. Sam began to picture her daughter's belongings. Her glitter lamp on the mantelpiece. Her photographs, posters and books scattered about. However, try as she might, she could not picture Cass herself. Cass idolised Neil. If she had to choose between them she would choose Neil . . . and Megan?

David grabbed her hand, derailing her train of thought as he pulled her along the landing, 'I want this to be our room. It's big enough to section off a corner and create an ensuite.'

Sam surveyed the room. The low, thick windowsill was crying out for cushions. The little wrought-iron fireplace would scrub up nicely. Sam looked at the wall opposite, picturing a brass four-poster bed.

David was smiling at her. 'What do you think?'

'I'm overwhelmed, I don't know what to think,' Sam admitted.

Standing behind her, David wrapped his arms round her, resting his chin on her shoulder. 'I have so many plans for us, for this place.'

'It won't be easy,' she said hesitantly.

'I know it'll be hard work . . .'

'I meant with the children.'

'Josh and I get on fine. I'll build bridges with Cass.'

He made it sound so simple. She found herself daring to hope. This could be their bedroom. She stared at the place where she had already mentally put the bed. For so long she had yearned for him. Wondered. Her heart thumped at the expectation. Finally, she would know this man as a lover and not just as a friend; they would build a home together, a life.

There would be sunny days in the garden, chilly evenings in front of the fire and passionate nights. Her breath caught in her throat. They would have the rest of their lives to explore and discover, to delight in one another.

But what about Neil?

What about Neil? she demanded of herself, angry that he had intruded into her thoughts. He was drinking with his mistress in Spike's. *Roses and jasmine. He doesn't care.* But even as she thought it, she knew it wasn't true. He was angry, not indifferent. Anger suggested emotion. He still cared and so, if she was honest, did she.

'And I thought this could be Josh's room,' David said, leading her along the landing once more.

'It could be lovely,' she agreed.

'The fourth bedroom is slightly smaller than the others.' He ushered her across the threshold, then, standing behind her once more, he put his hands on her stomach and kissed her neck. 'In time, I thought it would make a perfect nursery.'

'A what?' Stunned, Sam turned in his arms.

'A nursery,' he said, smiling.

'You want us to have children?' she stammered, shocked.

'A couple would be nice,' he admitted. He obviously hadn't noticed her surprise because his smile broadened as he said, 'I always imagined I'd be a dad one day.'

Sam pictured him cradling a baby.

'I'm rushing you again, aren't I? I can't help myself,' he admitted with a grin. 'I'm just so happy.' He took her face in his hands and kissed her. 'I want to give you the world, Angel. Please say you'll let me.'

Sam extricated herself from his embrace and walked to the window. The garden was a good size, with two fruit trees at the back. She pictured a hammock strung between them, her lying upon it, drifting back and forth in a gentle breeze, a baby asleep on her chest. A toddler playing on a blanket at her feet. His children. They would be just like him: passionate, impulsive, bounding through life full of enthusiasm.

David's dark, Celtic good looks would be a strong contrast to her own colouring. Viking, he'd called her once; blonde and blue-eyed. Who would their children take after? Surely, his dark colouring would overpower her own? The children would be little replicas of him.

Sam felt a frisson of excitement rush through her but it was quickly pegged back as she thought of the practicalities of one pregnancy and possibly more. She was not old but certainly past the first flush of youth. There could be complications but even if everything went smoothly did she really want to endure the hormonal upheaval, the bone crushing tiredness, the sheer hard work? What would further children do to her body? She had exercised furiously after the births of her existing children, determined to regain her figure. It had been a slog but she'd done it. Was it possible to do it again now? Would her young husband still desire her with broadening hips and a rounded belly?

She stifled a laugh. In the space of a couple of minutes she had married, had two children and was contemplating the prospect of her new husband cheating on her, she realised.

'I'll make you so happy,' David said. 'And I'll always be true to you. I'll never give you a reason to doubt me.'

It's as though he read my mind, Sam thought.

'Why don't I come to Cass's gig tonight? I could buy you all dinner afterwards?'

'No, it's bound to be late.'

She saw the hurt look on his face before he could mask it.

'You don't want me to meet her. Why not? He's with Megan, isn't he? Your marriage is over, isn't it? Why can't I take you out? Why can't I meet your daughter?' His tone was petulant.

She didn't entirely understand it herself but something was holding her back.

'This has all happened so fast,' she said.

The petulance faded, quickly replaced by a smile. The sun chasing away the clouds. 'Dinner at mine tomorrow then,' he said. 'Don't go expecting too much. My culinary skills aren't up to yours.'

'I don't care.'

It was a tacit acceptance of his invitation. A date. To discuss their future. 'Or you could come back to mine, now.'

The electricity of attraction tingled through her. It would be so easy and yet her day was mapped out. 'I can't,' she said. 'I have appointments.'

'Cancel them.'

Was this how her new lover was going to be? Demanding, insistent? Common sense reasserted itself and she took a step away from him. 'I can't,' she said, more forcefully.

'Why?' A hint of petulance returned.

'Because I can't go cancelling appointments at short notice and even if I could, I wouldn't,' Sam admitted. She took his hand in hers. 'I need to think about all of this.' She gestured to the house. 'My head is spinning.'

He nodded and kissed her fingers. 'I wanted to play it cool, take it slowly but somehow my emotions always get the better of me when I'm with you, Angel.' He smiled.

They went back downstairs and through the entrance hall to the front door. The sun was pouring through the coloured-glass panels, throwing a rainbow up the bare wall.

'Seven o'clock tomorrow. Don't be late,' he implored, kissing her cheek.

'I won't be.'

She turned as she reached the pavement. David was leaning against the doorjamb, watching her, his thumb hooked through the loop of his jeans. He quickly raised his hand to wave and she waved back.

Sam returned to her car in a daze, not even pausing to glance into Spike's as she passed by. The last hour had been surreal. She grappled with her emotions: excitement vying with doubt, worry battling with joy. Was tomorrow going to be the day everything changed?

Chapter Fifty-Nine

Spike's was heaving when Sam, Connor and Josh arrived. Sam had no idea that open mic night was so popular. As Connor jostled his way to the bar to get them some drinks, Sam craned her neck to search for Cass but it was Neil she spotted first. He was helping Tobyn set up the drum kit.

'Never thought of Neil as a roadie,' Connor commented as he returned with their drinks. 'How many songs do they get?'

'Three.' They turned as Cass spoke.

Sam took a deep breath. Her daughter was dressed in skyscraper heels, ripped jeans and a tight tee shirt emblazoned with *Global Warning*. Her blonde hair was carefully tousled, her eyeliner was heavy and her lips were purple.

'Liking the look,' Connor said with a whistle.

'What are you playing?'

'I promised we'd play an REM song for Dad, then one of our own called "If Only", and we're finishing with a Snow Patrol song.'

'Good luck.'

'Slay 'em, sis.'

'Thanks, Josh.'

'Good luck, darling.' Sam kissed her cheek.

As they watched her walk towards the stage, Connor bent his head to Sam's. 'Have any of you actually heard her sing?'

'Not since she was in the choir at junior school.'

'This could be interesting.'

As Cass took to the stage, Connor let out an ear-piercing whistle followed by a cheer.

Sam saw Neil look in their direction and then quickly away. She could see no sign of Megan.

As soon as the band started to play and Cass began to sing, Sam felt herself relax. The kids had been force-fed REM songs from the cradle by Neil. As she got to the chorus so the crowd began to join in and by the end of the song everyone in the bar was singing.

As the crowd quietened Cass said, 'This is a song we wrote called "If Only"'

Cass's voice was pure and strong. Sam listened to the lyrics. *If only I could make you stay, be mine for just another day. But like a fool I let you leave, instead of trying to believe. I watched you walk away, I should have made you stay. If only.*

Across the room, she saw Neil look her way.

As the band launched into their final number, Neil made his way over. Connor ushered Josh to one side.

'Some performance, eh?' Neil said.

'Incredible.'

'You know she wrote "If Only" for us.'

'No, I didn't know that.'

'Can I come and see you at home tomorrow night? We need to talk.'

Sam nodded. 'I'd like that very much.'

Neil smiled. 'Better go. Set will be winding up soon. I've got to help get all this gear back in the car.'

Connor nudged her shoulder. 'I'll look after the kids tomorrow. They can sleep at mine,' he said with a wink.

*

Sam rang David the next day.

'What do you mean Neil's coming round? What does he want?' David's tone was sharp.

'To talk.'

Sam knew that while she could put Neil off, arrange to meet him another night and still go to David's, she needed to hear what Neil had to say.

'Maybe it's for the best. It'll give you the chance to tell him about us. I want to be there when you do.'

'No!'

'I still have questions about the accident, questions only Neil can answer.'

'He won't answer them. Leave it, David, please.'

'I can't.'

She heard the pain in his voice.

'I live with the consequences of that accident every bloody day.'

'I know but confronting him isn't going to help.'

'It might. Many's the time I've thought of going to his office. Perhaps if I speak to him tonight . . .'

'No! Please don't come here tonight. If you love me like you say you do, let me speak to him alone. Promise me, David.'

She heard him sigh.

'I promise.'

Chapter Sixty

Sam picked up her phone. 'Hello?'

'Can I speak to Sam Davenport, please?'

'Speaking.'

'My name is Lauren Brightwell. I understand you've been trying to get hold of me? I'm in Abbeyleigh at the moment visiting my parents. I could meet you for a coffee if you still want to talk. It's about David, isn't it?'

'Yes.'

*

The Northey Hotel was packed with Christmas shoppers enjoying afternoon tea. Sam had been lucky to bag a table close to the fire. She watched the tide of people coming and going through the hotel's double doors.

Finally she spotted her. A blonde woman, unwinding a long scarf, undoing the buttons on her military-style red coat. She lifted her hand. The woman turned and nodded but something was wrong. The woman heading towards her wasn't Lauren.

'I'm sorry, there must be some mistake,' Sam said.

The woman hesitated, one glove off, the other part way. 'Are you Sam Davenport?'

'Yes.'

'Then there's no mistake. I'm Lauren Brightwell.' She took the remaining glove off and sat.

'You're not the woman I saw.'

'I don't think we've met before.'

'You . . . someone was waiting outside my office, watching. At the auction house. At my home . . .'

Lauren looked alarmed. 'Are you accusing me of stalking you?'

'David said you wanted to know about us, he said you were obsessed with me. You snatched his phone . . .'

The woman looked confused. 'I haven't seen David or spoken to him since I left in January.'

Sam rubbed her forehead, her mind racing. 'But David said . . .'

'David says a lot of things. Usually whatever gets him what he wants. Are you his new girlfriend?'

'No. It's complicated.'

Lauren smiled. 'With David it's always complicated. It took me two years to realise that. I should have left sooner, only I felt sorry for him.'

'But to leave him the way you did, in the hospital like that . . .'

'It was my chance to escape and I took it. You can't blame me for that. If he'd have been well he would have come after me.'

'I don't understand.'

'With David it's all or nothing. Surely you know that? I think it's because of the way he lost his parents. He felt abandoned when he was just a boy and he's been trying to find a home ever since. It's sad really because the harder he tries the more he pushes people away. He's a twenty-four-seven type of person who takes things to extremes. It's exhausting being with him. He doesn't love someone like a normal person loves someone.'

Sam thought about the photographs of her on his phone. They were the product of an obsession. His obsession with her.

'You must know what it's like. It's why you called me, after all.'

'Tell me what it was like for you,' Sam said quietly.

'To begin with he made me feel like a million dollars, the centre of his world, but slowly things began to change. Little remarks about how I dressed, my friends, my co-workers. He wanted me to give up my job, stop seeing my friends. He wanted to shrink my world until it was just him and me left in it because he was scared of losing me. Being with David is suffocating. He's like one of those snakes that squeezes the life out of you. He doesn't mean to do it. He can't help it. He's so scared of being abandoned again that he clings to people too tightly.

'I began to see someone else, someone who let me breathe. I knew I had to end it with David but I just didn't know how. When the accident happened I saw my chance and I took it. I know it was cruel but I had to get away.

'Even then he was harassing me over the phone. Texting me all hours of the day and night. I had to get my lawyers to threaten him with an injunction – that was when he finally left me alone. That, and by then he'd probably met you. Transferred his affection. So what exactly has David McAllister been saying about me?'

Sam recounted all that had happened since David had arrived at her office unannounced in October. When she had finished speaking, Lauren said, 'I don't know who the woman was but she certainly wasn't me. Maybe he got someone to pretend to be me.'

'But why would he do that?'

'Isn't that obvious? You picked your husband over him and he wanted you back.'

'By scaring me witless? That's not how you show someone you love them.'

'He told you I snatched his phone and sent it to your husband with a note to look at the photos?'

Sam's mind spun. 'It was all an elaborate charade so that he could send Neil the photographs without me ever thinking he was to blame.'

Lauren nodded.

'He knew if Neil saw the date and time they were taken we would be over,' Sam said.

'And David would then happily supply a shoulder for you to cry on.'

Sam could see the sympathy on Lauren's face.

'He was unstable enough before the accident,' Lauren continued. 'If he's been suffering from post-traumatic stress disorder as you say, I hate to think what that has done to his state of mind.'

Sam saw again the flashes of anger that had occasionally surfaced over their months together, the petulance when he couldn't have his own way. How much more had he kept hidden from her?

'I imagine his love for you will only be matched by his hatred for anyone who gets in his way. You and your husband need to be careful.'

Chapter Sixty-One

Neil waited with trepidation for the door of Meadowview Cottage to open. The chocolate-box house they had both worked so hard to make a home looked splendid. Sam's touches were evident all around him from the weathered chimney pots planted with winter-flowering pansies to the shutters at the windows to the bay trees either side of the front door covered with Christmas lights.

It could be their home again, he resolved as he checked the bouquet, turning it slightly for maximum impact ready for when Sam opened the door.

White peonies. Traditional. Gorgeous. Outrageously expensive out of season. A peace offering but also a declaration. *If I can put aside my anger over your relationship with McAllister and the fact you were with him when Josh was in the hospital, then you should be able to put aside your anger over Megan and the money.* Tit for tat. Grievances even.

He took a deep breath as she opened the door.

'Neil.'

'These are for you,' he said with what he hoped was a winning smile.

'Peonies in December? Thank you.'

He followed her through to the kitchen, watched as she took down a vase, filled it and hastily arranged the flowers. 'They're beautiful,' she said, turning to him.

Her smile made his heart flip over.

'Ruinously expensive too, I wouldn't wonder.'

'You're worth every penny. More besides.'

She carried the vase through to the TV room and stood it on the side table.

'Connor's taken the children out?' he asked.

'Yes.'

He'd been delighted to discover Connor was back from America and that the younger man had quickly agreed that Cass and Josh could stay with him. Neil had taken it as a good sign. Connor was paving the way for him and Sam to spend some time alone together. Therefore, he must want them to be reconciled. Was he taking his lead from Sam? Neil wondered. He hoped so. If all went to plan, he would be making love to his wife before the night was out.

Sam was fiddling with the flowers. She looked ill at ease, he thought, but who could blame her after the way he had treated her these past few weeks?

'Sam.'

She turned to face him. Her arms were folded in front of her defensively. 'What do you want, Neil?'

'To talk.'

He sat down and she sat too, but on the very edge of the seat, he noticed, coiled like a spring.

'I want us to start over,' he said without preamble. 'I want to come home.'

She looked alarmed.

Neil was taken aback. To expect her to welcome him with open arms had perhaps been hoping for too much, but this?

'I needed to cool off. I over reacted. I'm sorry.'

She stood. 'You went to Megan.'

'I never went to her,' he said, rising.

'But you said . . .'

'I wanted to hurt you. I saw those pictures of you and McAllister and they broke my heart, Sam. I lashed out. I thought telling you I was going to her would hurt you more than anything else.'

'It did.'

'I never went to her.' Neil could tell she was struggling to believe him. 'I stayed at The Northey Hotel for the first couple of nights. Since then, I've been house-sitting for a colleague.'

'But I saw you together.'

He frowned. 'When?'

'Yesterday. At lunchtime in Spike's.'

'That was my leaving do. Everyone was there.'

'Everyone?' Sam sank back onto the sofa.

'Yes. Nothing has been going on between Megan and me all year. I might have given the impression that something was.' He shrugged, embarrassed now by his actions. 'But only because I wanted to hurt you. I've been a fool.' Neil sat beside her, taking her in his arms, holding her close. He felt her arms tighten round his neck. It felt good to hold her again. To be held. But there was more he had to say. He set her back and, hooking his finger under her chin, he lifted her face so that he could look into her eyes. It was a truth he didn't want to confront but he knew he had to.

'Those photos. You were so in love with him. How did I not know?'

'You were working so hard.'

'That bloody promotion.'

She reached for his hand. 'I didn't plan it, spending the afternoon with him was a spur-of-the-moment decision. One I'll regret for the rest of my life. If I had thought, for one second, that you and Josh needed me, I would have been there in an instant.'

It was a conclusion he'd reached long ago. *If she had known.* He had punished her anyway, for not answering her phone, for not knowing, just because he could. Now, he crushed her to him. 'We can make this right,' Neil whispered. 'With time. With care. We can fix everything.'

Gently, he nudged his lips against hers. He felt her push back and away from him but he held her tightly, not prepared to let her go until she understood just how sorry he was. This woman was his world and he wanted her to be in no doubt of it. She softened, then, in his arms, her lips parting, and he kissed her ardently. This was his chance, perhaps his last chance, to prove to her how much in love with her he truly was.

When, finally, they broke apart, he caressed her cheek. 'How close did I come to losing you?' he asked quietly.

There was panic in her eyes. His heart went cold.

'That close, eh? I can't blame you. How can I? I started it. If there had been no Megan, there would have been no McAllister. I got my pay-out from the firm today. I've replaced all the savings I took.'

'Neil . . .'

'Just hear me out,' he pleaded. 'We've both done wrong but if I can forgive you, surely you can forgive me? We can start over. Forget Megan. Forget McAllister. Concentrate on us and the children. We can be happy again.'

He'd expected a tearful reunion followed by hot, frantic sex. Her reticence unnerved him. He could see she was upset. His heart skipped a beat.

'What is it, Sam? What aren't you telling me?'

They both turned at the sound of the doorbell.

'I'll go,' Sam said.

A moment later the reason for her reticence was standing in the doorway. *McAllister*. Sam was standing behind him, trying to pull him away.

When had it happened? he wondered. Sometime in the last three weeks? While he had been nursing hurt pride, letting her think the worst, McAllister had come back into her life. Neil felt like a fool.

How he now regretted his casual parting words *'I'll be at Megan's'*. He had never considered seeking solace with her, not for a moment. He'd always intended to come home. He'd just wanted Sam to hurt as he'd been hurt.

'What's he doing here?' Neil snarled.

Sam looked distraught.

'I have some questions for you,' McAllister said.

As nonchalantly as he could, Neil poured himself a double scotch. He flopped into one of the studded leather armchairs, determined to look and sound as calm as possible.

'Neil,' Sam began.

'Did you set this up, Sam?'

'Of course I didn't,' she said, sounding shocked.

'And you're together?' He hated that he had to ask, the evidence was right in front of him and yet he had to know, had to hear it from her lips.

'Oh yes,' McAllister responded triumphantly.

'Sam?'

Sam gave him an anguished look. He didn't have the heart to push her. He gulped at the scotch, desperate to steady his rattled nerves.

'You needed to know we were together. Now you do,' McAllister said.

'Jolly decent of you.'

'Neil . . .'

'What do you want, Sam? My blessing? Go to hell.'

'Don't speak to her like that.'

Anger spiking, Neil stood. 'She's still my wife. This is still my house. I'll speak to you both however I damn well please.'

Neil watched Sam turn pleading eyes to McAllister and motion towards the door.

Ignoring her, McAllister folded his arms. 'I want to know about the accident.'

'Don't remember much,' Neil replied bullishly. 'I'd had a bit to drink.'

'How much?'

'I wasn't counting.'

'You should have been. Were you over the limit?'

'Probably.'

'But you insisted on driving? You must have known you were drunk?'

'I didn't say I was drunk.'

'Being over the limit means you were drunk.'

'Not necessarily.'

'I'm not here to argue semantics with you,' McAllister said. 'You knew you shouldn't have driven. Why did you?'

'Because I felt fine.'

'Clearly not fine enough to take responsibility,' McAllister said scathingly.

'Do you want me to say I'm sorry? Is that why you're here? If it is, you're going to be sorely disappointed. Hell will freeze over before I apologise to you after what you've done to me.'

'What *I've* done to *you*? Tell me what it is you think *I've* done to *you*.'

'Taken the only woman who has ever meant anything to me and made her love you.'

'I didn't *take* anything. You gave it all away.'

Had he?

Neil turned his back on them, sank the scotch, poured another.

'You spent the evening at the Northey,' McAllister persisted.

Neil nodded. 'I had a couple for the road. I didn't think it would make much difference. In fact, I'm not sure it did. I wasn't breathalysed so we'll never know if I was over the limit or not,' he declared smugly, facing them once more.

'A couple for the road?' McAllister was incredulous. 'I've still got pieces of that road embedded in my thigh, you bastard.' He was by Neil's side in seconds, grabbing him. Sam screamed. The glass fell from Neil's hand and rolled away. Scotch bled into the carpet.

Sam clawed at McAllister's arm. 'Let him go, please! This isn't helping.'

The punch to Neil's jaw sent him sprawling. He saw McAllister swat Sam away and before he could react, the younger man was pinning his wrists to the floor with one hand whilst grabbing the poker from the fireplace with the other.

'How many blows do you think it will take for me to shatter *your* leg?' David raised the poker.

Neil braced himself.

'How many until the bone comes through the skin? Three? Four? 'Cos I'll keep going until it does. I hope you've got a high pain threshold because you're going to need it!'

'*David!*'

'Get out, Sam. This is between me and him.'

Neil could see the wild look in David's eyes. He struggled under the man's grip but it was no use, there was no way to free himself. McAllister was younger, fitter, fuelled by anger.

'How many months of rehab will it take for you to walk again, do you think? Shuffling round with a frame and then a cane like an old man. Or maybe I'll do so much damage you'll never walk again. You'll need a fucking drink when I've finished with you, I can promise you that!'

Neil closed his eyes. Let him take a hit. How bad could it be? He could bear it. One blow. Then maybe McAllister would release his grip a little and he could free himself.

'Open your eyes, you coward. I want you to see it coming.'

Neil opened his eyes. 'You were riding that bike like a fucking maniac. If you hadn't have been, I would have seen you.'

'I cannae believe you've got the nerve to try and make this my fault. Did you even stop at the junction?'

'My reaction time might have been slower because of the drink,' Neil conceded. 'But you came out of nowhere.' He had the satisfaction of seeing a look of doubt creep into McAllister's eyes.

'Did you stop?' McAllister repeated.

'Not exactly.'

'Not exactly?' McAllister exploded.

'It was late.'

'It was a *stop* junction.'

'I looked.'

'Not hard enough.' David lifted the poker.

Neil braced himself for the inevitable blow. Above him he could see Sam grappling for the end of the poker.

'*David, stop it!*'

'I told you to get out, Sam.'

'I'm not going anywhere. Put it down.'

'Why the hell should I?'

'Because if you hit him with it, I will never forgive you. Do you hear me, David? Never! You wanted us to be together. You did everything you could to make it happen. I know the lengths you've gone to. Everything you've done. You hit him, it will all have been for nothing.'

With a visceral cry of rage, David threw the poker across the room and tossed Neil aside.

Wiping the blood from his lip, Neil scrambled to his feet. 'No one could wish the accident hadn't happened more than me,' he shouted. 'It cost you a broken leg. It looks like it's cost me my marriage. Ultimately, I'd say I paid a higher price.'

'You don't know anything about what I've been through.'

'I know plenty,' Neil retaliated. 'I'm the man you sued, remember? I've seen your psych report. Does Sam know about the nightmares, the flashbacks, the fact you can't even walk down the road in which the accident happened, let alone drive down it? Haven't

ridden your bike since it happened. Too bloody scared.'
He sneered.

'Neil, stop it!' Sam said.

'You've seen my psychiatric report?' McAllister
asked looking bewildered.

'I demanded the insurance company ran everything
by me. A little unorthodox but being a partner in a law
firm does have its benefits. I know for instance that
you're still having counselling and that you've bought
a shiny new bike with one of your interim payments
but you don't have the nerve to get on it. Is the counselling going to help do you think or are you going to
run scared for the rest of your life? Have you warned
Sam that you're damaged goods?'

'You bastard.' McAllister spat contemptuously.

'Yeah, that's me. A bastard. At least you had Florence
bloody Nightingale to hold your hand through it all.
You were looking for answers, I've given them to you.'
He gave McAllister a shove. 'Now, piss off out of *my*
house.'

'Do you feel any remorse?'

'I did before I knew you were screwing my wife.
Now I wish I'd knocked you down and reversed over
you until you were dead.'

David went to hit him again. Neil sidestepped
the blow.

'*Stop it! Both of you!*'

Fuming, Neil said, 'Do you love her?'

'More than I can say.'

'You're not worthy of her.'

'Probably not.'

'We were happy.'

'Was that before or after Megan?'

Neil sprang forward but Sam placed herself between the two men. Her hands on Neil's chest, forcing him backwards. 'Please go,' she said, turning to McAllister.

Throwing a black look at Neil, he nodded and said, 'I got what I came for.'

✳

The night air was sharp with the cold. David turned to find that Sam had followed him outside.

'You should have let me hit him. He deserves to know what it feels like.'

'I told you not to come,' she hissed.

'I had to know he didn't stop at the junction.'

'I told you that.'

'I had to hear it from him.' He blew his cheeks out, watched his breath mist in the chilly air. The cold took the heat from his anger. *Damaged goods*. Was that what Sam thought?

He turned to her. 'I haven't been able to go down the Stebbingsford Road since the accident. I bought a new bike. She's a real beauty but I can't ride her. I've tried. I lose my nerve. How pathetic is that?'

'It isn't pathetic, not after what you've been through,' Sam said, her tone softening.

'You don't think less of me?'

'Of course not.' She looked over her shoulder. 'I need to go back inside.'

'To him?'

'Go home, David.'

'You could come to mine, after . . .' he gestured to the house.

'No.'

There was a finality to the word that pierced his heart.

'I need to be on my own tonight.'

Reluctantly, he walked to his car.

'We'll talk tomorrow,' she said.

He nodded. She was angry with him for going against her wishes. He couldn't blame her but he hadn't had a choice. He should have confronted Neil the second he'd got out of the hospital but if he had would he and Sam have shared the summer, he wondered?

She was everything and he'd got so close to making her his. He pictured her hair as it had been that afternoon at The Rectory, a glorious golden halo. He remembered its silky softness through his fingers, the way it had fallen back, just so, into place. The smell, fresh and clean, mixing with the gorgeous scent of her perfume. All the plans he'd made, the hopes and dreams. Did they stack up favourably against so many years of marriage? Could they?

He had known for a long time now that his guardian angel was another man's wife. That, because of it, he might one day have to let her go. Would he be strong enough to do it, he wondered, if that was what she truly wanted?

*

'That shouldn't have happened. He shouldn't have come here,' Sam said returning to the TV room.

Neil was on his knees, mopping up the spilt scotch. 'When did you and he . . .'

His words tailed off. Sam watched the cloth move mechanically back and forth over the carpet.

'I saw him again for the first time yesterday.'

'Yesterday?' Neil's surprise was apparent. 'So, you and he haven't . . . I mean, he hasn't been here, with you?'

'No.' She took the cloth from him. 'Let me,' she said.

He gave her a strained smile as he stood. 'You were always better at that sort of thing.'

'I got more practice,' she said wryly. 'You should call a cab. You can pick the car up in the morning.'

'Are you going to be okay?'

'I'll be fine. We can talk again tomorrow.'

'The man's got a screw loose, you do realise that? Has had ever since his parents died. His psychiatrist reckons he's on the verge of a nervous breakdown now thanks to the PTSD.'

'I can see that.' *With the gift of hindsight, anyway.*

'I should call the police. Get him done for assault.'

'You'll do no such thing!'

'He threatened to break my fucking leg.'

'He's a sick man, Neil. Not a bad one. He needs help not locking up.'

'And let me guess, you're going to be the one to supply it.'

'It's our fault. We're the ones who pushed him over the edge, Neil. You and me. Actions, however great or small, have consequences. We did this to him and somehow we have to make things right.'

*

Alone with her thoughts, Sam poured herself a large glass of wine and took it into the conservatory. She settled back into the generous cushions of the sofa, resting her head against them, letting them enclose and soothe her with their softness.

She was angry with David for defying her wishes, causing a scene she would never have wanted to endure. Yet questioning Neil was clearly something he'd needed to do.

I live with the consequences of that accident every day.

As do we all, Sam thought.

He'd lied to her. Made up the reconciliation with Lauren purely so that he would have a way to release the photographs to Neil without any blame attaching itself to him, hoping it would split them up for good this time and he would be there to pick up the pieces. She wondered who the woman was he'd roped in to help.

She took another sip of her wine. Her heart hardening as she remembered how frightened she had been every time she'd seen her. *Lauren. Not Lauren.*

The hundreds of photos of her on his phone were testament to an unhinged mind. She should have realised as soon as she had seen them, particularly the ones of her sleeping. He had spent his life looking for a home. Holding on too tightly, loving too hard every chance he got and he'd thought he'd found a home with her.

'*I want to give you the world, Angel. Please say you'll let me.*'

Sam pictured Neil's face as she had seen it from the doorway, when he'd first seen David. He'd looked crushed and Sam's heart went out to him, just at the memory of it. His words earlier that evening came back to her.

'*With time. With care. We can fix everything.*'

Could they? Should they?

Neil wanted to recreate the world they had once inhabited before their own actions and those of others had threatened it. David wanted to create a new world, with her at the centre of it.

What do I want?

If she were to reconcile with Neil they would have to work hard to put the past behind them, to learn to trust one another again. Their relationship had certainly been tested but could it survive?

Whilst with David the doubts came because their relationship was largely untested, Sam realised, struck by the irony. In time, she was sure she could forgive David for lying to her because his spirit had been wounded. She could see that now. He needed help. *Professional* help. More help than she could give him. But she had seen enough of the man underneath to know that she could still love him, wound or no wound. But then what?

All fire and passion, they'd never had to deal with the daily routine of domesticity. Would they have as much to say to one another after years together as she and Neil still did? Could all that fire and passion embrace the mundane and still thrive?

There were things she didn't know about David. Question marks and blank spaces that were as unnerving as they were exciting. Whereas she knew everything about Neil, perhaps more than was good for them.

Sam swirled the wine in her glass. What about children? The ones she had now and the children she might have? If she moved in with David, Cass would find it hard to forgive her. Sam could picture her daughter, hands on hips, chin tilted belligerently, demanding to live with Neil. *Could I stop her, if that was what she wanted?*

And then there was Josh. He would hate having his world turned upside down but, ultimately, he would enjoy living with David. Doubtless, Neil would find that fact hard to cope with. Josh's relationship with David was likely to be a constant source of friction between them all, Sam realised.

And what about babies? Sam pictured the scene she'd conjured whilst at the house: a baby asleep on her chest, a toddler playing nearby. Dark-haired, brown-eyed replicas of their father. Could she do it? Did she *want* to do it?

Of course, there was nothing stopping her and Neil from having another child, but Neil had often made remarks along the lines of 'When the children leave home . . .' As though he was already looking forward to the day when it was just the two of them again. She had thought she felt the same.

However, she couldn't dislodge the pictures from her mind: a tiny baby nestled in her arms, David bursting with pride as he looked at her . . . *and the sun will shine and all will be well*, Sam thought wryly.

Meanwhile, back in the real world, there would be dirty nappies and sleepless nights, husband and child competing to have their needs met and her in the middle, not knowing which way to turn. A fragile husband at that. There was no escaping the fact that babies were hard work. Worth it though, Sam thought. Worth all the pain and effort of childbirth, the ruined clothes, the non-existent social life. Just to have that tiny hand grip your finger, to see your baby smile, to smell their sweet skin.

Sam sighed, in a quandary. If she and David were to have children, then it wasn't something they could put off, because of her age. They would have little time for David to heal and for them to get to know one another and enjoy each other's company before she fell prey to mood swings and cravings. It was a lot to ask of a fledgling relationship but that was the way it had to be if they were to have children and Sam knew she couldn't deny David the chance to be a father. It wasn't fair to make him choose. If she did, she was sure he would one day resent her for it. *But, if I go along with his plans, will I end up resenting him?*

Sam finished her wine, no clearer about what to do than when she'd started. She decided to take a long, hot bath and have an early night. Perhaps she would see things more clearly in the morning.

*

Sam slept fitfully, tossing and turning, her troubled dreams full of Neil and David, houses and babies. Waking at five, she showered and dressed, then fixed some toast and tea for breakfast. She ate and drank robotically, her mind, like a pendulum, swinging back and forth between Neil and David, as it had done all night.

Deciding what she needed was physical exercise to tire her body out and give her mind a rest, Sam quickly threw her swimsuit and a towel into a bag and, grabbing her keys, headed off to Park Place.

Their early bird sessions in the pool started at six. There were two other people in the pool when she arrived. The water was warm, such a contrast to the frost, which lay thick on the ground.

The three swimmers each ploughed their own lane, the wash from their bodies rippling across the surface. Sam concentrated on her strokes. Four lengths of front crawl, four of breaststroke, four of backstroke. She had never mastered butterfly, though Neil had tried to teach her once on holiday, in the pool at their villa in Italy. Five strokes had been her maximum and then she had sunk ignominiously, much to the children's delight.

Neil. She edged him from her mind. Concentrated instead on counting her lengths, alternating her strokes. She pushed herself to go harder and faster. Worked on her breathing. Emptied her mind.

She swam with such focused fury she did not notice the other swimmers leave. Until, finally, panting she clutched the side of the pool, her chest burning. She shook her hair away from her face, ducking it under the water, smoothing it back. Then, she hoisted herself out of the pool.

She knew what she had to do next.

*

David cast around for something to take his mind off the empty hours of waiting for Sam to get in touch. His gaze fell on the motorcycle helmet. *I could take the bike for a spin. Then, if I want, I could head out towards the Stebbingsford Road.* The idea grew in his mind and, somewhere between his flat and the lock-up he rented, the journey took on a greater significance. *If I face my demons, maybe Sam will come back to me.*

With determination, David straddled the bike, flexing his hands inside his leather gloves, before firing up the engine. Beads of sweat stood out on his forehead even though the day was cold.

You don't have to do this, he thought. Then, as quickly, *Yes I do. I'm letting that accident hold me prisoner. Until I do this, I will never be free.* He put his visor down and set off. A quick circuit of the town.

A loop out onto the bypass and then back, to settle himself.

Nervous, he stayed well back from the car in front, reacting to the traffic lights, slowing down long before he needed to. His hands were shaking. Once, he had dodged in and out of traffic, not thinking, not caring. Instinctive. Had he been driving like a maniac as Davenport had suggested? Had he thought of himself as invincible? Maybe once, certainly no more.

He was alert to the car at the side turn. He watched it intently. It stopped, waiting for him to pass. He let out a sigh of relief and reminded himself why he was doing this. It was time to consign the accident to history.

He turned onto the Stebbingsford Road. The road where the accident had happened nearly twelve months before. The junction was just a few hundred metres ahead. He checked his mirrors. The road was deserted. It was just him and his demons. No one would know if he pulled up now.

I'd know. He turned the throttle. *It's time to get this monkey off my back.* His heart raced as he rode past the turning. No car waited at the junction. It didn't matter. He'd done it. He'd set himself free from one demon at least.

He pulled up past the junction, killed the engine and took off his helmet. His heart was thumping as if he'd run a marathon. The junction lay behind him. It was just another junction on just another road. A bad thing had happened there once but now it was time to move on. With a steadying breath, he pulled the helmet back on and started up the bike.

He made a longer loop around the town than he'd originally intended, enjoying the feel of the bike once more. Remembering all the things that were good about riding instead of just the bad. A weight had been lifted. Three quarters of an hour passed before he pulled back into the car park at the Old Mill.

He let out a sigh, his breath frosting in the air. Proud of himself, there was only one person he wanted to tell. He wondered if she'd rung while he'd been out. He pulled his phone from his jacket. She'd sent him a text.

Meet me at The Rectory. Ten thirty.

*

Neil lifted his certificates off the wall and carefully stowed them in one of the two cardboard boxes he'd brought in with him that morning.

His uncle knocked on the door. 'Morning, Neil.'

'Edward.'

'You never had to leave, you know.'

Neil smiled. 'Yes, I did.'

Edward gestured over his shoulder. 'Can I have a word in my office?'

Neil dusted off his hands. He was wearing jeans and a Ralph Lauren polo shirt, no point getting dressed up in a suit if he wasn't seeing clients.

He took a seat opposite his uncle.

'Off to Ellis and Son in Stebbingsford?' Edward began.

Neil nodded.

'May I ask what level you're going in at?'

'Associate. We've agreed to review the situation after a year. I'm in no hurry.'

Edward templed his fingers. 'Harry Tilden's wife has been taken ill.'

'I'm sorry to hear that.'

Edward nodded. 'She wants to go home to Ireland. Harry handed in his notice last night.'

Neil couldn't stop himself from laughing. 'What will you do now?'

'Ask my nephew if he'll change his mind.'

'You thought I was too young and inexperienced.'

'I still do but I could work alongside you for the first year, guide you.'

'And the others?'

'They're happy with that. No one wants you to leave. We never did.'

Neil stared out of the window. A squally shower was whipping the bare trees. He hesitated for just a heartbeat, then said, 'I appreciate the offer . . .'

'Don't let hurt pride be the determining factor here, Neil.'

'I'm not,' he said evenly. 'It's true, I wanted the job desperately. Only once it had been denied to me, however, did I stop to think about all that it would have entailed: the endless hours in the office, the egos of my fellow partners, the sheer grind of all that extra paperwork. Now, I've come to the conclusion that I've had a lucky escape.'

'There's nothing I can say to change your mind?'

Neil shook his head. 'I lost the promotion but I regained my life. Hard to argue with that.'

Edward stood, proffered his hand. 'Good luck at Ellis and Son. They're a fine firm and lucky to have you.'

'Thank you.'

Neil returned to his office. Abandoning the packing, he sat and watched the rain lash the window. The promotion he had coveted for so long had just been handed to him on a plate. How the man he had been six months before would have loved that. He was a different man now though and, while he'd hesitated for just a moment, he hadn't really been tempted to accept the offer. There was more to life than work. If only he'd realised that sooner, Sam might still be his.

He had tried so hard not to think of her last night and again this morning when he'd collected his car but it had been impossible. He'd been so tempted to let himself into the house to speak to her but caution had stayed his hand. If he pestered her, there was a danger he would push her into McAllister's arms. Let her have the time she needs, he thought.

Neil massaged his eyes. The waiting was hell.

*

David opened the door of The Rectory as soon as Sam entered the front garden.

'You've made a decision?'

'Yes.'

They went through to the kitchen.

'Sam . . .'

'This house will make someone a beautiful home one day,' she began.

'But not us?' David said flatly.

'No, not us.'

'Is it because I said I wanted children? Because I can live without them.'

Sam touched his face. 'I could never deny you the chance to become a father,' she said. 'It wouldn't be fair because you'll make such a great dad, but I've had my share of child-rearing. I don't want to go through it all again, not even for you.'

'That's fine. I don't mind.'

Sam smiled sadly. 'Maybe not now, but you would. In time, you'd resent me or try to change my mind. It's not just a question of children, though. I know you were never reconciled with Lauren, that you made the whole thing up.' She watched him crumble into a seat at the kitchen table.

'How did you find out?'

She was relieved he hadn't tried to deny it. 'I reached out to Lauren. We met.'

'I just wanted . . .'

'I know.' She went to him. Held him. 'I know why you did it. It wasn't just your leg we broke that night, I realise that now. We broke something inside you, too. Who was the woman?'

'Just someone I knew. I paid her.' He gripped her hand. 'All I wanted to do was break you and him up. I didn't think you'd be so scared but once I started I had to see it through. I'm sorry.'

'You need help, David. You need someone with whom you can work through your feelings.'

David's face hardened. 'He showed you my psych report, didn't he?'

'He didn't have to.'

'I drove down the Stebbingsford Road today, past the scene of the accident. It was actually easier than I thought it would be. I really do think I'm ready to put the accident behind me and move on. I'm not damaged goods, like he said, Sam.'

'I didn't say you were but you still have unresolved issues from the time of your parents' accident, don't you?'

He balled his fists. 'I hated them for dying on me, for leaving me alone, if that's what you mean. It's like a tangle of knots in the pit of my stomach. It's been with me ever since the day they died. It never goes away. I loved them so much, you see. Ever since, I've been searching for something, someone, to give me back what I lost. I thought I'd found that in you.'

She stroked his face. 'The answer doesn't lie with anyone else. It lies with you.' She withdrew her hand. 'That night at the cottage, did you give me something to make me sleep? I know the doctor gave you sleeping pills. Did you give some to me?'

His gaze slid away from her.

'You did, didn't you?'

'I just wanted you to stay.'

'Did you touch me?'

He shifted in his seat.

449

'David, did you touch me?'

'Not like that, no. I wanted to but I didn't.'

Sam swallowed. 'What did you do?'

'I lay down beside you and put my arm around you. I wanted to pretend, even if it was just for a few hours, that you were mine.'

'You need to speak to someone, someone who can help you make peace with the past. There's a clinic. A place where they help trauma victims recover. You can talk about everything that's happened. They'll help you heal.' She pulled the literature out of her bag. 'This is their brochure. Neil and I will pay the bill.'

'You want to lock me away?'

'No. No one is locking you away. This place isn't like that. There aren't bars on the windows or locks on the doors. Whether you go or not is entirely up to you. I can't make you. No one can. But as your friend I'm telling you that I think it would be the right thing for you to do.'

'My *friend*?' He gave her a sullen stare. 'That's it then? We're over.'

She nodded. 'You need time and space to get your head together. There'll be someone there you know. A friendly face to welcome you.' She put the brochure on the table and pushed it towards him.

'Who?'

'Jane.'

'From the hospital?'

'I spoke to her this morning. I wanted her advice. She's been retraining. She works at the clinic now.'

'You told her about me?'

'Because I want you to get better. She gave me her card. She said to tell you to give her a call.' Sam held the card out. When David didn't take it she laid it on the table beside the brochure. 'I need to go now, David.'

'To him?'

Sam nodded.

'Even though I'd give you everything and he broke your heart, it's still not enough?'

'What we shared was special but no, it's not enough.'

'Because you think I'm broken inside?'

'It's got nothing to do with that. You'll heal. I know you will. Because you're strong. Stronger than you think. But I need to be with him.'

She turned to walk away. David grabbed her wrist. Standing, he took her in his arms. Their kiss lasted a moment and a lifetime and was more passionate than any they had shared before. A fitting valediction to a love met too late.

Sam eased herself out of his embrace. She went to speak but he brought his finger to her lips.

'I'll think about your fancy clinic. You go on now,' he said and he raised his eyes to the door. 'Do it like you did before, Angel. Keep walking. Don't look back.'

*

Neil was still packing his belongings into boxes as Sam entered his office.

'There's cold coffee in the mug, if you want to throw it over me,' he said, recalling the last time she'd been there.

'Why would I do that? Have you done something wrong?'

'It feels as though I haven't done anything right in a long time.'

He gave her a wry smile.

'Tilden's wife has been taken ill. They've offered me the position of senior partner.'

'What did you say?'

'I said I didn't want it.' He gestured to the boxes. 'You'd think I'd have more to show for all the years I've been here.'

'You can't put hopes and dreams into a cardboard box. He came back into my life a couple of days ago, offering me the world,' Sam said without preamble.

'Lucky lady.'

'I turned him down.'

Neil's gaze leapt to meet hers.

'I've tried to persuade him to seek help. A private clinic. We're paying the bill. Don't even think about arguing.'

Neil rubbed his neck.

'I fell in love with him but I don't know whether it was with the man himself or just the idea of him. It was probably a bit of both. You see, he'll forever be the perfect blank canvas because you can never know what a relationship can be until it's been tested. David and I will never have a blazing row followed by passionate sex. We'll never share the tedium of a long car journey when I want to listen to Radio Four and he wants to listen to pop music. We'll never fight over whose turn it

452

is to take out the rubbish and then both end up doing it. We'll never watch in awe as our children grow. We'll never look at one another and feel so overwhelmed by love that we're rendered speechless by it but I've done all of those things with you and so much more and I wouldn't have it any other way.

'We think of marriage as being about the grand gestures; the wedding, the honeymoon, the anniversaries. Actually, it's the little things that matter most. The mundane things that make up our days, the moments that weave themselves into our souls.'

Sam moved to stand beside him. 'I can't deny that David carved out a space in my heart but the rest belongs to you. It always did.'

Neil searched her eyes. 'You're coming back to me?'

Mirroring his smile, Sam said, 'I don't think I ever really went away.'

As Neil swept her into his arms, Sam was sure there was no better place on earth to be. After so much heartache, the joy was even sweeter than she'd imagined it would be. This man was hers and she was his and nothing could change that. They had been tested. How they had been tested! But they'd come through.

When he set her down, they smiled at one another. *I won't look back or brood or wonder*, Sam thought. *I've made my choice and I'm content.*

Neil took her hands in his and kissed her fingers.

'Have you lost your father's ring?' he asked.

'No. I took it off. I decided I'm not that little girl any more. I don't need to be afraid.'

With a smile, Sam picked up one of the boxes. 'Why don't we take this stuff home?'

Neil grinned at her as he hoisted the other box under his arm, his hand in the small of her back. Intimate. Tender.

They walked out past Neil's colleagues who had gathered to wish him well. At the back of the group, Sam noticed Megan. Their eyes met. Megan looked away first but not before Sam saw her tears. She loved him too, Sam thought, and it was pity, not fear that filled her heart.

They left the office and walked to the car park. His affair was over. Her dalliance with David, too. Sam was confident they would pick themselves up and go on from this moment, stronger than before.

In time, she mused, *distance will bring a perspective that's impossible to imagine now, and when it does the events of this year and last will fade into the fabric of our lives. A series of dropped stitches and nothing more.*

Neil turned on the engine. The sound of REM flooded the car. Sam grimaced and then laughed. Grinning, Neil reached for the dial. 'Why don't we give Radio Four a try instead?' he suggested.

Reviews are crucial to all novelists whether they be established stars or just starting out.

If you would like to, you may leave an honest, short review of *White Lies* on Amazon or Goodreads.

If you would like to find out more about me and my books:

Please visit my website at www.ellieholmesauthor.co.uk or follow me on:

Pinterest: https://uk.pinterest.com/EllieHWriter/

Twitter: @EllieHWriter

Facebook: http://www.facebook.com/EllieHWriter

If you would like to be among the first to hear about my latest releases why not join Ellie's Readers' Group via my website. You can sign up by clicking on the link:

http://www.ellieholmesauthor.com/ellies-readers-group/ 4591358893

As a thank you, you will receive a free gift –
Three Quick Reads – to enjoy.

You will also receive monthly instalments of my newsletter serial which is exclusive to my readers' group for two years from the date each serial starts. Don't worry if you join part way through, a catch up will be available.

Love, Ellie x

Acknowledgements

To my family for always believing in me. To my best friend, Simon, and to Vicky, Sheila and John for keeping the faith.

To my beta readers: Mel, Angela, Lesley K and Deborah – your insightful comments were invaluable.

To everyone at Frinton Writers' Group – your support and encouragement has been greatly appreciated.

To Adele Blair for suggesting the name of Cass Davenport for Sam and Neil's daughter. It suited her perfectly, thank you!

Finally, to everyone who has made this book a reality including the incomparable George Edgeller – you are the best – my fabulous cover designer Berni Stevens and my lovely editor Jill Sawyer.